FEARLESS

Books by Robin Parrish

Relentless

Fearless

FEARLESS

THE DOMINION TRILOGY: BOOK 2

ROBIN PARRISH

BETHANY HOUSE PUBLISHERS

Minneapolis, Minnesota

Fearless
Copyright © 2007
Robin Parrish

Cover design by Brand Navigation

Published by Bethany House Publishers
11400 Hampshire Avenue South
Bloomington, Minnesota 55438

Bethany House Publishers is a division of
Baker Publishing Group, Grand Rapids, Michigan.

Printed in the United States of America

ISBN   978-0-7642-0518-7

The Library of Congress has cataloged the hardcover edition as follows:

Parrish, Robin.
    Fearless / Robin Parrish.
        p.   cm. — (Dominion trilogy ; 2)
    ISBN 978-0-7642-0178-3 (alk. paper)
    1. Heroes—Fiction. Supernatural—Fiction. 3. London (England)—Fiction.
I. Title.
    PS3616.A7684F43   2007
    813'.6—dc22   2007011983

For Mom.

You don't believe in superheroes,
but I know they're real.

Because you're mine.

PREVIOUSLY . . .

ON AN ORDINARY DAY, one man steps off the bus and sees . . . himself, standing across the street.

Grant Borrows has been Shifted. He discovers he has a new identity and a Ring of Dominion melded with his finger that gives him extraordinary powers.

And he soon discovers he's not alone. Others have been Shifted. They are called "Ringwearers" or "Loci," and each has a special gift.

Morgan remembers *everything*. Alex can manipulate emotions. They're joined by Grant's sister and Daniel Cossick, a guilt-ridden scientist. Brought together, seemingly by chance, these individuals slowly realize they have one aim: Discover the identity behind a secret organization thousands of years old—the Secretum of Six.

The Secretum guards a prophecy of which Grant seems to stand at the middle. He is called "The Bringer"—but the bringer of what?

Pursued at every turn by a ruthless assassin, a corrupt cop, and a sword-wielding warrior with superhuman speed who calls himself "The Thresher," Grant soon feels he is being manipulated.

He is. The puppet master calls himself "The Keeper," and he'll stop at nothing to provoke the Bringer into unleashing his full power, even arranging the murder of the woman closest to Grant.

But Grant does not give in to rage. And together with the sword-wielding Payton with whom he allies, they foil the Keeper's plans.

Still, all is not well. Loyal scientist Daniel Cossick has killed a man in revenge, and the Secretum's true aim still remains shrouded.

The world, however, is in need of heroes—and Grant, Alex, and Payton find themselves with no other choice but to become . . .

FEARLESS

Two Months Later

Grant Borrows awoke on the ground.

A sharp yelp roused him, and Grant was instantly aware of three things. First, he was flat on his back, staring into the black snout of an imposing bronze horse statue, which sneered down at him from above. Second, the sky behind the statue was a dismal gray while in his periphery he saw the vivid greenery of trees on all sides. Third, what startled him awake was that he was holding someone's wrist.

Someone's wrist that didn't belong.

Rolling his neck to the left, Grant came face-to-face with a boy who couldn't have been more than fifteen. Bright eyes offset shaggy blond locks, which framed his oval face in a messy sort of way. A faded polo shirt was untucked over a pair of jeans that looked like their best days were long behind them.

"You *are* him!" the boy exclaimed, eyes as wide with wonder as they were with fear. Grant turned loose of the boy's wrist and slowly sat up.

What? Where. . . ?

He was in the center of what looked like a very small park, surrounded on all sides by trees, a circumference of parked cars outside of them. Beyond the vehicles, a quadrant of buildings loomed, enclosing the park in a box-like perimeter.

The buildings were very old. Historic, even.

A dark-colored statue of a man riding a horse stood atop a white cement pedestal on his right, opposite the boy.

Grant's recognition of it was vague. He was sure he'd been here before, and he was quite certain he was still in London.

But how long. . . ?

And why was I asleep out here in the open?

"Who're you?" Grant rasped, his voice dry, his thoughts spinning in too many directions at once.

Why can't I remember anything?

His heart rate was increasing with each new possibility that occurred to him.

"Didn't mean nothing by it, man!" the boy cried, tossing Grant's wallet back to him. "Just wanted to see if you had a real name, is all."

But Grant wasn't looking at the wallet. His eyes were still on the boy's wrist, which was bright red where Grant's hand had been.

He lifted one hand and found blood. His other hand was bloody too . . . and there were similarly dried stains scattered across his clothing . . .

Yet he felt no pain.

A chill stopped his pulse.

This blood was not his. And it wasn't the boy's, either.

Reflexively, he reached out with his mind and touched the minds of the Loci, checking off his friends, one-by-one. The process was a mere flash, lasting less than a second, and his heart skipped a beat when he felt it.

One of the Loci—one of his friends—was missing from Grant's internal radar. A single voice from the chorus, gone without a trace. As if there were a hole where that person had once been.

No!!

His eyes stubbornly refused to focus on anything but the blood covering his hands as his heart raced and the grass beneath him seemed to melt away.

For the first time in a long time, icy cold fear gripped the heart of the most powerful man in the world.

The Bringer was afraid.

1

Los Angeles, California
Eight Days Earlier

Leeza Martz never knew what hit her.

All of Los Angeles had gone mad, so she couldn't quite manage any shock that she'd fallen victim to the group insanity. The riots outside were loud, gunfire only blocks away. Fires spread through what seemed like every other building, and screaming came from all directions.

But the sight of her own blood oozing from her forehead . . . that hit a little closer to home.

"It's okay, baby," said the monolith of a man holding the pistol. "Just relax. Don't scream or nothing and I'll make sure you enjoy the ride as much as I do."

Leeza's young, desperate eyes searched for salvation. But the ramshackle apartment building in South Central where this predator had chased her was all but abandoned and practically falling apart as she watched it. She knew better than to let a crazed client chase her into an empty, enclosed space . . . The other girls had warned her, even Shade had given her strict guidelines . . .

You don't run into a place that makes it easier for the guy to kill you when he's done with you. . . .

Her auburn locks fell across her heavily made-up face, mingling with the blood and dripping onto an expensive, sequined, black halter top and gold skirt. The copper smell was an incredibly strong sensation—perhaps her only remaining foothold on anything resembling reality.

But then, reality had changed, hadn't it? All over the world it had changed, but especially here in L.A. . . .

"You scared?" the big man asked as he hunched over her shivering body on the floor.

"Y-yes."

"That's real smart," he replied, burying the gun's nozzle in her temple. "You *should* be."

Leeza began weeping openly just as a soft, calm voice from behind her assailant wondered aloud, "What *is* it with men and guns?"

The gun spun around dizzyingly fast and was instantly trained on this newcomer, while at the same time Leeza found herself pulled to her feet, choked in a vicious headlock.

Facing them both with an air of tranquil curiosity was a girl not much older than Leeza. She stood relatively short, with wavy brown locks. She wore no makeup. A simple tank top and a well-worn pair of jeans covered a slender frame.

Her appearance couldn't have been any more different than Leeza's if she tried. There was no jewelry around her neck, no watch on her wrist, and no shoes on her feet.

"So," she regarded them, cocking her head to one side, "is this little encounter a free-for-all or do I have to take a number?"

A long silence filled the air. Looting and rioting must still be going on, but in that moment only the building could be heard; the immediate surroundings were deathly silent.

"What?" the burly man finally answered in a bewildered voice.

"I saw what was up," the plain-dressed girl replied, tossing a fleeting glance at the half-opened fly in his pants, "and was hoping I could get a turn."

She's a junkie, Leeza thought.

Please, whoever you are, help me!

The woman's voice was light and airy, her hands casually clasped behind her back as if the riots, the city collapsing around her, were an everyday occurrence.

The attacker's demeanor suddenly changed. He loosened his grip on Leeza's neck and smiled. "Oh yeah, baby. I'll even let you go first."

"You sweet-talker, you," the girl replied, a grin spreading over her face. "You're going to get me *all* riled up."

The man turned loose of Leeza and flung her against a wall, where she fell into a heap on the floor.

"Don't go anywhere, sweetheart," he said, winking at her, still smiling with a wicked glee. "This'll be five minutes, tops."

He turned and approached the brunette, who stood there waiting for him, unmoving and apparently unconcerned with the danger she'd just placed herself in. Leeza looked about for an opportunity to crawl away. To her right, ten feet down the hallway, she saw a door cracked open leading to what was likely a derelict apartment. If she could only get there, maybe once the two of them were at it, they might not notice . . .

"Five minutes?" she heard the strange girl repeat, incredulous. "That all you got?"

Despite herself, Leeza couldn't keep from watching the two of them. The big man quickly turned gruff and ill tempered.

"No," he barked, stepping right up into the girl's face, "five minutes is all you *get!*"

The girl's arms crossed across her chest and the smile disappeared. When she spoke, her voice had changed from casual to cold as ice. "Sweetie . . . in five minutes, you won't even have *bladder control.*"

Incredibly, this only seemed to excite the man even more. He grabbed the girl by the shoulders, but a distant look crept across her face as she locked her eyes onto his.

In seconds, he fell suddenly to the floor, hot tears streaming down his cheeks. He clutched his knees to his chest, lying on his side. His reddened face was howling in . . . was that *agony*?

The plain-dressed girl stepped around him as if he were a dilapidated ottoman and glanced at Leeza. Suddenly, it felt as if they were the only two people in the room. She approached carefully, kneeling next to Leeza, who still lay terrified on the floor.

"My name is Alex," she said softly. She stretched out a hand and carefully asked, "What's yours?"

"Um . . ." Leeza stammered, still trying to figure out what just happened, "Leeza."

"Are you okay, Leeza?" Alex asked in a kind voice. It wasn't a question about her physical well-being; it was as if Alex were asking if she was going to *be* okay now.

And somehow Leeza knew that she would. That this ordeal was
over, and that she would be fine. The soothing sensation washed over
her, and with it came a bravery that had escaped her only moments
ago.

She nodded slowly.

Alex smiled. "Come on," she said, helping Leeza to her feet, "let's
get you out of here."

Leeza stood on shaking knees. She was still unable to take her eyes
off of the man in the fetal position on the floor, who continued howling
as though he were a newborn having a nightmare. "What . . . What
happened to him?"

"Fear's a powerful weapon," Alex replied with knowing eyes. "The
ones who try hardest to make others afraid are always the first to want
their mommies when things get *really* scary."

Leeza felt a wave of nausea but quickly found Alex's arms stabiliz-
ing her. She was so tired . . . so tired . . .

Like everyone in this city, she was so tired of being afraid.

Alex watched her as they walked down a creaking set of stairs, a
steadying hand braced against wallpaper that was peeling off of the
wall beside them.

"This life you lead," Alex said carefully. "You're burned out, aren't
you? I can see it in your eyes—a newfound resolve, a readiness to start
life over and get things right this time."

Leeza was amazed to find herself nodding, tears forming in her
eyes. She knew this girl called Alex was right, yet she had no explanation for why she'd suddenly made a life-altering decision on the spot,
why she knew it was right, and why accepting it felt so good.

As Alex kept her eyes on her, Leeza immediately felt as though the
fear and shock and trauma had been flushed out of her body. Her skin
began to warm, her pulse steadied, and her equilibrium returned.

She felt an overwhelming sense of resolve sweep through her, and it
struck her as astonishing that she'd ever been afraid of the sad, weeping man that lay coiled in the hallway behind them.

"I know a place you can go to get a fresh start," Alex was saying as
they walked carefully outside. Leeza simply nodded gratefully, overwhelmed by all this.

The center of the riot seemed to have moved west toward downtown; the immediate area looked safer now than it had when Leeza had first run inside.

A cab was already at the curb waiting for them. Alex helped Leeza enter the backseat first, then she gave the driver an address. Alex was about to take the seat beside Leeza when she froze and looked into the distance. She seemed to be listening, but Leeza couldn't figure out what she was listening to. She gave a barely perceptible nod to no one in particular.

"I'm sorry," Alex said, shutting the car's door and sticking her head inside the window. "I can't come with you—they need me," she explained, without ever bothering to clarify just exactly who "they" were.

"But you're safe now, I promise," Alex said, a strong grip tightening around Leeza's hand one last time. "Things are going to get better."

Alex glanced at the front seat and caught the cabby's eyes in the rearview. "Protect her until she safely reaches her destination," she said in a tone that left no room for discussion.

The driver gave no argument. His shoulders seemed to set firmly and a new determination lit up his otherwise dull eyes.

As she saw it happen, Leeza finally understood what was going on. The realization shocked her as all of the pieces of this puzzle fell into place. It all made sense now.

She knew who this Alex was.

"You . . . you're one of. . . !" she cried excitedly. "You're with *him*!"

Alex smiled, and then she turned and ran.

2

Los Angeles burned.

The city raged with the most virulent outbreak of fear and panic it had ever known. And like predators trapped by circumstances beyond their control, most of the city's residents lashed out at one another in fear.

Nothing of this magnitude had ever been seen by most of the eyes watching the shocking events unfold on live television, all over the world. Few were surprised when gangs used the opportunity to settle scores with rivals, but throughout most of the city, there was no premeditation to the acts of violence. It was everyday men and women, displaying a brand of fear and panic found only when it is believed the world is coming to an end. Wherever three or more of them gathered, anarchy ensued.

Those not engaged in the fighting were simply trying to get away. Flee the city. Find shelter. Seek refuge wherever they could find it.

Or wherever they could *take* it.

The real threat came from the fires. Over seven thousand separate instances of burning buildings erupted across the city in less than two hours' time—an act so impossible, it left many reeling from the same panic that had gripped downtown one morning two months ago, when it seemed that the sky had turned to flame and was threatening to rain down upon them. No one had seen anything of this scale on American soil since Sherman marched through Atlanta during the Civil War.

Open looting was videoed from news helicopters circling above;

throngs of rioters could be seen like ants emerging from malls and shopping centers carrying mostly expensive electronic merchandise, but also armfuls of clothes, designer shoes, furniture, toys, and even stacks of books. A few here and there took their time, taking refuge in the handguns they wielded—or more crude weapons like hammers, box cutters, or anything heavy that could be thrown. But most simply counted on speed for safety, running as fast as they could with the bundles they carried.

The mayor's pleas for calm and order fell on ears that could not hear him over the roar of the widespread flames. The thousands of burning buildings churned out black smoke that was just beginning to coalesce above the city as though a volcano had exploded.

Major highways were clogged or blocked altogether by traffic jams and accidents. Local 911 services were overwhelmed from the flood of calls that broke out in the first ten minutes alone; firefighters and police were vastly outnumbered, and the governor of California had ordered a National Guard deployment just ninety minutes in, though they had yet to mobilize for the deployment.

One news crew on the ground caught what would become a defining image of the riot: just to the southeast of LAX, a pregnant woman's head stuck out of the third floor window of a burning building, begging and crying for anyone to help her. An angry man who would later be identified as Nick Jensen stood on the street corner beneath her, waving a loaded gun in the direction of anyone who attempted to rescue her. His face was the very picture of the riot itself: madness, desperation, anger, fear. His eyes were bloodshot, his cheeks puffy and burning from hot tears.

Most would never find out what exactly the situation was here— was Nick the child's father? a scorned lover? or was he simply insane?—but several pedestrians tried to slip around the man or overpower him. None succeeded. One fireman was shot point-blank while trying to enter the building behind Nick. The firefighter was dead on the spot.

It was when the police began to converge on Nick's location from both sides of the street that things got *really* bad. That single action set the stage for the world to witness something that no eye had ever seen before.

Samuel Levinson had never witnessed anything like this, which was saying something. At seventy-eight years of age, Samuel had fought for his country in two wars, survived more than twenty earthquakes in sunny California, survived triple bypass surgery, escaped a forest fire that nearly consumed the beachfront neighborhood where he and his wife had lived for more than fifteen years, and managed to keep his loved ones safe during the '92 riot following the Rodney King incident.

But *this* was new. Never had he seen an entire city gripped by the same hysteria. Everywhere he looked people were running, screaming, throwing, punching, crashing, spitting, dying.

They were raging against the entire world for changing its rules so drastically without asking their permission.

The scale of it made Samuel doubt his old eyes could really be showing him reality.

His well-kept '75 Buick Regal weaved cautiously around the wild crowds and abandoned vehicles filling Imperial Highway. Someone from high above on the 105 interchange was throwing rocks and food down to the surface roads, and a carton full of eggs splattered across Samuel's hood.

Any other day, such damage to his precious Regal would have seemed like the end of the world. Today he simply turned on the wiper blades to remove the excess splatter on the windshield and pressed down on the gas pedal a little harder.

Samuel rarely said it aloud, but for his part, he was inclined to blame these new superhumans that were popping up all over the place. If they couldn't use their so-called superpowers to help everyone else and stop all these disasters, what good were they? The media had split its nonstop coverage between this unprecedented global phenomenon and the strange natural disasters that continued to break out all over the world, and Samuel's question was one that came up frequently among the reports. The superhumans didn't seem to be doing anything to prevent the disasters, so why not blame them for everything that was going wrong?

The disasters had begun following the appearance of the very first of the superhumans right here in L.A., about seven weeks ago. China took the first hit; an outbreak of an unknown contagion decimated three cities in the southern Jiangxi Province, killing nearly a million people practically overnight. It happened much too fast, caught everyone off guard, and too many people became sick simultaneously for health officials to successfully identify a first patient. But the first official medical report about the contagion, showing the earliest time stamp, was for a businessman surnamed Zhuan. So it became known as the Zhuan Virus.

The virus, which caused blood to clot *inside* of human veins, killed so quickly that the devastation had been done before it was contained. The entire province remained under complete quarantine even now, but no further fatalities had been recorded since that first forty-eight hour period. Health officials speculated that either Zhuan had mutated or the remainder of the population had developed the antibodies necessary to defeat the disease. Foreign travel to and from China was severely restricted.

Samuel reacted to this gruesome pandemic with the same detached fascination as the rest of the United States—unable to look away from the gripping, heartbreaking news coverage, yet unable to invest himself personally in a plight so far on the other side of the world.

Two days later came a situation he couldn't disengage himself from so easily. An unseasonably early Category Five hurricane—which had been projected to dissipate in the middle of the Atlantic, having never touched land—inexplicably and without warning shifted its track and drenched most of New York and New England. Carving a path of destruction thousands of miles long, Hurricane Austin left over a dozen feet of water standing for weeks in Central Park and Boston Common, and only in the last few days had the ground again become touchable by human feet. The devastation of American soil was without precedent, and Manhattan Island itself had all but disappeared beneath the ocean.

The news coverage, inveterate in its focus on drama and desolation, had repeatedly insisted on zooming in on shots of hundreds and thousands of bodies floating atop the water.

Samuel's thoughts returned to the present as the Regal was forced to slow to a crawl. He couldn't stop blinking due to the smoke seeping in from everywhere and stinging his eyes. The world was on fire.

Helen gasped beside him in the passenger seat, stifling a scream as a pair of college-age girls, happily drunk with beer bottles sloshing in their hands, started banging their palms against Helen's side window. Samuel couldn't make out all they were saying but he thought they were trying to get money.

His eyes darted to the door locks for the eighth time since starting the car. He moved on, barely noticing the yells, rude gestures, and then laughter from the girls in his rearview mirror.

In the center of the street ahead, a man wearing nothing but a sandwich board waved a megaphone around, screaming the same message that was painted on his dual signs. Samuel recognized it as the usual "the end is near" garbage that always got spouted by the crazies after or during a major disaster. He mashed his car horn down, but the man in the street refused to budge. Samuel was forced to take his time, wait for an opening in the fender-to-fender traffic, and finally go around.

In the weeks since Hurricane Austin, the world had witnessed one indescribable disaster after another. Stifling heat waves plagued India and Africa, bringing droughts and death in their wakes. Wildfires ate away at forests and vineyards in southern Europe. A massive sinkhole had opened up near Sydney, Australia, causing drastic shifts in the city's geological structure. There had been many cave-ins of buildings and highway bridges. The most recent disaster had come in the form of more than a dozen volcanoes across Central America and the West Indies that all erupted simultaneously.

The entire global economy was in turmoil over the loss of sources of so many basic essentials used by people the world over. Simple items like a bar of soap or a loaf of bread cost four or five times what they had only a few months ago.

It was madness, all of it, Samuel concluded. Sheer madness. The rules of how this little planet worked weren't meant to be changed so quickly and so drastically, and the earth itself was protesting as loudly as it could. And of course, a suffocating fear had clutched the hearts of those who dwelled upon it.

L.A.'s citizens were simply the first to act out.

What they were seeing today, Samuel's instincts were telling him, would soon engulf the world. It would spread and the world would soak in blood . . .

It was as this thought passed through his mind that he jumped in his seat. A nearby gunshot was accompanied by a splattering of blood against his right cheek.

3

Five-year-old Gina Levinson tried to do as her grandfather told her and crouch low in the floorboard, in the backseat of his car. But the gunshot and someone yelling, "OUT OF THE CAR! NOW!!" just outside was more than she could resist.

Slowly she lifted her head to see her grandfather's hands hovering above the steering wheel in a gesture of surrender. Something red was on the side of his face. Was he bleeding?

Where was he hurt? Or was it her grandmother?

She screamed, unable to catch her breath, too many thoughts clashing in her brain at once, and the gunman outside turned the gun in her direction.

Her grandfather immediately stepped out of the car and offered to toss his keys to the man with the gun. "Just let me get my family out first," he pleaded.

"GIMME THE KEYS, OLD MAN!!" the man with the gun screamed, his finger on the trigger and the gun still pointed at Gina.

Samuel's heart seemed to stop.

No! Mercy, no. Please no.

"The girl goes free!" Samuel firmly stood his ground. "If you want a hostage, you can have me! But *she* walks away."

The man pulled the trigger.

The rear passenger window shattered with the shot, but Gina was too low in the floorboard to be anywhere near the bullet. Dozens of onlookers nearby turned to watch the drama unfold but none had the courage to intervene.

Worse still, Samuel spotted not one, but two separate camera crews filming the event from several hundred feet away.

Why were they *filming* this instead of helping him?!

Frantic, Samuel eyed the man he would later learn was named Nick, and Nick returned the favor. There was evil in those eyes, something primal and desperate and animal. Samuel had seen it before, during his time in the Marines as a young man. And he knew without question that there was no good way out of this situation.

Nick would wreak death and destruction on all he encountered, because he knew how to do nothing else. Remarkably, Samuel found himself pitying this man, this hate-filled creature who was unequipped to hold onto his soul in a world gone mad. This vile killer who had murdered his Helen.

"Give. Me. The. Keys," Nick said, voice low.

"Gina, get out of the car, honey. Right now," Samuel said loud enough for her to hear.

Gina opened the rear driver's side door where her grandfather stood and slowly walked toward him. She clutched at his right pant leg, watching the gunman with big eyes and a blank expression, as her grandfather threw the car keys at him. Her breaths came in shallow gasps and she reflexively retrieved an inhaler from her pocket and breathed in its medicinal contents.

The man with the gun circled the front of the car, gun still pointing at her grandfather, and entered the driver's side. And just like that, the car and her grandmother were gone.

Once the drama was over, the rampaging crowds on all sides swarmed into and through the spot where the car had stood like oxygen filling a vacuum. Gina and her grandfather merely stood there in shock, not knowing where to go or what to do.

Finally, her grandfather found his voice and said, "Help us," in a small voice. It gained strength and intensity every time he said it until he was shouting it at the top of his lungs. "HELP US!!"

"I'll give ya a hand, pops," said a broad-shouldered brute who passed by, flying gang colors. He slugged the elder man viciously across his temple and kept moving with the crowd. In no time at all, Gina's grandfather was lying flat on his back, and she cuddled atop him, trying her best to keep from being trampled by the sea of adults running around them.

Samuel squeezed his eyes open through the tremendous pain that now seized his forehead, and caught a blurry image of the mass of humanity that was running, hopping, and stomping across him. He tried to raise a hand when he saw Gina kneeling over him, tried to protect her or caution her, but he was too drained. Too weak to do anything.

Feet trudged over his body, crushing his legs, ankles, and abdomen. He did his best to shield his face but knew he wouldn't last long. A sharp chemical smell overpowered him and he felt something tacky and wet on his face. It was spray paint. Someone was spraying graffiti on his face and body.

He was glad Gina wasn't old enough to read yet, for fear of what the paint probably said.

Samuel could only pray that he himself would bear the brunt of the meaningless attack, and that somehow Gina would survive this. Because he had failed her, just as he had failed Helen. The whole city had gone to Hell and there was nothing left to hope for. . . .

Samuel felt a great *whoosh* and suddenly the crowd around him was replaced by a wide, full view of the hazy gray sky above. He squinted his eyes to see that the crowd had fallen back several yards away, many of them lying in a circle with a ten-foot radius around him. It was as if a small bomb had been dropped and he was in the exact center of the explosion; everyone else was on their backs, just outside of what might be considered the blast radius.

But no, he was wrong.

One person was still standing.

A tall man with sharp blue eyes, brown hair, and a grim focus stood at Samuel's feet, his brown leather jacket framing his stance in the hot, smoke-filled wind like a billowing cape. He placed himself between Samuel and everyone on the ground around him.

Between Samuel and certain death.

The man's head turned sharply in the direction that Samuel's car had disappeared into only moments ago, and he stretched out his hand in that same direction.

A screeching of unmoving tires on pavement could be heard in the distance.

Gina had closed her eyes, afraid to look. But when the commotion stopped, she peeked just as everyone else did. A streak of the red spray paint on her grandfather's face had caught the ends of her hair, but other than a few bruises, she was unharmed.

She blinked in recognition at the man who calmly stood just inches from her, his arm out.

"Grandpa, look!" Gina cried, smiling. "It's *him!*"

Hearing her exclamation, the standing man turned to look at her and a softer expression washed over his features.

Gina clapped her hands in glee.

He was here.

"It's Guardian!" she shouted.

4

Grant had to force himself not to wince at the sound of the name the public had given him. It wasn't their fault he had to remain anonymous, after all—and the name they'd selected for him could have been worse.

Still, he felt wholly unworthy of such a name.

And the camera crews nearby had caught the whole thing on tape. He fought the urge to sigh. Once again, the one man in all the world that nobody could identify, yet everyone recognized, would be the top story on the six o'clock news.

He advanced toward the old man and his granddaughter, who still lay on the ground, as the others around them got to their feet. Some ran away in fear, others stood and marveled at the sight of him.

A boy of no more than fifteen stood a couple of yards away, a paint can in his hand. Grant glanced at the can and it exploded, showering the boy in his own shade of bright red paint.

At this, half a dozen other young men stepped forward from the crowd.

Crips, Grant thought, steadying himself at the sight of the familiar gang colors.

"So you the big dog, now, huh?" one of them shouted, pulling out a knife.

"Yeah, we heard about you!" another joined in, brandishing a pistol. "Can't wait to be the one to say I put a bullet in your sorry—"

The weapons in their hands leapt into the air as one. The gang members did double takes at their guns, knives, brass knuckles, and even a grenade, jumping into the sky and hanging there, several feet above their heads. The more complex pieces of weaponry disassembled themselves in mere seconds, all the way down to their core pieces of metal.

The man that had brandished the gun was livid. "You sack of—!"

The gunman suddenly stopped talking. His hands went to his throat, where he tried to pry something loose. He was breathing, but he couldn't make any sound come out of his mouth.

"Now, gentlemen, I *know*," Grant said without shouting, his right arm still pointed at the old Buick in place several hundred yards down the road, "that we've had this conversation already. Same tune, different verse. I've squeezed off your voice box, because I don't want to go through it again. It's growing tedious. As I've told you many times now, you and your crew are *done* in Los Angeles."

Grant had had several run-ins with the city's major street gangs over the last few months and had succeeded in driving thousands of them out of town. But he found that they were like roaches—always plenty more hiding in some unseen crevice, ready to pop up and multiply at the first opportunity.

"L.A.'s ours and always will be!" another one hissed, threateningly. "We ain't givin' up our turf to no—"

"You *have* no turf," Grant said with a voice that was quiet but unarguably authoritative. "Los Angeles is under *my* protection. Get out now under your own power, or later under *mine*."

The tires on the car were screeching loudly as the Regal came into view, inching toward them in reverse. Everyone in the surrounding area had stopped what they were doing and watched the scene unfold. No one dared interfere.

A sea of gang members appeared from the edges of Grant's vision, and took up positions alongside their brothers. The new players drew out enough weapons to supply a small army. Switchblades, baseball bats, and guns of all kinds—even a few semi-automatics—appeared and all of them were aimed at Grant.

Grant could practically feel the news cameras on the sidelines zooming in to catch his reaction.

"Perhaps you didn't hear me," Grant offered. He held out his other hand and as he spread his fingers wide, every weapon that was visible flung itself upward, joining the others that were suspended above their heads. One gang member who stubbornly refused to let go of his gun was thrust up into the air with it, dangling freely as if hanging from a cliff. Finally he turned loose and landed with a dull thud against the pavement.

Grant made a fist. The hundreds of pieces of metal above their heads complied by mashing and twisting themselves together into something resembling a large ball of gleaming silver and black gunmetal. Grant tossed his fist casually to the side the way an office worker might toss a wadded up piece of paper into a trash can. The ball of metal shot impossibly high and away, miles and miles into the horizon, toward the ocean.

"There will be no more violence here," Grant evenly stated, finally bringing the squealing car to a stop. Inside, Nick frantically tried to get out, to shoot a hole in the driver's side window, but his weapon had joined the others in the sky through the already-broken passenger window, and the driver's seat belt pinned him tightly against the seat.

Grant let go of the car. Now both of his hands were free.

"We still got fists, dog!" one of the gangbangers shouted, and the rest of them seemed reinvigorated by this outburst.

"Yeah," another yelled. "You gonna pull *those* off us too?"

As one, the angry mob began running toward him on all sides.

Grant's head ducked down in concentration, but his eyes remained fixed on the horde stampeding straight at him. He opened his hands, arms down at his sides.

The ground shook as hundreds of small pieces of the paved road cracked and tore free and shot toward the mob. Many of them were nicked in the head, leg, or stomach. It was enough to slow them down or even send some of them to the ground in fierce pain.

A handful remained rooted to where they stood, still trying to look tough but unsure of what next move to make.

"Don't make me do something you'll regret," he said to the ones still standing.

That was enough to deter most of them, but a few lingered, as if deciding that their reputations might be worth risking it. One bold teenager ran straight at him, but he was knocked off of his feet by more pieces of pavement that collided with his shins. He screamed in pain, and Grant felt a momentary twinge of regret at having to harm the boy.

But then, Grant had learned not long ago that some lessons could only be learned on the other side of pain.

Grant's eyes went out of focus, and his thoughts went to . . .

Hector.

No definable command was given, no verbal message sent. But Grant immediately knew that Hector had received the summons and was on his way. Just as he knew from a sense deep within that Alex had just arrived nearby and was deterring some of the onlookers with her powers of emotional control. Nora he could feel nearby as well; the man still struggling in the car would be left for her to deal with.

He turned slightly to glance over his right shoulder; one of the gang members stood there, a cinderblock raised to smash against Grant's head. This guy was older than most of the others, probably in his late twenties.

"Your friends will recover," Grant said quietly, glancing at the large brick in the man's hands. "Do this, and I promise you, you won't."

The block was dropped to the ground, and the man ran after his friends.

Grant returned his attention to the old man on the ground and his young charge, who was breathing unnaturally fast. She had hollow eyes that looked as if they'd known nothing but fatigue and fright for a very long time.

Hector arrived. His round body quickly knelt down on one knee, his big eyes closed, his palm pressing lightly against the old man's forehead. The man's eyes, buried beneath the red paint that covered his face, blinked to life and Hector opened his own.

Alex. Nora.

"See what you can do about spreading some calm," Grant called out without looking in their direction. They never used names in the field; it was too dangerous.

Grant exchanged a glance with Hector, who said nothing. But then, Hector hadn't said a word since joining Grant and his team. Not a single word.

Grant and the others were still unsure if their Hispanic friend was genuinely mute, or simply chose not to speak. But he had proven an invaluable ally. Most of the Loci thought of him as a healer, but the truth was that he was able to control the body's functions by taking command of the mind's regulation of those functions. It was a powerful ability, but he mostly used it to force the minds of others to heal their bodies at a vastly accelerated rate.

A nod was all it took from Grant, and Hector replied in kind. Always running from one victim to the next, soon he was gone, off to heal someone else who needed him.

"Guardian! Sir! Can we get a statement, please? Sir?" A female reporter was running toward him, trailed by a cameraman. She held a microphone out far enough ahead of her body that she might've been carrying a bomb.

He was still deciding how best to avoid the reporter when a loud crash from far above was followed by a scream from the little girl on the ground.

Grant turned a sharp one-eighty upward in time to see a gleaming silver tractor-trailer that looked like it was carrying some kind of toxic liquid. It had punched through the cement barrier lining the westbound 405-to-105 overpass high above and was now falling straight at him and the old man and the girl and the reporter and dozens of onlookers like a hundred-thousand-pound bullet. He'd barely caught sight of it when it was right on top of them.

But just as it should have crashed and exploded in a spectacular display, Grant's arm was in the air, palm like a baseball catcher's mitt. The hurtling truck was frozen in place, its grille maybe a foot away from Grant's fingertips. The driver was frozen as well, though not by Grant's doing. His face was drained of color and his hands still frantically white-knuckled the steering wheel.

From the sidelines, Grant heard the reporter whisper to her cameraman. "If you didn't get that on tape, I'm going to scratch your eyes out."

Gina felt her jaw drop at the sight before her but couldn't will it back into place beneath her upper lip. She was staring at the most incredible, most outrageous thing she'd ever seen. It was him—the one everyone called Guardian—holding a tractor-trailer just above the ground.

Suspended by nothing.

Hundreds, perhaps thousands, of people—even Guardian's companions—had stopped whatever they were doing to marvel at the sight.

Seeing a cross-sectional view of both Guardian and the truck from her perspective, it was as if the truck were a missile pointing diagonally down at Guardian like an arrow. Guardian stood as the target, keeping it at bay with a single arm.

And despite the showdown with the gang, despite the weight of the truck, despite even the brown leather jacket he wore on this warm day . . .

Guardian hadn't even broken a sweat.

Later, whenever anyone would ask Gina about what she saw that day, she would swear that Guardian had paused for a moment before settling the truck safely on the ground, and half-swiveled his head in her direction, as just a hint of a smile teased the edges of his mouth.

5

Washington, D.C.
J. Edgar Hoover Building

"Over seven thousand acts of arson, more personal injuries than officials are currently able to count, open looting in broad daylight, four-
thousand-some-odd vehicle accidents, defacement of government property, gang wars brewing throughout South Central, and local
emergency services so overwhelmed that Governor Bowman called for
a full National Guard deployment throughout Los Angeles County less
than *two hours* after the riot began. Agent Cooke, I hope there's some
sort of happy ending on the last page of this very dramatic report of
yours."

FBI Special Agent Ethan Cooke half rolled his eyes in what could
be interpreted as a brazen act of insubordination. But he gave such
concerns little thought and eventually met the glance of his superior,
Director Lindsay Stevens, who sat opposite him near the head of the
table, while absently scratching at one of his many scars, this one on
his left bicep.

Ethan had ultra-short blonde hair and green eyes highlighting a
round, boyish face. Easygoing creases framed his mouth, hinting at a
smile that came very easily. And his body always seemed to be in
motion. Even if he collected himself for a meeting like this one, one or
both of his knees would bob up and down relentlessly.

It was one of the many things about himself that he knew Director
Stevens hated.

"As a rule, I try *not* to draw conclusions, Director," Ethan coolly
replied. "I'm a field agent, here to collect and present you with the

known facts. As I understand it, drawing conclusions is reserved—particularly in this case—for agents above my pay grade. Such as yourself."

Stevens's eyes flared, almost imperceptibly. Ethan had fired the opening shot. One point for the visitor.

His fingers fidgeted, tapping on the tabletop.

Seven other members of various intelligence committees and agencies sat around the table, here under utmost secrecy to be briefed with the latest information about the world's new status quo and determine a recommended course of action to deliver to the president. Yet for now, none of them spoke; most seemed content to watch the battle brewing beneath the surface between FBI Director Stevens and the Agency's leading expert on the man known as Guardian.

Stevens, wearing her customary crisp blue skirt and jacket over an impeccable white blouse, appeared right at home in this setting, a private briefing room. Ethan, on the other hand, even though he'd dressed in his best denim and long sleeve button-up, felt completely out of place. He belonged outside, in the field, pounding the pavement. He hated the indoors, preferring a setting that would let him take unrestricted action.

At a meager twenty-eight, Ethan had racked up more field experience in various other agencies—police, the state bureau of investigation, military—than the rest of his graduating class at the Academy. He'd also had the lowest qualifying test scores of the group that made it in.

But that was almost three years ago now, and one need only look at his rapid rise through the ranks and the glowing recommendations of his various superiors to see that he was among the Agency's finest, particularly in the field, where he thrived. What he lacked in psychology or business degrees, he more than made up for with solid instincts, deductive reasoning, charisma, and old-fashioned determination. And despite his lack of graduate studies, his intelligence and quick thinking on his feet were unquestionable.

Put simply, Ethan Cooke was the agent assigned when you had to have results and you had to have them now. And everyone in the Agency knew it.

Despite this, he knew it remained something of an irritant to many in the upper echelons that this agent with only a handful of years under his belt had been named the company's top man on the Guardian situation.

Director Stevens was one of his most vocal critics. And right now, she was doing everything in her power to underscore the fact that he was out of his league.

She lobbed his report onto the tabletop and fixed her unflagging gaze on him. "If Guardian is on-site at the riots *now*, as your report suggests, perhaps you would be good enough to explain to us why a vigilante with such extreme power at his command is being allowed to operate unsupervised. Or more to the point, unhindered."

Ethan hesitated; his tapping on the table stopped. He stifled the initial sarcastic response that entered his head. "As I understand it, there *is* no one available on-site to deal with the Guardian situation, with the riot still in progress as we speak. I would be there right now myself, had I not been ordered to report to this meeting. And as my reports over the last three weeks have made clear . . . with all due respect, Director, if there *is* a way to 'hinder' this man, in any fashion, it has yet to be found."

"Yes, yes," Stevens replied impatiently. "We've all heard about how he can do anything. Yet how much of this is verifiable truth? All we know for certain is that he appears to be the most powerful of the superhumans, with the ability to manipulate any object—great or small—in his immediate vicinity. Which makes him potentially a walking, breathing, *living* weapon of mass destruction."

"I'm afraid I have to take issue with such a categorization," Ethan replied. A few of the others in the room stiffened. Ethan knew he'd spoken out of turn, as it was uncustomary to speak up in a briefing of this nature unless addressed—but this could be his only chance. "What little evidence we do have—along with dozens of firsthand reports—suggests that Guardian and his band of fellow superhumans are using their powers not offensively, but defensively, and most often in rescue operations or the prevention of crime.

"A Hispanic man with some kind of healing ability has been seen at three different hospitals this morning alone, after which all the patients in all three ERs—even the most critical of cases—were given clean bills of health and discharged. Two women identified as members of Guardian's team have helped stabilize numerous violent situations that threatened to spiral out of control. Just today, Guardian himself has been documented using his powers to save lives, end crises, and avert disasters.

"Forgive me, Director, but I must wonder if the issue at stake here today is clear. Are we investigating Guardian's capabilities or his *intentions?*"

Stevens's eyes narrowed on him. "Your weakness, Agent Cooke, is that you believe there's a difference. The situation in Britain demands that we consider the safety and sovereignty of maintaining authority over this nation. But you *have* misinterpreted my concerns, which is unsurprising. Considering your position on this task force, it is not Guardian's intentions that are foremost among my concerns here today. It's *your* intentions that have my full attention. You have repeatedly showed a proclivity for sympathetic terminology in your reports on Guardian and his activities. Such actions force me to wonder if your priorities might be misplaced."

Ethan paused, swallowing this pill that went down bitterly. It wasn't that she'd come right out and said it, in front of all of these important people. It was that she'd taken her time getting around to it, making sure that he played into her accusations as fully as possible.

That was a big misstep, he thought. *Allowing yourself to be so transparent? Director Stevens, I thought you were smarter.*

He leaned forward into the table, framing his next words with deliberation. "One thing I think we can all agree on is that our world has become a powder keg that's ready to ignite at any time. What's happening in Los Angeles today is just the first salvo. But there's an elephant in the middle of this room that no one is acknowledging."

Stevens sat back in her chair and crossed her arms over her chest. *Educate me*, she seemed to be telegraphing. No one else said a word, waiting on Ethan to continue.

"The global disasters taking place virtually nonstop around the world," he explained. "I'm sure no one has forgotten the mysterious atmospheric disturbance that took place over Los Angeles shortly before Guardian first appeared on the scene? That was the day everything began. There's an almost *systematic* quality to the way these disasters have played out. China, New York, Africa, Central America, and all the rest followed that initial event—an event which Guardian and his followers were present for, and some assign credit to for quelling. Can we really allow ourselves to be so blind as to believe that these various global phenomena are random and coincidental to the sudden appearance of the superhumans? That just when the world needs saving like never before, a team of . . . *superheroes* arrives on the scene?

"Director, distinguished guests. Do not mistake a presentation of unbiased facts for sympathy with a potential enemy of mankind. We are talking about a man who wields unprecedented power in the palm of his hand. His actions tell one story, but his very *presence* tells another. Why is he here? Where did he come from? Why can we not identify him, with all of our vast resources? These questions plague my every waking thought, as they *should* plague yours. What are this man and his friends playing at?

"Allow me to be perfectly, unwaveringly clear. I was placed on this task force because I am a blunt instrument. In my observations, most members of this Agency are more comfortable sitting in offices and *talking* about policy, rather than doing the kinds of things I do every day. Guardian and those like him are a clear and present danger to the safety and sanctity of not just the United States, but the entire human race. We are talking about an individual who can use any object in his immediate vicinity as a weapon. He could be, in a word, *unstoppable.*

"I'm on a flight to Los Angeles the minute this meeting is concluded, and no matter the hurdles, I *will* find him, and for the sake of our entire way of life, I will show no hesitation in personally bringing this entire business to a very swift, very *definitive* end."

Stevens was quiet for a long moment, her mouth bordering somewhere between a frown and grim acknowledgment of Ethan's plainspoken truth. He was right, and he could see how much it bothered her.

She rose from her chair in a signal that the briefing was over, but before moving away, she looked on him one last time.

"Find him," she ordered.

6

Grant couldn't get the image of that little girl out of his head as he pulled his car to a stop in front of the warehouse. His car was a used SUV they'd purchased not too long ago to replace the Corvette that had been destroyed in the collapse of the Wagner Building; he'd decided that a less flashy car would help preserve his anonymity as he came and went as needed. A forged license plate completed the effect.

There was something about the haunted, hollow quality of the girl's eyes that Grant couldn't shake. The light had burned out in them long ago; they'd known only fear and pain for quite a while: He'd personally escorted her and her grandfather until they were safely ensconced in one of several safe shelters that had popped up behind police barriers throughout the morning.

Am I partly to blame for that? For taking hope out of the world for normal people because I can do so much more than they can?

No, Grant could hear Julie's voice in his head correcting him, *you're the one* bringing *them hope.*

He got out of the Blazer and marched toward the entrance of the warehouse. In the wake of the events under the Wagner Building, Daniel's warehouse was the only remaining place for the Loci to take shelter. Protecting its location was of paramount importance.

Daniel was holed up in his office upstairs, but allowed them to convert the main floor downstairs for their needs. Last Grant heard, there were at least thirty-seven of them staying here now, including non-Ringwearers like Julie, Lisa, and Daniel.

"Fletcher?" Grant asked, striding confidently through the main side door. "What's the word?"

"Most of the violence seems to be dwindling," Fletcher replied from his massive computer workstation-slash-cubicle. "Right now it looks like the overall focus is shifting to rescue and cleanup. Not to mention putting out the fires—of which there are still thousands. Careful with the names; we've got 'newbs' in the house."

Just as they never used names in the field, anytime newcomers were accepted into the group, no one was supposed to reveal their first names to the "newbies" until they'd been there at least a month.

Fletcher's work area was a three-sided rig of metal, steel, wood, and wire framework, atop which sat every computer he could get his hands on. Several large flatscreens were on his eye level, with smaller and more outdated monitors above and below. A keyboard extended toward him from the center section, and his desk chair had long ago conformed to the shape of his wiry body. The screens' lights flashed and changed colors unceasingly.

When the group had reorganized itself a few months back, everyone had been encouraged to find a role that suited them. Fletcher took it upon himself to become the eyes and ears of the team, which to him felt like a logical extension of his self-presumed role at the old asylum.

With the help of several of the more technically inclined members of the Loci, including Grant, who had once worked as an IT professional, he had hacked into hundreds of surveillance cameras positioned around Los Angeles. He also had live, ongoing news coverage showing on several of his monitors, twenty-four hours a day. And he'd gained backdoor access to numerous civilian and government top secret databases. From this one workstation, Fletcher kept track of the team's movements, coordinated their efforts, and offered crucial information to those in the field. His unique ability to process more than one thought at a time made him an ideal fit for this job—a job that would require multitasking on a grand scale.

"Alex checked in lately?" Grant asked.

"She's still over near the 405 interchange, working cleanup. She's fine."

Grant nodded; he knew it was true from the sense he had of her, but it was always good to know details. "I've got to get back, just wanted to make sure you guys are safe here." Grant squared his shoulders and turned to go, but something caught his eye.

"What's up with the new décor?" Grant asked, nodding at a large, bright, and rather gaudy banner that hung from the center of the converted warehouse. In big, bold letters, it read, "WHAT DO YOUR EYES SEE?"

"Ask your sister," Fletcher replied.

The words were no sooner out of his mouth than Julie came running across the room, a stack of folders clutched to her chest, and grabbed him in a gigantic bear hug, dropping the folders as she did. "Thank God you're okay! That was *too close*."

He smiled and returned the hug. "You saw the thing with the truck."

Julie had been carrying a stack of manila folders over a foot high in her arms when she approached. There were Ringwearers applying to join Grant's team within the folders, approval of which was one of Julie's primary responsibilities.

As she loosened her hug, she turned and saw the folders, hovering neatly in their stack, right where she'd turned loose of them.

"Every time I think I've seen it all, you do something that blows my mind all over again." She placed a quick peck on his cheek. She couldn't stop looking into his eyes.

One of her knees buckled slightly, as if the muscles had simply given out. Grant steadied her at once, while guiding the folders to rest on a nearby table. He smiled at her, and she allowed him to cradle her in the crook of his arm.

For the hundredth time that day alone, he found himself thinking of her illness and how much he hated it. It was still in its early stages and would take several years to fully deteriorate her motor control, but he despised it. He *reviled* that despicable disease, in every possible way that hate could be felt.

And he loved her more than ever for the millions of little ways she fought it.

He pretended to be looking at the folders—knew they must be profiles of the new applicants she was screening—so he could blink back hot tears that threatened to spill from his eyes. Because there was no way he would do that to her. Not here, not today.

"Took your meds today?" he asked her softly.

She nodded, concern still written on her face for him and his adventures.

"I'm okay, really," he comforted her. "The truck thing wasn't even a strain."

"It's not that . . ." she said, smiling even more broadly. "I've been glued to the TV, and I just—I saw what you did. And I'm not talking about your amazing feats of telekinesis, or whatever. What I saw was *raw* and real. What you did, those people you saved . . . The gentleness, the fierceness, the compassion, the strength . . ." She swallowed. "You were magnificent. I love you so much—not because you're my brother, but because of the man you've chosen to be."

Tears spilled down her cheeks, and he saw a slight shudder in her gait. He kissed her on the forehead.

"I want you to know," she said, "I have never been more proud of anyone than I am of you, right now."

Grant felt his cheeks redden. He smiled but looked down. It was too much, she'd gone too far . . . Julie's words, coupled with the exhaustion he felt from the day's events . . .

"Hey, where do you want these two?"

Grant and Julie released each other and turned to face Lisa, who stood off to the side with two men just behind her. One was enormous, the size of a bodybuilder or professional wrestler, the other was frumpy and mousy, with greasy black hair and a few bits of stubble scattered across his cheeks and chin.

Both of them wore gold rings with burgundy gemstones upon their right middle fingers.

New recruits, Grant recognized.

If Lisa knew she was breaking up a sentimental moment, she didn't show it. She appeared more bored than anything.

"Oh, um," Julie said, switching gears, "I'd like you to meet Henrike—is that how you say it?" She nodded at the big bull of a man who wore a camouflage tank top to show off his intimidating muscles, and he nodded back. He had earrings in both ears, and a crew cut that looked like he had somehow managed to bleach blonde what little hair there was. "And this is Wilhelm." Julie nodded at the little guy, who seemed to be trying to figure out a way to melt into the cement floor.

"They're joining us from different parts of Europe."

That was nothing particularly new. As more Loci found them, increasingly they were showing up from places of origin that were great distances away from Los Angeles.

Henrike was clearly awed by Grant's presence, though he puffed out his chest even further than it already was. Wilhelm briefly glanced up at Grant before returning to his examination of his feet.

"I still need to talk to you," Lisa abruptly said to Grant. She'd been trying to get him alone for days now, and Grant was sure he knew why.

He sighed, glancing at the stairs to his right. "If it's about *him*—"

"It's not," Lisa replied, staring him down. He wouldn't have blamed her if it was, but he was as tired of that conversation as Daniel was. Daniel had made his office upstairs home and was rarely seen by anyone on the ground floor. Lisa's unrequited feelings for Daniel were widely known among the group, though never discussed openly. Everything had changed for both of them the night he pulled the trigger on Matthew Drexel, the corrupt police detective.

Grant sighed again. "I have to go back out, help the others finish the cleanup. We'll talk when I get back."

Lisa walked away. The new recruits followed her.

"You need to rest. I *know* you're exhausted," Julie said. "You've been going nonstop for hours."

He smiled for her benefit, but even his powers weren't strong enough to wipe the weariness from his face.

"What is that?" Grant overheard one of the new recruits asking Lisa as they walked away. It was the heavily accented voice of the big man, Henrike, and his finger was pointing to the loud banner hanging over the center of the room.

"I was wondering the same thing," Grant mentioned softly to Julie.

"It's a reminder, so we don't forget," Julie answered, loud enough for everyone to hear.

She put an arm around Grant's shoulder and ushered him into the center of the warehouse, where a makeshift Common Room had been pieced together. It resembled the original Common Room, from Morgan's converted asylum, in name only. No walls separated this area from any other part of the warehouse, save the sleeping quarters in the northwest corner, which were cordoned off with sheets and drapes.

Much of the old building had been quickly converted over the last few months into an all-in-one central hub for the Loci.

Those in the room stopped to regard Julie, who stood in the center of the Common Room with her brother on her arm.

"What do your eyes see?" she recited the words from the banner. "Are you letting perspective and purpose guide your actions? When you open your eyes and look around, do you see the trivial, the mundane, the routine? Or do you see the profundity of what we do? The changes we make upon the world? The miracles we spread?

"What do your eyes see?" She said it again. "Where is your *focus*?"

The room was filled with silent contemplation, and it was several moments before anyone realized that Julie was finished and they could go back to what they were doing. But now they attacked their work with more vitality in their movements.

"You," Grant said softly so only Julie could hear, "are the most amazing person I know."

She gave him a tired, shy smile. "We're growing so fast—more Ringwearers find the Railroad every day—and a few days ago it occurred to me that everyone could use a noble idea to rally around, a mission statement that defines why we do *what* we do. I made it as loud and ugly as I could just so it would be hard to overlook or forget."

He smiled again, appreciatively. "If you weren't around to think of these things, I don't know who would."

Julie shrugged. "We're in the business of handing out second chances. We can't forget that *everybody* deserves one, and why."

Grant looked away, something about the phrase "second chances" stirring up feelings in him he'd fought to bury. He turned in Julie's direction when he felt her hand holding his.

"You never talk about it," she said softly, "but I know you miss her." *Hannah.*

He blinked back the rising emotions. No. Not on this day would he allow himself to go down *that* road, see her face as he held her and watched the life drain out of her. . . .

He smiled, and squeezed her hand. No matter how many amazing feats or displays of power he could unleash, he would never feel superior to his sister. As far as he was concerned, if there was one person deserving of the title of "hero" in this building, she was the one.

"Thank you for doing this," he said, squeezing her hand and gazing up at the banner again.

"You better see this—the Brits are at it again!" Fletcher called out.

7

Fletcher had dubbed his cubicle "command central"—though no one but him referred to it that way. His work area was near the side entrance that everyone used, which was adjacent to the stairs that led to Daniel's office.

Grant and Julie quickly returned to Fletcher's station, taking in the scene on the largest monitor, directly in front of him.

Two weeks ago, a second group of Loci had appeared on Grant's internal radar; they were all in London, and Grant counted five of them. Fiercely patriotic to their homeland, this new team had also been using its awesome abilities for heroics, but their agenda and tactics left much to be desired. Instead of hiding their faces from the cameras, they appeared often on British television, using the media as an added tool in their arsenal. Grant had no idea what their powers were, but they had pulled off a number of astonishing feats, all in the name of keeping the motherland safe.

Their spokesperson—an older gentleman with a clipped accent, bushy mustache, and roguish demeanor—stated often and loudly that they would do "whatever is required" to keep Great Britain safe in the wake of the world's unending calamities.

British authorities were supposedly in an uproar, but so far had found no way to deter the group's actions. They referred to themselves with the unabashedly pretentious name, "Upholders of the Crown."

On Fletcher's computer, he was displaying a full-screen live feed from CNN, which brandished a red "BREAKING NEWS" banner at the bottom of the screen.

A red-cheeked reporter with male pattern baldness and a little too much makeup was breathlessly giving an account of some sort of upheaval.

"What is it?" Julie asked.

"Forced lockdown of some kind," Fletcher replied, inching up the volume.

". . . Local authorities are at a loss but promise not to rest until the heart of the city is reopened. With no information coming out of the quarantined area, we have no idea who is responsible for this startling turn of events. The only thing we know for certain is that no one can get in or out of a significant portion of the city—a portion, I should add, that includes key edifices such as the Houses of Parliament and Buckingham Palace.

"Speculation from local law enforcement is that the group calling itself the 'Upholders of the Crown' may somehow be responsible; others believe the prime minister or Parliament took drastic measures to ensure a working government, in response to the riots erupting around the globe. Shelley, back to you," the reporter signed off, still trying to catch his breath.

The camera shifted to a perfectly coifed redhead sitting behind an anchor desk. For a second, she looked terrified, but composed herself and, obviously improvising, said, "If you're just joining us, this is breaking news, so please bear with us. Charles, do you have any idea at all what method or methods have been used to cut off access to the city?"

The reporter in London shook his head. "I'm afraid not; details on this subject are particularly hard to come by. All we know is that no one can get in or out. I heard a rumor a few minutes ago that attempts to get live satellite feeds of the quarantine area have brought back nothing but static. As you can imagine, the friends and loved ones of those trapped within the quarantined zone are both fearful and outraged, demanding action from the police. We've heard rumors that MI-5 is considering this to be an unlawful action, and I personally have heard the word *terrorism*, but they've not yet released a public statement using those terms. Until a course of action can be determined, access to all of London proper, north of the Thames, is completely cut off."

"Thank you, Charles," the anchorwoman returned. "We're expecting a briefing from Washington momentarily with their response to both the new situation in London and the day's events in Los Angeles. . . ."

"It's crazy." Julie shook her head. "Did *they* do this? Those 'Upholders' people?"

Grant frowned, concentrating. "They're definitely in London somewhere; I can feel that much. But I'm not familiar enough with the city to tell you where they are, exactly. It looks like they're just sitting around a table together, chatting."

Fletcher cleared his throat. "Am I the only one wondering where this group came from to begin with? Without the Keeper around to plot and scheme, who's out there passing out rings? And why have all of these new wearers popped up in London—and at the same time?"

"You're not the only one wondering," Grant replied, his eyes still on the news report. He suddenly felt very tired.

"All of this can resolve itself later, honey," Julie said in her most motherly tone. "You've been running from one crisis to the next for over *six hours* now. You need to get some rest. Surely the firefighters and police have things more or less under control by now."

He shook his head. "No, I have to get back. It's way too much for them to—"

"The entire world is talking about what you did today," Julie said, looking into his eyes. There she saw remnants of the lives he hadn't been able to save, the fires he couldn't make it to in time. "They're crediting you with a new world record for the number of lives saved from immediate danger in a single day."

"The Fansite already has pictures," Fletcher added offhandedly.

"The whatsite?"

"You didn't know?" Julie grinned, taking his arm again to steady him. "There's a full-fledged 'Guardian Fan Club' and everything."

Fletcher's fingers danced over his keyboard and a monitor to his right switched to a website, the front page of which bore a blurry photo of himself from about an hour ago, holding the eighteen-wheeler in midair. He saw links to news articles, a photo gallery, and some sort of message board where members could post "Guardian Sightings."

Grant's shoulders slumped. "I can't believe people . . ." he whimpered. He wasn't even remotely kidding. He knew Julie couldn't help teasing him, but even she must see the danger in this sort of hero worship . . .

"You should see the boxers in the merch section," added another voice. A noble, intelligent voice with an impeccable British accent.

Grant turned to the building entrance, where Morgan was closing the door behind her, smiling mischievously.

"The prodigal librarian returns," Grant mused, thankful for the opportunity to change the subject. He smirked curiously in the elder woman's direction.

"And bearing gifts, no less," Morgan added, indicating the bag full of books in her arms.

"You could have checked in," Fletcher said irritably. "You must not have noticed that there's a *war* going on out in the streets. It's not safe out there, and we had no idea where you were or what you were doing. As usual."

"Fletcher, your observational skills," Morgan coolly replied, "as always, are on par with the great detective, Sherlock Holmes himself. I do apologize for leaving you in the dark about my whereabouts, but I was quite safe and quite far from any danger."

"Is that all we get?" Grant teased. "No details?"

"For now," she replied. "But very soon, you will know everything I know, I promise. And you have my word it will be worth waiting for."

Starting several weeks ago, Morgan had taken on the habit of disappearing from the warehouse, sometimes for hours, sometimes for days on end. But before leaving the first time, she had approached Grant and asked him, on their friendship, to do her a favor: She requested that he not use his awareness of the Loci to find her or look into her activities. All would be explained in due time, she assured him.

It wasn't a hard decision. He was as curious as everyone else, but he trusted her.

Remarkable to see her actually enjoying *being outside again*, Grant mused as he watched her.

Their conversation over, Morgan turned to Julie. "Do you remember our conversation from a few weeks ago, about books worth reading again and again?"

Julie smiled warmly. "Of course."

Morgan and Julie, over time, had developed a close mother/daughter type relationship. This particular new habit they'd developed— exchanging favorite books—Grant found amusing, since Morgan had an overwhelming advantage. Since her power allowed her to perfectly recall every detail she was exposed to, and since she was a former librarian and an avid reader, Julie had a very hard time finding books to recommend that Morgan had never before gotten her hands on. Morgan, on the other hand, never experienced any difficulty recommending books to Julie. She was a walking encyclopedia and often quoted from literature as reflexively as most people inhale oxygen.

Morgan herself had undergone a drastic change thanks to Grant and the events surrounding his life. Once a reclusive hermit, Morgan fled her home for the first time in years when it was destroyed by an enemy of Grant's in a terrible fire. Forced outside, she'd felt a sense of renewal or rebirth, and though she now made her home alongside Grant and the others at the warehouse, it was rare that she wasn't out and about, doing . . .

Well, no one really knew *what* she was up to, Grant had to remind himself. Morgan was relishing the mystery and theories her actions were igniting among the group, but was in no hurry to offer an explanation for her activities.

"Well," Morgan continued talking to Julie as if no one else were there. She retrieved a hardback from her satchel and handed it to Julie. "I know this book backward and forward, and yet sometimes I find I simply *crave* reading it again, slowly. I can't recommend it enough."

The book was entitled *The Remains of the Day*, by Kazuo Ishiguro.

Julie glanced at the book's cover. "I hate to admit it, but I'm not sure when I'll have a chance to read again anytime soon. Things are so hectic around here—"

"Oh, no worries, dear. A story as profound as this one deserves to be held onto for a special occasion," Morgan replied, casting a sideways glance at Grant.

Grant's attention wandered off, his eye catching an image on

another of Fletcher's computer monitors—a different news channel
reporting on a large nursing home in L.A. that had caught fire from an
adjacent property. A text scroll at the bottom said that more than seventy people were still trapped inside and rescue workers were having
difficulty reaching them.

"Where is that?" Grant asked.

Fletcher swiveled in his chair, his fingers doing a quick dance
across the keyboard. "Union Avenue, off West Sixth."

"Tell Alex to meet me there five minutes ago," Grant said, moving
toward the door. He stopped one last time to turn around as Lisa
passed by, offering him a hardened gaze that told him he would be held
to his promise to talk to her as soon as he got back.

An image floated through Grant's mind of a single man, alone
somewhere and facing a very dangerous situation. He didn't recognize
the man's surroundings.

"What about Payton?"

More than one look of alarm greeted this question, but Julie offered
a calm reply. "What about him?"

"Has anyone heard from him lately?" he asked.

Fletcher made a kind of alarmed bark and quicky turned to his
workstation, pretending not to listen.

From several yards away, Lisa, her voice worried and disappointed,
was the only one to answer. "Do you really think we *will?*"

8

Paris, France

There really was nothing else quite like the sound of a man's jaw breaking.

Payton considered it a truly singular, remarkable sound—one he relished. It was without equal.

A second security guard backpedaled away from him on his hands and feet, crab-like, as the first landed on the floor nearby with a *thud*.

"S'il vous plait!" the guard cried. "I speak English! Don't kill me!"

Payton almost smiled.

French nancy boys . . .

"Please! I have a wife, son—"

"Sucks to be you, mate," Payton said. In a flash, he whipped out his sword, flipped it end-on-end, caught the blade, and sideswiped the man on the floor with its hilt.

Two security guards now lay on either side of the front lobby door to the small building on the outskirts of the French Government Plaza, out cold. It was early morning, long before dawn, and the building was all but empty.

Payton eyed the ceiling for any sign of cameras while sheathing his sword; the building seemed to have very low security measures, with only a minimal staff and no electronic surveillance that he could detect.

A small computer workstation rested on the far wall to the right, which included a telephone and walkie-talkies holstered in battery chargers. Payton darted to the station and turned it into shards of metal and plastic in seconds with his long steel blade.

His footfalls echoed loudly as they clomped across the foyer's shiny black tile. Very little light was available in the empty space, though as always, Payton had no interest in stealth.

Besides, he hated this place. Almost as much as he hated his reason for being here. He would not waste his greatest talents on this task.

He burst through a set of walnut double doors and broke into a sprint. He never slowed to check for additional security or orient himself to his position in the building. There was no need. He knew exactly where he was going.

He was here tracking down a hunch. A hunch that annoyed him significantly.

France, after all, was the location of his death and rebirth. The place where the love of his life had left him to die after a cave-in, without attempting to dig him out or call for help. The place where he'd first heard the word *Secretum*.

And the French are rotten little gits.

Every last one of them.

Several turns, more running, and a swish of his sword that broke through a padlock, and he had arrived at his destination: an enormous records room. A domed, rococo glass ceiling showed an ocean of stars and the moon sailing through it high above. Opulent pillars held up the high ceiling throughout the room, which stretched at least three hundred feet long and one hundred and fifty wide, accompanied by elaborately patterned carpet and entirely too many paintings adorning all four walls.

In the center, on a large raised platform that took up most of the room, resided a series of twenty colossal rolling file cabinets, each at least twelve feet tall, with flashy golden knobs about the size of steering wheels on the end of each cabinet. Payton mused that it was built to look like the strength of Hercules himself would be required just to turn one of these things and make the cabinets roll. It wasn't hard to figure out how the mechanisms were operated. The trick was not to roll a cabinet without checking to make sure no one was inside the aisle, in its path. Each cabinet had a lock that held it in place once moved to expose the desired files.

Whatever, Payton thought. He had neither time nor patience for caution.

He dared not turn on any lights due to the skylight; anyone outside might see.

So in the darkness, he found that the files rolled quite smoothly and quietly, and it was only minutes before his skilled hands were searching through the particular files where he believed he would find what he was looking for.

His gift—incredible speed and dexterity—meant it was only minutes until he'd narrowed down his search to the correct shelf, and then the correct file. Inside a cardboard box he dug until he came across a manila folder that bore a very familiar name.

And just as expected, *it* was there. The tiny marker in the upper right corner of the file's hand-written label. It was a symbol, which to the untrained eye might be nothing but the doodle of a pen. But Payton recognized the shape at once.

That same moment, the vast room's lights came on from overhead, and the cabinets on both sides of him began to contract inward, squeezing the space in which he stood. The row he was in was over thirty feet long. Two more adjoining cabinets on each end weren't moving along with these two that threatened to squish him, so escape was impossible on both sides.

As the cabinets inched closer, barely allowing him room to move, he zipped the file inside his black jacket. He drew his sword and punctured the back wall of the cabinet on his left. Grabbing the over-long hilt of the sword, he swung himself up and over the top, like a gymnast. He barely had time to rip the sword free—breaking the top of a cabinet in the process—before the two cabinets closed shut beneath him.

The cabinets rolled beneath him again. He ran until he reached the end of the cabinet closest to the exit. He leapt at incredible speed to the ground and rolled until he was next to the door, but gunshots from behind pulled him up short.

He sheathed the sword and came up off the ground with his hands up, but didn't turn around. He counted at least six voices, all shouting orders to him at the same time. He had no idea what they were saying, but he suspected it was the usual: "Get your hands up." "You're under arrest." "Turn around."

He slowly turned and allowed them to see him yawn as he did. The shouting escalated as six handguns were pointed in his direction by six angry French guards.

"Sorry, lads. I don't speak frou-frou," he said under his breath. And then a little louder, "If you intend to shoot me, do it now. I have places to be."

The guards looked at one another—all except the youngest of them, who stood on Payton's far right. A squirrelly looking boy with sweat on his brow, he was clearly the team's rookie.

His gun went off, the bullet in its chamber fired point-blank at Payton.

The guards all started and looked at their companion in horror. A glistening of light radiated from Payton, and all six of them stared at his drawn sword. There was the tiniest *plink* as the flattened bullet fell to the floor.

A tiny whiff of smoke rose from a small spot on the sword where the bullet had impacted, but the blade showed no sign of damage.

Their shock and hesitation was all Payton needed. In a burst, he was in the center of them, on his knees and sweeping his arms around to bring all six of them down on the ground. Half of them were knocked out by the abrupt fall. The others floundered, scrambling to pick up their lost guns.

One Payton grabbed by his shirt and flung into the wall on the far right, where he cracked the plaster and slumped to the ground. A second man was already aiming his gun at Payton, his finger on the trigger, but Payton sidestepped the shot with ease, and grabbed the guard with his single free hand by the throat. He squeezed as the third man rose and lunged at him, but Payton merely raised his sword, and the man ran his own body through at his shoulder.

The one he had by the throat passed out, and Payton let him fall to the ground. He retracted the sword from the impaled man, who collapsed in pain, clutching at his wounded shoulder.

He looked the men over carefully. These were no security guards. Their uniforms bore the insignia of the French police. Which meant they wouldn't be here alone . . .

Would've been easier to kill them, Payton thought. It wasn't as if he didn't want to. But he'd promised his employer no one would die on this job, and he considered it an interesting challenge to defeat without killing. It required a finesse that was typically lost in his more straightforward missions.

The easiest way not to kill someone, he'd found, was to be gone when they arrived, so Payton ran, sprinting flat-out for the main entrance, which was a winding hallway path and several hundred feet away, straight through the ornate main foyer.

He didn't see the wire until he was too close to it to stop. It had been placed right across his path, tied to two pillars there in the foyer, and it tripped him hard, breaking a nearby flag stand in the process. The sword flew from his hand and landed over one hundred feet away, sticking into the tile grout right by the front door. He was on his feet quickly, but he made no move toward the exit. A five-foot piece of the broken flagpole rested near his feet.

He found himself standing directly in the center of the foyer, encapsulated by a concave ceiling high above. A modest chandelier hung in the center, and it flickered to life as he stood.

Payton sighed calmly. "No need to be dainty, fellows. Who do we have?"

A baritone seethed from the edges of the circular area. "A battalion of the National Police's finest. You're a wanted criminal and we've been onto you since you first set your dirty feet on our soil," the guardsman said, in heavily accented English. "We don't take kindly to crimes committed on government property, particularly from foreigners."

Around the borders of the circle of light, Payton watched over twenty French police officers step into view, most of them large, and all of them well armed, with hungry looks on their faces.

Payton thought he saw one of them slurp back a bit of drool.

He kicked at the tile, and the wooden flagpole rose in the air before him. He clutched it in the middle and twisted it like helicopter blades up over his head and then brought it to a rest with one of the broken ends touching the floor.

"Clearly, Paris has taught you lot how to heft about as many bulky weapons as humanly possible," his gravelly British voice intoned, still the embodiment of cool and collected. "And here I stand, with nothing but a broken wood stick."

The guards reacted by bringing every weapon they had to bear upon him, ready to lunge.

"Right, then." Payton eyed his prey patiently, hungrily. "Let's break something."

9

The nursing home Grant and Alex approached burned fierce and blindingly hot. Inside, dozens of elderly patients huddled in terror, unable to escape under their own power. The entrance was blocked by a collapsed cement and wooden porch, with roaring flames pouring through the doorway's outline.

He'd seen a lot of terrible things this day, but this was one of the worst.

"We have to get in there!!" Alex screamed over the roar of the flames. "I can feel their fear, their panic!"

"How many?" he cried.

"At least fifty, I think, maybe more."

He looked around, desperate to find something he could use.

Fifty. . . !

The city's firefighters were still pushed past their limits, most of them committed to a special operation intended to keep the wildfires of the city from spreading to the surrounding countryside. But as usual, the news crews were here, watching and waiting to see what Guardian would do.

The sight of the burning facility made Grant's mind flash back to the asylum, the former home of the Loci, which had collapsed under a similar fire-induced strain. There, he'd used his abilities to push all of the building's walls high into the sky. The walls carried the fire with them, eliminating the problem. But the trapped victims there were younger and of better health; most of those inside the facility in front of him were much too frail to risk something similar here.

He'd never been able to control wind, despite repeated efforts. There simply wasn't enough tangible substance to the atmosphere to manipulate.

What he needed was a way to put out the—

"Hydrant," said Fletcher in his earpiece. *"Half a block south and across the street."*

Alex fell into step after Grant, who was already running toward Fletcher's suggestion.

The two-lane street they crossed was filled mostly with wrecked cars and pedestrians who either watched with morbid fascination or tried to escape. L.A.'s usual melting pot of races was entirely accounted for among the crowd, and while many of them were cheering him on, Grant got the distinct impression that there was a well-represented segment that was waiting to see him *fail*.

Don't think about that now . . .

In the far corner of the adjacent block, he spotted the red fire hydrant.

The top of the hydrant tore off with a simple thought, but the plume of water it created high in the sky was too far away from the nursing home, over two hundred feet, at least . . .

Alex was already scanning their surroundings before he'd finished the thought. He knew what she was looking for . . .

His eyes landed on a pickup truck about twenty feet away. The truck's hood ripped itself free and Grant guided it into the air with a single hand until it was directly above them. He carefully positioned it so that it created an angled surface for the water to bounce off of, until it was aiming at the nursing home.

But the water was still too far away. Gravity took hold a good eighty feet before it could reach the burning building.

"Over here!" Alex shouted.

He spun in place, his left arm still holding the pickup truck's hood above them. Alex stood by a tiny yellow VW Beetle, pointing at its curved hood. He couldn't help a grim smile.

She's quick . . .

He yanked the hood from the car with his free hand and held it in midair upside down. He'd effectively created a scoop to redirect the falling water, which with some careful positioning and angling, he used to send the water straight at the front of the building. The fire went out quickly, but just as Grant was lowering the two pieces of metal safely to the ground, a *whoosh* was heard and the fire consumed the building once more.

He lifted the metal into the air and positioned it once more. "Something must be feeding it!" Grant shouted.

"Gas line, probably," Alex agreed.

"I'll hold this; see what you can do about getting those people out."

She was already running. He watched, arms outstretched, as she stopped in front of the large crowd that had gathered and focused her attention on a few burly men that stood off to one side.

"Anybody feeling overwhelmingly *brave*?" she said, willing the emotion into their hearts. Three men shouted back ferocious affirmatives and set off after her toward the water-soaked entrance.

Even with the fire out of the way, there was still a ton of rubble in front of the door. Grant had no more hands available, but he didn't really need them anyway. He reached out with his mind and pushed at the wreckage that lay at the threshold of the nursing home. . . .

He heard an ear-splitting bang from very close by, and suddenly he felt his body losing strength.

The wreckage safely out of the way, he allowed himself a quick glance down and saw a big red stain spreading on his shirt, right above his stomach. Time seemed to slow and he was aware of many odd details: the taste of copper on his tongue, sweat pouring off of his body in sheets, and a bitter cold that threatened to swallow him whole.

"Who's the man now!? Huh?" taunted a voice from behind.

Grant struggled to keep himself upright, to not pass out, as he turned slowly to look behind . . .

"Yeah, baby!" said the man proudly holding a pistol at point-blank range, less than four feet from where Grant stood. He was wearing some very familiar gang colors on his arm.

Grant had been too distracted; he'd never even heard anyone approach. . . .

His eyes kept trying to roll up into his head, but he fought to stay awake and upright. He was vaguely aware that Alex and her new friends were pulling victims from the burning building and needed more time. He had to keep the water aimed at the nursing home, but he was starting to waver. He let out a loud moan as he struggled against the pain that washed over him, the two sheets of metal in the sky above swiveling and flailing.

"Saw what you did to my boys this morning!" the man shouted. "It was all over the news, man! You think you could just *get away* with that kind of disrespect?! Not in this—"

Grant wasn't entirely sure what happened next, only that the man was no longer talking and no longer standing. He was on the ground and several civilians were pinning him down, wrestling control of the gun from his hand . . .

"NO!!" Alex screamed, spotting him from the front of the building. She ran toward him while her three helpers continued pulling the elderly patients from the building. But everything had slowed and Alex ran as if frozen. She'd never get there in time to . . .

To what? What *could* she do?

A wave of nausea overtook him. Grant had to swallow hard to keep from vomiting. He could feel his body trying to shut down, the hole burning through his insides, rupturing organs . . . the hot blood spilling out of his front and back, seeping down his legs . . .

But still more victims were being dragged from the building by the men whose help Alex had enlisted, so he stood his ground.

Something else caught his attention as his eyes began blurring in and out of focus. A man stood on the roof of the nursing home, watching him calmly. He couldn't explain it or describe the feeling he got from the man in the state he was in, but everything about this man was wrong.

He certainly looked out of place, this man with olive skin and silver hair. He had a stately presence that was underscored by the tailored suit he wore. Hands in his pockets, oblivious to the danger he was in standing astride a burning building, he looked at Grant with a keen detachment. He couldn't have been any more out of place if he tried, yet he simply stood there, watching Grant's every movement.

Grant's thoughts came rocketing back to the present with another unbearable surge of pain from his gut.

No! he thought, bearing down against the rising exhaustion. He squeezed his eyes closed against the pain and the sweat and clamped down with every ounce of strength he had left.

Not until they're out of the building! You stupid little piece of metal, you're not taking me down!

He faltered, stumbling to his knees, but held tightly to the car hoods redirecting the water flow above his head.

I. WILL. NOT. GO. DOWN!!

He cried out in agony, fighting against the fatigue that was over-taking him . . .

NOOOOOO!!!

A wave of fatigue poured through him, his muscles spent, his blood running thin . . .

Alex was close now, horror written across her features. She was close enough to catch him. . . .

He blacked out.

10

Grant slowly opened his eyes. He was lying on an EMT gurney, next to similar gurneys in use by victims of the nursing home fire. His back was against an ambulance, and in his periphery he could see a number of other patients nearby.

His mind screamed *get up!* but his body refused. His vision was slightly blurred, off-kilter, and his head pounded with an intense migraine. The first of those he'd had in a long time.

But he was breathing. He was alive.

"Grant! You're okay!" Alex was sitting at his side. "You're okay. . . ." She nodded assuringly, as if she was talking to herself more than to him. She let out an audible sigh of relief.

"If I'd known you were so eager to be a martyr, sweetie, I could've given you some easier options," she attempted to joke, but didn't quite pull it off. Something about her body seemed weak, deflated.

He allowed a small grin, closing his eyes. His mouth was incredibly dry, but his strength was already returning. With some effort, he raised himself up on his elbows, trying to sit. But he froze halfway there and looked down at his abdomen. His shirt had been ripped off, and the blanket that covered him fell away from his motion.

There was no wound. No sign of a bullet hole. Nothing, except for dried blood staining his skin, and the IV fluids pumping into a needle in his arm.

Now that he thought about it, he felt no residual pain from the attack, save for the headache.

"Fletcher managed to get ahold of Hector," Alex explained. "You lost a lot of blood, but otherwise you're good as new. More or less."

"More or less?"

"Well, it's just . . ." she faltered, frowning. "Toward the end, before you passed out . . . there was this thing in your . . . I mean, I thought I saw—"

She stopped talking when she saw Grant eying her curiously. "It was nothing," she said. "Forget it. You've got a clean bill of health."

Grant smiled faintly, then shook his head. "Hector is truly a wonder."

Julie had once confided to him her belief that Hector had so much energy—constantly running from one thing to the next, one person who needed his help to another, despite his rotund frame—because he conserved so much energy by never speaking.

The sun was farther along in the sky than where he'd left it, but it couldn't have been more than an hour or two since the attack. It was late afternoon.

His eyes narrowed suddenly. "The shooter, did they catch—?"

"Caught, arrested, and thrown *under* the nearest jail cell, if the crowd had anything to say about it. No less than *eight* pedestrians attacked him as soon as they heard the first shot. The police hardly had to do anything. We got everyone out of the building, by the way. If you hadn't held out as long as you did . . ."

Grant looked over her shoulder to see a gathered crowd standing behind yellow caution tape. Easily a hundred people waited there, perhaps more. He couldn't quite see the whole crowd; an EMT van blocked part of his view.

He saw hastily-written posters and signs held high in the air by the onlookers that bore expressions of gratitude and love, well wishes and prayers. All for him.

He found himself shaking his head, almost involuntarily.

Alex turned around to look, and someone in the crowd noticed the motion.

"He's awake!" one of them cried.

And then the most remarkable thing happened. There were no shouts, no murmurs among the crowd. No one tried to break the yellow tape and run toward him and Alex. A silence fell over the crowd as every eye focused on Grant, who gazed wordlessly back at them.

One person began to clap. She was joined by another. And another. And soon the entire crowd thundered with applause. The signs and posters danced in the air animatedly, and a few individuals put fingers to their mouths and whistled in appreciation. Fists pumped into the air, and a fair amount of whooping was heard.

Alex turned back around to face him, a smile on her face but her eyebrows high above their usual position. He was quite sure she was enjoying this considerably more than he was.

A hand was placed on his shoulder from behind. "Thank you," said a husky male voice.

He swiveled to look as a fireman walked around the gurney to stand at Grant's feet. It was then that Grant noticed the man's badge. This was no mere fireman—he was the fire chief. Of Los Angeles County.

The chief looked as if he wanted to say something, but unspoken words passed between his eyes and Grant's. Grant knew the look on his face, because he felt it on his own. Too much had happened today, more horrors witnessed by both than any single person should see in a lifetime. Grant knew that all of the chief's firemen had given everything they had to the struggle today, every one of them a hero. And Grant saw a reflection in those eyes of all of the lives that had been lost—all of the ones he and his firefighters hadn't been able to save, including some of their own who had no doubt fallen in the line of duty.

It was a face filled with grime and soot and sweat and puffed out eye sockets. It was a face that must've looked an awful lot like his own at that moment, Grant surmised.

Despite all this, the fire chief smiled at Grant. It wasn't a big, beaming smile, or a kindly look of admiration. It was the grim look of a man who was taking in someone he considered his better, far more than an equal, and had no idea what to say to such a person.

"Thank you," he said finally, nodding at Grant. He turned loose and extended his hand to Alex, who accepted it with a nod of her own. "Ma'am," he said with an air of gratitude.

Then he simply turned and walked away.

Grant looked at Alex. Alex looked at Grant.

She reached up to his forehead and brushed his mussed hair away from his face. "You need to rest a little more, doctor's orders."

Grant looked down at his prone body on the gurney once more. "I don't think my insurance will cover this," he remarked. It was a joke, of course. He had no insurance because he had no public identity on record.

"Somehow I think the city of Los Angeles will be able to underwrite this one," Alex replied. She turned and left him alone to do as she'd requested.

Grant studied her as she walked away, unsettled by the uncharacteristically maternal gesture from the young woman. She had truly become his partner in the field over the last few months, and the closest thing he had to an equal. No one understood what he faced every day better than she did.

Still, something about the sincerity in her voice caught him off guard. His thoughts shifted back to the fire chief, the crowd, the victims that lay next to him . . . These thoughts and many others collided and bounced off of one another in his head. Resting was the last thing he wanted to do. He'd rested enough while he was unconscious. He needed to get back on his feet and get back out there.

Earn all of this approval he was getting from everyone around him. Somehow.

11

Alex sighed. She was tired, though she knew it was nothing compared to how Grant must feel, what with the gaping stomach wound just a little while ago.

The thought of it made her queasy, but not because she'd seen the wound itself. She just didn't like the thought of Grant at death's door. After all, he should be indestructible.

"Is Guardian okay?" called out a voice.

She hadn't realized it, but as her thoughts wandered, so had she— closer to the crowd behind the barrier. The voice came from a small boy who wore a T-shirt with "Guardian" emblazoned on it and a Zorro-style mask over his eyes.

Her heart melted at the sight of him; he couldn't have been more than eight years old.

"He'll be fine," she said, walking a little closer to him. "He's a super-hero, remember? Bullets can't hurt him as easily as they hurt everyone else."

The boy grinned and nodded. But then a thoughtful expression passed over his face. "What *can* hurt him?"

Alex knelt close to the boy and peered into his eyes, which were barely above the yellow police tape marking off the boundary where civilians shouldn't cross. "What do you mean?" she asked.

"You know, like Superman is hurt by kryptonite," the boy said. "What's Guardian's kryptonite?"

Alex tousled the boy's hair playfully. "He doesn't have one. No green meteorites for Guardian."

If only that were true . . . she thought. A simple bullet had almost done the job today.

"You! Young lady!" A television reporter covering the dramatic events pushed his way to the front of the crowd and held out a microphone. A cameraman was attached to his hip. "Are you on Guardian's team?"

Alex was flustered, and slightly annoyed at the rudeness of the reporter breaking up her moment of fun with the little boy. "Well yes, but—"

"What is your power? Are you related to Guardian? What's your superhero code name?"

Alex stammered, struggling to respond to the barrage of questions. It was the last one that caught her attention most.

"I've given this some thought, actually," came Fletcher's voice in her ear. She tried not to roll her eyes; as happened so often in the field, she forgot he was listening in. *"How do you feel about 'Emoticon'?"*

Alex frowned and cleared her throat, forcefully. "We don't actually use code names. 'Guardian' was an invention of the press, if I'm not mistaken—"

"Who is that talking to Guardian?" the reporter interrupted. Alex turned to see Grant rising from his gurney and putting his shirt back on, blatantly ignoring her insistence that he get some rest. A stooped, elderly man, probably in his late seventies or early eighties, was gesturing wildly at Grant. Strange sounds that sounded nothing like normal speech could be heard coming from the old man's mouth.

The reporter kept asking questions, but Alex was no longer listening. She immediately moved to join Grant, but she quickly stopped short. She'd received a mental signal from him to stay away.

"Rrrrrrrrrrrrrrrr . . ." the man blustered. There was no stutter; he simply couldn't create words or anything else beyond basic, guttural sounds. He wore a pair of baby blue pajamas and a matching pair of slip-on bedroom shoes. He had bushy white hair and a scraggly but full white beard. Old-fashioned spectacles with bold frames sat atop his nose. He was a good head and a half shorter than Grant, though it wasn't clear whether that was because of age or bad posture.

The man was undoubtedly one of the residents of the nursing home, now displaced by the fire. From the looks of it, he'd led a difficult life. He was missing one hand; a prosthetic limb took its place.

The harder the old man tried to get Grant to understand, the more unintelligible his gibberish became and the more visibly frustrated he obviously felt. It was a vicious circle.

Grant had no idea what the old kook wanted, but it seemed that he wouldn't be able to get rid of him until he'd conveyed whatever was on his mind.

"Rrrreehhhhh," the man went on, his eyes wild now over his own inability to communicate.

Grant thought about maybe something to write on would help, but where would he get his hands on something like that out here?

"Rrraaaann . . . ttt."

Grant froze. Had this old man just said his name?

"Grant?" Grant whispered his own name.

The old man's eyes grew even wider, and he nodded vigorously.

"How do you know that name?" Grant whispered.

The old man put his hands up and swept them back and forth, a gesture Grant interpreted as, *never mind that*.

Grant was startled when the old man grabbed his hand with his one good one and balled up Grant's hand into a fist. With jerky, quivering movements, he roughly but slowly unfolded Grant's fingers one at a time until three of them were standing up. Then he let go and stepped back, motioning with his fake hand at what he'd done.

"Three? You want to tell me there's three of something?" Grant concluded.

Another excited affirmation from the old man.

Who *was* this weird old relic?

The man grabbed Grant's hand again and pointed wildly at the watch he wore.

"Time?" Grant asked. "Three times?"

Frustrated again, the old man shook his head violently and motioned at Grant's watch again. This time he traced the circular shape of the timepiece, but he traced it backward.

"Backward time . . . A countdown?" Grant pondered. The man

reacted positively. "Is something counting down from three?"

The man grabbed Grant suddenly by the shoulders and nearly hugged him, so overwhelmed was he that Grant was finally beginning to understand.

But Grant wasn't. He had no idea what any of this meant.

"Looks like you've made a new friend, Mr. Wood," said a jovial voice behind Grant.

A black woman appeared, dressed in bright-colored scrubs—the kind used by nursing home employees. Her name tag read "Teresa" and had the nursing home's name and logo off to one side.

"Do you know him?" Grant asked.

"Of course. Mr. Wood is one of my favorite patients," she said smiling.

"He keeps you laughing, huh?" Grant prodded.

"If only," she said with overstretched sadness. "Poor old soul took brain damage to the part of his brain that controls speech some time ago. He can barely say anything at all."

"How did that happen to him? What happened?"

"I don't know the details," Teresa replied. "But it must have been some kind of blunt-force head injury."

"Did he lose his hand at the same time?" Grant couldn't help asking.

"I don't know, honey," Teresa replied, her eyes slowly dawning with recognition of just who she was talking to. "Oh! I'm so sorry, sir. He shouldn't be bothering someone like you, just let me get him settled in here somewhere. I'm sorry about this . . ." Her voice trailed off as she spotted a vacant wheelchair nearby and quickly retrieved it.

"It's no bother, really," Grant was saying.

Just as Mr. Wood sat in the wheelchair Teresa had brought him, he snatched a small pad out of her large front shirt pocket, along with a pen. She was startled by the action and nearly screamed.

"Now what do you want with that?" she asked him over dramatically. She seemed to think it was pointless for him to try to write anything with his spasmodic movements.

The old man ignored her and scribbled something on the pad and then hurriedly handed it to Grant.

Grant could barely make out the letters that had been scrawled across the blank paper in red ink; it was something a few steps worse than a small child's handwriting. The "c" and the "s" were backward, but if Grant wasn't mistaken, the word Mr. Wood had written was "acts."

"Acts? Is that what you've been trying to tell me?" Grant asked, looking into the old man's eyes.

The man nodded and then pointed at Grant's hand again. Grant's mind spun, piecing it together.

"Three acts? Three things are going to happen . . . and *that's* the countdown? A countdown from three?"

The old man closed his eyes, smiled, and sighed a great, heaving sigh, as if a tremendous weight had been lifted from his shoulders. Whatever it meant, Grant had figured it out.

Teresa, oblivious to their talk, was still busy preparing to cart off Mr. Wood. She circled the chair, grabbed the handles, and pushed him away from Grant with another quick apology.

"But a countdown to what?" Grant called out. "A countdown from three . . ." he mused. "Three *events* will count down to something?"

It was a full minute before he realized that Alex was standing beside him. He had no idea if she'd heard him talk to himself.

"What was that about? Who was that guy?" she asked. "And why did you want me to stay out of it?"

Grant didn't reply, only put out an arm to steady himself from a sudden wave of dizziness. His hand landed on her shoulder.

"We've talked about the inappropriate touching, sweetie," she said playfully. "Respect the personal space. And you're supposed to be resting anyway—"

Then she looked into his eyes for the first time, and she dropped all pretenses. "You're scaring me, Grant. You look spooked. What is it? What did that man say to you?"

Grant's mind was racing to places and times and possibilities very far from here. "I honestly don't know."

12

A deep red sunset came and went.

Grant watched it disappear while quietly eating a quick supper, until what he saw was replaced by darkness. Red skies at night usually meant good tidings, but in no way could Grant imagine this to be the case tonight. *Maybe,* he thought, *the sky is mourning for the earth. It soaks up the gallons of blood that were spilled on it today.*

Even though his body had healed, he still found himself horribly sore, both from the shooting and from the day's exertions. Hector stopped at his side briefly to dispose of his plate for him. The large man offered an encouraging smile, and then he was off again.

It was not Grant's custom to eat alone. He and his sister usually made a point to eat with as many of the others as possible. But he didn't feel like dealing with everyone's pointed stares and answerless questions tonight. Even now, he would spot them taking fleeting glances at him from the corners of their eyes, though they'd quickly look away if he caught them in the act.

He denied Julie's comforts as well; even her mothering was tiresome on rare occasions like this. After all, it wasn't every day you almost died.

It wasn't every day you had to watch so many other people die.

The day had been dreadfully long. He just wanted to be alone someplace, where the rest of the world couldn't intrude for just a few minutes of solitude. Was that too much to ask?

Mostly, he wanted time to think about the old man he'd met and the "three acts" that would countdown to . . . something.

It sounded important. Formal, even. Like something from a prophecy. Grant had had plenty of experience with those, thanks to that slab of rock he'd come to hate that was known as the Dominion Stone.

He didn't want to think about it, but that was where his mind jumped. Was that crazy old man trying to tell him something about his prophesied role as the Bringer?

Wow, he thought. *There's a word I actually haven't thought about in weeks.*

But no, it couldn't be about that. There *was* no Bringer. He'd denied his supposed destiny and made his own choice as to what to do with his life. That prophecy crap was nonsense, and he'd proven it by refusing to fall into the trap of the Keeper. His grandfather.

Grant ached all the way down to his bones; his muscles protested every movement. But there was no time for that now . . . Alex had *dragged* him back here to the warehouse for some downtime. She and Julie had tag-teamed, insisting that he get something to eat and at least six hours of rest.

He obliged only because he felt like he might fall over if he didn't rest soon. But it would be no more than six hours, he promised himself. A little shut-eye, and then back out to help with the cleanup. With so much property damage and loss of life, it would be weeks before Los Angeles could put the pieces back together and resemble its old self again—if it ever did.

But before he was allowed to sleep, Lisa grabbed him. Not known for subtlety, Lisa ignored his protests and desire to sleep, and yanked him away to an isolated corner of the warehouse where she'd set up shop with a modest desk.

With Daniel refusing all company—except for Grant, on occasion— she'd considered leaving the group, but her feelings for Daniel still ran stronger than she liked to admit. So she had found a use for herself in overseeing the group's financial obligations. Paying rent on the warehouse, transportation, utilities, food, and other supplies—she kept track of it all, because no one else did.

There in her corner, she finally had her conversation with Grant. True to her word, the discussion was not about Daniel in any way.

It was a twenty-minute conversation with voices lowered enough that no one else could hear anything that was said. Lisa did the majority of the talking, making a confession to Grant and swearing him to secrecy. Though stunned by her admission, he agreed there was no reason that any of the others needed to know what she'd told him.

But he would certainly never look at Lisa the same way again.

After their conversation, Grant longed for bed once more. It was only nine o'clock, and many of the team members were gathering around the television for the latest news coverage, while others turned in for bed. His mere appearance near the Common Room area made him the center of attention again. It was to be expected, after all that had transpired in the last eighteen hours, but it made him feel squeamish.

Grant also found that he couldn't stop thinking about Daniel. Despite all of the other thoughts racing around inside his head, despite everything he'd seen and done and everyone he'd encountered today . . .

Something about the color of the sunset had caused him to think of the crime that had been committed on the floor where he now stood.

Unable to get the thought out of his head, Grant nonetheless hesitated as his feet pounded on the steps that led upstairs to Daniel's lab. He sighed heavily and frowned. Any trip to see Daniel these days was something to be dreaded.

Then again, it wasn't very long ago when most of these good people probably felt the same way about seeing me. . . .

Grant took the remaining stairs two at a time. A quick left turn led him down the narrow hallway to the door that still bore an unpolished, scratched brass nameplate that read "Dr. Daniel Cossick, PhD". Grant barely registered the disarray that had once been Lisa's outer office, making a beeline straight for the second door.

"*She* send you again?" Daniel asked without looking up as Grant opened the door with his mind, before he had ever come near it. Daniel was intently reading a computer screen, but he was barely recognizable as the man Grant met three months ago.

"*Everyone* sent me," Grant replied. "We're worried about you."

"I'm fine. I have a smaller comm link design that will fit more comfortably in your ear; I'm sending it to Fletcher for production now."

Daniel hadn't had a haircut in two months; his face was lucky to be shaved once a week. His clothes hadn't seen the inside of a washing machine in at least as long. The only familiar thing that remained was his glasses, perched at the tip of his nose, and the intense focus of his eyes behind them.

"Hector brought takeout for everyone," Grant surreptitiously offered. Lisa repeatedly suspected he wasn't eating well, though they couldn't prove it. "It's downstairs if you want any."

"I'm fine." He scratched at the scruffy stubble about his cheeks, as he continued studying his computer.

The others couldn't seem to find out much about Daniel's state of being at all, as he refused to see anyone except Grant. And then only to get or give information about Grant's technical needs in the field. Whatever technology they needed to perform their missions, Daniel provided. He also crafted training equipment from time to time. Otherwise he was engaged in what appeared to be long, arduous hours of self-loathing.

His body was more or less healed from the attack he'd suffered months ago at the hands of Detective Matthew Drexel, though Lisa mentioned often that he never quite seemed to move or function the same again. Daniel had slowed down, was rarely seen walking, and had lost a good ten to twenty pounds. He sat at his desk whenever Grant visited.

Grant considered sharing his encounter with the strange old man at the nursing home today with Daniel, but scratched it. That sort of thing would be more up Morgan's alley, anyway.

He switched to a more direct approach. "Are you planning to stay up here indefinitely?"

"As long as we remain in this building. Or until you no longer need my help."

Grant was one of only two people in the building who knew the reason Daniel remained up here. Downstairs, in the very center of the Loci's new home, despite much cleaning, was a blood stain. Nobody else knew what it was and a rug covered it, but still it waited there in the central Common Room area where chairs, a sofa, and a large television resided.

"There's nothing to be feared down there, you know," Grant said tentatively. "It's just us. Your friends."

"No it's not. There are . . . memories."

"Daniel, talk to me. You can't bottle this up; believe me, I know. *Pretend* that we're friends, if you have to," Grant said.

"We *are* friends," Daniel replied, pulling back from his computer at last and looking up. "But this has nothing to do with you."

Grant sighed. How could he convince this man that he didn't have to carry his guilt and pain alone? That he didn't have to bury himself under the weight of his own sins? That self-flagellation would never be enough penance to rid himself of this Hell he was living in?

Daniel was nearly too far gone into his own world. Soon he'd be untouchable.

"You're going to have to find a way to move on from this," Grant said bluntly. Aloud, it sounded much more inadequate than it had in his head. "We need you."

Grant hesitated, then added, "*She* needs you."

Daniel wouldn't meet his eyes.

Grant grasped for something to say, but what was there? He had no frame of reference for what Daniel was feeling. Well, there was that one time he thought he'd killed the mercenary Konrad . . .

"What happened to Drexel was unfortunate, but it's not like—"

Daniel's head popped up. "Don't! *Don't* say he had it coming. Or that I was 'under duress.' Or that deep down, you know I'm a good person. Don't try to fix it, all right! Just . . . spare me."

Grant was at a loss.

"The truth is," Daniel said softly, "in my heart of hearts, I think I created that entire situation, because I wanted—"

"Justice? Drexel reaped what he sowed, and he was so deeply covered by the system, it was the only way he ever would have been punished for his crimes. He will have no more victims; people's lives have been saved because of what you did, Doc."

Daniel shook his head. "It wasn't justice I was interested in, and we both know it. But history repeated itself. Once again, I got exactly what I wanted, regardless of the cost."

Grant was too tired, too emotionally drained for this. He knew Daniel was referring to his past, to the devilish deal he struck with the company called Paragenics Group years ago to save his own life, but which also buried an unspeakable truth. He understood it all.

But Grant couldn't get himself to sympathize with the man. He was just too spent. Resigned to leave Daniel to his misery, he stood.

"I, uh—I heard about the truck thing," Daniel said, his hungry interest betraying the layers of walls he'd built around himself and his emotions. "Did you try that new focusing technique?"

Grant nodded, unsure whether to be happy or sad over this display of life and passion that remained inside his friend. He returned to his seat. "Worked flawlessly. I did it before entering the situation, and everything came so naturally after that. . . . More and more, I'm finding I don't even have to concentrate and focus to use my abilities. It's becoming second nature, I think."

Daniel's eyes flared with excitement, but he quickly looked down and away, searching his desktop for something. "Now that you've mastered fine control of your psychokinesis, I've been thinking you might turn your attention to honing other aspects of your power."

"What other aspects?"

"The Forging, for starters," Daniel replied. "Your link to the others. Just as your psychokinesis was at first, this telepathic link with the other Ringwearers is very reflexive right now. You've even learned to send them rudimentary signals and orders. I wonder what might be achieved if you tried pushing this ability further?"

The notion had never struck Grant before. He found it intriguing.

"Try this," Daniel said. "Find one of them in your mind, and hold onto that image."

Grant closed his eyes. "Okay," he said, eyes still closed. "I've got Alex. She's downstairs talking to Julie and Fletcher. I think they're at his workstation."

Daniel leaned forward on his elbows, which were positioned atop the desk. "Even though you're locked onto Alex, you can see your sister and Fletcher, and his equipment, all within your field of vision?"

"Yes, mostly."

"Hold tightly to that image, but imagine you're looking through a camera's lens, and try pulling the camera back. See if you can widen the field of vision, and see more of their surroundings."

Concentrating hard, Grant pulled back as instructed and surprised himself. "I can see Fletcher's entire work area now, and—"

Something caught his attention. He zeroed in on one of the monitors, but as soon as he removed his focus from Alex, the image vanished from his mind. His eyes popped open.

"What happened?" Daniel asked.

Grant was still processing the image he'd seen on Fletcher's monitor, and then he refocused his thoughts onto one of the Loci, attempting to trace her location. . . .

"The usual—big trouble," he concluded and darted from the office. The office door shut itself behind him.

13

"Where is she?" Grant demanded, descending the stairs rapidly.

"Who?" asked Fletcher.

"Nora!" Grant replied. "I just saw her on one of your television monitors, and she's in danger, I can feel it."

"It's okay, honey," Julie soothed him. "I sent her out on a Railroad errand. She's meeting a contact."

Though Ringwearers were finding the Loci often, from all over the world, none of them could be considered "new." Their Shifts all dated back to the same time period as the rest of the Loci—between Morgan, the first Ringwearer, and Grant, the last. These newcomers had remained in hiding after the trauma the Shift caused, only choosing to step out of the shadows now that they were discovering a new purpose in joining Grant and the others like themselves.

That is, everyone but the British team they'd watched on television earlier in the day. No one knew where they had come from, only that they were a very recent addition to the Ringwearers' numbers.

But elsewhere, news had spread fast. To ensure that no one untoward infiltrated the group, but that those Ringwearers who needed to find them could, Julie and Fletcher had set up a complex system of checks and balances. Applicants had to ask the right people, undergo a series of background tests, and much more, just to find out the location of the warehouse.

They named this covert system of entry to the team "the Railroad," in honor of the Underground Railroad made famous during the American Civil War.

On a daily basis, Grant found himself in awe of his sister. Not only did she single-handedly oversee the Railroad, but she had resigned from her professorship at UCLA to devote all of her time to their work here. She probably put in more hours than anyone else on the team.

And she *was* a member of the team—powers or no powers—as far as Grant was concerned.

Alex piped up. "Did you send her alone? With everything going on in the city?"

Julie blanched. "I didn't think. I'm sorry."

"Where did you send her?" Grant asked.

"The contact was to be made at Dodger Stadium," Julie replied.

"She's nowhere near there," Grant said with conviction, shaking his head. "Fletcher, can you trace her?"

Fletcher spun in his seat and engaged his attention fully upon his computer feeds. Every member of the team had tracking devices built into the earpieces they wore in the field. "That's confirmed. Looks like she's down at . . . huh."

"Fletcher . . ." Grant warned, impatient.

"She's at the Metro Center Station."

Julie got it immediately. "Isn't that where—?"

"It's where I fought Konrad the day I was Shifted," Grant replied. "Below the Wagner Building."

"Why would she go there?" Alex pondered.

"You said she's in danger?" Julie asked.

Grant nodded, closing his eyes. "Some kind of big fight going on, all around her. Dozens of people involved, from the looks of it, maybe more."

"Nora can handle herself," Fletcher pointed out.

Alex and Grant exchanged a meaningful glance, but said nothing. Nora could handle herself far better than most of the team knew, including Fletcher.

"Put a team together," Grant ordered. "We'll back her up." He sighed, still longing for rest. "Hector?"

"I think he's asleep," Fletcher replied.

"Then let him sleep," said Grant. Hector had trouble sleeping, everyone knew. His energy level was like that of a child's; it made it very hard for him to find rest at night.

Alex turned to him. "Why don't we make this a training exercise? We'll take those two new guys along. What were their names again?"

"Henrike. Wilhelm," Fletcher spoke into a headset as he placed it over his spiked hair. "Please report to command central, on the double."

"I want to know what Nora's doing down there," Grant said softly. "*There*, of all places . . ."

"And now she's in a big scuffle," Alex noted. "Is it my imagination, or does she attract this kind of trouble wherever she goes?"

Grant sighed. "I'm getting tired of her antics. She doesn't seem to understand the concept of 'teamwork'."

"Then she should be cut," Fletcher suggested. At their looks of surprise, he continued, "People are *dying* out there, and Nora is taking time to blow off steam in a random fistfight? Don't we have bigger fish to fry? I'm just asking—because no one else is—in the grand scheme, is she really worth the trouble? Does she matter that much?"

Grant started to answer, but Alex beat him to it.

"Everyone matters," she replied.

There was no Wagner Building anymore of course, but the subway station below the surface had been repaired and opened to the public again just a few weeks ago.

Alex and Grant approached the station from the sidewalk above, trailed by the beefy, muscular Henrike, who looked ready to take on the world, and Wilhelm, who was clearly unprepared for being thrust into action so quickly. The spot where the Wagner Building once stood had been cleared and converted into a downtown parking garage that had just opened days ago.

Grant took in the changes to these familiar surroundings with interest, but still he was struggling hard to keep his eyes open. His knees were wobbly and kept trying to give out.

As they approached the top of the stairs leading down to the subway, they were met by a handful of policemen putting on riot gear. Their clear shields were cracked and broken, and their worn eyes betrayed similar spirits. They all sported bruises and bandages of one sort or another. Clearly the city's resources were still maxed out, if these four wounded and worn out cops were all they could spare.

Sounds of fighting, screaming, and panic could be heard from the massive stairwell leading down, and every so often, a pedestrian or two emerged from the stairs and ran for their lives out onto the streets.

Grant approached the policemen, who were off to the side of the stairwell, still suiting up in their gear. "It's all right, guys," he said, "we've got this."

As one, all four of the policemen looked up and their shoulders fell upon seeing Grant and hearing his words. There was no frustration or disappointment on their part, only relief.

"Oh, thank God," one of them said under his breath.

"Are you sure?" another asked. "We're under orders—"

Grant conjured up a smile for them. "We're here now. Go get some rest. I insist."

This was met with a chorus of grateful nods and a couple of thank yous.

He turned toward the stairs and saw that Alex stood right at his side, as always. But she was facing away from the subway.

"Okay, guys," she said to their two trainees with a mischievous grin. "Class is in session."

14

Underground, pandemonium raged. Over one hundred men and women battled with fists and feet and packages and purses and whatever else they could get their hands on. It was like a free-for-all at an Old West saloon; no one seemed to be fighting for any particular reason, nor did they care to find one.

It was pure, unbridled aggression. Most likely further reaction to the world spinning out of control of late, Grant guessed. The real question was how it had started.

The fighting filled almost the entire station, spilling over across the tracks to both sides of the platform. A few dozen crazed souls even fought down on the train tracks, oblivious to any oncoming danger.

He sensed Nora was right in the thick of it on this side of the platform but made no move to intervene on her behalf.

"Do you mind. . . ?" said Grant. He remained near the bottom of the stairs and crossed his arms, resting his fatigue against a side wall.

"Getting old and feeble on me?" Alex teased.

"Hey, I got *shot* today," he retorted.

He had no idea what powers these two possessed, but despite his weariness, he was curious to find out.

Alex faced Henrike and Wilhelm. "Gentlemen. You have just walked into a highly dangerous situation involving a hundred or more pedestrians, and a member of your team is located smack-dab in the middle of it. You need to put a swift end to this situation without doing permanent harm to anyone, and you need to pull your teammate out of danger. How do you handle this situation?"

The two men merely looked at her.

"That wasn't a hypothetical, guys," Grant offered, unmoving from his spot against the wall. "Step up and show us what you've got. Now."

Eager to please, Henrike moved forward first, at the edge of the stairs, and spread his bulky arms wide. His brow came together in intense concentration and focus, and his muscles flexed and rippled all over his body.

Grant waited for something to happen but saw nothing. Had Henrike tricked them somehow, perhaps weaseling his way onto the team with a fake ring?

He was just about to tell the big man to give it up when he felt it. Cold.

The temperature had dropped inside the station. And despite his earlier feeling that whatever Henrike was doing was taking a long time, once Grant saw his own breath he realized just how fast Henrike had worked.

There was no blast of arctic wind, no tangible signals of what had caused the change. The temperature all around had simply lowered to a frigid state. In moments, the room had been rendered an enormous meat locker.

The fighting slowed as the cold spread throughout the station. Momentarily, everyone stopped, searching for the source of this drastic climate change.

"Not bad," Alex said.

Henrike smiled, as pleased as if he'd just gotten a gold star from his favorite teacher. "And it is not merely cold I can induce. I can cause the temperature to increase also."

"What you *can't* do," Alex noted, "is talk and still hold onto your concentration." She nodded toward the station.

Henrike turned, horrified, realizing that by explaining his abilities to Grant, he'd broken off his meditation. The room was already returning to normal temperatures.

Punches flew once more, and the fighting resumed as if there had been no pause.

"No!" Henrike cried. "I'll do it again—"

"That's okay, you did fine," Alex said, placing a hand on his shoulder and pulling him backward. "Let's give someone else a try."

The small man, Wilhelm, stepped forward timidly, arms hanging limp at his sides. "I don't know if I—" he said softly.

"Don't worry," Grant said reassuringly. "This isn't a test. We just want to see what you're capable of."

Wilhelm registered a worried expression on his face and still never quite met Grant's eyes. He turned slowly to face the fighting crowd. But unlike Henrike, he never screwed up his face in concentration, never bore down on anything or even raised a finger.

Without warning, a bright blue bolt leapt from one of his hands hanging at his side and jumped down to the nearest human body on the ground level. From there, it branched out instantly, from body to body, connecting them all in a blinding electrical current. It arced down onto the metal train tracks and surged up into the light fixtures hanging from the ceiling, which instantly exploded and went out.

And then it was over, nothing more emerged from Wilhelm's hand, and the room was dark. Emergency floodlights came on throughout the station, but all other sources of electricity were dead from electrical overload. All the people who had been fighting now lay on the ground, awake but in shock.

All of it happened in less than three seconds.

Grant kept looking back and forth between the small man and the crowd on the ground below him. His jaw hung open, but he couldn't form words.

"What just happened?!" Fletcher cried into their earpieces, his surveillance equipment no doubt going haywire. *"What did he do?"*

"How . . ." Alex stammered, registering the same shock as Grant. "How did all of that come from a *mental* ability?"

"Thoughts are just electrical impulses traveling through gray matter," Wilhelm said quietly, and then he stepped back, again trying his best to become invisible.

It was a futile effort, for now nearly every eye in the structure had turned to look upon him.

15

"What was *that*?" called out a voice from below.

Like everyone else, Nora was on the ground but was slowly recovering, getting back to her feet. She moved toward Grant and the team, while they moved toward her.

Like so many of the Loci, Nora was unique. Aside from her well-known power to render normal humans unconscious, she was equally known for her unpleasant disposition. They'd taken a gamble in letting her onto the team, as she'd had a criminal record before the Shift, but that was ancient history. Morgan vouched for her, and that was good enough for everyone else. And she'd proven a valuable team member in the field, even if Grant and Alex often found her hard to handle.

Most of the other Loci whispered amongst themselves that it was best not to get on her bad side. (Grant thought they would soon be adding Wilhelm to that list as well, after what he'd just witnessed.) Strong-willed and defiant, Nora had no inclination to avoid confrontations. Instead, she seemed to thrive on them.

Displeased, she cast squinty eyes on Grant. "Did you do that? I was just gettin' warmed up!"

"Who started this fight?" Grant asked in a tone that implied, *It better not be you.*

Nora pointed to one of the men on the floor nearby. "His girl mouthed off at him and he laid into her with both fists flyin'. Couple a' Good Samaritans tried to bail her out, and it turned into a free-for-all from there. Ask me, people just needed to work off some aggression."

Grant raised his voice. "Everyone go home. *Now*," he ordered. "This is over."

The crowd slowly rose from the ground and dispersed, no one daring to argue with Guardian. But Grant held the man who'd instigated the fight pinned to the ground.

"I have a zero tolerance policy when it comes to abusers," he said slowly. "I've seen too many of you, and I'm running out of patience with it. So you're going to pack your bags, you're going to leave your girlfriend alone, and you're going to get out of Los Angeles. I don't care where you go from here, but *stay out of my city*. I ever see your face again, I'll remove it from your head."

As Grant released him, the man cast a nasty look in his girlfriend's direction. But he exited as ordered.

"What were you doing here?" Grant rounded on Nora the minute they were alone after returning to the surface above.

"Julie said she sent you to Dodger Stadium," Alex added.

"Contact got twitchy, called and asked to move the meeting to someplace with more people. Jerk stood me up anyway, though. What's the big?"

"You're supposed to notify Fletcher of any change in plan, and you know it," Alex replied forcefully.

"Hey, big G here knows everywhere I go, every move I make, anyway," Nora replied, cocking her head at Grant. "Nothing I do can change that, right?" She walked away toward the SUV.

Alex and Grant turned to one another and shared a look of frustration. Alex became pensive. "Do you really think that was wise, back there? Sending that man off to someplace else, outside L.A.? Won't he just find someone else to victimize?"

Grant was tired of talking. Why was Alex questioning his decisions? And why now? Couldn't she see how exhausted he was? "What *should* I have done, Alex? Can't turn him over to the police—local jail cells are bursting at the seams already after today. Should I have just killed him and removed the threat from society?"

"No! I don't know," she replied, waffling. "But I don't believe you're in the position that you're in for the benefit of just one city."

"The whole world is too big a place for us to fix. We're a small group—"

"—of superpowered people—" Alex interjected.

"—who have limited means and resources. And L.A. keeps us plenty busy as it is. Who has time for international travel? Our faces are famous; how would we be able to leave the city without being mobbed? Or even arrested? Just because LAPD appreciates our efforts doesn't mean the rest of the world would. It's too much for me to stop it all—"

She cut him off with a wave of her hand. "Then we do what we can. And we inspire the rest of the world to do the same." With that, she joined Nora and the two men at the car.

Women, Grant thought.

As he stood there on the well-lit street corner in front of where the Wagner Building had once been, his phone vibrated.

"Yeah."

"Hello, Grant." It wasn't a familiar voice. The guy spoke with a South African accent, sounded very refined, upper-crust even. "I've waited a long time to make your acquaintance."

"Who is this?"

"My name is Devlin, though you will find that piece of information unimportant. What will matter to you is that I am the Keeper of the Secretum."

Grant didn't respond. He couldn't think of anything to say.

"I infer from your silence," Devlin went on, "that your grandfather told you to expect another to be appointed to take his place."

Grant found his footing and remembered how tired he was. He wasn't the same person the Secretum was used to dealing with; he had no use for their games anymore and saw no reason to put up with them.

"What do you want?" he asked.

"Merely to introduce myself. I think you saw me earlier today, at the nursing home fire you handled so readily and sacrificially."

The man in the tailored suit, standing on the roof . . .

"You've been watching me," Grant stated. *He's probably watching me right now.*

Grant spun in place, taking in his surroundings. He observed the pedestrians strolling the streets on all sides, the nearby office buildings with a few lights still on here and there, the cars passing by. There were rooftops so high in the darkness that any number of people could have been on one of those buildings, watching him right now.

He could be anywhere. Anyone.

"Of course I have," Devlin replied. "That's why I'm calling. I knew you'd spotted me this afternoon, and I feel you deserve to know who you're dealing with. It's important to me that you know that though I am officially the Keeper, I am *not* your grandfather. Your relationship with me will not be as it was with him."

"We aren't going to *have* a relationship."

"I noticed you don't wear his bracelet anymore," Devlin said in a mildly curious voice, not an accusational one.

Grant glanced down at his empty wrist.

Devlin kept talking. "Your grandfather's methods may have gotten results, but they were not without controversy within the Secretum. Many of us regarded his tactics as barbaric and extreme. He repeatedly placed your life in danger, and that is unacceptable."

"I'm in danger every day. It's what I do," Grant replied smoothly. "So why am I still talking to you?"

Devlin laughed, once. "I think you know why . . . The game is still in play."

A cold feeling Grant hadn't felt in a long time slinked down his spine. "Not for me, it's not. I'm done with you people. And you have to know you'd be a fool to try anything against me now."

"Believing our own press these days, are we? Yes, I do recall hearing one of them say recently that you are 'afraid of nothing'."

"Not nothing," Grant replied. "Just not *you.*"

"Nor should you be," Devlin said encouragingly. "As I said before, I've no intention of harming you in any way. But it *is* my function to finish the work your grandfather started. I will complete preparations for you to fulfill your destiny."

"I've chosen my own destiny. You're not in it."

"Don't be obtuse, boy. *You are the Bringer.* You will bring into being—" Devlin's voice trailed off, as if he wanted to say more, but held back.

"What? I'm supposed to *bring* something? Bring *what*?" Grant demanded.

"In a matter of days, all will be known, and all will be fulfilled. I'll see you then."

Click.

Grant stared at the phone in his hand. *Call terminated*, it read. *Swell.*

All thoughts of sleep jarred from his consciousness, he speed-dialed a number stored on his phone. It rang for a few moments before Morgan answered.

"If you're not at the warehouse, get there now," he said.

16

It was after one in the morning and the overhead lights were out in the warehouse when Grant and Morgan settled into a quiet corner. Even Fletcher's workstation was dark, though at least one light was still on upstairs in Daniel's lab.

Grant and Morgan found some folding chairs and arranged themselves so Grant could see any late-night lingerers.

"I had a phone conversation with the new Keeper today," Grant said without prelude.

Morgan was just taking her seat as he said the words, and she sat far back to fully process what he'd said. Her eyes grew slightly, but she made no reply, only waited for him to continue.

"His name is Devlin. He thinks I'm still going to become the Bringer and . . . *bring* . . . something."

Morgan looked away, her eyes darting to and fro, betraying wheels turning inside of wheels in her mind.

"You're not surprised by this, are you?" he asked, coming to a realization.

She glanced at him as if considering lying, but finally said, "Not at all. We always knew the Secretum was bigger than your grandfather. He himself told you their work would continue without him. Though it would seem you've been outside their sphere of influence for many weeks, it would be foolish to assume that they were inactive during your respite. One must conclude that their plans for you extend far beyond the reach of Maximilian Borrows."

Grant was silent as he allowed her time to ponder this. Morgan had always been a woman of many secrets. Grant often found himself wondering just how much was going on inside that perfect mind of hers that no other living soul would ever know about.

"There's something else," he said softly. "Devlin led me to believe that events are going to be coming to a head very soon. And there was an old man I met at the nursing home. Very strange. Unsettling."

"In what way?"

Grant took a deep breath. "He seemed to think that there were going to be three acts or events that would take place, as a countdown to something."

Morgan eyed him gravely. "Three acts?"

He nodded.

She looked away again, trying to hide an intense shock.

"Why do I feel like you know what he was talking about?"

She regarded him carefully, cautiously. Forming her words with deliberation, she replied, "It could be a reference to the Three Unholy Markers."

Grant was incredulous, wondering if he'd heard her right. "What are 'Unholy Markers'?"

"Disruptions of the natural order of things. Perversions of physics, or of the way the world works. A passage on the Dominion Stone referred to Three Unholy Markers that would take place in the days of the Bringer."

Stunned, Grant leaned forward. "If you knew this was on the Dominion Stone prophecy, why haven't you ever mentioned it before?"

"Grant, the Dominion Stone prophecy is over three thousand words long. I had no way of knowing which passages were of greatest significance until you came along and fulfilled them. Even now, there are parts of it that seem completely nonsensical to me."

"Did it tell what the Three Markers are?"

She nodded and swallowed. Grant recognized the gesture. She was about to recite something from her perfect memory.

"In the days of the Bringer,
there shall be three unholy acts of Creation,
a perversion of all that was made and all that is good.

These Markers shall serve as a sign to those with eyes to see:

The heavens shall turn to fire
and ash will rain from the sky.

The most fertile soil shall bleed,
and forever stain the firmament.

And the end shall be marked by a scar
revealing man's deepest hollow."

"The first one has already come true!" Grant cried, doing his best to whisper to stifle his shock. "The sky turned to fire the day we defeated my grandfather!"

"Yes," Morgan replied, already aware of this. "And I take no pleasure in making the connection, Grant, but I believe it is of utmost importance to point out that *you* caused that 'unholy' act to occur."

"You think *I'll* be the cause of all three Markers."

"The Secretum thinks so."

"I still can't believe you never told me about any of this."

"Even if I had, would you have been interested in hearing it?" Morgan retorted. "I've warned you many times that nothing about the prophecy changed just because your grandfather died. But your focus has been elsewhere of late."

What do your eyes see?

Grant looked down, realizing his frustrations were more rightly pointed at himself, not Morgan.

"In any case, this confirms my findings of late," Morgan continued.

"Findings?"

"Yes. I'm afraid we must wake everyone at once. As of this moment, time is too precious a commodity to waste on sleep."

"You want to wake everyone up? Are you sure?"

She cast him a stern glance.

"Okay, you're sure."

17

Henrike hated himself.

Hated what he was doing. What he was about to do, or let happen.

At the beginning, he'd had no mixed feelings about agreeing to do this thing for the FBI agent named Cooke. He was available, he was needed by the United States government, and it would pay well. Possibly even enough to allow him to pay off some very volatile men to whom he owed money. Men who weren't intimidated by his powers.

But now, after having met the man called Guardian and having seen firsthand what he was about . . . What if he'd picked the wrong side in all this?

He put change into one of the last pay phones in L.A. and dialed the number he'd been asked to memorize. Agent Cooke answered.

"About time," Cooke said anxiously. "You were supposed to report in hours ago. Do you have what I asked for?"

Henrike hesitated, momentarily debating, but ultimately decided it was pointless to resist. This *was* the government, after all. As a foreigner on their soil, they could make his life much more complicated than it already was.

"Yes. I have the address."

Grant willed the bright overhead lights to come on, and much commotion ensued from the far corner where the sleeping areas were draped off.

Morgan remained momentarily in the small corner she and Grant had occupied. She told Grant she needed to make a quick phone call to confirm something, and then she would meet him and everyone else in the Common Room.

And she would tell them everything she could about her recent activities.

Slowly, one by one, Grant's friends—his team—emerged from their beds. All were groggy and wiping away sleep from their eyes, and no one was terribly happy about being woken up.

Alex was the first to speak up. "This better be life-and-death, sweetie."

"Come on, come on!" Morgan shouted, appearing over Grant's shoulder. Apparently her phone call was done. Her proper British accent added greatly to her commanding tone of voice. "All hands on deck! Everyone! Gather round!"

She turned to Grant. "I should like Dr. Cossick to join us as well."

Grant harrumphed. "I bet you would."

"The doc doesn't make house calls these days, remember?" Alex added before yawning long and hard.

"Grant, surely you could persuade him to join us?" Morgan offered.

"Doubt it. He won't come down here, not for anything."

Morgan glanced at the stairs. "His light is still on, he's awake. Leave him no choice in the matter," she concluded with a cold casualness.

"Oooookay," Grant replied.

Within minutes, Daniel was protesting loudly as his desk chair— with him still seated in it—floated on air, gently descending the staircase to the ground floor. By the time he and Grant reached the Common Room, he'd folded his arms and fumed silently to himself.

Less than five minutes—and a number of bleary-eyed complaints— later, everyone present was gathered in the Common Room area. Grant sat on one end of the faux-leather couch, Julie at his side. Fletcher seated himself next to her, and Alex was directly across from them in an armchair. A folding chair groaned under Hector's weight, threatening imminent collapse, while Nora sat alone on the floor at the far edge of the circle. Wilhelm also sat alone along the periphery, though by his own choice.

Many of the others sat elsewhere on the floor or in other chairs that

Grant had pulled into the circle with his mind. He didn't see Henrike and concluded he must be a heavy sleeper.

His eyes fell upon Nora. His thoughts focused again on the black woman, thinking back to when she had found the group about the same time as Hector. Unlike most of the others, she'd had difficulty integrating into the group, preferring to work alone. As Grant understood it, she had a history of abuse and violence and had spent more than one night in jail. She isolated herself often, which was understandable, given her power, but also had the effect of keeping her from integrating with the others.

Nora rarely felt like she belonged here, a fact that was painfully obvious. The only time she seemed to enjoy herself was when they were on a mission and she was able to unleash her abilities. The first time Grant had seen her do it, it had chilled him to the bone.

But she was a powerful asset to the team—one of their most valuable members. Everyone believed her ring gave her the ability to render others unconscious.

And Grant was content to go on letting them believe that. If anyone knew the truth . . . it could be disastrous.

Morgan sat in another armchair not far from Alex. Dozens of bleary, sleepy eyes stared back at her. Her own manner lost the excitement she'd displayed just moments ago, and now settled into a foreboding resolve. She settled back into her seat and interlaced her fingers, looking slowly around the room.

She offered no apology for waking everyone up at this hour. She was contemplative and subdued.

"I've been working on a personal project," she began. "Honestly, I'm surprised none of you determined on your own what I've been up to. I don't think it could be any more obvious. I've been trying to decipher the mystery that is the Secretum of Six," she quietly announced, her voice filled with introspection. "And I think I've found the answers I was looking for."

Silence followed her statement.

"Which answers are those, exactly?" Grant asked.

Morgan's eyebrows bunched together, and her eyes became unfocused. "All of them," she focused on him at last. "The rings. The Dominion Stone. The prophecy. The Bringer. I think I've figured it out."

18

Sagging heads perked up around the room.

Morgan was silent for so long, seemingly lost in such deep thought, that Grant spoke up. "Are you going to tell us?"

"Yes and no," Morgan replied. "There are parts that you simply are not prepared to accept. There are truths about the Secretum that are too fantastic, too astounding for you to believe without proof, and rightly so. But I have seen things of late . . . And I know the truth. You will soon know the full truth as well, but until then, my words will fall on ears ill equipped to understand what I have to tell you."

Murmurs swelled through the room; several sounded angry.

"This doesn't make any sense," Alex noted. "What are you playing at?"

Morgan leveled an even but unforgiving gaze on Alex. "This is no game. After the kind of day you all have had, after the last few months and all of the terrible things that have been happening to our planet . . . I would never be so trite as to belittle our work by teasing you about it.

"Understand me clearly: I am not withholding information to be cruel or coy or secretive. I *intend* for you to know everything I know. But before that can happen, there are things you will need to discover on your own—things you must see with your own eyes—that you would not accept as hearsay from me or *anyone*."

"You're saying an awful lot of absolutely nothing," Grant said.

"I'm not a fan of Oscar Wilde, but he was right on one count: 'The truth is rarely pure and never simple.' We have shaken off the coils of the past and carved out new lives for ourselves. Free of the plans the Keeper had for us, we've made something new, something better. And I can't tell you all how proud I am of you for this. The events of this day alone have shaken us all, but still we stand firm, holding to what's right. It would have been so much easier for us to take an alternate, more comfortable route. . . ."

She drifted off, lost in thought for a moment. Then she cleared her throat. "No matter. I tell you this because I don't wish to lead any of you to believe that I disapprove of our recent activities. Quite the contrary.

"Still, despite this newfound purpose you have embraced, I've found it difficult letting go of the original purpose for which we were intended. Or more precisely, the ones who intended it for us. I am speaking of course of the underground organization responsible for empowering us with the Rings of Dominion and Shifting us into our new lives. The Secretum of Six. They sit in places of great power and authority, and their actions are not idle. They move with precision of purpose and a plan that will lead to the ruin of everything we hold dear."

Many of those listening shifted and squirmed uncomfortably in their seats. Unsettled glances were exchanged, dismay on the faces of many.

"Come on, Morgan," Lisa spoke up. "Is it really necessary to go down this road again?"

But Grant's ears perked up as his mind returned to the odd conversation that afternoon with the sickly old man.

"'For what a man would like to be true, that he more readily believes,'" Morgan recited. "I know you don't want to think about this, but someone *must* take responsibility for bringing the Secretum to justice, and undoing whatever grand plan they have set into motion through all of us. Who else is there to do this? It's no secret that whoever they are, wherever they come from, they are skilled, resourceful, and deft at keeping themselves hidden. All that is required for them to accomplish their goals is for us to look away and do nothing."

Grant remained attentive but couldn't get the old man's face out of his head. Something about Morgan's words was causing an odd itch inside his head.

"Finding information about them—even records of their very *existence*—has proven more challenging than even I expected. But we managed to turn up a symbol that I believe may lead us to—"

"We?" Alex asked. "Have you been working with someone outside the group?"

Morgan hesitated, and Grant felt very uneasy at the look on her face.

"It's Payton," she replied resignedly, to much shock among those gathered round. "I asked him to help in my investigation, to be my eyes and ears in the field. I realize this may come as a surprise, considering our history . . . But the two of us have one thing in common, and that is a powerful desire to see the Secretum's plans exposed and ended once and for all. After all of the lies that organization fed him for the last nine years, you might say Payton is feeling a bit . . . bloodthirsty."

"So when he left after everything that happened with the Keeper," Fletcher said, three steps ahead of everyone else per usual, "it wasn't because he didn't want to stay. It was because you sent him off on this mission to track down the Secretum."

"That's right," Morgan nodded. "Payton is what he is, and I know he makes many of you uncomfortable. He makes *me* uncomfortable. I thought his absence might make things run more smoothly for the group. So this plan killed two birds with one stone. And his help in this task has proven invaluable."

More murmuring. Grant was displeased that she'd kept this to herself, but understood her reasoning. Still, Payton had been a huge help in the end with their struggle against his grandfather. He still believed the Englishman could make a valuable addition to the team, if he could learn to tone down his casual lethality.

"You mentioned a symbol?" he said, bringing everyone's focus back to the matter at hand.

"Yes," Morgan replied, clearly grateful to get back to her point. She took out a piece of paper on which she'd scribbled a symbol by hand. It was a series of lines that connected to form a six-pointed star, with an identical star inside of that, its lines half as long. Another star was inside the second one, only half as big, and so on, until the center was a bulging mass of lines too close together to make out.

"Do you recognize this?" she asked, turning it slowly so the whole group could see. She handed it to Alex, who examined it and passed it on so the entire group could get a closer look.

"Maybe," Grant replied. "I'm not sure."

She produced a photograph and handed it to Grant. "What about now?"

The picture was a familiar one. It was a photo of his parents when they were younger that he'd uncovered months ago at his old family home. His dad was leaning over his mom, who sat at a desk. They both wore military uniforms, and they had turned to the camera and smiled.

A tiny "x" had been marked in ink on the photo long before he'd ever found it. The "x" marked a very small tattoo that was visible on his father's wrist, if you knew what to look for.

The tattoo was tiny, but Grant held the photograph close to his eyes.

And there it was. It matched Morgan's symbol. Right before his eyes, he'd seen it a dozen times.

Of course!

19

Grant looked back up at Morgan, eyes wide.

"I believe this symbol is the insignia of the Secretum," she explained. "I have a theory that they use it as a marker—for their strongholds, their assets, their files and information. Anything—or any*one*—that belongs to them, is identifiable by this symbol."

"Seems kind of simplistic for such a powerful secret society, doesn't it?" Alex asked. "I would have expected something more . . . I don't know . . . elaborate?"

"Ah," Morgan's eyes flashed, "but you're ignoring the cunning of creating a secret symbol around a common shape. It's the symbological equivalent of 'hiding in plain sight.' To an untrained eye, found on any document or scrawled on a wall somewhere, it could be nothing more than a smudged asterisk. But looking closer reveals lines on top of lines, smaller and smaller inside the primary shape. It's terribly clever."

"What does it symbolize, exactly?" Grant asked.

"I've put considerable thought into this, and honestly, I'm still not certain. But I believe the shape itself could be less significant than the number it represents—denoted by how many points the star has. They are known as 'the Secretum of Six,' and here we have a six-pointed star. It could be just that simple. Or perhaps it goes deeper.

"The number six is steeped in tremendous historical significance. There are six points on the Star of David—the symbol of Israel, one of the oldest civilizations in the world, and Judaism, one of the world's oldest religions. The first humans are said to have been created on 'the sixth day of creation.' Even our measurements of time—minutes, hours, days, months—are numbers built around increments of six. Mathematically speaking, six is the first 'perfect number', and there are six sides to a cube. From a scientific point of view, six is the atomic number of carbon—and every form of life known to exist is built upon a foundation of carbon compounds. . . ."

"Good grief, woman," Nora mumbled loud enough for all to hear while stifling a yawn, "we get it. Six is all that and more. So what?"

Unmistakably annoyed, Grant slowly turned in her direction. "This is the *listening* part of the meeting. Keep the commentary to yourself."

Morgan watched and waited as Grant and Nora studied one another. Alex shifted in her seat, no doubt feeling the sudden tension in the room.

"Go on, Morgan," Grant said, still looking at Nora.

"I sent Payton to France, back to the cave where he was buried alive nine years ago. If you'll remember, he and I were there together at the time, looking for a fragment of the Dominion Stone. The cave is a historical monument, and therefore overseen by government agencies. His investigation led him into a government records building, where he discovered a file belonging to a company called Trigate International—a company I believe to be one of many used as fronts for the Secretum—that supposedly provides labor and maintenance for the government division in charge of national historical landmarks in France. The file he found bears a small, handmade mark that matches the symbol of the Secretum."

She paused to allow everyone a moment to let that sink in.

"Payton tells me that this file contains references to other holdings by this same front company—mostly international deals similar to their deal with the French government. All of which I suspect to be forged information. But there was one reference in the file to something that had an air of authenticity to it—it was a reference to some sort of repository."

"Repository?" Grant asked.

"I've no idea what kind," Morgan replied. "It could be information, it could be supplies, or it could be . . . an army. If we ever want to know, there's only one place we'll be able to find out: London."

Grant registered surprise at this, as did most everyone else. "England?"

"This dummy corporation's headquarters are located in Great Britain. Though it won't be easy getting there, as I'm sure you're all aware of the events that have played out today in London. And Fletcher, before you ask, yes, I've considered the possibility that the lockdown in London could be connected to Payton's investigation of Trigate. The company's home office *is* inside the quarantined zone."

The room was silent for a few minutes. No one seemed to want to speak, but Morgan waited patiently. There were too many implications in her suggestions, too many truths that none of them wanted to face.

"Wouldn't it be easier to just send Payton to London?" Alex asked. This suggestion got nods of approval from others.

All except for Grant, whose thoughts were miles away, locked on the eyes of an old man who was missing a hand.

Three events . . . Three signs . . .

A countdown.

"He will be joining us there, but you're still not grasping the magnitude of this," Morgan replied. "The rest of the world has no idea that the Secretum is out there, but we have tangible evidence in hand that it *exists*. This symbol may very well be the key to locating and confronting the Secretum once and for all. For all we know, they could even be located at or near this Trigate International headquarters in London! Do we really dare send one man alone to bring them to justice? Considering all of the resources they *must* have at their disposal, it seems the only logical course of action is to take them on with everything we can."

It was Grant who eventually broke the silence. "But how do we do something like this?" Grant put a voice to the hesitation etched on every face. "Are you suggesting we just pull up stakes and hop across the ocean? *All* of us? And what if this turns out to be a wild goose chase? What about the people of L.A.—they need us here, *now* more than ever. How are we supposed to just *leave*—"

Morgan jumped to her feet. "*Stop* it!" she shouted. It was a rare display of anger, of indignation—so rare, the gigantic warehouse was deathly still in the pauses between her words. Even Grant had never seen her so indignant. "Stop making excuses! Don't let yourself think for one instant that any of what I am saying is a *suggestion*.

"If you have ever believed my words or respected anything I have done for you—for *all* of you—then *please*, you *must* believe me now. I have a great deal more information at my disposal than I have shared with you, and I *know* I'm right about this. The Secretum can be found, and it's our responsibility to find them. And they must. Be. Stopped.

"The Secretum is connected to us, and we to them through the Rings of Dominion, whether we like it or not. Whatever it is they *do*, whatever reason they exist, they are not a force for good. And there is no one else in the world that has any chance of finding and stopping them. The fact that we haven't seen or heard from them in a while means *nothing*. According to the prophecy on the Dominion Stone, this group waited *millennia* for the coming of the Bringer. They have not been inactive for the last few months, despite all appearances to the contrary."

She shared just a hint of a glance with Grant, but didn't press it.

"I'm sorry to put it in such terms, but I must say it: *It's us or them.* Choose now. We must find them before they are able to finish what the Keeper started."

"And just exactly what did the Keeper start?" Alex asked. "Do we even know?"

"All we have to go on is the prophecy that was on the Dominion Stone," Morgan replied. "The Stone spoke in vague terms about the coming of the Bringer, the 'man of miracles,' who would wield the Seal of Dominion. One passage in particular spoke of a clash between the Bringer and the wielder of a weapon of silver. Their battle would 'bring forth a day unlike any other. No act of man, no work forged of his hands, can prevent the torment that day will herald.' There's much more than that, about the Thresher, the Forging, the Keeper . . .' "

"Sounds like a fight between Payton and Grant," Alex replied. "I mean, the Bringer fighting someone who has a silver weapon? Come on."

"No," Morgan explained. "The exact wording of the passages states, 'He who wields the weapon of purest silver will stand between the Bringer and the day of torment.' That doesn't necessarily mean Payton."

"The Keeper," Grant said. "He wore a silver ring. But he was buried under thousands of tons of earth, and his ring with him. And he told me that ring was one of a kind. Wouldn't that mean we're in the clear, as far as this—"

Grant's entire body flinched as his head snapped around sharply to look behind the couch, off into a distance too far away for the others to see. Julie was so startled by the movement, she jerked away from him.

Everyone fell silent, watching him. He jumped to his feet, and the entire room registered alarm.

What was his name again? The big guy Julie introduced me to this morning?

Henrike.

Oh, no.

"Leaving the country is sounding better all the time," he said, his voice barely above a whisper. "Fletcher, execute Emergency Code Black. *Now.*"

20

The federal strike team held its high-powered rifles ready, beams of light sweeping across the darkened warehouse floor. Thick, murky clouds of gas meant to render anyone inside unconscious swirled and billowed throughout the vast room.

Special Agent Ethan Cooke motioned for his men to fan out and cover the entire building. Like the rest of the team, he was dressed in black from head to foot, his weapon held out ahead with a light attached to the barrel, and a balaclava and gas mask covering his face.

The warehouse was nearly pitch-black, the only light filtering in from streetlamps outside through cracks in the boards covering the windows high above.

"Infrared indicates no warm bodies, sir," another agent spoke softly into his earpiece.

"We may not be able to trust infrared," Ethan reminded him. "Or any other means of detection."

Still, he was well inside the building now, and by all appearances, it had been gutted and abandoned hours ago.

"Federal agents!" he shouted as loud as he could. "Show yourselves!"

"Sir?" someone squawked in his earpiece. One of the flashlight beams was dancing about sixty feet away. Quiet and cautious as a cat, Ethan approached the spot with his weapon at the ready.

"What is it?" he whispered.

The agent replied by shining his light down at the ground before them. There, on the cement floor, was a barely noticeable red stain, no bigger than an apple. It bore signs of having been scrubbed, an attempt to wash it clean.

"Tag it," Ethan ordered, moving on.

The agent complied by placing a small flag on the floor to mark the spot and prevent the other agents from stepping on it.

Fifteen minutes later, he pronounced the building officially secure. There was nothing here—no people, no equipment, no documents, nothing—though he expected to find plenty of trace amounts of DNA throughout the facility once forensics arrived. He'd sent an agent to find the building's breaker box and turn on the lights almost five minutes ago. But the man hadn't reported back yet. . . .

"I'm curious," a voice called out in the dark. Ethan spun to see a man standing in the main doorway entrance. The details of his appearance were obscured by the lights behind him outside. All Ethan could see was a black silhouette of the man's body.

Dozens of guns were drawn to bear upon the stranger. Ethan considered ordering them to stand down, but knew it was pointless either way. If this was who he suspected it was, their weapons were useless.

"What's the going price," the man asked, "to get a superhuman to betray the rest of us?"

Ethan swallowed. *The rest of* us.

"Twenty large," he replied, stepping slowly forward. He decided to be honest; not knowing the full extent of what this man was capable of, it was better to start out on the right foot. "I apologize for the deception, sir, but as I'm sure you know, you're not the easiest man in the world to find. I would have used one of my agents with a facsimile ring, but word on the street has it that you'd know the difference."

Guardian took three steps inside the door, his hands clasped casually behind his back. Ethan saw his face for the first time and matched it to the photos and television coverage he'd seen.

Adrenaline surged, his heart pumped. It was him.

"Poor Henrike," Guardian said, referring to the man who had betrayed him and his friends. "He threw away his first and last chance to do the right thing."

"Did he?" Ethan replied, grim.

"I'd suggest you take my advice and leave him be. He's already on the run, and we made sure he won't be of further use to you."

"Yes, I know," Ethan conceded.

Ethan had found Henrike a little over an hour ago, sitting on the sidewalk near the same pay phone he'd called Ethan from. But he wasn't the same man Ethan had met a few days ago. The burly Henrike was lost and confused and terrified. He had no idea where he was or what he was doing there.

"What do you want from me?" Guardian asked.

"Don't you care to know who I am? Who I speak for?"

"Henrike told me that much," Guardian replied. "Not that I needed the confirmation. We knew Uncle Sam would come looking for us sooner or later. The only question is why? What do you want?" he repeated.

"We want to know who you are. Where you come from. How you gained your special abilities. What your agenda is, and that of your group. I assure you we mean you no harm," Ethan took another step forward, changing his tactics. Perhaps he'd respond to an offer. . . . "We know about all that you've done recently to help the people of this city, the countless lives you've saved, and we're grateful. Washington would like to open the lines of communication with you, and find out if we could work together, coordinate our efforts somehow."

"So," Guardian replied thoughtfully, "you want to be my best friend . . . and to convince me of your sincerity, you brought an *arsenal*?"

"Our weapons are for defense only, we honestly mean you—"

"No harm," Guardian finished. "You mentioned that. Just as we mean *you* no harm. Now, do you believe me when I say that?"

Ethan hesitated. "I want to. But my superiors won't find it acceptable to take the word of a man who goes to such great lengths to keep his identity a secret. Let's face it: you're not even a taxpayer."

Something akin to amusement passed across Guardian's features.

"Won't you at least tell me your name? Your real name?" Ethan tried, blinking back the sweat that stung his eyes. He had to consciously force himself *not* to let his eyes shift to the two members of his team that were sneaking in the back door behind Guardian. If his pupils twitched even slightly . . .

Guardian ignored the question. "My people and I are to be left alone. We are not your agenda. We are not a mystery for you to unravel. We are *nothing* to you. As far as you are concerned, we do not exist."

"I'm afraid Washington will disagree," Ethan replied, trying to hide the quiver in his voice. His men were slowly and silently raising their weapons to bear on Guardian . . . if only they could tranquilize him . . . "As will every major world leader around the globe."

"If you get a shot, take it," another agent whispered over the frequency Ethan's entire team shared, a message intended for the men sneaking up behind Guardian.

NO!! No no no!

But how could Ethan countermand those orders without alerting Guardian?

Two loud shots caused everyone in the room to retrain their weapons on Guardian, but Ethan knew immediately that something was wrong. Those shots were much louder than they should have been.

His two agents behind Guardian lay on the ground, the rifles gone from their hands, but the fronts of their black jumpsuits were smoking.

The bullets had never left their guns. They fired, but the guns exploded in their hands.

Guardian's demeanor changed ever so slightly, and he made the tiniest of gestures with his eyes. The two men on the ground flew up into the air and smacked their backs against the ceiling. They remained there, lying *up* against the roof, as if gravity were reversed.

"Do you still mean me no harm?" Guardian said slowly, menacingly. "Because my feelings on the matter are changing as we speak."

"It was a mistake, I'm sorry—"

"I'll say it again, since you didn't seem to hear me the first time," Guardian continued. Still he stood rooted to his spot, unthreatened and unconcerned for his own safety. "Stay. Away. From us. I would take no pleasure in destroying you, but *don't push me*. This is the only warning you will get."

Guardian gave a fleeting glance to the weapon in Ethan's hand. The flashlights on all of their weapons went dark, while Ethan's gun fell apart and out of his hand. Its dozens of metallic parts clanged on the ground. The only light in the building came from the indirect glow of the streetlamps outside.

Then he turned, exposing his back to them, and walked away slowly. Confidently.

Guardian walked calmly away until he was almost out of sight, and Ethan had to appreciate the man's bravado. Why *wouldn't* he show them his back, indifferent to whatever other hidden weapons they might have? They could throw twenty grenades at Guardian, and what good would it do?

Guardian paused just outside the door. Ethan looked up in time to see the two men on the ceiling plummet facedown toward the ground. Three feet from the floor, they froze and hovered for an instant before they fell again and smacked unconscious against the cement.

Ethan looked up and Guardian was gone.

INTERREGNUM

Substation Omega Prime
The Secretum of Six
Ruling Council Inner Chamber

"DO THEY KNOW THE TRUTH?"

"They know nothing."

"We have reports that the one they call Morgan may know. She has discovered much of late. Too much."

"Then the threat must be eliminated."

"Agreed."

"What if she reveals her findings before we can intervene?"

"It does not matter. She cannot stand between the Bringer and his destiny. No one can."

"He draws closer, doesn't he?"

"Yes. But closer to finding us, or closer to his destiny?"

"They are one and the same."

"Are we certain of that? Is there no chance he could fulfill the prophecy elsewhere—"

"No. Remember the words of the Ancients. At the appointed hour, the Bringer will meet his destiny in this most sacred place. It can happen only here, and so shall it be."

21

*Flight 910
39,000 feet over the Atlantic Ocean*

First class held a group of ten people with odd appearances. *Eccentric rich folk*, most of the other passengers thought, *living the weird life.* The first-class passengers certainly looked nothing like Grant Borrows and a team consisting of his most powerful friends.

But it was them.

Grant wasn't sure what to be more amazed at—that Lisa had managed to secure the entire first-class section of the plane for their team, or that Julie and Fletcher had already had a stash of disguises hidden away for just such an occasion. Their collected materials included wigs, fake beards, nose appliances, shoes with lifts, odd clothing, glasses, hats, a few colored contact lenses, and even a cane for Daniel.

The disguises wouldn't measure up to Hollywood's standards, but they would do well enough to get them to London undetected. Especially Grant, who had the world's most recognizable face these days.

At least, they hoped the disguises would work.

Fletcher had quickly cooked up a fake photo ID and passport for each one of them to go with their new looks. Grant, having no desire to go all out with his disguise, instead opted for a dingy trucker's cap, sunglasses, and hooded sweatshirt to cover most of his head. He looked like nearly ninety percent of the young men at malls these days. It was a bit conspicuous, but with everyone else sporting more eye-catching disguises, he guessed that few people were likely to notice him at all.

As for the public plane ride, it was the only solution that fit with the group's current budget and short notice. Grant had suggested renting a private jet at one point, but Lisa was forced to point out that the money and resources his grandfather had given him months ago had been burned through all too quickly, and they simply couldn't afford to blow such a huge chunk of money on what she referred to as "a hop across the ocean."

Grant took comfort in knowing that the people he cared about most in the world were right here alongside him, as well as the most powerful Loci he could find, and all of them were ready to take this headlong leap into the unknown. Julie, Alex, Morgan, Fletcher, Nora, Hector, Daniel, and Lisa surrounded him. The final member of the team was the new guy, Wilhelm, who Grant had asked to join them at the last moment on a hunch that his powers might prove useful in the field. Payton, as Morgan had pointed out last night, would meet them in London at some point. The other Loci who had lived with the team in L.A. were given strict orders to report to a reserve safe house Morgan had secured just outside the city limits and keep a low profile until Grant and the others returned.

Leaving behind the people of Los Angeles, venturing out into a world that feared them, even attempting to locate the Secretum and put a stop to their machinations—it was a lot to digest for everyone. And it was taking its toll on each of them. For the first time in a long while, Grant saw anxiety and uncertainty written across his friends' faces.

But this was hardly the only thought occupying Grant's time during the flight. His sister's illness was cause for unending concern. Aside from his chosen role as protector of the innocent, Julie's welfare was his top priority. Then there were wild cards like Nora and Daniel, who were both demonstrating increasingly unpredictable behavior.

And what to make of his phone call from the man named Devlin? *Was* his destiny as the Bringer still in play?

Grant found himself momentarily pondering the Secretum of Six, where it came from, how it operated, and who it was. How had his grandfather come to be a part of their ranks? Devlin must have known his grandfather if both of them were such high-ranking members of the Secretum; Devlin no doubt knew more about his grandfather than Grant ever would. Where was Devlin right now? How was it that the Secretum came upon the unimaginable resources and influence it possessed? How did the Dominion Stone and the rings fit into things?

And just what *was* the destined role of the so-called Bringer, anyway?

His thoughts drifted to the world thousands of feet below, teetering on the brink of madness. He wondered what horrific event would hit the globe next and what nations and peoples would be affected by it. And what about his exodus from L.A.? It was only a matter of time before the media realized he and his friends were no longer there. How would the people of the world react to the thought of *him* potentially arriving on their doorsteps?

Stop it, stop this! You're going to make yourself crazy.

"What do your eyes see?" he reminded himself. *Stay on point.*

Don't give in to worry or doubt. Are you going to let fear overpower you or keep you from what you're meant to do?

No. Never.

Some lessons, after all, only had to be learned once. And after all that had happened to him at the hands of his grandfather, this particular lesson was one he had down cold.

He glanced at Julie, who sat next to him. She was listening through earbuds to some in-flight radio station and fiddling on a laptop she'd brought along that looked like it contained her entire Railroad database, among other things. He surmised that she and Fletcher were already cooking up a replacement for Daniel's warehouse, so that when they returned to L.A. the Railroad could reboot and the group would have a new headquarters.

Her dark brown hair was hidden beneath an ultra-short, wavy blonde wig that was surprisingly convincing. Her ears and fingers were adorned with sparkling jewelry, and she wore a crisp, fashionable gray pantsuit. Grant had no idea if it lived up to the "high-powered female executive" disguise it was meant for, but the laptop should be enough to put her over the top as long as no one scrutinized her too closely.

Cooking up convincing disguises for all ten of them hadn't been easy. But then, when you have a roomful of some of the world's smartest people, it could be a lot harder.

For a brief, fleeting moment Grant thought of how much easier it would be to pull this off if Hannah were here. Her powers of misdirection would come in very handy right now.

And having Hannah herself here would be . . .

No. Don't do that.

He sighed. Nothing good ever came from letting himself linger on those thoughts. There was no changing the past, no magical Ring of Dominion that would allow anyone to rewrite history. Or wake the dead.

Stay on point. Focus on today. Tomorrow will see to itself.

He settled back into his seat as conflicting thoughts and ideas struggled to attract his attention. Somewhere along the way, his eyes closed and he drifted off to sleep.

22

Julie waited until she was sure Grant had fallen asleep.

A live report on the news radio she listened to through her headphones had detailed the latest disaster: an enormous iceberg had broken off of the Arctic shelf and slammed into northern Alaska near a tiny Native American village called Wainwright. Fortunately, the injuries were few, and there were no fatalities.

When she was satisfied that her brother was out, she quietly unlatched her seat belt and slid out of her seat. Two rows back, she found the people she was looking for.

Morgan sat next to Nora on the fourth row; Alex sat next to Fletcher on the third.

"Switch with me for a sec?" Julie asked Nora, who shrugged indifferently. "But don't wake him," Julie said as they passed one another.

Julie slid in beside Morgan and tapped on Alex's and Fletcher's shoulders in front of her.

"There's been another disaster," she whispered, low enough so that only the four of them could hear. She explained the situation in Alaska, while the others listened with rapt attention.

"Thank God there was no further loss of life," Morgan remarked.

"Why are we talking about this without Grant?" Alex asked.

"He's napping," Julie replied. "And I wanted to get your reactions to it . . . where he can't hear us."

"That's not like you, Jules," Alex observed. "You and Grant don't keep secrets from each other."

"I was just thinking . . ." she replied, hesitant to say her thoughts aloud. But she'd come back to their seats for this very reason, so she might as well get it over with. "Remember the fire in the sky over Los Angeles, the day Grant confronted our grandfather?"

"Oh, I get it," Fletcher jumped in with his persistent ability to make the connection faster than anyone else. He always felt compelled to share his early insights as well, cutting right to the chase to save everyone time. If he knew how annoying it was to everyone around him, he never showed it.

"Grant caused that 'disastrous' weather anomaly over L.A. subconsciously," he explained, "so now you're wondering if he might have any similar connection to the other disasters taking place. You know, Professor, your mind is much more cunning than you're given credit for."

Julie squinted at him, glaring, while Morgan and Alex struggled with how to formulate responses.

"I know it's an unsettling thought," Julie said consolingly, "but it's a possibility we should consider."

"There's no denying Grant is powerful," Morgan conceded. "He could potentially be the most dangerous man in the world. But he's *good*. He has *chosen* to use his power for good, even if that power is rooted in darkness."

"I agree," Alex quickly added. "Not a chance in the world would he do something like this. *Not Grant*. Not ever." She was frowning, her arms crossed. Her feet, uncharacteristically stuck in white tennis shoes, nervously tapped the floorboard.

Fletcher faced her, a curious expression on his face. But for once, he held his tongue.

"That's just it, though," Julie persisted, still whispering. "He'd never do anything like this on purpose . . . but what if it's happening and he's unaware of his influence over it?"

The others looked at one another in silence.

"Well . . ." Morgan swallowed. "There was something I failed to mention in the meeting just before we left L.A.—something else that occurred to me while I was researching the Secretum. It's a terrible thought, and I don't want to believe it. All of us look to Grant to set the course that we follow, so it's most unsettling to think that he could be—"

"Just spit it out," Fletcher said, his impatience brimming to the surface.

"It's the prophecy," she said. "The Dominion Stone prophecy, that said that Grant was supposed to become this mythical figure called 'the Bringer'?"

"Grant chose a different path than that supposed destiny," Alex refuted. "His own path."

Morgan hesitated and then whispered words that she didn't seem to want to hear herself say. "Did he?"

Julie sucked in air. Alex frowned severely. Fletcher mashed his eyebrows together, thinking this through.

Morgan pressed her argument, still whispering. "We have to consider the possibility. What if somewhere along the way, he became this Bringer . . . and *we missed it?*"

"If that were true," Fletcher stated dispassionately, "then he would be to blame for the worldwide disasters."

"I can't believe I'm hearing this," Alex spoke at last. Exasperated and ticked off, she continued. "After all he's been through—after all *we've* been through *with* him . . . He's not the same man he used to be."

"But Alex, *think*," said Morgan. "It *does* seem terribly coincidental that the disasters began almost immediately after Grant's triumph over his grandfather that day in L.A."

"You're all crazy!" Alex cried, her voice climbing a bit too loud now in anger. She rose to her feet. "I'm not listening to any more of this. Let me out of here."

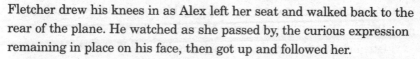

23

Fletcher drew his knees in as Alex left her seat and walked back to the rear of the plane. He watched as she passed by, the curious expression remaining in place on his face, then got up and followed her.

When Alex had walked as far as she could go, she opened a lavatory door and entered. As she was closing the folding door, Fletcher's hand stopped it and pushed it back open again.

He stood there studying her, with his eyebrows raised. A smirk teased the edges of his lips, and his eyes flashed.

Alex didn't know *how*, but *he knew*.

She grabbed his tacky striped racing jacket and pulled him inside the lavatory, locking the door behind him. There was barely enough space inside for one person to stand, so with two, they were smashed up against one another.

"You have feelings for Grant!" he whispered a little too loudly.

So he knew. *Of course* he knew. Fletcher always figured out all the things that no one wanted known.

She didn't even bother asking how he'd figured it out. It was his particular talent: making connections that no one else could, thanks to his ability to process more than one thought at a time.

I should have known he'd put it together.

Venom filled her face. "If you tell *anyone*—!"

"Nobody knows?" he asked.

She glared at him and then shook her head.

"Does Grant know? Does he have any idea at all?"

"I don't know." She hesitated, looked away. "I don't think so."

Fletcher grinned. And not in the cocky, self-assured, smug grin he usually displayed when he knew he was right about something. For once, he seemed to actually be displaying a hint of playfulness. Even mischief.

"Then what are you waiting for?" he said. "Life is short! Why don't you just tell him?"

Now Alex looked at him as if he were just plain stupid. "For a hundred reasons, and sweet fancy Moses, I can't believe I'm talking to *you* about this . . ."

He said nothing. She sighed.

"Why don't I say anything? Because he has much, *much* bigger things on his mind than romance. Because I don't want him to know that I had ulterior motives for contacting him back on that first day we met. Because he's still grieving for Hannah . . ."

Fletcher's mind seemed to be spinning like wildfire, and Alex noted with no small amount of chagrin that he was warming to this idea quickly. She'd never seen him play matchmaker before, but upon seeing the seeds of it form across his features, it didn't seem as out of place as she might've expected.

"You mean you've been in love with him this *whole time*? Since the day you met?" he asked, still smiling.

Despite herself, she let her guard down slightly. "Longer," she admitted. "I watched him when he was Collin Boyd, living out his boring life, all alone. I can't explain what happened, I just watched him and followed him as he walked through his world, and I think something in me *grieved* for the life he led. . . . He was so sad and lonely and mad at the world. He'd lived such a bitter existence all his life. Growing up in that horrible orphanage, being abandoned by everyone who ever loved him . . . And then one day he was suddenly Grant Borrows, and he became noble and strong in ways no one dared dream he could. He's remarkable. I see in him everything I want to be."

Her gaze had drifted away as she spoke, but now she peered back into Fletcher's eyes, which were only inches from her own in the cramped little room. He was grinning even wider than before.

"Fletcher, I *swear*, you tell *anyone* about this—!"

"I won't!" he insisted. "But you should. You may have been too love-sick to notice, but this group leads a fast-paced, high-risk lifestyle. You may not get too many opportunities for romance along the way. When one comes along, you should think about grabbing hold of it."

Alex shook her head sadly. "Not now. I can't. The world is all screwed up. There's no room for romance anymore."

24

"Nick, talk to me," Ethan said into his earpiece as he dodged pedestrians at a rapid clip through the LAPD main office.

"We got a match on the blood traces you found on the floor of the warehouse," replied his associate at the local FBI office. "They belong to an L.A. police detective named Matthew Drexel. Guy disappeared off the map about two months ago."

Terrific. As if the LAPD wasn't being difficult enough to deal with already, let's add evidence of a dead officer to the mix, who happens to be one of their own . . .

"What do you want me to do with this evidence, dude?" Nick asked.

"I'll have to take it to Stevens, which means our friend Guardian is about to find himself a wanted man." He stopped walking when he arrived in a hallway just outside an interrogation room.

"It's not right, Ethan. Just because he showed up at that warehouse while you were there doesn't mean he had anything to do with this detective's murder," Nick pointed out. Not a big surprise; Nick was a *huge* Guardian fan. "Evidence indicates that the blood isn't exactly fresh. And the detective *disappeared*—we don't know if he's really dead or not."

Ethan frowned, a thought crystallizing in his mind that had been lingering since that night at the warehouse. Nick was right to defend Guardian; Ethan felt it in his gut. He'd looked directly into Guardian's eyes, and he didn't find the soul of an evil man there.

But despite his intuitions about the man, Guardian had still picked up stakes and run away. And if he knew anything for certain, it was that only the guilty run.

"It won't matter," Ethan said with genuine regret. "This is about to get ugly, Nick. There's too much heat coming down from Washington. Everybody's looking for a scapegoat for the global disasters, and a link this close to a potential murder will be way too juicy for them to ignore. This guy's a hero but his blood is going to end up on my hands, I just know it. I've got a witness to question. Sit tight with what you've got and I'll get back to you."

Ethan snapped his phone shut and pocketed it. He opened the door before him and found a frightened-looking young woman sitting at the bare table, waiting nervously in the dark room all alone.

"Ms. Martz?" he asked in a carefully practiced tone of voice that was neither threatening nor pleasing.

"I been here for four hours! You finally going to tell me what for?" she snapped.

He seated himself in the chair across from her, then folded his hands on the table top. "It's come to our attention that you were recently given aid and protection by a young woman known to be an associate of the man the media calls 'Guardian'. *This* young woman," he slid a portrait-sized photo of the young woman in question across to her. It was a black and white still image that had been taken from a video recording of what looked like news coverage from the riot. Leeza did her best not to react when she saw the image, but Ethan saw her throat constrict and her eyes flicker, very briefly.

"Bein' rescued a crime now?" she asked.

"No, ma'am, of course not. We would simply like to meet this 'Guardian' and offer him the gratitude he deserves. Unfortunately, he seems to be a bit publicity shy. We've identified several known *associates* of his, and we were hoping you might be able to identify this young lady who's often seen with him, since you've met her in person."

"Sorry," Leeza replied, leaning back in her chair and crossing her arms. "Don't know a thing."

"You're denying that she helped you?"

"I ain't denied nothing. But we didn't become best girlfriends after she helped me out."

Ethan sighed. "Is there anything you can tell us about her at all—

any distinguishing marks on her person, any accent to her speech . . . Did she happen to tell you her name?"

Leeza's eyes shifted. "Nope."

Liar.

"Ms. Martz, I feel obliged to point out that we ran your records and know all about you, including your . . . occupation."

Leeza squinted at him. "Hey! I've been in a safe house, man! I ain't had nothin' to do with that scene since Alex—"

Her eyes went wide.

"Alex," Ethan repeated, mentally jotting down this name. It wasn't much, but it was a start. "Thank you, Leeza. You can go now."

Moments later she was gone, and Ethan remained in the interrogation room alone, thinking. What to do . . . Did he give Stevens the evidence he'd collected? The blood of the presumed-murdered detective and the name "Alex" wouldn't get her very far. But the political climate being what it was, he was certain it would result in an international crackdown on Guardian, driving him even further underground. And making Ethan's job of finding him that much harder. But he had a duty to do, and if Stevens found out later that he'd withheld evidence . . .

Ethan didn't react when his phone vibrated in the sound-protected room. After a few rings, he reflexively detached it from his belt.

It was an email message, but it was sent to his personal account, not his FBI address.

> Want to be dealt in, Agent Cooke?
> You'll need more than help from a hooker if you
> want to win *this* game.

Ethan's head turned all around, but no one was nearby. The interrogation room door was shut and he was alone.

The red light on the video camera high up in the corner of the ceiling was still on. It had never stopped recording since his meeting with Leeza Martz. He thumbed the phone and typed a clumsy reply with the phone's number pad.

> who r u?

Only seconds after the message was sent, the phone vibrated again.
Another email message.

> Forget me. You need to know who *he* is.
> He has a real name.
> Go to Metro Center Station, look for a blue
> arrow.

Ethan blinked. That was nonsense. He'd been to Metro Center Station before and knew it to be a stop for the Blue Line train. It would be
full of blue arrows on the station's signage.

Despite his misgivings, his adrenaline spiked at the intrigue of all
this, so he exited the building immediately and drove his FBI-issue
black sedan until he found a parking spot just outside Metro Center.
He descended the stairs two at a time and scanned the interior of the
underground installation. It was the middle of the afternoon; fifteen or
so people were dotted about, waiting for the next train to stop. All
looked nervous. Things had calmed in L.A., but it still seemed as
though the next explosion could happen at any time.

This is ridiculous, Ethan thought. As expected, there were signs all
over pointing the way to entries, exits, rest rooms, and trains, all using
blue arrows. He moved about the station quickly, taking in every sign
he could find, looking for anything unusual or out of place, anything
that might be a clue.

On the opposite side of the station from where he'd entered, he
stopped, frowned, and gave up. It was on his way out that he spotted a
tiny blue mark on one of the station's round cement pillars. He moved
closer. The small mark was an arrow that appeared as if it had been
made by hand with . . . was that crayon wax? It pointed straight down
at a crack in the cement.

No, that wasn't right. No natural deformity in the cement would be
this perfectly straight. Cement was brittle and always broke in frag-
mented, disjointed lines. To be this even, the crack must have been cut
into with some sort of high-powered hand saw.

He leaned in, examining the crack closely. If he hadn't been standing right on top of it, he would have missed it. A folded piece of yellow
paper was stuck deep inside the crack. He retrieved a pocket knife

from his pants pocket. A few seconds of digging and scraping inside the crack, and he had it.

It was a page torn from a standard legal pad. Ethan unfolded the paper and found large words scrawled with the same blue crayon.

His name is
Grant Borrows

He's not what
he appears to be

Find him before it's too late

25

Grant was surprised to find Morgan sitting to his immediate left, in the window seat, when he awoke.

"I thought we should talk."

"About what?"

"The prophecy."

Grant's head fell back onto his headrest, and he began to snore loudly.

"Not funny," Morgan said. "Just because you'd rather not have to think about it anymore doesn't make it untrue."

Grant opened his eyes. "I'm going to pretend I understood what you just said, so we can get this over with."

"Why do you think you were given your extraordinary powers? Why were you given the Seal of Dominion—a dark weapon forged before time began?" she asked.

He perked up slightly; this wasn't the approach he was expecting from her. "This is old news, Morgan. The ring and the power it gives me may have been intended for evil purposes, but I'm using it for good. I'm making my own decisions now. No more outside manipulation. I'm using it to help people."

"No one is more proud of that fact than I," Morgan said gently. "You are more than I ever had any right to hope you would become, after all that you've been through. You're kind, compassionate, strong . . . You place the welfare of others above your own. You are a hero, Grant."

Grant offered half a smile for Morgan's benefit, but words of praise never sat comfortably with him.

"But it isn't enough, is it?" she added quietly.

Grant wasn't entirely sure what she was getting at, but made an effort to respond in kind. "Some days," he admitted, "I can't help wondering if we're making any real difference. I have all this power, but I'm only using a fraction of it. I could *really* change this world if I wanted to. I've never unleashed the full scope of what I'm capable of."

"How do you know you could make life better for everyone on earth if you did?"

"I don't, but what if I never find out?" he counter-argued. "What if the world isn't getting any better because I'm too timid to take it all the way?"

"This power we wield . . ." Morgan said gravely, casting a gaze down at her own ring. "It is savage. It is black and raw. And it *longs* to be unrestrained. I only feel it in fleeting moments, so I cannot imagine how strong its pull must be on you."

Grant didn't answer. He didn't have to.

"Your ability to keep its influence at bay with mere will power is nothing short of remarkable. But we would be the greatest of fools to let ourselves forget where this power originates."

Grant let out a frustrated breath. "But *do* we really know where the power comes from? All we have to go on is the ravings of a world-class sociopath—a psychotic old man with delusions of grandfather-hood. The power is ancient and primal, yes, but that doesn't automatically make it evil. Maybe it's just . . . I don't know how to put it . . . Maybe it's *pure* in a way we could never comprehend. Like, undiluted by man's influence. Part of . . . linked to something that existed in an age before life as we know it was born. And old enough to tap into the very fires of creation . . ."

Grant's voice had grown increasingly distant as he'd spoken, and now his gaze was very far away. When he snapped out of it, he found Morgan studying him with the kind of worry only a mother could conjure.

"Grant, why do you choose to do what's right? Why do you do what you do?" Morgan asked.

"I guess . . . because I feel like I was meant to. If I'm not using this power to help people, it would be a waste, wouldn't it?"

"Yes, it would. And for the record, I'm glad you're using your power to do good. But to what end?"

"I'm not sure I know what you're getting at. . . ."

"You save people from harm, from injury, from death. You help the helpless. But what are you *accomplishing*?"

"I'm making the world better," Grant replied with the only words he could conjure.

"Ah!" Morgan exclaimed, clearly happy that they'd arrived at her intended point. "Making the world better is a noble goal, and I commend you for it. But there are some things that superhuman abilities can't fix, prevent, or rescue. *Real change*—the kind of change that *is* required to change the world—is not something you can *physically* cause to happen, not even with your immense power."

Morgan watched him, waiting patiently for his response. "So what, then? Are you saying I have to find a way to change the human heart?"

"No," Morgan replied knowingly. "Despite all of your awesome abilities, changing the heart is the one thing you *can't* use them to accomplish. The heart of every newborn baby is deceitful and prideful and selfish. It is the condition by which each of us enters this world, and rescuing helpless people from calamities will not alter this fundamental state of being."

Grant leaned back in his seat, resting his head and taking this in.

He cut his eyes across at her.

"Are you worried about me?" he asked. "I'm not the bad guy, no matter what others may have intended for me. The ring doesn't control me, you know. I'm the good guy, and that's not going to change."

Morgan sighed, frowning. Grant got the distinct impression that he had missed entirely whatever point she was trying to make.

"I'm the good guy," he repeated, waiting and hoping for her to affirm the statement.

Morgan studied him briefly. "There are people in this world who are capable of all manner of dreadful things. Unimaginable pain and contemptible cruelty they leave in their wake. And those people . . . they are me and they're you."

His eyes met hers, ready to argue the point.

"There is no great chasm between 'us' and 'them', between the 'good guy' and the 'bad guy'," she explained. "Our powers do not make us better than everyone else. And the tiniest of distances—a single bad choice—is all that separates you from those you fight against. Don't for one moment let yourself believe that you are incapable of being what they are. Be very mindful of your choices."

He pursed his lips. "I thought you wanted to talk about the prophecy."

"Why do you assume I haven't been?"

Grant suddenly gasped as if seized by a jolt of lightning that surged through his body. He leaned forward in his seat and clutched at his head, seeing something far, far away that was too terrible for his eyes to withstand.

"Grant!" Morgan shouted.

He doubled over in his seat and pressed his hands to the sides of his head.

Everyone in first class and several others at the front of the economy cabin were standing or leaning forward to see what the commotion was. Julie was out of her seat and kneeling in front of Grant almost as soon as Morgan had shouted his name.

"What?" Julie shouted, taking one of his hands in hers. "What's going on?"

"I can see them! They're dying," he said. "So many of them . . ."

26

Before Morgan or Julie could ask for a further explanation, Grant was on his feet and moving. He stopped at the door to the cockpit as a flight attendant appeared to block his path.

"Sir, please return to your seat," she said. When he persisted, she added, "I'll have to summon the air marshall if you don't return to your seat right now."

Grant pulled back his hood, removed his hat, and took off his sunglasses. As the woman in front of him gasped at his now very familiar face, Alex appeared at his side.

"Do you know who I am?" he asked.

"What's going on?" Alex interjected. "What are you doing?"

"No time," was his reply. At her confused expression, he stopped and added, "Do you trust me?"

"With my life."

He turned back to the flight attendant. "If you know who I am, then you know what I can do. Now move," he ordered.

Her jaw was still slackened as she silently sidestepped, but her eyes remained trained on him.

Three feet out from the locked cockpit door, Grant reached out with his hand and grabbed the metal door with his mind. He pulled back with his arm and the door followed, crumpling as it wrenched itself free from the doorway and then remained in midair. Grant tossed the door aside; it landed on the floor beside the main exit.

Inside the cockpit, the pilot and co-pilot were already scrambling for the gun that was locked in a small metal box between them.

Grant pulled the metal box through the air with a thought and caught it. "Do either of you recognize me?" he asked, stepping fully into the cockpit. He slipped the box backward through the opening and handed it to Alex.

"Yes, I do," the pilot replied. The co-pilot nodded.

"Listen, I know this will be hard to understand. There's an emergency happening in Israel right now, and I need to be there. If you were to change course now, how fast could you get me there?"

The pilot swallowed. "I, we can't . . . Regulations prohibit us from deviating from our flight plan unless—"

"We don't have time for this," Grant interrupted, his voice leveling to a deadly threat. "Maybe it's an inconvenience, maybe it violates all your regulations. Thousands upon thousands of people are *dying* while we're having this conversation. So you're going to change course right now, or I'll have you rendered unconscious and do it myself."

The pilot hesitated, but finally acceded. "Very well," he said, clutching the controls nervously and manually changing their course. The man was visibly shaken, but struggling to maintain the detached calm that pilots are trained for. "If I don't declare our change in destination, international authorities may view us as a terrorist hijacking."

"This is a rescue operation," Grant corrected him.

"I still need to declare the change in our flight plan, sir."

"Fine, whatever. Just get us there."

Grant left the men to their work and returned to his seat. Every person on the plane seemed to be staring at him now, including his friends in first class. Their cover was clearly blown, but he didn't care.

"What's happening?" Julie asked desperately.

Grant turned to Morgan. "Why didn't you tell me Payton was in Jerusalem?"

"I didn't know he was," she replied honestly. "What's he doing there?"

Grant sat back in his seat slowly, clutching the armrests as if he could *will* the plane to go faster.

And for a moment, he wondered if maybe he could.

"Why are we going to Jerusalem?" Morgan asked.

"I caught a glimpse of what's happening there right now, because

Payton is there," he explained. "In my mind's eye, I can see him in his surroundings. And it looked like . . . it looked like the city just . . . just *sank*. As if a fissure opened, and the entire city collapsed in on itself. Payton's conscious, but just barely. I can see him clearly, and I can see a lot of people on the ground around him, through smoke and debris. . . ."

First class grew silent as Grant's voice drifted.

"What's the population of Jerusalem?" Julie asked, her voice nearly a whisper.

Morgan spoke up, knowing the question could only have been directed to her. "Seven hundred and fifty thousand, at last census. With tourists and religious types on pilgrimage, the total could rise above one million."

Everyone at the front of the plane—even the flight attendant who still lingered and was listening off to one side—grew silent at the idea of *a million* people hurt, lost, or dying.

It was staggering. Another disaster on an epic scale.

"This is the captain speaking from the flight deck. If I could have everyone's attention, please," said a voice over the speakers above their seats. "An unexpected turn of events has forced us to divert to Israel, where we've just received word over the wire that there has been an earthquake."

Mumbling spread throughout the plane as the captain continued. "The American known as 'Guardian' is onboard the aircraft with us, and he has requested that the crew take him to Jerusalem in the hope that he may be able to help there somehow. I apologize for the inconvenience this will cause to your travel plans, ladies and gentlemen, but I think I speak for the entire crew in saying that the people of Jerusalem need him right now more than the rest of us need to be in London."

27

Fifty miles outside of Jerusalem

As the plane began its descent four hours later, Grant returned to the cockpit to get a look at what lay ahead. Alex followed. They'd changed out of their "disguises" and into clothing more appropriate for rescue operations: sturdy jeans, T-shirts, boots, and the like. Against Grant's protests, Alex insisted on going without footwear as usual.

They were still too far out to land and the sun was beginning to go down, yet the destruction was already visible. White smoke rose high into the sky—higher than the plane flew.

One of the oldest cities in the world, Jerusalem rested on a hill, with valleys on all sides, for thousands of years. Now the entire plain on which the city was situated had collapsed to a level below the valleys that surrounded it. Nothing had been spared: the old city, where Solomon's Temple once stood, as well as modern-day Jerusalem, where business and government hubs resided. All of it was simply gone. Fallen into a crater in the earth bigger than the city itself.

The pilot and co-pilot sat awed by the sight. No one spoke.

The newly formed basin had to be over one hundred square miles, Grant thought, staggered by the sprawl of it. And it was churning up smoke in slow billows, drifting up into the air to become a narrower column of smoldering white that divided the sky.

Miniature flashing lights danced across the rim of the crater; emergency workers were already on the scene.

Grant couldn't have imagined the size of the destruction; like trying to conceive of the vastness of the universe, it was simply beyond anything he was capable of picturing in his mind's eye.

What can I possibly hope to do to help in a situation on this kind of scale?

Alex had a hand over her mouth as she took in the view beside him.

"What about the airport?"

"Looks like it's still standing," the co-pilot replied, pointing into the distance before them. "The runway, at least."

Grant couldn't see anything. "Where?"

"Ten miles due north," the pilot replied, not turning around. "I wouldn't expect a friendly reception if I were you," he added.

"Why not?" Alex asked.

"Jerusalem International was handed over to the IDF several years back; it's effectively a military base now, and not open to commercial flights. But it's by far the closest runway to the city. Our landing may be seen as an act of aggression, assuming anyone is still alive down there to see it."

"IDF?" Alex whispered sideways.

"Israeli Defense Forces," Grant whispered back. "Captain, as soon as my people and I are on the ground, I want you out of here. You should probably resume course for England."

"No can do," the pilot replied. "Getting here expended more fuel than we were meant to use; we'll need refueling before we can make it that far."

"Then get in the air and hop over to a nearby airport—I don't know, Tel Aviv or Cairo or wherever—someplace where you can refuel. Do what you have to, but get these people out of the area immediately. And from the density of that smoke, I'd say we need to do this fast so you can get back in the air before nightfall."

The pilot nodded. "There are no working Jetways or catwalks at JIA; we'll have to dump you right on the tarmac with an inflatable slide."

Grant and Alex watched the devastating remains of Jerusalem draw nearer for a few minutes until the pilot spoke up again. "You're going to need to buckle up for landing."

"Of course," Grant replied, still studying the devastation on the ground laid out before them.

"If it's all right with you, sir," the pilot said, "I'd like to make an announcement over the speakers letting everyone know what we're about to do. We should ask if there are any medical or emergency practitioners on board who would be willing to stay behind with you and lend a hand. I'm sure those folks down there on the ground can use all the help they can get."

Grant placed a grateful hand on the pilot's shoulder. "Good man."

"Not really, sir," he said, turning to face Grant. "My sister and her family live in Los Angeles; she talks a lot about you and your friends. *You* are a good man. I'm just a pilot."

The expected military reception never happened. The plane descended through the murky white haze to a wobbly landing on the broken asphalt at Jerusalem International Airport without incident. The entire country must've been focused on rescuing the demolished city.

Not counting Grant and his team, over thirty passengers volunteered to leave the plane with him and help the emergency efforts. Less than half of them possessed any medical or rescue qualifications, but one look out the side windows at the hellish conditions on the ground was all it took to convince them, even though the entire plane had been glued to the news coverage all afternoon. More than one hundred remained on board and would continue with the plane to Great Britain.

As the jet lurched to a stop, Grant looked up to see Daniel using his cane to limp toward him.

"I've been thinking," Daniel said quietly so no one else could hear. But Julie, who had returned to her seat at Grant's side, was listening in as well. "Maybe your sister, Lisa, and I should continue on to London."

"Why would we do that?" Julie asked, surprised.

"We have no special abilities. I don't see us being a big help out there, and I assume that once this crisis is dealt with, we'll be resuming our original mission. Perhaps the three of us could go ahead of you, scout things out, secure a place to stay . . ."

"All I need is a shovel," Julie said with an air of finality. She slung her own bag over her shoulder, just as Grant had, and swept past them toward the exit.

Grant regarded Daniel sternly. "We're a team, Doc. You're either on the team, or you're not. Your call."

Lisa walked past them both just then, carrying her own bag toward the inflatable yellow slide that led to the ground. She was focused on getting out of the plane and did not pause for either of them.

"Whatever you decide, it's all or nothing." Grant ended the conversation. He followed the others out and hopped onto the slide.

Daniel stood in place for a moment as the civilians who chose to help filed past him and down the slide as well. The plane was already powering back up as the last of the civilians followed and jumped out of the plane.

Daniel let out a very audible sigh and hobbled toward the exit.

28

Jerusalem International Airport sat utterly deserted.

Working together, the group quickly located an antiquated passenger bus inside a collapsed hangar near where the plane dropped them off. Grant had to remove what was left of the hangar before they could reach the bus.

There was only one problem: the bus refused to start. Whether it was out of gas or simply too old to run anymore, they couldn't tell from the damaged instrumentation.

"I could probably hot-wire it," Daniel offered.

"No need," Grant said, and then he called out, "Everyone find a seat and brace yourselves."

Grant placed himself in the driver's seat and found that the steering wheel was the one part of the console that still functioned. He looked at the broken gear shift, willed it into neutral, and started the wheels beneath the bus turning with nothing but his mind.

Recalling the mass of rescue vehicles he'd seen from the air on the lip of the newly formed crater, he steered the bus in that direction, applying his own brand of gas and brakes as needed to get them there as fast as possible. The bus rumbled over the jagged terrain, resisting the beating it was taking, winding through brush and desert. But Grant refused to slow down.

Night had fallen by the time the bus pulled to a stop in the overpowering, swirling dust clouds that marked the edge of the fallen city,

which now sat invisible, cloaked in thick dirt and smoke that tasted of
death and sulfur.

A large crowd of several hundred local relief and emergency workers had gathered here, at the edge of the city. Rescue vehicles were
parked haphazardly, blocking one another's paths. Grant had just
stepped off of the bus when he heard a voice shout over a bullhorn.

"Es gait nit!" the voice cried in frustration. A man stood atop an
ambulance, its lights still flashing, and he stared into the abysmal
destruction that lay before them.

As the others carefully exited the bus behind him—the Israeli
emergency workers were too focused on trying to see inside the city to
notice their arrival from behind—Grant carefully squeezed his way
through the growing crowd until he was close enough to the ambulance
to see the man on top of it properly.

"You in charge here?" he called out.

The man spun angrily. "Who wants to know?" he replied in English.
The flashlight in his hand scanned the crowd until it fell upon Grant,
whose hand was raised in the air.

He sucked in his breath and muttered something in Hebrew.

"Let him through! Let him through!" he bellowed through his bullhorn, motioning for Grant to join him.

Grant carefully made his way through the crowd until he reached
the ambulance. He climbed the hood and then jumped up onto the top
of the vehicle to stand next to the man with the bullhorn.

Grant extended a hand. "I've got thirty able-bodied doctors, emergency workers, and volunteers ready to help. Not counting my team,
which is here as well."

The man accepted his hand gratefully. "Jehovah be praised, you
have come when our need is gravest. I am Amiel Yishai," he said, offering his hand as a nod to American custom. "It is an honor. I have been
placed in charge of the rescue and cleanup operations by my government. But I do not know where to begin. How are we supposed to rescue anyone when we cannot see through this accursed smoke of Jerusalem Stone?"

Grant examined the column of white smoke that lay before them,
many miles wide.

His thumb rubbed the underside of his ring, back and forth, as he thought.

"Maybe I can do something about that," he resolved.

Can I, really? he wondered. He couldn't manipulate air, but there were so many particles of dust and dirt and ash in *this* air, maybe he could reach out and . . .

Grant swallowed and took a deep breath. He closed his eyes and quickly ran through the focusing exercises Daniel had helped him learn. When his mind was at peace, he opened his eyes and looked straight ahead into the fog. He jutted out both of his arms, palms out, toward the smoke that covered the city. The massive sandstorm that covered Jerusalem split perfectly down the middle, breaking forward from the point where Grant stood.

Brow furrowed, heart rate skyrocketing, his breathing became hard and heavy, as he slowly began separating his arms. The sandstorm followed suit, parting in a perfectly straight line before them all.

A powerful gush of wind nearly knocked Grant and Amiel off of the ambulance as air rushed into the vacuum of empty space created by Grant's actions. But he refused to relent, pushing with all his might, until the dust and dirt and smoke and ash were moved far out of sight. It took almost five full minutes, with the roiling clouds threatening to break free from his grip at every turn. But he held the smoke unwaveringly, and every time it threatened to spill over into the gap, he beat it back.

When it was done, Grant bent over and braced himself with his hands on his knees. He was spent and out of breath.

The hundreds of individuals present would have been in awe of his display of raw power had their eyes not inevitably settled on the city the very second the smoke was gone.

Grant finally looked up when sounds from inside the city carried to where they stood. He heard weeping and screaming. He heard the sounds of the lost and confused and dying.

It was remarkably loud, like a crowd the size of twenty football stadiums, all cheering at once.

A vast canyon stood before them as if scooped out of the earth. Dark and boundless, it stretched out much farther than the eye could see. What once had been a hill had collapsed into a bowl. Yet much of the city still stood, even though the ground had pressed so far into the earth—over one hundred feet below the altitude where it had once stood. What buildings remained upright were fractured, broken, and many of them were perilously close to falling over.

The recognizable walls of the Old City stubbornly clung to their foundations, but many of the interior structures had caved in or disintegrated. Many modern buildings elsewhere had fallen, but a few skyscrapers still projected into the night sky. The golden Dome of the Rock, one of the city's most recognizable structures, still gleamed, wholly intact, though it was much too far away from Grant's position to see if the building beneath it remained undamaged as well.

As for her citizens, Jerusalem's survivors could be seen wandering the streets, looking for loved ones or screaming at the heavens, with faces both dirty from soot and soaking wet from tears. Thousands of others simply lay on the ground, sprawled out with arms and legs at rest in unnatural positions.

Grant didn't snap out of his initial shock until someone started shouting behind him.

"This ain't a spectator sport, people!" It was Alex. He turned and saw her stepping forward from the crowd. "People in there need help, and they need it *now*! What are you waiting for?"

As if awoken from some communal nightmare, the crowd broke and began pouring over the edge of the crater as one. Vehicles rumbled to life and found roads that would take them into the heart of the city.

Grant looked at the Jewish man beside him, Amiel. He'd been weeping silently, agape at the ruined city before him. He glanced at Grant with a fearful, hopeless expression. He merely shook his head back and forth, unable to speak.

"Never surrender to anger or despair," Grant offered, quoting the words he lived by. "Never give up; never give in."

"Our shining pearl of the desert . . ." Amiel whispered. His eyes turned slowly upward until he was facing the heavens. "Why have you abandoned your people when they need you most?"

"Hey," Grant said, a hand placed gently on the Jewish man's shoulder. Grant waited until Amiel looked at him, and he held his gaze confidently.

"Hope lives," said Grant. "And we're going to show this city what it looks like."

29

"So not only did you fail to apprehend the suspect," Director Stevens explained, "but you allowed him and his associates to hijack a commercial aircraft."

Ethan sighed. *Hundreds of thousands of people are dead or dying in Jerusalem, and she's* still *playing her games?*

His recent discovery in the L.A. subway had left him with little patience for Stevens's petty power struggles. And he resented her summoning him here at a time like this. FBI Headquarters was the last place he needed to be.

"It's not accurate to categorize Guardian's actions on the plane as a 'hijacking.' Even the pilot is willing to testify to that. By all accounts, he commandeered the plane so he could effect rescue operations in Israel—"

"Cut the crap, Agent," Stevens replied, testy. She was well aware of Ethan's impatience for being here, but she chose to ignore it. She was at this meeting, which featured the same attendees and location as the one a few days ago, ready for a rematch. "Did you or did you not find blood from a murdered LAPD detective on the floor of the warehouse that Guardian and his associates called home? Did he or did he not take control of a commercial flight for his own purposes? And did he or did he not first come to light the same day as the unexplained meteorological disturbance in Los Angeles, by your own account?"

Ethan knew there was no way to come out on top today. This "debriefing" was nothing more than a public dressing-down of him, and he doubted anyone in the room couldn't see that.

But he still had an ace in the hole. He knew Guardian's real name. Did he dare play that card?

"Yes ma'am, that's factual information. All of it."

"Then let me give you some more factual information, Agent Cooke," her curt voice replied. Ethan wasn't sure, but he thought he almost detected a hint of a purr in her demeanor as she settled back into her chair, relishing the moment. "You are still on the case. But from now on, you're going to do things *my* way."

Ethan swallowed his pride and managed, "Understood."

"You will leave immediately for Jerusalem, tracking Guardian's movements there until you have ascertained his true travel intentions. But you *will not engage* the target under any circumstances. Am I clear?"

"Completely," he replied. "But if I may ask . . . his 'travel intentions'? Why is that relevant?"

Stevens smiled, anticipating this question and zeroing in for the kill. "You don't understand," she said with clear pleasure. "Guardian booked his flight to England. *England*, Agent Cooke, not Israel. He booked this flight *before* the disaster took place in Jerusalem. If it was his intention all along to wrest control of the plane and venture to Jerusalem, then that proves your own theory that he is somehow complicit in these worldwide disasters."

"But," Ethan picked up her line of reasoning, "if he *was* planning to go to London all along, then that means he knew nothing of the crisis in Jerusalem until *after* it took place. Which means he's innocent."

"Perhaps," she conceded. "Either way, pressure is increasing from the Beltway to settle this 'Guardian question' once and for all. And *that* is precisely what you are going to do. But now you will do it under my constant supervision."

The first seven hours after the dust had cleared over Jerusalem, Grant and Alex systematically worked their way throughout the city using a borrowed, open-top IDF Jeep. Their vehicle was equipped with a basic medkit, high-beam flashlights, and radios so they could call in help as needed.

Hector rode with them for a while but got on and off so frequently, helping anyone he spotted who was hurt, that they'd been forced to leave him behind after a few hours. There was just too much ground to cover to keep stopping so often. Their task was to focus on the areas of town with the largest concentrations of trapped people and get them out.

Using her empathic abilities, Alex zeroed in on the locations with the most frightened people, and Grant used his psychokinesis to clear away the rubble so that emergency services could come in and offer the victims aid.

Nora joined them four hours in, but soon had to recuse herself from their fast-paced efforts. Grant had never seen her so focused and intent, yet so tremendously vulnerable. Her usual walls were down, and he saw her reach out to many survivors with a tenderness and humility that she'd never displayed before. He knew her remarkable gift would come in handy today, relieving the trauma of many a survivor.

Early on, Grant received permission from Amiel to place all of the rubble that he cleared away in one of the outlying valleys surrounding Jerusalem. It had taken over an hour, but Amiel arranged to have a powerful spotlight shine straight up into the air from the center of the valley, so Grant could find it quickly, regardless of his orientation to it from within the city.

It was taxing work, hefting hundreds of tons of wood, bricks, concrete, and other materials high into the air, and then guiding them in the direction of the spotlight shining so far off in the distance. After several hours of work, fatigue set in, and his eyes tried to convince him that he was seeing the wrong light. But he would always shake the cobwebs away and refocus.

The work proved perhaps most trying upon Alex. Repeatedly, she found it difficult to concentrate because of, as she explained it, the swarm of "intense emotions" surrounding her. The hundreds of thousands of survivors inside the city were overwhelming her senses with pain and sorrow and grief and panic . . . And she was having a hard time blocking it all out, which caused pronounced headaches. From how she described it, Grant kept picturing someone trying to tread water in the ocean in the midst of a hurricane. She had to stop every so often just to catch her breath.

Three hours in, Grant had contacted Amiel and asked if he could order his workers—which already numbered in the thousands and were growing all the time—to try and rein in their emotions, just to see if it would make any difference on Alex's senses. It didn't.

On they drove, for hours upon hours. Farther into the heart of the ancient city.

Grant was surprised to happen upon Wilhelm as the sun was rising.

The small man with slicked-back black hair was seated next to an electrical generator outside of a major hospital downtown. He explained upon seeing Grant and Alex that Hector was here also, inside the building, putting his skills to good use.

Wilhelm was holding a pair of wires that snaked along the ground and up inside of the generator. The wires' protective coverings were exposed, and Wilhelm touched them with his fingers. The generator was humming with life, powering the emergency systems inside the hospital.

Or rather, Wilhelm was powering it.

"Until today," he explained, "I never realized that my electrical powers could be put to a constructive use. I thought they were only good for hurting people, and I never wanted any part of that."

He went on to confess that he felt alive for the first time in years, and he couldn't wait to find more ways to help.

Grant was standing at the Jeep, about twenty feet away, and talking to Morgan on his radio, when he saw two children wander out from inside the hospital. A local boy and girl, around four years old, Grant surmised. They were dirty and confused by everything going on around them, not understanding the magnitude of what was happening to their home.

They spotted what Wilhelm was doing and questioned him about it.

Grant saw the man's eyes soften as soon as the children came into his field of vision, and his features radically changed. No longer timid, awkward, or self-conscious, Wilhelm's face was reshaped into something warm and gentle and kind.

The language barrier came between him and the two children, of course, and Grant was tempted to end his conversation with Morgan so he could intervene.

But as he watched, Wilhelm smiled at the children, and they responded in kind. He let go of the wires with one hand and placed his free hand on the little girl's face. His forefinger and thumb spread apart and upward, making her lips curve into a smile. She pulled away and giggled, but then tried doing the same thing to the little boy. Once they'd all tried it, the children looked to him again for another trick.

He took the girl by the hand and placed her palm on his own nose. He coached her into pressing on his nose, and when she did, his tongue popped out of his mouth, as if in response. The girl screamed with delight and clapped her hands. The boy reached out to Wilhelm's nose and tried it too.

Grant and Alex were called away, but as they left Grant watched his new friend in wonder, laughing and playing so calmly and naturally with the two children, until he could see them no more.

30

Morgan and Fletcher declined the offer of a vehicle and opted instead to set out on foot through the city, looking for survivors that others might miss. Also, they'd been given the task, at Grant's request, of locating Payton.

As the hours passed, they worked their way toward the octagonal Dome of the Rock, led more by Morgan's intellectual curiosity than anything else. The building held steadfast to its foundations atop the Temple Mount, though many of the mosaic tiles on its outer walls had broken free and shattered on the ground. The glistening golden dome itself still stood firmly in place, and remarkably, it didn't appear to have suffered any damage at all.

They carefully made their way up the many stairs that led to the shrine's entrance. When they'd entered the outer door, Fletcher asked, "What?"

Morgan had stopped walking and her eyes were closed. She was perfectly still.

"This place," she replied quietly, reverentially. "It's so rich with history . . . The walls themselves whisper to us. Don't you hear it? Don't you *feel* it?"

Fletcher dutifully listened but heard only ambient sounds of water trickling and rubble breaking free and falling.

"It's overwhelming . . ." Morgan said, still lost in her own world. Her eyes snapped open, and Fletcher jumped.

"Did you know that the Dome of the Rock was the original location of Solomon's Temple?" she asked.

Fletcher opened his mouth to respond that yes, he did in fact know that already. But she didn't stop talking.

"On this very ground we stand upon once rested what many believe to be the single most important historical artifact in human history."

"What artifact?" Fletcher prodded.

"The Ark of the Covenant."

"*The* Ark of the Covenant? As in, *Raiders of the* . . . ?"

Morgan nodded slowly, smiling. She pointed straight ahead, to the center of the main chamber, where a massive slab of granite rested directly beneath the enormous dome. "The 'Rock' the Dome is named for is believed to be part of Mount Moriah, the very location where Abraham almost sacrificed his son Isaac upon God's orders."

Fletcher's eyebrows popped up at this, despite his personal ambivalence toward history.

"There are catacombs, caves, and ancient tunnels beneath this structure that are *thousands* of years old. Think about that! Tunnels carved into the earth that predate most of modern civilization, and they're still down there, still intact."

Fletcher watched her and waited. He knew her well enough not to interrupt now.

"I don't know what it is, but something about being here, in this place, and knowing who else and what else once existed here as well—*right here*—it's a profound feeling. It's as if somehow, everything in the universe and every strand of history is connected to *us*, here, in this moment. We are playing a part in the same history that Solomon and Abraham are part of. We've arrived at the stage, and our curtain call is about to begin."

Fletcher was beginning to understand, even if he didn't fully grasp her level of intuition and emotion. "Are you saying we were meant to be here, somehow?"

She looked upon him for the first time since entering the building. "I want to say yes, but that doesn't feel like strong enough of a word."

Fletcher was pondering this when they heard clanging sounds from deeper inside the building. Following the sounds, they found a teenage boy and girl beyond the building's many internal pillars and supports, standing off to the side of the Foundation Stone. They were stuffing Islamic relics into a large burlap sack.

Fletcher stumbled on a crack in the floor, and the teens were startled. The girl pulled out a pistol and cocked it in their direction, her hand shaking nervously.

"Don't," came a voice from behind them on the other side of the structure's interior. A very familiar voice.

In a blur, the gun was knocked out of the girl's hand before she could pull the trigger, and then Payton stood between the teens and Morgan and Fletcher.

He was bruised and had blood stains across his bald head, and he wore the casual clothes of a tourist. Otherwise he looked just as Fletcher remembered him.

He drew his sword in a split second and waved it in the direction of the teenagers. "Drop the stash, and leave Jerusalem. *Don't* come back," he warned.

Stunned, they let the bag fall to the ground and ran, their footsteps echoing for several minutes.

"You're all right, then?" Morgan tentatively asked, approaching him with Fletcher trailing behind. She maintained a healthy distance from her former lover.

"Never mind that," Payton answered dispassionately. He looked Morgan in the eye, and Fletcher saw a familiar loathing in that gaze. "I found something. You better have a look."

"Later," Morgan replied, resolute. "The city is in ruins and people are dying. Whatever you've found, it can wait."

"No," he replied bitterly. "It cannot." He turned and marched to a spot some twenty feet away. They followed him across barriers meant to seal off the Foundation Stone, now fractured and broken on the ground. Payton stepped onto the Stone itself and continued walking.

"You shouldn't be up there!" Morgan cried, her knowledge of the Foundation Stone's historical and religious significance weighing heavily upon Payton's every footstep. If anyone caught him walking over this thing . . .

"Wait there," he said, and he dropped inside a tiny hole on the far side of the Stone.

Despite her misgivings, Morgan and Fletcher climbed up onto the giant white rock and looked down into the hole Payton had disappeared into.

Minutes passed, and they heard echoes of movement emanating from the darkness. But they could see nothing.

"What's down there?" Fletcher whispered.

"A small cave known as the Well of Souls," Morgan replied. "Though I should think much of it collapsed when the city fell. It's connected to the catacombs I mentioned, and some believe that the voices of the dead can be heard within the Well."

Fletcher shivered in the dark candlelight of the building's interior and shifted his weight away from the hole. "Thank you for choosing to share that right now."

"If you liked that, then how about this?" she said. "According to Jewish tradition, the creation of the world originated with this particular rock. Which, if true, would make the Foundation Stone the oldest existing object there is. Sound familiar?"

Fletcher's beady eyes nearly jumped out of his head. "The Dominion Stone! You said it was the oldest object on earth. Do you think the Dominion Stone came from *here*?"

"I haven't the slightest," Morgan admitted. "But it's an enticing notion, is it not?"

At last the sounds drew closer again, and they leaned over the edge of the small, round hole once more.

It wasn't Payton that came up through the hole. Instead a large, flat piece of metal was flung upward from it, and Morgan and Fletcher recoiled instinctively. It landed next to them atop the white stone, approximately three feet across and two feet tall.

There were words inscribed upon it. Morgan and Fletcher were examining it in disbelief as Payton climbed out of the hole.

"See anything you recognize?" he asked.

Etched into the broken piece of stainless steel was a very familiar lettering that bore the words:

SUBSTATION TAU EPSILON

31

"Found it this afternoon, about an hour before the quake hit," Payton explained a short time later. Amiel had insisted that Grant take a break after more than twelve solid hours of work, and Morgan brought him here, inside the Dome, to rest. Amiel's people had sealed off the building and placed it under guard to avoid any further looting or desecration of the site. But he'd given Grant and his team access as a courtesy.

Payton detailed his story for Grant, Alex, and Julie exactly as Morgan and Fletcher had heard it earlier.

They sat on the ground near the Foundation Stone, the tarnished piece of metal on the ground between them.

"So what were you doing in Jerusalem?" Julie asked. "Morgan said you were investigating some front company for the Secretum in Paris."

"That investigation led me here. In the file I found in Paris, I came across a list of longitude and latitude coordinates. One of the coordinates was the exact spot where Morgan and I found the first fragment of the Dominion Stone all those years ago. I realized the list contained coordinates for finding all of the pieces to the Stone. An intriguing find, but no longer useful, as all of the fragments have already been found.

"Elsewhere in the file, I found another set of coordinates scribbled in pencil at the bottom of a work order. These coordinates were accompanied by a depth relative to sea level. We're standing about five hundred feet above that depth. I found the wreckage of this 'Substation Tau Epsilon' down there and had fished out this piece of a door as evidence, but when I neared the surface with it, I heard voices echoing through the catacomb tunnels—some kind of religious types on a tour, I believe. So I hid the metal and made my way to the surface when their backs were turned, planning to return after dark and retrieve it. I never got that chance, for obvious reasons. After the city fell, I awoke and set about finding my way underground again. I'm as surprised as you are that my way back led here, of all places."

Grant and the others stared in silence at the metal sheet with the words inscribed across it, absorbing the implications.

Alex, who sat next to Julie, leaned over and whispered, "Are his adventures always so . . . death-defying?"

Julie didn't turn. "There's usually more violence."

Morgan finally spoke up, her impatience getting the best of her. "Do I need to say it out loud? Do we all grasp what this means?" she asked, gesturing at the steel plate.

"It means the substation beneath the Wagner Building was not the only one. There must be others," Grant replied. "Which, more importantly, means that—"

Morgan could hold it in no longer. "The Secretum's resources are larger than we ever conceived of."

"But this substation was abandoned, wasn't it?" Julie asked. "Payton said it was 'wreckage.' Don't you think that's an important detail?"

"Perhaps," Morgan replied.

Grant sighed. "You all can ponder this all you like," he said, standing to his feet, "but I've had my obligatory twenty minutes of downtime and I have to get back outside."

Once he began moving, Alex was hot on his heels. Soon everyone else followed, including Payton. But Morgan and Fletcher stayed behind, examining the steel door fragment once more.

"Is he not taking this seriously enough?" Fletcher asked when they were alone.

"No, he gets it," Morgan replied. "No one understands the stakes better than Grant."

It was almost thirty-six hours before Ethan finally set foot inside the disaster zone. It required all of the FBI's resources to get him across the ocean quickly, but Israel's airports were closed down, so he had to fly into Cairo and take a car from there.

In the car, Ethan listened to the radio as the Israeli president issued a statement declaring a state of emergency. The borders were locked down, IDF was on high alert and ready to scramble at a moment's notice, and though he didn't word it as such, he had effectively placed the entire country under martial law.

He cited concern that Israel's enemies might try to take advantage of his nation's vulnerable state right now as reason for the tightened security.

Old fool . . . Ethan thought bitterly. *You're playing right into your enemies' hands. Let's just hope it's a long while before they realize that.*

Not that he could blame the president. There really was no other responsible course of action for him to take, both professionally and politically.

Two hours after hearing that decree over the radio, Ethan used his FBI credentials to get through the locked-down borders. Stevens had phoned ahead to their diplomatic consulate to assure that he would have a smooth entry.

Ethan tried to use his drive to Jerusalem to prepare himself for his mission but all that vanished when he brought his car to a stop at the edge of a road that simply dropped off at the outer edge of the crater. His heart raced at the sight of the city midday. A surprising amount of it still stood—more than the TV reports were leading everyone to believe. He'd seen countless shots of the area from the sky, which were largely obscured by the dissipating smoke and dust that persisted throughout the entire region. But those sky-cam views were worlds apart from the view here on the ground.

He retrieved a backpack from the trunk of the car, and from inside the bag a pair of binoculars. He scanned the city's interior, especially the areas where there was a high concentration of activity. Grant Borrows proved an easy man to spot; his eyes merely followed the walls that were rising into the sky on their own and then hurling themselves off to some spot Ethan couldn't see miles away in the distance.

The IDF was doing its best to create and maintain a perimeter around the crater to keep others out of danger. Ethan spotted several groups of onlookers behind the perimeter holding up signs of adoration for Guardian and cheering whenever they caught a glimpse of him.

But despite the attempted perimeter, anyone who really wanted to get inside could. Ethan just slipped down inside the crater and began his trek on foot toward Guardian's location.

By late afternoon on the third day, Grant, Alex, and many of the others were sifting through the streets of the Old City. They led a procession of emergency workers, searching for any last survivors that might be located in this most ancient part of town.

Over two hundred thousand bodies had been uncovered across Jerusalem, with twice that many found alive. That left anywhere between two and four hundred thousand more unaccounted for.

Grant's face was drained, lifeless. He'd seen too much death over the last forty-eight hours, held too many hurting victims, washed his hands too many times from all the dirt and soot and blood. He had no passion for going on; he merely willed himself to keep moving, keep searching, even though the number of survivors they were finding dwindled sharply.

King David Street was a total loss. Formerly it had served as a bazaar—a crush of stands for authentic local knickknacks and walk-in stores where tacky souvenirs could be purchased. The timeworn cobblestone paths were lamented by locals for being overrun with signs, rugs, and even stringed instruments hanging at eye level, all to loosen the purses of foreign travelers.

But now the buildings on either side of the street had fallen in and taken out most of the street with them.

Some of the emergency workers were talking quietly amongst themselves in the rear of the line when Alex suddenly stopped walking and turned to them.

"Quiet!" she called out. "Listen!"

Silence fell across the old street, and Grant's eyes lit up when he heard it: the unmistakable cry of an infant.

"Where?" Grant asked, turning to Alex.

Her eyes were closed, and she was concentrating hard on the location. Grant had learned something new about her abilities from this experience: children were often easier for her to locate than adults, because their emotions came from a purer place within. Whereas adults had a tendency to try and stifle their true feelings and put on a front of some kind, there was less clutter to get through with children.

Babies, paradoxically, were often the hardest of all to get a bead on, because they relied so heavily on instinct that their emotions were often too primal for Alex to easily grasp.

"In there!" she pointed toward one of the indoor souvenir shops, which was really the bottom floor of a much larger structure—all of which had collapsed in. Alex grabbed Grant by the arm. "I think it's hurt," she whispered. "It's *bad*."

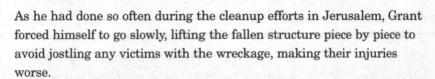

32

As he had done so often during the cleanup efforts in Jerusalem, Grant forced himself to go slowly, lifting the fallen structure piece by piece to avoid jostling any victims with the wreckage, making their injuries worse.

Hector! he thought desperately, willing the healer to get here as fast as possible. Through his mind's eye, Grant couldn't tell where Hector was exactly from his surroundings. One pile of rubble tended to look like every other. But chances were, he wasn't anywhere nearby.

Minutes passed, and the baby's cry began to weaken. "Come on, come on!" he shouted, watching the recovery workers sift through the debris, looking for the source of the sound. His imagination worked overtime, thinking of the helpless infant crying out for the basic needs of safety, food, and love. He began to shake nervously.

He hefted several heavy wooden beams and tossed them high and away into the pile outside the city.

"Here!" one of the strong-armed men called out. "It's here!"

Alex ran inside and saw the edge of an overturned stroller beneath a soda machine that had fallen over.

"Move this thing!" Alex shouted.

Grant flung the machine into the air with a thought, while racing inside. The baby's cries were barely audible now.

Alex already had reached into the stroller, which was lying on its side, and unbuckled the infant from its seat. A young olive-skinned woman lay dead beside it, her cold hand still clutching the handle of the stroller. Alex cradled the child—a boy—in her arms, stark horror spreading over her face. Grant could practically feel it emanating off her as he approached.

Grant watched as the infant coughed one last time in her arms, and a tiny spurt of blood flew out of the baby boy's mouth, splashing across Grant's face. Water spilled down his cheeks as his eyes moved from the baby's empty face down to a piece of floor tile that was stuck into the side of its abdomen. Its tiny hand wrapped around Alex's forefinger and squeezed it, but then suddenly it turned limp and let go.

For the first time since they'd met, Grant saw Alex break down and cry.

It was too much. So much pain and death and grief. Blood ran from the wound in the baby's side and fell in tiny droplets to the ground, where it seemed to vanish among the brown earth and stone.

Rage seared through Grant's veins, and he ran back outside and into the street. With every muscle in his body clenched, he raised his hands toward the heavens and screamed. The bone-chilling sound could be heard, carried by the wind, for miles around. He reached out with his mind, needing something, anything, *right now*, that wouldn't hurt anyone. . . .

The ground shook with his anger, and suddenly what remained of the mighty walls that surrounded the Old City surged upward into the sky. Higher and higher they went, until they abruptly exploded into white powder at the exact moment Grant fell to his knees. Specks of old Jerusalem Stone gently rained down on them all like light hail.

Spent, Grant hung his head, sobbing.

He looked up to see that Alex had collapsed similarly inside the broken building, but still she held the dead infant in her hands. She cradled him with great tenderness.

Something about this child had brought out a side of Alex that Grant had never seen before. It was as if something had been awakened within her, something profound and terrible.

He approached and tentatively took the baby from her arms. He handed him off to a rescue worker and then sank to his knees in front of Alex.

She instinctively reached out and wrapped her arms around him, crying uncontrollably into his shoulders. She held him tight for a long time.

Daniel wandered alone through the governmental district, finding few souls he could help. But he was not alone out of self-pity.

Walking through the ancient city had aroused in him a profound sense of reverence. History saturated every single thing he laid his eyes upon; holy sites for three major religions were all around.

Mosques for the Muslims. Churches for the Christians. The Temple Mount for the Jews. He had never been exposed to any place like this that held so much prominent human history.

The Tower of David. The Shrine of the Book. The Mount of Olives. The Al-Aqsa Mosque. The Church of the Holy Sepulchre.

So much history, and most of it was still standing, though quite a bit worse for wear. Daniel stopped near the Shrine of the Book. Built to house the Dead Sea Scrolls, it was a one-of-a-kind edifice which at its peak had a lovely white dome that unexpectedly curved up and in at the top to meet at a round hole well above the dome's main structure. Now crumbling pieces of Jerusalem Stone broke off and shattered from the wall and the dome that had once been surrounded by a pool of water on all sides. But the earthquake had done away with that. An enormous wall of black basalt was built opposite the dome to offset and enhance its dramatic appearance.

Daniel remembered reading once how the shape of the dome had been built to resemble the lids of the jars inside which some of the Dead Sea Scrolls had been found.

Just outside the Shrine, a courtyard made entirely of white Jerusalem Stone blocks was dug into the earth, providing a few shaded places to sit while waiting to enter the building.

Daniel was about to make his way down to the courtyard and go inside to check the safety of the Scrolls—arguably the greatest archaeological find of the last century, and thus his responsibility as a scientist—when an elderly woman, sporting a traditional Jewish *tallit* that covered most of her head, appeared in the courtyard and ran into the Shrine's entrance. She was crying loud enough that he could hear her from where he stood at street level above.

It was mere moments before two large men exited the Shrine,

dragging the old woman along behind them. They tossed her roughly onto the ground in the center of the courtyard, spat on the ground near her, and returned inside.

Daniel's mind immediately began formulating possibilities. Were the men Orthodox Jews who had taken it upon themselves to guard the Dead Sea Scrolls? Were they Palestinians, attempting to claim the site or its contents? Or were they merely common criminals, nosing around in places they didn't belong?

He would probably never know. His mind returned to the present as the sound of weeping reached his ears. The woman on the white ground below remained on her hands and knees, sobbing loudly and not caring who heard her.

Cautiously, he found his way down from his perch onto the main ground where she lay and approached her, his cane clanging loudly against the stone walkway.

"Ma'am?" he said softly.

If she was aware of his presence, she didn't show it. Her weeping continued unabated.

He gently placed a hand on her arm and attempted to hoist her back to her feet. "Are you all right?" he asked.

The woman took one look at him and screamed in horror. She riddled him with a flood of Hebrew, none of which he understood. But her body language and her facial expressions communicated clearly enough to break the language barrier.

Daniel froze in shock as he gazed into the old woman's eyes. The expression she gave him was as harsh and fearful as the one Lisa had shown the day he'd murdered a man in cold blood.

It occurred to him that with his shaggy hair, bushy beard, and ragged clothes, he didn't look all that different from the men who'd thrown her to the ground just moments ago.

He backed away from the woman, who continued railing at him in Hebrew. "I'm sorry," he tried to say as he continued to back away, chilled to the bone. But it did no good. She shouted even louder; he was uncertain if she was trying to attract attention to her plight from anyone who might be nearby or simply scare him off.

She rattled off an unending diatribe in Hebrew, and whatever she was saying, he got the message. He turned and ran from the sight of her fearful eyes.

33

Twelve hours later, the entire team had come together to continue the search for survivors. Payton had joined them as they migrated to an area of town known as Manahat, one of the few remaining areas of town they hadn't yet covered. Historically rich with agricultural significance, the neighborhood had been transformed in modern times to a sophisticated urban sprawl, complete with a hillside housing development, a high-rise devoted to technology advancement, a shopping mall, a contemporary football stadium, a train station, and more.

Much of Manahat's beauty had been lost in the quake, with many of the hillside homes swallowed up by the earth, but Grant barely noticed the aesthetic damage. He was emotionally numb, worn out, but persisted in going through the motions of searching the wreckage. He had to. He couldn't stop until he was sure there was no one left to save.

Payton spent his time carting bodies out of the wreckage, or hacking his way into places blocked by piles of rubble. He never spoke a word, no matter how many bodies he carried away. He just kept working.

Most of the others behaved similarly. Alex had barely spoken since they found the dying baby. Morgan seemed to have run out of interesting historical anecdotes to share, as now she and Fletcher had dedicated themselves to manual labor, like everyone else. Julie, Lisa, and Daniel were sifting through dirt with shovels. Hector and Nora worked silently too.

Only Wilhelm seemed to still have some signs of life left in him.

Somehow his spirit hadn't shattered as everyone else's, and he was often found playing with local children or raising the spirits of the adult survivors. Everyone he came into contact with seemed enlivened by his newfound warmth and kindness.

But otherwise it had been a silent day. The few times anyone spoke, Grant thought he heard quiet talk of growing tensions throughout the region. He himself had taken time to stop a small insurgency's attempt at infiltrating the city late the previous evening. And every time he spoke to Amiel, be it in person or over the radio he'd been given, the rescue operations supervisor spoke of new security restrictions that had been put into place throughout Israel.

The Holy Land had been laid waste. A battlefield with no battle. And what remained of Israel stood convinced that the battle was yet to come.

Grant was retrieving a dead body from the rubble of the fallen Technological Centre and placing it in the large pile of corpses they'd collected this day, when he spotted Amiel running toward him through the building's central plaza.

Amiel was screaming, "Guardian! Guardian, my friend!"

When he caught up with Grant, he seized him by the elbow and spun him around. "You're in danger. You and your people must leave at once!"

"What?" Grant asked. "Why?"

"Word has reached my government of the destruction to the walls around the Old City—"

Grant was downcast. "Please, I'm sorry about that. I deeply regret—"

Grant was cut off when Amiel held up a hand. "They were merely walls. Anyone who has been here and seen the things that all of us have seen knows that such things no longer matter. After all that you have done for us . . . And truthfully, the absence of the walls has made getting supplies in and out of the Old City an easier task on all of us.

"But outside of this place, the perspective is not the same. My government intends to apprehend you by any means necessary for damaging what they see as 'an irreplaceable piece of our history.' There is also talk about your 'hijacking' of an airplane. I believe they are misguided, but they will not hear my words."

"Don't worry," Grant reassured him. "I'm not going anywhere until this is done. There's no power in the world that can force me to leave."

Just over Amiel's right shoulder, Grant saw Payton's eyes focus on something far away, in the distance. He followed Payton's gaze and saw a man standing at the top of the nearest rise, about half a mile away, hands in the pockets of his tailored suit and watching them all. He had silver hair and a passionless face.

Is that Devlin. . . ? No, it can't be.

Unless it is . . .

Grant's gaze returned to Payton's position, but he was gone, vanished from where he stood. The silver-haired man atop the hill turned and walked away.

What just happened?

"My people are bringing more than mere *guns*," Amiel answered, urgency evident in his voice. "Entire infantry divisions are being mobilized. I have no doubt that you could defeat them all, after what I have seen your awesome powers accomplish. But at what cost? If you try to fight this, the survivors of this city will get caught in the crossfire.

"I am sorry, but I must plead with you to leave, my friend. Your work is done, in any case. No survivors have been found for over ten hours now; we both know there is nothing left to search for. You have done more than five hundred men could have in the same amount of time, and my people will not forget this."

Grant stopped what he was doing, at a loss for words, his shoulders slumping. "I never meant for it to end like this. What will you do? Where will you go from here?"

"We will rebuild, of course," Amiel replied as if it were obvious.

Grant merely shook his head, taking in the sights of infinite misery and destruction around them. "How?"

Amiel's features hardened, his back stiff. "This is not the first time our jewel of a city has been destroyed. My people are used to overcoming odds where others see the insurmountable. We learned the importance of hope long before your people first sailed to America's shores. And you and your friends have reminded us of that hope. I was wrong when I asked God why He had abandoned us in our hour of need. He did not. He sent you."

Grant offered a worn smile at Amiel's profound words, but he was still distraught at the notion of running away. He looked to Alex for some kind of help, but her exhausted face seemed resigned to this fate. All of the others had stopped what they were doing as well to watch this exchange between the two leaders.

"I don't know how to just *leave* you all here," Grant lamented.

Amiel smiled. "No matter what our governments and leaders may fear you are capable of . . . *We know* what you have done for us, how you have saved us and cried for us and comforted us. Hundreds of thousands who were pulled out of the destruction owe their lives to you. All of you. We will remember this, and the story of what has happened here will be passed down to our children. History will know of the man named Guardian who stood between the City of God and the angel of death. Now I beg you. *Go*, my friend. You must, please go."

Grant sighed again as Amiel turned to go. It was time to leave.

But maybe not for all of them . . . A thought struck him just then.

"Amiel?" he called out, and the young Jewish man returned. "I'd like to leave one of my people here with you. One who doesn't have as famous a face as the rest of us, who could stay and help you all but could more easily be hidden than our entire group."

Amiel studied him, considering this. "We would be grateful for the help, but who of your people could you spare? Do you not need them all for whatever tasks lie ahead of you?"

"Wilhelm?" Grant called out.

Wilhelm stood from where he'd been sitting cross-legged and playing a game of jacks with some locals. He ran up to Grant's position eagerly.

"It's time for the team to leave," Grant explained. "It's not safe for us here anymore. But if you're so inclined, I'd like for you to stay behind and continue to help out here. For as long as you feel up to it."

Wilhelm was taken aback by this. "But . . . But why me? You don't even know me."

"I trust you," Grant replied simply.

"My powers won't help these people."

"That may or may not be true. But I've seen you with them, and they like you. They're put at ease by you, and you come alive around them. You need each other."

Wilhelm looked around, still confused. "I don't know . . ."

Grant placed a hand on his shoulder. "You'll be fine. And when you feel that you've done all that you can do, head back to L.A., to the reserve safe house, and wait for us there."

Wilhelm straightened himself. He was bewildered but determined to serve. "Very well. If these are your wishes, I will do my best, Guardian."

"It's Grant, actually," he replied, smiling at his young friend. "My name is Grant Borrows. I don't usually reveal that to people I haven't known very long, but I think you've earned it."

"Grant!" Morgan clutched at his arm. He hadn't seen her approach, but now she stood just over his shoulder. Her other hand was pointing to the mound where the bodies were being stacked.

Hundreds of the dead had been piled here, and on order of the local health administration would soon be set on fire to reduce the chances of any sort of plague outbreak. It was an uncivilized act undertaken in desperate times.

But Grant's attention soon focused on what Morgan was pointing at. It wasn't the mound itself, but the trickles of red liquid that flowed down its sides and pooled in the shallow ground below.

"The earth is bleeding," Morgan whispered.

"The fertile soil. . . ?" Grant replied, dumbstruck. He faced her.

"'The most fertile soil shall bleed and forever stain the firmament,'" she recited. "It's the second Unholy Marker."

Their eyes locked. A silence passed between them, an entire unspoken conversation.

I caused it, Grant said to himself, still holding her eyes. *It's the second Marker, and once again, it's my handiwork.*

"Of course!" Morgan cried, a realization dawning over her. "This entire region is unusually conducive to farming for a desert climate. In fact, the first known farming settlements in recorded history have been found here. It's been a mystery to scientists for centuries, how a specific region—this cradle of civilization running from part of Egypt up toward the Mediterranean and then across to the Persian Gulf—could be so accommodating to agriculture. This phenomenon prompted an Egyptologist from Chicago many years ago to coin a phrase that has come to describe this entire region. He called it 'the Fertile Crescent.'"

"Fertile Crescent," Grant repeated. The phrase sounded familiar.

He'd probably heard it in school as a child. "'The most fertile soil shall bleed . . .'" he repeated.

"And we're standing right in the heart of it," Morgan concluded.

Grant rubbed at his tired eyes, not sure if he was ready to accept all of this.

Alex approached, seeming to have overheard some of what they'd said. "What's she talking about, Grant?"

He hesitated, looking deeply into Morgan's eyes once more. "The Prophecy is coming true."

34

Flight 1004 to London

The team's flight from Israel to England was less eventful than their last flight. The disguises they had used before were all but useless now, so Fletcher hastily created new ones. Most of his computer equipment had been left behind in storage in Los Angeles, but he'd brought a few laptops along, just in case.

The new disguises were even less convincing than the originals, having been thrown together so quickly. Most of the team had had to settle for just trying to hide their faces behind sunglasses or under hats.

After lying low for most of the day following their exit from Jerusalem, they'd traveled to nearby Amman and booked a red-eye flight to London Heathrow from there. Lisa had once again used her unique talents to get them on the earliest possible flight, but they happily settled for whatever seats were available on this airplane. They sat scattered throughout the economy section, but Grant was just relieved that everyone made it onto the same flight.

Their numbers had dropped down to nine now, since Wilhelm had opted to stay behind. Payton never rejoined the group after he'd vanished from their midst in Jerusalem. Was that really Devlin they'd both seen in the distance? The man was so far away, it could have been anyone.

Morgan got a call from Payton a few hours later with a brief message that he would meet them in London in a few days.

The nine of them spent the first few hours of the flight trying to sleep after the toil and drudgery they'd left behind them. Exhausted, they slumbered, but the horror they'd seen did not quickly abandon them.

Grant had been through several of these days-long search and rescue operations now, beginning with the days following the destruction of Morgan's old home, the converted asylum where she'd once housed the Loci. It never got any easier. The way you lose parts of yourself to the pain and grief . . . a piece of you always stays behind in that place where you rescued some and couldn't help so many others. More than anything, the indignity and injustice of it all gnaw at you when you try to sleep, in the coldest, quietest part of the night.

It may not have been Grant's first time, but it was the rest of the team's first. So he knew exactly what they were feeling and how they would never quite be the same again from this day on.

Alex, seated next to Grant, slept only in spurts. No one talked about it, but she seemed to have come the most unhinged by the events in Jerusalem. It was understandable, Grant surmised. Never before had she been surrounded by so many ferocious, unfettered emotions at one time. It was too much to shut out; it was more than she probably ever thought she would be exposed to. Grant guessed that she'd been saturated with so much external grief and pain that maybe those powerful feelings were lingering in her system, refusing to leave her alone. Kind of like a hangover.

When Alex did manage to sleep, she woke up with bugged-out eyes. She refused any offers to talk about it, but the offers themselves were few and far between because everyone else had their own demons to wrestle with from their time in Jerusalem.

Daniel found no rest either. Everyone was used to his internal retreat, but when the flight attendant reminded him to buckle his seat belt before take-off, she'd had to say it three times before he registered her presence.

Julie, who sat next to Morgan four aisles in front of Grant and Alex, quivered more than usual following the hours of hard work she had put in. But as was her custom, she was working hard to hide it.

Grant's thoughts obsessed around Devlin. Was that really him? And if so, was his presence there in any way related to their discovery of another Secretum substation? Or was he merely watching Grant again?

He switched gears, wondering about this strange barrier that had been erected around much of downtown London. Would his powers help him get past the barrier? Were the Loci there—these Upholders of the Crown—responsible for its existence? Who were those people, and where had they come from?

And then there was the bleeding of the fertile soil . . . The second Unholy Marker. Leaving only one more to go. *The end shall be marked by a scar revealing man's deepest hollow.*

He was lost among so many thoughts when it slowly dawned on him that Alex was awake. Not only that, but her bleary eyes were fixed on him. In his peripheral vision, he could see her studying him closely, unblinking. Finally, he irritably turned to her and snapped, "What?"

Her eyes seemed to be searching her memory as she searched his face. "Your eyes are blue, aren't they?"

"Last time I checked. Why are you asking me this?"

"Hey easy, tiger," Alex said. "I couldn't remember, is all."

"Whatever."

"Don't 'whatever' me, pal. You're not the only person here who's having a hard time with the state of the world. The way you let your temper flare back in Jerusalem . . . I hope all that thinking you're doing includes some long and hard meditation on where that thing on your finger came from. I can feel the influence it wields over your emotions. You keep it in check, but it's always in there."

Grant glanced fleetingly at her own ring finger, then returned his gaze to his window. "If you're right about the influence my ring has over me, then you're not exactly pure as the driven snow, yourself."

Alex stared at him, crossed her arms, and to Grant's great surprise, had nothing to say for once. She merely sat back in her seat and looked straight ahead.

He suddenly felt very foolish. "I'm sorry, okay? I'm just stressed out. It never gets any easier, what we do."

They sat in silence for several minutes. Alex's entire countenance had changed during their time in Jerusalem. When he'd first met her she'd been so alive, so carefree, so articulate yet playful. Now, only a handful of months later, frown lines furrowed at the corners of her mouth, her eyes were puffy, and creases often showed between her eyebrows. She had been opened to a world of vulnerability and reality. She was no longer the person he first met.

Something occurred to him just then. Morgan may have been his guide, setting him on the right path. And his sister Julie may have been his conscience, holding him to that path.

But Alex had become his equal. No one understood the daily realities of what it was like to do what he did better than her.

She spoke very softly. "I can't get that baby boy out of my mind."

Grant nodded solemnly. He was right there with her.

"I keep thinking," she said, "about how alone he was, for so long. He cried . . . and suffered . . . for hours and hours. Can you imagine what that was like for him? He never even had a chance."

Before Grant knew what was happening, Alex had leaned sideways until her head was resting on his shoulder. She slowly drew her knees up and folded them sideways against the opposite side of her seat, her bare feet slipping out of the flip-flops she'd been required to wear to get on the plane.

It was an uncharacteristic display of weakness that caught him thoroughly off guard. But he wasn't bothered by it. A little human contact felt pretty good right about now, actually.

"Ask you a personal question?" he prodded carefully.

She remained rooted to his shoulder. "Sure."

"Who were you? Before you were Alex?" he asked, verbalizing a question that had been in the back of his mind for a long, long time. "Before the Shift?"

She sniffled but didn't raise her head. "No one that mattered," she gingerly said.

The answer stumped him a bit. "I thought everyone matters. Didn't you tell me that a few days ago?"

Alex never replied.

Instead, she fell into a fitful sleep, twitching and mumbling as if chased by an unrelenting jumble of thoughts and feelings.

35

Fourteen Years Ago

"Mom, I can do this myself."

A middle-aged woman named Nell with sagging skin and a somber expression gave a halfhearted roll of her eyes at the teenager she knelt in front of. "Becky, please don't start."

Becky, a bright-eyed fifteen-year-old who sat buckled into a wheelchair, narrowed her eyes in anger. "I am not helpless!" she protested. "I can tie my own shoelaces!"

Nell didn't respond. She merely finished her task at Becky's feet and then braced herself on the end of the small hospital room's adjustable bed. With visible discomfort and a bit of a lurch, she raised herself up.

This hospital room had been the mother and daughter's home away from home for the last six weeks, where Becky was monitored while recovering from her latest surgery. This was her fifth major surgery, which was required as her body grew and matured in order for her to have a chance at a normal life.

Born with a severe birth defect to the spinal cord known as Spina Bifida Cystica, Becky had lived in a wheelchair or locking leg braces her entire life. Her mother, Nell, was a single parent working two jobs to make ends meet for Becky and her brother. She bore the telltale signs of constant exhaustion that Becky knew would probably drive her mother to an early grave.

But today wasn't the day to think about such things. Today, at long last, Becky was being discharged and sent home. She couldn't wait to sleep in her own bed and play with her German shepherd, Barney.

I hope he still remembers me, she thought sourly.

She took a deep breath and braced herself to spring something on her mom that she'd been waiting days for the right opportunity to say.

"Steph and the girls want to take me to the lake for the day on Saturday to celebrate getting out of here," she said.

Her mother carefully sat on the edge of the bed, and as she did whenever the two of them had important discussions, said nothing for a few moments. She merely looked ahead and thought. The waiting killed Becky, as it always did, while her mother maintained a distant calm.

"Would anyone's parents be there with you?" Nell asked. "You know I have to work."

"I don't know," Becky answered honestly. "Lacey's dad might be there I guess—he owns the boat."

Nell's eyes grew for an instant, and Becky knew what that meant. The thought of her paraplegic daughter on a boat had probably caused her heart to miss a beat.

"Why does it have to be the lake?" her mother asked in a tired voice. "Couldn't your friends take you someplace safer, like the mall or a movie?"

"They know how much I love the outdoors, and I haven't *been* outside in a month and a half, Mom! C'mon, *please* . . ."

Nell sighed again and was about to speak when there was a knock at the door.

Olivia, her favorite nurse, appeared with Becky's little brother Mark in her arms. Mark, who was only two years old, was the product of a one-night stand between her mother and some truck driver. Becky wasn't supposed to know this, but like most of her friends, she knew lots of things her mother didn't want her to.

Olivia placed Mark on the ground, and he waddled over to Becky's wheelchair and reached his little arms up toward her. "Hey, little man!" she squealed.

Mark may have been an unexpected addition to their family, but he brought Becky more joy and happiness than anything else in the world. She loved him selflessly, more than she ever knew she was capable of loving anyone. And he adored her as well.

Their family was so well known at the hospital that Mark had been adopted by the entire nursing staff, who would often give Nell a break by entertaining him for half an hour or so. Olivia was just returning from one such break.

"I ride?" he asked in two-year-old speak, grinning at the chair.

She grinned in return. "Come on, you can do it," Becky coaxed him. He was already too heavy for her to lift, so he had learned to climb up her legs whenever she was in the wheelchair so she could give him a ride.

"Oh," Olivia the nurse said cheerily, "I'm sorry, Becky, but the ride will have to wait until you get home. And Dr. Bellarmo is waiting for you in the hall, ma'am," she told Becky's mom. Nell gave Becky a nervous smile and stepped outside, Mark waddling alongside her with his hand in hers.

"Well then," Olivia said, turning to Becky, "how about I gather the rest of your things and get you out of here!"

As Olivia vanished into the bathroom, Becky wheeled herself toward the door to the hall. It stood open a few inches, and if she could catch the gist of Dr. Bellarmo's instructions to her mom, she could save her mother the trouble of having to explain it later.

Olivia, meanwhile, clattered around in the bathroom, piling toiletries and belongings into a travel bag. Between the noises the nurse was making, Becky heard her mother's voice speaking in a lower register. Becky was alarmed to hear her mother suppressing a heavy cry.

"Are you sure?" her mother said. "You haven't seen any change at all?"

"I'm sorry," came the doctor's familiar, deep baritone. "It doesn't look like the spinal tissues have responded to the surgery. We're going to need to schedule Becky for another try, after she's had a few more months to fully recover, of course."

Becky twisted the wheels on her chair until she was facing away from the door and away from the bathroom where Olivia still plundered away. She looked out the big picture window at the green grass two stories below. Tears burned at her eyes, but she refused to let them out.

This was life. This was her life. Surgery after surgery after surgery. All in an attempt to provide what . . . a marginally better existence?

Certainly not for her mom, who carried the burden of caring for a handicapped teenager and a toddler all by herself.

"I hate this place!" she heard her mother half-shout from the hall-way. Her voice changed again, this time to the one she used when she'd reached the end of her rope. "I spend all my time working to save bread crumbs to pay you people with, and nothing you do makes any difference anyway!"

Becky heard Olivia emerge from the bathroom at the sound of her mother's outburst. She carefully closed the outer hospital room door so Becky would catch no more of this painful conversation, and then approached Becky from behind, saying nothing. She placed a gentle hand on the young girl's shoulder.

"I—I'm so sorry, sweetie," Olivia said.

Becky couldn't hold back the tears anymore; they spilled out and moistened her cheeks. But she didn't give in to it all the way; she refused to break down.

She realized in that moment that she hated herself and her life in every way possible.

Olivia carefully spun her around and knelt in front of the chair. "Your mother loves you very much, you know."

Becky nodded, looking away and trying to smile to cover her tears. "I know. I just wish I wasn't such a burden on her. She deserves better than this. So does Mark."

Olivia nodded, full of understanding.

"Sometimes I think everything would be better if I wasn't in their lives anymore," Becky admitted. She couldn't believe she'd said it out loud. She searched Olivia's kind face, waiting for the inevitable re-assurance that everything would be fine and that it was normal to feel this way, and she couldn't let these feelings consume her.

Instead, Olivia leaned in close and began to whisper.

"What if I told you that you could live a normal life? That you could have your wish fulfilled, that every burden would be lifted from your mother's shoulders, and yet you could live a long, happy, healthy life as a regular person? That you don't have to be a burden to everyone around you anymore?"

Becky was sure she had misunderstood what Olivia was trying to say. Maybe there was some life lesson that Olivia wanted her to learn and understand so she could heal emotionally.

"Have you got some kind of miracle cure hidden up your sleeve?" Becky joked, sniffling through her runny eyes and nose.

Olivia smiled. "I suppose I do at that. It's highly experimental and a huge secret. No one could ever know what's happened to you—not even your mom or your brother. Not that they'd believe you . . ."

Becky was shaking her head. "I couldn't do that to them."

"They would have a shot at a normal life. Your mom wouldn't have to work so much, and your brother would get all the attention from her that he deserves. And you'd come out best of all—you would get everything you've ever dreamed of. A normal life. And a chance to be whoever you want to be."

"I don't understand. . . ."

Olivia took her hand and looked into her eyes. "As long as this stays our secret, I'll answer every question you have, I promise. But tell me something first, sweetie . . . How do you feel about the name 'Alexandria'?"

36

It was midday as the dilapidated rental van came to a stop about ten blocks out from the edge of what the media was calling "the barrier" that mysteriously surrounded a key portion of London. It was as close to the barrier as they could get due to the swarming crowds of what looked like most of the rest of England milling outside the cordoned-off area.

Out of the van spilled Grant Borrows, his sister Julie, Alex, Morgan, Fletcher, Daniel, Lisa, Hector, and Nora, looking much worse for wear. Their spirits were defeated, as if hope and the wind had been knocked out of them permanently. Jerusalem was proving hard to get out of their systems; they had barely spoken to one another over the last twenty-four hours. What was there to say?

On the sidewalk, Grant began moving in the direction of the barrier. Alex and his sister followed immediately; the others barely noticed the movement and then struggled to keep up.

It was a typically balmy summer day in London, though the lack of sunshine left much to be desired. The city hummed with activity, with vehicles and people packed in tighter and tighter the closer one got to the quarantined zone.

Just to their north lay the Thames, the famous river that calmly twisted and wound its way through the heart of London. The parts of the city south of the Thames were still open; it was the area to the north that was the problem.

Strategically, whoever had cut off access to that part of the city certainly knew what they were doing. Just north of the Thames were Buckingham Palace, the Houses of Parliament, Big Ben, and countless other buildings that upheld the government of Great Britain.

Unfortunately, the quarantine zone also held the reason they were here—the Trigate International headquarters building, a suspected front company for the Secretum of Six.

If it *was* the "Upholders of the Crown" group blocking access to this area of town . . . then how on earth were they doing it?

"Hey," Julie said, walking faster to come alongside him. "Now that we're closer, can you feel anything else about those Upholders people?"

"Like what?" Grant asked. He wasn't sure what she expected him to find that he hadn't already.

"I don't know, more details about where they are. . . ?"

He shook his head. In doing so, he noticed the stares they were getting from the crowds. Soon throngs would push their way in closer, shoulder-to-shoulder. Was that a good idea, given their celebrity status?

Grant stopped, forcing the others to follow suit. "Wait—come with me."

They sidestepped into the foyer of a small restaurant. Grant examined them one by one, then made a quick decision.

"Lisa."

"Yeah?" she replied, stepping forward.

"Most of us are too recognizable to get very close. I want you to work your way to the front of the line and then try to talk a policeman or someone in charge into telling you what they know about this barrier."

While not entirely thrilled at the idea, she dutifully left the restaurant and proceeded on her way. In her absence, the team asked to be seated at a table inside the quaint building, which was decorated like a tasteful tourist attraction, and ordered lunch. Memorabilia and duplicates of historical artifacts native to England were placed on tables and hung from the walls. One primary wall was comprised of a hand-painted mural of downtown London.

Half an hour later, Lisa returned and joined them at the table. The group was used to eating fast and had already downed their food in silence by the time she arrived. She snatched her sandwich along with a to-go cup and followed them outside, where they continued the trek toward the barrier.

"Guy down there said they think it's some kind of 'energy barrier,' as weird as that sounds," Lisa reported between mouthfuls. "They don't know how else to describe it."

"Highly unlikely," Daniel muttered, his first words since they'd landed in London.

"Want to say that a little louder, Doc?" said Grant.

Daniel wasn't given to looking others in the eye anymore, so when his head popped up at Grant's remark, he immediately looked down at the ground again, leaning heavily on his cane as they walked.

"Assuming that whatever's keeping people out of the city is the work of a Ringwearer, and I think that's a safe bet . . . The scientific qualities of your unique abilities—and they are enhanced, measurable, *mental* capabilities, and nothing more—dictate that each ability that manifests should be an extension of something the brain can already *do.*"

"So what?" Grant replied.

"I've identified over two hundred potential ways the human brain could be enhanced, and none of them have anything to do with the pro-jection of . . . 'force fields,' for lack of a better term."

"Two hundred?" Morgan was taken aback. "Really? That many?"

Daniel nodded without looking up.

Grant glanced over at Morgan as she digested this number. And he had the distinct impression that it didn't fit with some fact she knew to be true.

Lisa spoke up again. "Actually, that lines up with what the police-man said. According to him, whenever a person approaches the barrier, they simply change their mind and decide not to go through to the other side. They've tried everything they can think of, but no one can maintain the desire to pass through it long enough to make it."

"Hm," Grant thought aloud. "Sounds like we're dealing with some-one who can affect will power. Have they tried placing a vehicle on automatic and just going along for the ride?"

Lisa nodded. "As soon as they hit the barrier, they're consumed with a desire to get back to wherever they started. They've had people jump from moving vehicles—driving over bridges no less—to avoid going inside."

Grant shook his head and focused on Morgan. "You ever hear of a Ringwearer that can affect hundreds of thousands of people all at once?"

Morgan shook her head.

"So the river marks this side of the barrier?" Grant clarified.

"And there's no way *across* the river," Lisa concluded. "All boat traffic has been stopped. All of the bridges are shut down. Even the Eye is closed."

Grant looked up and spotted the colossal white observation wheel known as the London Eye, a four hundred-and-forty-foot-high marvel of modern engineering. It stood deathly still, about five blocks to their right. Grant envied its chance to rest.

"What if we came at the barrier from the north?" Alex suggested, the first time her voice had been heard in a while.

Grant snuck a peek at her. Her eyes still looked hollowed-out and her shoulders still drooped, but a curiosity played at the edges of her expression. Maybe the curiosity of all these pedestrians surrounding them was empathically giving her an emotional boost.

"How big is the area?" Morgan asked.

Lisa looked up, remembering. "Guy I spoke to said they're not sure about the specific lines of delineation or exact square mileage, but they believe it's roughly rectangular in shape. He said they know it stretches from Paddington Station to some township called Poplar on the 'sides,' with the 'bottom' being the river. The 'top' is somewhere above . . . Izzington?"

"Islington," Morgan corrected. "At least two kilometers north of here, which isn't that bad, but going around Paddington or Poplar would certainly be taking the long way around this . . . whatever it is. With all of the major arteries clogged, it could take *hours* to get there in the car. Trying it on foot would be worse with the size of these crowds."

The crowd was noticeably murmuring now, as Grant and his team were weaving through the crowd, nearing its front. It wasn't long before all eyes were on them as they stood at the head of the crowd, just behind white beams on A-frames that were used by the police to keep the crowd at bay.

"You there!" shouted a policeman. A mid-sized man in a crisp uniform and checkered police hat trotted over to Grant. "You're—are you really—?"

"Yes, I am," Grant replied. "And this is my team. We've come to help."

The man showed signs of relief. "This thing takes anything we can throw at it. If you think you might have better luck, then by all means . . ." he motioned toward the riverbank, a hundred meters ahead. The policeman hefted the A-frame aside so Grant and his people could get through.

"Have you thought about restraining someone while they ventured through the barrier, but configure their restraints to open after they've reached the other side?" Grant asked the policeman.

"Certainly," the cop replied. "But the Chief won't sign off on it. And with good reason. Wait until you feel the pull of this thing for yourself—then you'll understand. It's like this awful sickness that settles into your gut, this feeling that you're going to *die* if you don't stop moving forward."

They were twenty meters from the edge of the riverbank when sirened cars burst onto the scene and blocked their path to the water. A dozen car doors opened and suited agents of some kind emerged. Multiple handguns were leveled on Grant and his friends.

The policeman stepped forward between Grant and the newcomers. "What's all this?!" he cried, irate.

"MI–5!" one of the officers near the front shouted, his gun hand steady and ready to fire. "Stand down, or we will use lethal force!"

37

"What are you on about?" shouted the cop. "They're here to help!"

"You're relieved," said the man in black, still aiming his gun at Grant's head. "MI–5 has assumed jurisdiction over this situation. Stand down immediately."

"What's the meaning of this?" Grant said.

At the simple movement of his mouth, the gunmen became twitchy, tightening their gun grips and shifting their body weight to better stances.

"We have our orders, sir," called out the man up front. "You are denied access to the barrier by Her Majesty's government, and you are ordered to come with us at any cost!"

Grant made a quick mental calculation.

"Down, NOW!" he shouted. All eight members of his team immediately dropped to the ground as an ear-splitting crack like a thunderclap was heard and a visible wave of energy exploded from Grant, rippling outward in a perfect circle and demolishing everything in its path.

Grant's team clung hard to the earth to avoid being tossed aside by the wave, but the MI–5 agents and their vehicles were not so lucky. The wave flung the cars up into the air and far out across the river as if they were shreds of paper blown by fierce wind. The policemen followed suit, some crashing into the cement fence that stood between the road and the river, others flying up high and soaring until they landed in the river itself.

A handful of trees, street signs, and riverside benches had been swept away by the blast as well. Nothing stood for a one-hundred-meter radius around Grant, save for himself. Everything else had been flattened or blown away.

Grant was careful not to release enough energy that it would touch the pedestrians, so the wave of energy he created dissipated before it ever reached them. It was a short-wave, but incredibly powerful blast.

Only a handful of people had ever witnessed Grant's utilization of this secondary ability he'd discovered not long before his final show-down with his grandfather. No one who was here now had ever seen it before, including Grant's entire team, who still clung to the ground, and they joined in the hush that fell over the crowd at this terrifying display of raw power.

"Come on, come on!" he shouted at them. "We have to go before more of them arrive!"

The group split up and melted into the crowd. Grant had the hardest time of this, of course, though anyone who saw him made sure to give him a wide berth. The team reunited back at the van an hour later.

"Well, any element of surprise or subterfuge we might have had on our side is long gone now," he remarked, revving the engine and driving south.

"Ya *think*?" said Lisa.

He glared at her from the rearview mirror.

Alex, voice still trembling, managed to change the topic. "The sun is already getting low, so we'd be lucky to make it around the barrier before nightfall. Even if we did manage it, we've got no guarantee that it would be any easier getting inside from there. If we're going to do this, it's got to be somewhere around here. The cover of nightfall should help, as long as we can come up with a plan to get across the river that . . . doesn't draw a lot of attention to us."

The others swallowed this in silence.

"We're ignoring an obvious question here," Fletcher said. "Why not go *over* the river?"

"Look up," Lisa retorted. "Do you see any helicopters in the area? Their pilots turn around just like everybody else. Whatever the barrier is, it reaches high enough into the sky to prevent access that way too."

"So," Alex wrapped her arms around her body. "What we need is to find a hole. Some gap in the barrier that whoever made it wouldn't have bothered to plug."

"Assuming there is such a thing, then yeah," Grant affirmed. "What about the Underground?"

"Closed down, according to the cop I talked to earlier," Lisa replied. "The tunnels have been checked; they're all affected by the barrier too."

"Um, I have a thought." Julie timidly rose her hand, turning all the way around to take in the river. "The river represents the barrier. We can't fly above it. We can't go *over* it, via a bridge. And we can't *cross* the river in a boat . . ."

"Right," Grant replied, eager for her to finish her line of thought.

"What if we went *through* it?"

"Twenty-seven oil fields in Saudi Arabia erupted in flames this morning, and experts have yet to determine a cause," said the talking head on the projected television screen that played at the front of the economy cabin, tuned to a twenty-four-hour news network.

Federal Agent Ethan Cooke watched with rapt attention from his aisle seat while others around him slept. He took notes on a small pad.

"The situation in the Persian Gulf is just the latest catastrophe in a series of unexplained disasters that have overwhelmed the entire world," the man on the screen said. "It comes hot on the heels of deadly mudslides that killed more than one hundred yesterday in southeastern Asia. Earlier in the week NASA announced that the orbits of ninety percent of all active, man-made satellites had begun to deteriorate. Those satellites—which number above two thousand—will reenter earth's atmosphere over the next month. The majority of them are expected to burn up upon reentry, though NASA expects at least ten percent of them to strike the surface, with only a fraction of those escaping the earth's oceans. Wall Street's telecommunications industries have taken an enormous hit from this news at a time when the global economy is already nearing worldwide collapse. . . ."

Ethan's body longed for sleep, knowing that this flight would be his one chance to get any decent rest before he arrived in London. But he couldn't tear his eyes from the screen. History was unfolding at a rapidly accelerated rate, and everyone knew it.

He had seen it firsthand. Per Stevens's orders, he'd watched in Jerusalem. He'd done nothing but watch as Grant Borrows and his friend—or was she something more?—Alex worked tirelessly for hours, even *days* on end, saving lives, sacrificially giving of their own energy and health and going the extra mile each and every time. When Borrows unexpectedly and quickly pulled out of the city, Ethan bit the bullet and consulted Stevens on his next move.

She had detained him by a few hours for a conference call during which he gave a full report on everything he'd seen "Guardian" do in Jerusalem. He did his best to keep his report unbiased, but it was hard to find anything negative to say about a man who gave so much of himself, yet had absolutely no obligation to even be there.

He was highly trained and duty bound to bring Grant in. But he was absolutely convinced that whatever Grant Borrows was, he was *not* the bad guy.

The problem now was how could he convince his superiors of this without becoming weak in their eyes?

Even with their amateur disguises, Ethan was able to follow Borrows and his people to the airport and watch as they booked seats on a flight for London. As Director Stevens herself had pointed out, the fact that they never meant to end up in Jerusalem would help Grant's case considerably.

The question now was what business did Borrows have in London? What could be enough to draw him there, along with so many of his people, and away from all of the pain and destruction in Jerusalem?

Ethan had no idea.

A police sketch of Grant's face popped up on the television screen, in a small box beside the talking newscaster. Ethan had never seen this drawing before.

"We have just received word that the unidentified man known as 'Guardian' has fled from Jerusalem under threat of military action from the Israeli government. Rumors have reached our newsroom that Guardian and his team have already been spotted today, now in Great Britain, where he had some kind of skirmish with local authorities. We cannot independently verify this information, but if true, we would speculate that his presence there could be in some way related to the quarantine phenomenon taking place in the heart of London.

"Meanwhile, we have learned from an inside source at the Pentagon that as of late this afternoon, Guardian has been placed at the top of the FBI's Most Wanted List. It's believed that this action comes in response to Guardian's destruction of invaluable historic property in Jerusalem and the fight with London authorities we mentioned earlier, in addition to some further evidence we're told involves a murdered Los Angeles Police detective. International law enforcement agencies around the globe have received detailed reports about this man and the danger he is believed to represent. An official statement from the FBI is expected first thing tomorrow morning."

What?!

Stevens had given him no warning that Guardian's official status had been upgraded. What on earth was she thinking, making him a wanted man? Was she even *listening* to the report he gave during the conference call?

Borrows left Israel for England, and she knows it—proving he had nothing to do with the disaster in Jerusalem. He had nothing to do with that Detective Drexel's death. And even if he did tear up some historic site in Israel, this is an extreme reaction—there's no logical reason for it. . . .

A phrase popped into his head that he'd learned a few years ago from one of his instructors at the FBI Academy. It was a time-tested, reliable aphorism that could explain the most irrational of actions.

When reason fails, fear prevails.

38

Dusk settled over the River Thames with no fog in sight. The surface stood eerily calm; no boats disrupted her. Not even a cool breeze blew. All was still.

Bright lights shown across the water—streetlights, docks, Big Ben, businesses, skyscrapers, hotels—and those lights were reflected in a bright orange hue atop the silky smooth surface of the river.

It was almost hard to believe that just across the river there were hundreds of thousands of people. Every so often, tiny spots of movement could be seen along the city streets as people walked to and fro, though none approached the Thames. No escape attempts from within had been seen since the barrier was put into place. The calm, everyday actions of those on the inside left outside observers with a strange sense of dread.

These were not the actions of people being held against their will.

Grant and his companions stood at the edge of the water near the far end of Jubilee Gardens, a small park adjacent to the London Eye. The docks and bridges were packed with crowds waiting, watching, but this dark nook didn't have as much of a view and so the numbers were thinner. In fact, they managed to secure a space along the shoreline more or less to themselves, and Alex dissuaded any pedestrians milling about from approaching by making them worried of the dark.

And it was dark, so dark that unless you were right next to someone, you couldn't make out their features. All the better for what they needed to do.

Morgan turned to Grant and gave him an unspoken signal.

He faced the London Eye, which was to the group's immediate left, and focused his mind on the enormous mechanical apparatus with all his might and the power switch in particular.

The Eye flickered to life, its multitude of lights and spotlights blinking on. And it spun.

A slow swell of curious murmurs from the crowds along the shore began to build, and numerous hands and arms were pointed in the direction of the giant wheel.

The spinning grew faster. The Eye was equipped with various colored lights, used separately from one another at nighttime for dramatic effect. Grant forced them to shift with the rapidity of a strobe light at a rock concert, and soon all eyes had turned away from the city across the river and locked onto the Eye.

Grant pushed it a bit faster, careful now not to strain the structure beyond its capability. Morgan reminded him earlier that it wasn't meant to move at high speeds and wouldn't be able to withstand a workout like this for long.

"Go," he whispered.

Hector carried a large duffel bag over one shoulder, which he placed at the edge of the water. With help from Alex, he unzipped it and allowed its contents to fall out. A long rope ladder spilled out; he secured one end of it to a park bench, while Alex fed the remainder into the river.

Once done, Alex knelt slowly over the rope at the river's edge. She had one foot on the ladder's first rung, the other dangled over the water. Quickly, one foot after the other, she descended until she hung just below the shoreline, close enough to touch the water.

"Ready," she called out softly.

Grant turned loose of the Eye's lights but left them on and gave the wheel one final nudge to keep it spinning for several more minutes. Then he approached the water's edge and climbed down after Alex until he was just above her on the rope ladder. Julie followed, readying herself at the top to follow once Grant was clear.

With slow breaths to calm himself, Grant focused his mind on the dark water below and pushed at it with his mind. Ever so carefully, so as not to noticeably disturb the surface or cause too much noise, he pushed down until a bubble grew, and Alex immediately descended the wet rope into the empty space he'd created.

Grant followed cautiously, his powers focused on the water, growing the bubble large enough to accommodate all of them, while never making it so big that it drew attention from above. Only a tiny hole of air at the top of the bubble breeched the surface, allowing them to enter.

Alex reached the bottom and Grant heard a squish as she landed in the mud on the bottom of the river. She whispered up, "The ladder comes up a little short. You'll have to jump."

Grant hopped down with ease into the slimy mud, but Julie, who followed, struggled to get her feet into the correct rungs of the ladder, and slipped.

Grant caught her, both of them landing flat on their backs in the muck. The bubble's edges quivered and threatened to falter as Grant's concentration lapsed for a split second when he hit the ground, but he snapped back to attention and held the bubble firm.

In truth, it wasn't the fall that made his concentration waver. It was seeing his sister's deterioration. She hadn't been the same after the long hours of toil she'd put in in Jerusalem. He would never say anything out of fear of making her feel worse about it, but he'd seen her several times on the plane having difficulty just sitting still.

He stood and helped Julie to her feet.

The others continued to descend the ladder until they gathered in a tight grouping at the bottom. Their breath came out in wisps of freezing condensation.

"Everyone all right?" Grant checked. "Are we all here?"

"This . . . this is really weird," Alex observed. "Plus, we don't get frequent flyer, onboard snack, or even a nice view."

"'To travel hopefully is a better thing than to arrive,' according to Robert Louis Stevenson," said Morgan, shivering and taking in the soundless void around them. "We're making a very strong case against that argument here."

It was cold under the river, the air as moist as a rain forest. They elected not to use any lights, relying only on the dim city lights that filtered through from above; the Thames wasn't all that deep, so using light down here would only draw attention.

"Explain to me again why this is going to work?" Fletcher whispered in the bizarre, now flattened bubble of air they stood in, water surrounding them on all sides. With one finger, he poked a hole in the bubble, but nothing happened aside from his finger getting wet.

Even with their eyes adjusting to the dark, it was almost impossible to see down here. Grant held Julie's hand tightly in his, and she shivered violently in the cold, caked in the freezing mud as she was. Grant put an arm around her shoulders to steady her and looked into her eyes.

She nodded affirmingly back at him, but she couldn't fully hide her fear. The sooner this was over, the better.

"We don't know that it will," Morgan replied. "We're twenty-five feet under the largest river in England. We're hoping that the barrier doesn't extend this far down. We know they tried boats and even swimming. But who'd plan for anyone walking across on the river bottom? It would be an easy oversight to make on the part of whoever's erected this barrier to not bother keeping it in place under the water. Conversely, authorities on the surface will likewise assume that there's no point in sending divers down. It's a loophole, we hope."

Grant began to walk and the bubble followed his movements, urging the others to keep pace. Aside from Julie, Daniel seemed to have the most trouble with it, his cane getting stuck in the mud more than once. Lisa approached him several times and tried to offer her assistance, but he wouldn't accept it. Finally she gave up and moved away from him.

Julie meanwhile couldn't stop trembling. Grant knew she'd refuse help if asked, but he did use his powers to keep her feet from squelching too deeply into the mud. The walk was taking forever.

A few minutes later, Morgan's voice broke the silence. "The river is thought to be the home of angels who have reportedly been seen floating across its surface like white specters."

"Super," Alex said. "Thanks for the trivia."

Morgan's random information didn't scare Grant, but his arms did get goose bumps as he peered through the dark water around them. They were over halfway there now, but the precariousness of their situation suddenly hit home, and the water felt a little more threatening, so dark and surrounding them wherever he turned . . .

Nobody spoke. They just walked. Muddy footstep after muddy footstep, the bubble inching its way through the water.

A few minutes of walking later, they came upon the riverbank on the opposite side, and with extreme concentration, Grant was able to send another length of rope up out of the water and onto land. If they'd hit the target area they were hoping for, there should be a white statue jutting out from the primary embankment upon which he could tie off the rope.

It was difficult, not being able to see the sculpture, but as his grandfather had taught him, it was *awareness* that mattered. Not line-of-sight. He pictured the statue in his mind and finally found its shape with the rope, a few feet south of where they stood. He tied the knot securely, and they began the ascent. Julie went first, followed by Grant directly beneath in case she should lose her grip.

As Grant neared the top of the water, Julie suddenly sprang upward as if pulled out of the water. He climbed frantically until his head popped out of the river. Right in front of his face was a wrinkled but strong hand with a meaty palm reaching down from above.

Leaning over from the statue's platform was an elderly gentleman with a bushy white mustache and a bowler atop his head.

"Lend a hand?" he asked casually in his stiff accent.

39

There were four of them. Standing side by side, they watched Grant's group once everyone was back on dry land. But Grant felt sure he'd detected *five* Ringwearers in London . . .

Front and center was a forty-something female in a large red hat. Dressed in a smart, high-end red dress with simple hair and tasteful makeup, she looked more like a Parisian designer than a British native. Her chin was jutted slightly up and out, so that whomever she looked at, she looked down upon.

Beside her was the older gentleman who'd offered to help Grant out of the water. He had beady eyes that were surveying the newcomers carefully and frown lines etched around his mouth. He looked leathered, as if he'd spent much of life outdoors, and his skin was dotted with liver spots. His attire matched his demeanor. A beige sweater that had been ironed so many times it was almost shiny covered his torso. A pair of neat white slacks gave him the hint of a golfer, though Grant couldn't get Sherlock Holmes's pal Dr. Watson out of his head when looking at him. Grant guessed he only had one expression for every occasion: a frown.

There was a girl who had to have been in her early twenties, if she was even that old. She wore a white tank top, pitch-black jeans, and had close-cropped black hair that was spackled into hundreds of tiny spikes. She watched them with contempt written on her features.

The last was a man who brought the phrase "street urchin" to Grant's mind—or maybe what a street urchin grew up to become.

Ratty T-shirt, denim with holes in the knees that hadn't been put there for fashion's sake, and basic white tennis shoes. Might have been in his early thirties. His dirty red hair was parted on one side, framing his face in a boyish way that made him look a good bit younger than Grant suspected he was. In stark contrast to the others, his expression was not unpleasant, but filled with curiosity.

All four of them had gold rings on their right middle fingers exactly like the ones the Loci wore. No differences that Grant could detect. He was reminded that this group of Ringwearers had appeared on his radar only five or six weeks ago, which put them on the map after he'd been given his ring, the Seal of Dominion. Until that happened, he'd been under the impression that there would *be* no more Ringwearers made. Perhaps Devlin and the Secretum had continued another part of his grandfather's work and started handing out rings again?

"Hello," he began. "You're the group calling itself the Upholders of the Crown."

"The Guardian graces us with his ruggedly handsome presence," said the woman in the big hat. Her lips moved very little when she spoke, and words came out with a droll superiority, as if everything in the world was part of some private joke only she knew the punch line to.

Alex seemed to prickle, coming unexpectedly alive. "Don't get used to the view. We're not here to stay."

"Easy, tiger," Grant quoted back at Alex, then turned to address the strangers. "I take it you realize that we are just like you. We each wear a ring; we all have unique abilities."

The woman almost shrugged. "Be that as it may, you are here uninvited. *Why?*"

"We mean you no harm," Grant said. "We're investigating the origins of the rings we wear, and those who gave them to us."

"And your investigation has led you here, has it?" the older gentleman asked.

"That's right. We need to find a company called—"

"Our only interest in this matter is your trespassing, sir," said the older statesman. "And there is only one thing we know for certain about the one doing the trespassing. *You* are a criminal."

Alex piped up, "A criminal? For what, ruffling a few cops' feathers on the other side of the river?"

"Your government has placed you at the top of their Most Wanted List," the woman in the hat replied. "Something about a murdered detective in Los Angeles."

Grant didn't let himself turn in Daniel's direction, though he wanted to very badly. Out of the corner of his eye, he saw the scientist stagger slightly, as if his entire strength was threatening to fail.

Grant changed tactics. "How would you know that? I thought there was no contact with the outside world from within this barrier of yours."

The man in the T-shirt and jeans laughed hysterically, as if Grant had just given the punch line to the funniest joke in the world. Just as suddenly, he stopped laughing and the curious look on his face returned. "It's cold out here I'm bored. My show's on the telly Can we go home?" The man's words seemed to spill out of his mouth in a jumble, as if his lips couldn't keep time with his thoughts.

The woman in the hat spoke up as if the plain-dressed man hadn't said anything. "There's been no stoppage of information coming *in*, darling. But we keep a tight lid on what's going out."

Grant was too tired for this increasingly bizarre exchange. "So you *are* responsible for the barrier. May I ask why you took it upon yourself to do something like this?"

"You could never understand," the young girl spoke up for the first time, rolling her eyes.

Grant was unmoved. "I understand that the same people that put me on the Most Wanted List are labeling *your* actions here criminal. They're wrong about me. Are they wrong about you?"

The woman spoke first. "Our loyalty to our homeland is not something you should question lightly."

"British law does not make allowances for vigilante justice, my friends," Morgan said, stepping forward. Her accent did not go unnoticed by her fellow Englishmen.

"The New Order was requested and sanctioned under secret order of the prime minister himself," said the woman. "Not everyone is bubbling over with gratitude, but they accept that it's for the best. Life goes on."

"No martial law?" Grant asked.

"Heavens, no. People still go to work and pay their taxes," the old man said. "It's just smoother sailing this way."

"To what end?" Grant asked. "How long do you plan to keep this up?"

"I have a better question," Alex eyed them suspiciously. "What happens to the ones who violate the rules of your 'New Order'?"

While everyone was talking, Lisa quietly walked to a nearby tree. She pried loose a medium sized branch near the bottom and returned with it.

She whacked Daniel in the back of the head with it as hard as she could. Pandemonium erupted among Grant's people, but their British counterparts remained perfectly calm.

"What are you *doing*?!" Daniel cried as the others rushed in around the two of them, some to protect Daniel and others to prevent Lisa from striking him again.

But Lisa had already dropped the stick, horrified at what she'd done. Daniel felt the back of his head and found a small bloodied spot there.

"*That* is what happens," said the woman in the hat in reply to Alex's question.

Grant got it immediately. Lisa wasn't in control of her actions when she struck Daniel. One of the Upholders had taken control of her. His theory was accurate—one of them was able to control willpower.

"*Don't* do that again," Alex threatened. Grant knew then that he wasn't the only person who understood what had just happened; most of his friends had grasped it as well. Alex looked ready to strike.

Grant had one eye on her and one on Daniel. Morgan had already placed a handkerchief over the back of his head to stop the bleeding. Lisa stood alone, several feet away, mortified. Everyone else was braced for a fight.

"Look," Grant intervened, "you leave us alone, we'll leave you alone. Deal?"

"Very well, then," she snapped in a sour tone. "But if you *harm* anyone . . ." She let her threat fade to silence.

Grant and his friends leered at their British counterparts as they passed by and vanished into the night.

40

The team split up upon entering the city. Grant convinced Alex to accompany him to Trigate International immediately, despite their mutual fatigue. Investigating Payton's lead there seemed crucial, and even though he was still covered in dried mud from the bottom of the Thames, he had no desire to wait till morning. Besides, the cover of darkness was always a better ally than any powers they could conjure.

Julie and Lisa were to locate the roomiest apartment or hotel room they could find, giving the group a place to call home base while in London, even though none of them expected to be there very long.

Trigate's home office turned out to be nothing more than a one-room space located in a single-floor business complex several blocks north of Regent's Park. With Grant's abilities, getting inside the office was simple. No fingerprints or other evidence of their entry need be left behind. Grant removed his still-muddy shoes and left them outside.

Once inside, a few sweeps of their flashlights across the bare floor revealed the office to be all but empty.

"If this actually *was* used by anybody as office space," Grant remarked, "they've been gone for a long time."

"I love being in London," Alex said, her tired eyes glazed over. Then a stricken look appeared on her face. "I have no idea why I just said that."

"You're thinking what we all are," Grant replied, walking deeper into the room. "It's something about being inside the barrier. Some-one clearly *wants* us to love the city so much we never think about leaving—just like everyone else inside. It's how they're keeping every-one in, just like an unwillingness to enter the city is keeping the rest of the world out."

"My money's on Queen Fuchsia," Alex said.

Grant laughed. He examined the blank white walls, ceiling panels, and fluorescent lights. The room hadn't even been carpeted.

"This sure takes the term 'dummy corporation' to staggering new heights," she commented.

"We flew halfway across the world and walked under a river to see this," Grant said in a take-charge tone. "Let's not get so impatient we miss something important."

"It's probably the jet lag," Alex said, yawning, "or maybe it's the living *Hell* we spent the last few days in, *or* it could even be the delegation from the Psycho Squad that failed to offer us the keys to the city . . . but could you remind me what we're looking for, exactly?"

"Morgan said the file Payton recovered in France referred to Trigate alongside a memo about some sort of 'repository' that's connected to the Secretum."

"Yeah," Alex quipped, "I'm so glad she wasn't in any way vague about that. Just tell me what I have to do to get out of here so I can go to bed."

"If the Secretum left clues of any kind behind, they'll be well hid-den. We need to scour every inch of this place."

Grant knelt to examine the concrete pavement beneath his feet. He felt along its surface, looking for . . . he wasn't sure what, really.

Alex unenthusiastically followed his lead, inspecting the walls. She began beside the front door and made a slow circle along the room's four walls.

"I have a question no one's asking," she said, making conversation. "What makes those Upholders people think they have any right to do what they're doing with this barrier? I don't care if she was telling the truth about having the Prime Minister's approval. What is *ever* solved by putting up walls between you and the rest of the world?"

"Protection," Grant replied simply as he knelt to closely inspect the floor. "That's what they want. The world has become a very dangerous place, and living in fear is a fact of life now. They did the only thing they felt they could do to keep the danger at bay."

"But that's ridiculous," Alex replied. "If an earthquake or a tidal wave or some other horrible disaster comes to claim London, what can this barrier do to stop it?"

"Nothing, obviously," Grant replied. "But I think maybe they're more worried about the human quotient than anything nature might do. Look at what happened in L.A. The world is ready to explode. They want to keep their little corner of it out of the fray."

"It'll never work—*because* of the human quotient," she concluded.

A few silent minutes of searching later, she was done. She found Grant standing in the middle of the room shining his flashlight at the ceiling panels above them.

She stood beside him and looked up, shining her own flashlight on the ceiling.

"What do you see?" he asked.

"I don't know, water spots?" she replied, uncertain what he was wanting her to find. A white foam tile in the center of the ceiling space showed telltale brown stains.

With a wave of his hand in the direction of the entrance, Grant turned on the room's main light switch.

"Whoa, what are you doing?!" she said, lowering her voice. They had intentionally avoided turning on the lights to stave off unwanted attention; the room had two small windows on one side, which were completely uncovered by curtains or blinds.

"I don't think those are *water* stains," he said softly, still looking at the ceiling.

She looked up. In the soft white light of the fluorescents, the small stains on the center tile definitely looked several shades brighter than standard brown. In fact, they had a hue that was almost . . . *red*.

With a mere look, Grant raised the panel from its resting spot atop the thin metal tracks, but once it was floating in the crawl space above the ceiling, it tipped sideways unexpectedly and something fell.

Alex jumped back involuntarily.

"Ow," Grant mumbled. The falling object had grazed him on the way down. Something scratched him, causing a tiny trickle of blood to surface on the back of his hand.

They both looked at the object without saying anything. Grant forgot about the ceiling tile and it fell back into place above them, though ajar.

"Is that. . . ?" Alex started but couldn't finish.

"That's a human hand," Grant announced the obvious.

"Okay," Alex said, weariness spreading across her frame, "first of all . . . *ew*. Second, I know I'm your partner in the field, but don't even *think* about asking me to pick that up."

"Not necessary," Grant replied, studying the hand, which was frozen in a relaxed position. At his gaze, the hand floated up into the air between them.

"How did it scratch you?" Alex asked, noticing the angry mark on the back of his hand. "Fingernails?"

Grant examined the floating hand. "Guess so. Don't see anything else that could do it." The hand *did* boast some sharp-looking fingernails.

"Doesn't look very old," he observed. "Wait, look—it's the Secretum's brand or tattoo or whatever."

Alex leaned in just enough to see the tiny, asterisk-shaped mark on the hand's wrist, inches below the point where it had been severed. She fought back a wave of disgust.

"Yeah . . ." she said, taking a step back and looking away from the floating hand. "If you're waiting for me to be impressed, you've got me confused with Payton. He's the one who chops up stuff like this. For all we know, he may have done *this* one. Can we go now?"

"No," Grant replied, something about a disembodied hand was very familiar . . .

Of course!

"It's . . ." he said. "It's a *left* hand."

"Yeah. So?"

"The old man at the nursing home back in L.A.! He was missing his left hand!"

Alex looked at him as if he were crazy. "You don't seriously believe this severed hand we found in *London, England* belongs to some kooky old man in Los Angeles."

Grant caused the hand to turn over where it hovered between them. "I'm starting to believe it," he replied.

Alex followed his stare to the hand's open palm, which was now facing up.

Two words were cut into the flesh in dried, maroon-colored blood. Something razor-sharp had been used to carve them into the skin, and probably not long before the hand was removed, since the cuts hadn't had time to scab over.

The first word was *omega* and the second word was *prime*.

"If a member of the Secretum went to all the trouble of carving the words *omega prime* into his own hand," Grant said slowly, "then those must be pretty important words, wouldn't you say?"

Alex put a hand over her mouth, swallowing her supper for the second time.

"We got what we came for," he said, rubbing absently at where the hand had scratched him. He thought back to when Payton had once given him a similar scar on his other hand, the day they first met. "Let's go."

She closed her eyes and put a hand to her stomach. "Just tell me we're not taking that thing with us."

41

Ethan Cooke had a reputation within the Agency for attempting dangerous stunts. It wasn't an everyday thing for him, but when an investigation called for it, he didn't back down. He was about to attempt one that had the potential to put him in the history books.

Director Stevens had almost refused to give a green light for this particular scheme, but Guardian's disappearance inside London's mysterious barrier was an unacceptable tactical disadvantage. Not only was he off the grid, he might as well have been off the planet.

So at the eleventh hour Stevens had come through, pulling every last string at her disposal to coerce British authorities into helping Ethan carry out his plan. Which, he was forced to agree with her words from their last conversation, was a plan that could only be described as "altogether psychotic."

Then again, he mused, she probably just wanted to see him crash and burn once and for all. This time, maybe literally.

He stepped inside the subway train. There was only one car, specifically placed alone on the tracks for this mission, thanks to Stevens's contacts. The train's engine was behind the lonely car instead of in front, where it was normally.

Chief Inspector Walden, a local acquaintance from an international case or two Ethan had been involved with, met him inside the car and directed him to the special seat they'd set aside for him. Handcuffs were attached to the seat, a pair locked onto the rails on each side.

Ethan's heart fluttered with excitement as he sat and Walden locked the cuffs around his wrists.

"You sure I can't talk you out of this one, lad?" Walden asked in his thick Scottish accent.

Ethan smiled at him. "It'll work. I'll be incapacitated and unable to control my actions, and the car's movement will be completely maintained by inertia. There's no way to turn back."

Walden clearly wasn't convinced. He placed a locket around Ethan's left wrist. No ordinary locket, this one had a small metal box attached and rigged to open on a timer device.

"You just be sure not to drop these," Walden said, placing the keys to the cuffs inside the lockbox on Ethan's wrist. "Once I set this, it'll open after ten minutes, come what may."

Ethan nodded. His heart was pumping like mad, but he savored the feeling. He was ready.

Walden ordered the rest of his men out of the car. Everyone was to clear the area, with the sole exception of Walden himself, who would activate the engine car behind Ethan. As the other British officers vanished one by one, Walden leaned in closely to Ethan.

"You'll do well to remember two things. First, whoever or whatever you encounter on the other side of that barrier will have no notion that you're coming, so I wouldn't be expecting a warm welcome. And second, there's no evidence that once you're inside the barrier, your mental state will return to normal. But there's not much we can do about that bit, is there?"

Yeah, thanks for pointing that out.

"I'm ready," Ethan said, adjusting his sitting position.

"We'll have no way of knowing what happens to you," Walden replied, "so best of luck to you, laddie."

That was a sobering thought. No one would come to his rescue if this went badly. He was about to be cut off from the entire world.

Walden clicked the LED timer on the device on Ethan's hand, and it began counting down from *10:00*.

The Inspector exited the car, shut the sliding side door, and disappeared from Ethan's sight. Ethan waited impatiently for the car to begin moving. A slight bump from behind was followed by forward motion, building faster and faster.

They had agreed to start the train half a kilometer out from the edge of the barrier. That would give them enough time to build up some nice momentum on the passenger car, but still allow the engine, with Walden inside, to stop before hitting the barrier.

At least, that was the plan.

The running lights inside the tunnel started to flash by at a steady rate, and Ethan suddenly felt the loss of speed as the engine braked from behind. The engine was stopping already? That was fast.

His passenger car kept moving forward, but he estimated the car couldn't have been going more than thirty miles an hour, and it was starting to slow. Would it be enough?

He pulled instinctively at the cuffs, enjoying the rush provided by his immobilization inside the moving train. He glanced at the timer on the lockbox. *7:21* to go and counting.

The train approached a red flag that had been planted marking the spot where British agents first began feeling the fearful sensations associated with the barrier.

The flag passed, and Ethan was instantly filled with an overwhelming desire to get off of the train. The need to turn back consumed his mind.

Why had he done this? What was he thinking?!

Absolutely convinced that his life depended on not being on this train, he worked up a terrific sweat straining against the cuffs. He tried squeezing his hands through the holes, but they had been fastened too tight. He grabbed hold of the steel sidebars the handcuffs were attached to and tried to rip them free. But he couldn't get good leverage on the bars in his seated position. He stood, his arms pulled behind him, and he tried yanking the entire seat free from the car.

He *had* to get out! NOW!

Panic filled every pore of his body, and his wrists had ugly red marks on them. He noticed that the shining steel cuff on one of his wrists was covered in blood, and he grew clammy and cold. He'd cut a vein, the same way suicidals slice their wrists. He'd seen it enough times to know what it looked like.

And then just as fast as it had set in, the fearful sensation was gone. The car slowed to a crawl, and he plopped back into his seat, out of breath. The panic and fear subsided. He'd made it.

But his wrist was bleeding out, and the timer on the key mechanism still had more than five minutes left.

The adrenaline coursing through his body masked the lightheadedness that kept him from returning to his feet. He was already feeling weak, and the blood was gushing out of his wrist, all over his clothes and the seat, and even down to the floor.

He couldn't get free from the cuffs to apply pressure to stop the bleeding for another four and a half minutes.

And no one would be coming to help him.

Ever so slowly, the car drifted to a stop in the middle of a nondescript Underground tunnel. Westminster Station, the Tube station they'd been aiming for, was nowhere in sight. Adding insult to injury, the tunnel was powered down here and completely dark. Whatever was happening inside the barrier, maintaining electricity in the Underground wasn't a priority.

Ethan wanted to pass out. Oh, how he wanted to sleep so very much.

Instead, he blinked through the sensation, and a glimmer shone in his eyes.

Well, he smiled determinedly, *this will be a new personal best.*

42

Dawn was about an hour away when Grant and Alex followed the directions Fletcher had given them to what would be their new safe house. When they arrived, they found it to be a three-story flat about five blocks northwest of the river. Already furnished, the apartment had three bedrooms, two baths, a kitchen, dining space, and a large living room. A small coffee table in the center of the living room had already been claimed by Fletcher, who was using it as a pared-down, makeshift version of his computer workstation in L.A.

Grant wasn't sure how they had managed to acquire such a comfortable living space. Given the secrets he was keeping about both Lisa and Nora, there were any number of possibilities for making something like this happen. He decided he was happier not knowing the details.

"Did you find anything?" Morgan asked as soon as they'd walked in the door.

"Hand over fist," Alex replied unpleasantly. "Literally."

Grant seated himself next to his sister at the quaint dining room table. Morgan sat across from him, along with Fletcher, who'd brought one of his laptops along and typed on it while they talked. Alex sat at one end of the table and Lisa took the other end. She waited first to see if Daniel would take the remaining seat, but he preferred standing in the shadows at the back of the room. Grant assumed that Hector and Nora were asleep, or at least trying to sleep, elsewhere in the apartment.

"Omega Prime," Grant said without preamble. "That's what we found. Sound familiar?"

Morgan's eyes lit up. "More Greek," she said knowingly. "Yes. Yes, yes, of course . . ."

"I don't follow," Lisa spoke up.

"Substation Lambda Alpha," Morgan explained. "That was the name of the underground facility beneath the Wagner Building in Los Angeles. 'Lambda' and 'Alpha' are both Greek letters. As are 'Tau' and 'Epsilon', from the door Payton found in Jerusalem. 'Omega' is also a Greek letter."

"'Omega Prime' must be the name of another one of these substations," Grant concluded, cutting to the chase.

"Also consider," Morgan went on, "that 'Omega' is the last letter of the Greek alphabet. It adds a note of finality or supremacy to the title. And the inclusion of the word 'Prime' is also likely a connotation of added importance or significance. We could be looking at something a bit more critical than just another substation."

Morgan paused, rubbing at her temples. A migraine, Grant surmised. She suffered from them frequently. But she was also thinking something through, adding another layer to the secrets she was keeping. Finally, she nodded to herself.

"You were expecting to find something like this," Grant stated.

"After a fashion," Morgan replied thoughtfully. "I had a theory that this 'repository' Payton found evidence of might be a collection not of books or information—but of *people*. Secretum of Six people. I think what we're talking about here—this Substation Omega Prime . . . it could be their primary base of operations. It could be *the* central location where their key players live and breathe and operate from. And if that's the case—"

"We have to find it," Grant finished for her. He understood now why she had kept this particular theory to herself; the ramifications were too big to get everyone's hopes up. "So where is it?" he asked. "I mean, we're assuming it's underground somewhere, right?"

"Highly likely," Morgan replied. "I've given this considerable thought, and I think we can narrow it down a bit."

"How?" Alex asked, leaning forward.

"Grant's grandfather told him that the Secretum had been 'waiting for millennia for the coming of the Bringer.' That means, rather obviously, that the Secretum has been in *existence* for millennia. Let's assume for a moment that they've been operating out of the same location for all these thousands of years. What would *that* tell us?"

"That this Substation Omega Prime," Fletcher spoke up, getting there faster than everyone else, "would be in a place of specifically *ancient* significance."

"Yes, precisely," Morgan replied. "Global civilization as we know it today did not exist thousands of years ago. An organization with the kinds of resources that the Secretum has at its disposal would have needed to remain in a fairly centralized location to the smaller civilizations of the time. Which means that wherever this substation is, we'll find it beneath a place that's been populated by mankind for thousands of years. For all that time, it's been part of the known world."

"Meaning they have to be in Europe or Asia," Julie added, catching on.

"Or Africa?" Alex offered.

"Yes," Morgan said. "So we've narrowed down the possibilities already. Next, we must consider the Secretum's affinity for prophecies and ancient objects such as the Dominion Stone. The Stone, this ancient location, the Secretum's obsession with manipulation . . . it's all about one thing."

"Power," Fletcher concluded.

"They would select a location of great symbolic power for their headquarters," Morgan nodded, concluding her theory. "Either a symbol of power or a physical location where power is believed to subsist. Possibly both."

Grant and the others digested this. "So, we're looking for someplace ancient and significant for being a seat of great power . . ."

"What do you mean—like the Bermuda Triangle?" Lisa interjected.

"Right line of thinking," Morgan replied, "but let's assume for the moment that they'd build their headquarters in someplace a little more accessible than miles beneath the ocean floor."

Brows furrowed all around the table. Alex spoke first.

"What about Stonehenge? It's *seriously* ancient, and it's thought to be some sort of temple or observatory, right? Wouldn't that be considered a 'place of power'?"

"I think," Morgan replied thoughtfully, "we can rule out Stonehenge. Given the number of excavations that have been done there and all the tourists that have trampled its sod, it's likely safe to assume that if anything more were there to find, it would have been uncovered already."

Alex frowned.

"But you're on the right track," Morgan added encouragingly. "I'm thinking of places like the Great Pyramid at Giza, Petra in Jordan, Mount Olympus, Mount Parnassus in Greece, the spring at Lourdes in France, Newgrange in Ireland, Teotihuacan in Mexico, India's Kailasa Temple, the Nazca Lines of Peru, or Machu Picchu, Easter Island—"

"I thought it wouldn't be anywhere in the Western world," Julie interrupted, the college professor in her coming out. She massaged a mug of coffee as she continued. "You said it had to be someplace that existed in the center of ancient society. Civilizations existed in the Americas then, but they were hardly at the heart of the global community."

Morgan shrugged. "Yes, probably not in the Americas. But it never hurts to be thorough."

"What's Mount Parnassus?" Grant asked.

"Ever heard of the Oracle at Delphi?" Morgan replied. "Mount Parnassus is where she made her predictions, though she owed more to the hallucinogenic ethylene gas emanating from a fissure in the rock there than to any supernatural conduit."

"Sounds interesting, maybe we should look into it," Fletcher remarked off-handedly, glancing briefly at Grant. "Didn't a lot of people seek her out for . . . romantic advice?"

Alex kicked him under the table. He flinched but covered it by continuing to type on his computer.

"Maybe it's beneath the Vatican," Alex offered, half-joking, in an attempt to change the subject.

"Actually, I wouldn't rule out *any* historic sites around Rome," Morgan rebutted. "From the Coliseum to the Parthenon, ancient Rome was rife with locales of significant power and influence." She sighed and then settled her shoulders. "We can't afford to waste time guessing like this; it could go on forever. If we want to *find* Omega Prime, it will require access to records we can't reach through the Internet or any other usual channels. Records that stretch back hundreds, even thousands of years into human history. Fortunately, such records *can* be found nearby, right here inside the barrier."

"You serious?" Fletcher asked with a single cocked eyebrow. "Never thought I'd see the day . . ."

"Desperate times," Morgan replied. "We'll leave in a few hours, after everyone has a chance to catch a few winks."

"What are you two talking about?" Lisa asked.

"The Library," Morgan replied, resolute.

"*The* Library?" Grant asked, surprised. "The *London* Library? That's the place where you used to work, before you were Shifted, isn't it? Wait, didn't you tell me the London Library was *where* you were Shifted?"

"I swore I'd never return." Morgan nodded grimly. "But it's time."

Barely any light illuminated the drab alleyway, making it even more difficult for Payton to check for traps. A recent rainstorm had left the ground wet; it reflected moonlight back at his face from the otherwise dark pavement.

He held one hand on the hilt of his sword at all times, prepared for anything. The alley may have looked abandoned, but Payton knew better than to trust his eyes.

He walked through narrow passages, following the signs that had been left for him. The signs in question were nothing more than scratches against old buildings, shutters, and doors, but Payton recognized them all too well. The buildings on either side of him were several stories tall—old storage facilities for moving grain, meat, and other commodities.

A barely perceptible scratch on an overhang above his head caught his attention.

This would be the place.

His eyes fell upon the door behind the post. It was hingeless, instead sliding on rusted bearings, and Payton flung it aside.

The interior of the building had a high ceiling with catwalks two stories above. The ground level was cordoned off with thatched wire fencing. Only moonlight cast any shadows.

But Payton knew he was not alone.

"You've been sticking your nose in places it doesn't belong," called a voice from the blackness. "A propensity you've long had, as I recall."

Payton didn't bother looking up, though his instincts told him exactly where on the catwalk the voice had originated.

"Yes, well I learned from the best, didn't I?" he responded calmly.

He heard footsteps clanging against the catwalk, and then the footsteps were descending. Payton could only assume there were stairs somewhere up there.

"Hello, Payton."

Payton turned; his opponent had managed to appear behind him. His body stood silhouetted in the still-open doorway. His silver hair gleamed in the moonlight, his outline formed by a knee-length trench coat.

In a flash, Payton had withdrawn his sword and was holding it in a defensive position.

"Devlin," Payton acknowledged, noting a very important accessory that Devlin wore. "The ruling council has placed you in charge?"

"I am the Secretum of Six," Devlin replied, repeating an ancient recitation. Fitting to their location, Devlin had chosen an Italian accent today. "In all matters, I speak and act on behalf of they who serve the Great Task. I am their hand. I live in the in-between and the everlasting. Thus shall I serve, until my dying breath."

Payton was unimpressed. "If you have not summoned me here to put an end to your existence, then you're about to suffer a grave disappointment."

"I thought we should have a chat," Devlin replied, clasping his hands in front. "Yes, I lied to you. The Secretum lied to you. For years, you were trained and tasked to carry out our purposes under false pretenses. I know how much you must hate me for this—"

"You really don't," Payton replied, his teeth clenched tightly.

Devlin allowed a courteous nod. "Fair to say. But I have to believe that somewhere beneath all that anger there is still *some* modicum of respect for your former mentor?"

Payton didn't reply. He merely tightened his grip on the hilt of his sword. His breath came out in hot wisps of air.

"Whether you like it or not," Devlin went on, "you have served the Secretum's interests, and served them well. So we are offering you a chance at a reward."

"I want nothing that passes through your hands."

"It's not a material *thing* I came to offer you," Devlin calmly replied. "I simply want you to know that it is not too late. You can still take your rightful place as a servant of the Secretum. You could be a great military leader among our people. Come back to the fold, and all will be forgiven."

Payton didn't take time to consider the offer. He merely spat on the ground, very close to Devlin's high-priced shoes.

"You went to all this trouble to get me here so you could tell me I can *come back*? Why am *I* so important to you? I thought your interest was in the Bringer." Payton found that he still had trouble speaking that title without anger boiling in him inwardly. They had trained him to destroy the Bringer, and they had done their jobs very, very well.

"We each have our own agenda. *You* wouldn't have come all this way without one of your own," Devlin countered.

"I don't have to know what your end game is," Payton replied slowly, "to know that you will never succeed. You have seen with your own eyes what Grant Borrows has become. He has not conformed to your plans for him. He is charting his own destiny, free from your influence."

"Is that what you think?" Devlin replied, unperturbed. "More to the point, is that what *he* thinks?"

"It was all for nothing, you know," Payton continued. "All your meticulous planning, all those thousands of years of scheming and plotting. Antiquated ideas by an organization that outlived its usefulness a very long time ago. For your own sakes, let this thing go. Grant will *never* do your bidding."

Devlin let out a gust of air that was akin to a laugh. "He's made a believer out of *you*? The great Thresher himself is now one of the faithful? Then the Bringer is *truly* without limits!"

The tip of Payton's sword was suddenly pressed against Devlin's chin. Devlin made no display of alarm at this but held perfectly still.

"Going to kill me, Payton?" Devlin asked. "And where did you *get* that lovely silver weapon you cling to so tightly? Where did you learn those lethal skills for which you are so well known? From us. From the Secretum. From *me*. I know you better than you know yourself. You are neither blind nor foolish. And I say your part in all of this is not so resolved as you wish me to believe."

"Do not summon me again," Payton warned, circling Devlin but holding his sword under the elder man's chin as he moved, "unless you are prepared to kill me. I vow in blood," the sword pricked the skin beneath Devlin's chin, "nothing less than my death will keep me from destroying you. Whatever you have planned, I will not rest until it is undone."

44

"The London Library is not like any library you're familiar with in the States," Morgan studiously explained as she, Alex, and Grant exited their taxi at the center of a large square surrounded by buildings. Grant had noted signs designating this as "St. James's Square."

They walked toward the northwest corner, in the direction of a sprawling white building with majestic columns that reminded Grant of the White House or the Supreme Court. The building appeared to have been added onto many times, expanding outward in numerous directions.

They'd decided that morning that taking everyone along would be too conspicuous, and their best chance of getting inside would be with whatever minor disguises they could quickly pull together, used by a small number of team members. Morgan's presence was mandatory; she was the only one who knew what they were looking for and where to find it. Grant of course went as well, and Alex had refused to leave his side since Jerusalem.

"This Library is a self-sustaining, non-profit organization, independent of government influence," Morgan was saying in the maddeningly precise tone she used whenever reciting something from her flawless memory, "and it is not open to the public. A paid membership is required just to get in the door."

"Why here?" Alex interrupted.

"Sorry?"

"You said this would be the place where we can find records that may lead us to this big 'Omega Prime' HQ thing. Why will that be here?"

Morgan cleared her throat. She was having a hard time disguising her enthusiasm for sharing her intimate knowledge about this place. But there was an edge to her voice as well.

She experienced the greatest trauma of her life in this building, Grant reminded himself. *And she hasn't been back in fourteen-some-odd years.*

I'd be antsy too.

"You're about to enter the largest independent lending library in the world," she replied. "It contains over one million volumes, some dating back as far as the sixteenth century. There are few places on earth where you can find older or more exhaustive historical records.

"I brought enough money to purchase memberships for the three of us. I read recently that a major renovation is under way to modernize the Library, but in the meantime don't be surprised if it feels a little . . . aged."

From the southeast corner of St. James's Square, Ethan watched as Grant, Alex, and a woman with white hair opened wide the doors to the London Library and entered.

He'd tourniqueted his bloodied wrist, but red soaked the strip of fabric he'd torn off his undershirt. He shivered in cold sweats, his skin pale and clammy, and he felt nearly delirious. But he couldn't risk going to local authorities or doctors, alerting them to his infiltration of the barrier. After all, how was he to know who could be trusted, who wasn't in the pocket of whoever had put up the barrier? It was too risky, so he made do alone.

The bandage was dry now at least, meaning the bleeding had stopped. But he'd lost too much blood before he could escape the sub-way car, and had nearly blacked out several times. Adrenaline—his drug of choice—was all that kept him going.

He'd managed a few hours' sleep last night when he could walk no farther, under a heavy cluster of trees in St. James's Park. After buying some food from a small shop, he landed a break. Pretending to be a homeless man, he overheard two policemen talking about "some sort of business with the superhumans that happened last night" on the Victoria Embankment, directly across from the Eye.

From there, Ethan interviewed a few locals and was able to track the white-haired woman from Borrows's group to a flat not far from the Mall, which itself was near Buckingham Palace. There he'd waited, picking up the homeless routine again, until Grant Borrows himself had emerged with the girl, Alex, and the white-haired woman that morning. A cab ride later, and he was fairly certain he'd managed to follow them to their destination undetected.

He scanned his surroundings, considering his options. Was it time to make a move? Here, now? It's not like he was operating at his top capacity, but he'd suffered worse injuries than this.

Negative, he could hear Director Stevens's voice in his head saying. *Find out what they're up to.*

They're in an enclosed space, he replied to his internal monologue. *I may never get a better chance.*

Absolutely not, he knew Stevens would reply. *You will maintain cover until you have ascertained Guardian's purpose for being in London.*

He searched the skies, looking for what wasn't there. Those were the strict orders she'd given him before he'd entered the barrier the day before. Stevens was calling him three to four times a day now to check on his progress.

Or at least, she had until he'd crossed the barrier, where all communication with the outside world was cut off.

He looked again at the Library entrance, and despite his beleaguered physical condition, his adrenaline surged once more at the thought of Borrows *this close* to his grasp.

Too bad you can't stop me, he thought about his superior.

He cut diagonally across the small park in the middle of the Square, on a straight-line course for the Library.

Morgan wasn't kidding, Grant decided after they were granted permission to enter.

The Library didn't just look old. It looked like Noah might have built it after parking the Ark.

It was as if the modern world outside had passed them by and time were standing still inside this cramped, hallowed space. Dozens of other patrons browsed the aisles or searched card catalogs or small computer stations for their treasured prize, and all maintained a hushed reverence.

Row after narrow row of books stretched from floor to ceiling, reminding Grant of Morgan's dangerously stacked piles of books at the old asylum. Musty and drab, the majority of the building's interior light came in through tall windows. It smelled of leather bindings and decaying paper.

Morgan wasted no time as she led the way, winding through the ultra-narrow aisles, up stairs made of rickety metal gratings, and into an area she said was dedicated to historical texts. Her experienced fingers traced the tomes as they turned down an aisle, and she produced three gigantic volumes filled with weathered brown maps that looked like something Columbus might have once used. The pages were inside of clear sleeves, protecting these precious artifacts from human touch.

Grant, Morgan, and Alex seated themselves in cushy brown leather seats near a far wall and began slowly turning the pages.

"There's something else we should check, as long as we're here," Morgan said absently.

"What's that?" Grant replied.

"Sorry," Morgan said, snapping out of an internal thought. "I meant 'here' as in London. The British Museum is rumored to hold a secret repository, off-limits to the public, called—believe it or not—'the Secretum.' It's believed to contain mystical artifacts from ancient cultures."

Grant's curiosity was piqued at that.

"Don't get too excited," Morgan went on. "It's probably nothing, and widely regarded as an urban myth. Still, it's worth looking into, just in case."

"Is the Museum inside the barrier or outside?" Alex asked.

"Inside," Morgan replied.

"That's a relief," Alex said sincerely. Then she shook her head irritably, clearing cobwebs. "Ech, I still can't get past this feeling like I never want to leave London."

"Right there with you," Grant comforted her. "We'll look into the Museum later, if we get a chance. Let's focus on one thing at a time."

"What are we looking for, again?" Alex whispered.

"The symbol of the Secretum," Morgan replied. "The asterisk-like shape I showed you back in L.A. You hold in your hands some of the oldest surviving maps in existence. If any of them contain the symbol, then that spot is almost certainly a place of great importance to the Secretum and could quite possibly be the Omega Prime facility itself."

Grant paused flipping through the pages. "So we're looking for their mark on maps drawn by hand that date back to hundreds of years ago? Do you honestly think the Secretum had enough influence in society that long ago to manage something like that?"

"Do you honestly think they didn't?" Morgan replied.

Grant didn't want to believe it but wouldn't be able to prove her wrong until they'd searched every map and document on Morgan's to-do list. So he returned his attention to the volume in his lap.

Ten minutes passed, and nothing.

Grant was already growing bored. "So tell me something," he said softly. "Is it *after* we've found this Substation Omega Prime that you're finally going to share your big secrets with the rest of us, or sometime before?"

"This is not all for nothing, Grant," she explained, slightly ruffled that once again she was being chastised for keeping her secrets. "You think I *enjoy* keeping you in the dark? Do you think it's *easy* for me to be back here in this—"

Her voice faded, and her complexion turned stone white.

Grant and Alex followed her gaze twenty feet away in the direction of a smartly dressed woman in her late forties. She was returning a book to a nearby shelf, oblivious to their presence. When she was finished with her task, she briskly returned to wherever she'd come from.

"What?" Grant whispered urgently. "Who was that?"

"That . . . was the head librarian of the London Library," Morgan replied, still in shock, facing the corner where the woman had turned and disappeared.

"So you know her?" Grant replied, relaxing back into his seat.

She faced him, her complexion pale, her features gaunt. "I *am* her."

"HE IS CLOSE. TOO CLOSE."

"Agreed. He could discover everything."

"And so he must, before the end. Perhaps this is part of his journey."

"I concur. Don't let your fears guide you, my friends. It was destiny that brought him to London, just as destiny will bring him here."

"But what if Morgan leads him to the Library? Our operative in London will be flying blind because of this accursed barrier. What if he finds the—?"

"*Enough.* It does not matter *what* he finds. It is all part of a larger plan—a plan much larger and older than any of us. Too much has been set into motion. It cannot be stopped now."

"There is another matter. The Bringer's companions. They will be required in the end, but the Bringer's path must ultimately be walked alone. The ones who surround him know too much. They are becoming a liability."

"Then the time to act is now."

45

Grant Borrows awoke on the ground.

A sharp yelp roused him and Grant was instantly aware of three things. First, he was flat on his back, staring into the black snout of an imposing bronze horse statue, which sneered down at him from above. Second, the sky behind the statue was a dismal gray while in his periphery he saw the vivid greenery of trees on all sides. Third, what startled him awake was that he was holding someone's wrist.

Someone's wrist that didn't belong.

Rolling his neck to the left, Grant came face-to-face with a boy who couldn't have been more than fifteen. Bright eyes offset shaggy blond locks, which framed his oval face in a messy sort of way. A faded polo shirt was untucked over a pair of jeans that looked like their best days were long behind them.

"You *are* him!" the boy exclaimed, eyes as wide with wonder as they were with fear. Grant turned loose of the boy's wrist and slowly sat up.

What? Where. . . ?

He was in the center of what looked like a very small park, sur-rounded on all sides by trees, a circumference of parked cars outside of them. Beyond the vehicles, a quadrant of buildings loomed, enclosing the park in a box-like perimeter.

The buildings were very old. Historic, even.

A dark-colored statue of a man riding a horse stood atop a white cement pedestal on his right, opposite the boy.

Grant's recognition of it was vague. He was sure he'd been here before, and he was quite certain he was still in London.

But how long. . . ?

And why was I asleep out here in the open?

"Who're you?" Grant rasped, his voice dry, his thoughts spinning in too many directions at once.

Why can't I remember anything?

His heart rate was increasing with each new possibility that occurred to him.

"Didn't mean nothing by it, man!" the boy cried, tossing Grant's wallet back to him. "Just wanted to see if you had a real name, is all."

But Grant wasn't looking at the wallet. His eyes were still on the boy's wrist, which was bright red where Grant's hand had been.

He lifted one hand and found blood. His other hand was bloody too . . . and there were similarly dried stains scattered across his clothing . . .

Yet he felt no pain.

A chill stopped his pulse.

This blood was not his. And it wasn't the boy's, either.

Reflexively, he reached out with his mind and touched the minds of the Loci, checking off his friends, one-by-one. The process was a mere flash, lasting less than a second, and his heart skipped a beat when he felt it.

Morgan was missing from his internal radar. Her entire presence gone without a trace. As if there were a hole where she had been.

No!!

His eyes stubbornly refused to focus on anything but the blood covering his hands as his heart raced and the grass beneath him seemed to melt away.

Was the blood Morgan's? What happened to her? And what about Alex? He had a faint impression of her, but it was as if she'd gone blind. He could only see her surroundings, but it was as if she were surrounded by nothing. He couldn't even tell if she was conscious or not.

For the first time in a long time, icy cold fear gripped his heart.

What have I done?

He stood slowly, blood swimming in his head. There was an odd throbbing pain on the side of his neck, and he massaged it. "What's your name?" he asked the boy.

"Stephan."

"What day is it, Stephan?"

"Saturday," the boy replied.

Saturday!?

It was Thursday when he'd entered the Library with Alex and Morgan. Forty-eight hours, gone, just like that.

What's happening to me?

"You know who I am, Stephan?"

"Of course! I mean yes, yes sir."

"Then run straight home, right now. Tell anyone about this, and I'll *know*," Grant said in his most threatening voice. "Am I clear?"

"Entirely," Stephan replied with big eyes. He turned and ran, as instructed.

Grant took a moment to get his bearings. *The Library*.

He found its familiar outline behind the trees and began to walk. Soon he was outside the park and crossing the street that ran between the park and the outlying buildings.

What was the last thing he remembered? He remembered himself, Morgan, and Alex entering the Library two days ago, searching through very old records, until they encountered . . .

The head librarian. Who was really Morgan. Or rather, Morgan's old self, the person she'd been before the Shift. Why would that person still be here, fourteen years later? Why maintain the façade for all these years?

"Grant? What's happened to you?" said a voice from behind.

Grant spun. The man who stood there, face pale and weary, was unfamiliar. He looked sick, looked as though he might fall over his own feet, in fact.

"It's Ethan," the man explained as if Grant should already know this. "Ethan Cooke? I helped you out yesterday. . . ."

Hearing the voice again finally clicked it in place for Grant. "You're that FBI agent I met in Los Angeles. Didn't I warn you to stay away from me? How do you know my name?"

"You don't remember?" Ethan asked, suddenly concerned. "What did they do to you?"

He made a move forward, but Grant matched his step backward.

"Grant, we met yesterday afternoon. I helped you stay hidden while you were on the run."

"I don't know what you're talking about," Grant replied.

"You have to trust me, Grant. You already decided you *do* trust me; they just made you forget. We've got to get you out of sight. You're covered in blood; you're not even wearing a disguise. If anyone sees you like this . . ."

"Don't," Grant warned, raising his hand threateningly. It was then that he noticed the angry red marks on Ethan's wrists, and a bandage covering one that was soaked in blood.

"Grant, listen to me," Ethan said with slow, labored breaths. "They've erased your memory—I don't know how. But I met you yesterday afternoon, just outside the Library, over on the other side of the building. You were weakened, and I offered to help you, protect you. We were pursued, but they got the drop on us. I wanted to earn your trust and help you and your people. I have to keep up appearances that I'm hunting you, in case anyone is watching, but I told you that you have a friend now inside the FBI. You really don't remember any of this?"

Grant shifted, suddenly nervous. "You know about Drexel, then."

"I know he got off easy," Ethan replied with a knowing look. "And I know his death was not at your hands. Your addition to the Most Wanted List was not my doing, and I tried to prevent it, but the higher-ups are too paranoid about you and what you can do. They haven't seen what I've seen."

Grant stared the FBI agent down, not sure what to make of all this.

"Normally I wouldn't have been able to approach you so openly," Ethan went on, "but the barrier around London created an opportunity too good to pass up. You don't have to believe that I want to help you, but believe that you have enemies that have orchestrated this situation and are preparing right now to take advantage of it. We *need* to get you out of here.

"Check your jacket pocket," said Ethan. "I saw you put my business card in there last night."

Grant found the business card exactly where Ethan said it would be. "If you're trying to manipulate me—"

"I'm not. But *they* are manipulating you. Again."

"They who?"

"You know better than I do," Ethan replied with confidence. "And if you don't get away from here quick, they're going to quarterback this twisted little game all the way to the end zone."

"Fine, I'm going inside," Grant replied, and he turned toward the Library.

"You're going back in *there*?" Ethan cried. "Again? That's the *last* place you should be right now! Maybe I should come with—"

"*No*. The Library is the last thing I remember. So it's the first place I'll start. You stay away from me. I don't know you and I don't trust you."

"You're playing right into their hands . . ."

"We'll see."

46

A library worker near the door tried to stop Grant from entering. "Sir, you mustn't come in here looking like that! I shall summon the police at once if you take one more step."

Grant didn't look in the man's direction. "You do that."

Instead, he looked around, searching for . . .

There.

Not very far from the entrance, he approached the main desk. "I need to see the head librarian. Now."

The young girl seated there hadn't looked up from her computer workstation as he spoke. She did so now and flinched in alarm at his appearance. "Right," she mumbled, taking that as her cue to get as far away from Grant as possible.

"I expected you earlier in the day," said a familiar-sounding voice, even though he couldn't remember when he'd heard it last.

He turned. Standing over his shoulder was the woman Morgan had identified a few days ago as her former self—the face and body she had worn before the Shift, before she and Morgan had traded lives. He was unsurprised to note that the symbol of the Secretum was tattooed on her wrist.

But that didn't compute, just as it hadn't two days ago when Morgan first said it. All of the individuals whom the Ringwearers had been Shifted into had been volunteers from the Secretum's acolytes. "Husks," his grandfather called them, "and nothing more."

Then again, Morgan was the first to undergo the Shift. Maybe the rules weren't put into place until after her time. What if the person she'd traded lives with was *more* than a husk?

"Please, step into my office," the woman said with impeccable, business-like precision. Her clipped, fast gait forced him to keep up as she led the way to her office—a tiny room on the first floor with a single floor to ceiling window. Grant noted that the room was on the "far side" of the building from St. James's Square—which was where Ethan, the FBI agent, claimed they'd met.

The librarian circled the room and sat behind her desk. Grant stepped inside but refused to sit.

"Who are you?" he growled.

"I imagine you're wondering where your two friends are? What's become of them?" she pondered with a tilt of her head.

Grant didn't answer. There was no need. She was holding all of the cards here, and they both knew it.

"As you've no doubt gathered, some . . . events transpired after you and your companions first arrived here at the Library two days ago." She laced her fingers together, elbows resting on the desktop. "I wonder how far the most powerful man alive would go to retrieve memories that have been stolen from him?"

"You're not going to have to wonder very long," Grant said, stepping fully inside. But the moment he did, he felt light-headed. He landed in the seat in front of the librarian's desk with a flat thud and felt like he might throw up.

"Careful now," the librarian warned him in a low, throaty tone, though her posture and seating position never changed. "You probably shouldn't have gotten to your feet as quickly as you did. I imagine you're still weak from the . . . ordeal."

"What ordeal?" he asked angrily, even though he was looking at his feet, willing his body to not feel sick.

"I am the only person alive who knows the full extent of it. Only I know what happened to you and your friends over the last two days," the librarian said. "So if you wish to know the truth, you will do exactly as I tell you."

So. Ethan was right. The whole thing *was* a setup. Whoever this woman was, she knew *everything* and had orchestrated this entire situation to manipulate Grant into doing her a favor.

"I'm not moving from this spot—and neither are you—until you tell me where they are," he rasped, clutching his temples, which had begun to throb.

A hint of a smile tugged at her mouth. "You're assuming they're even *alive*. That blood on your hands? It belongs to one of them."

Grant looked up at her at last. If he wasn't fighting the urge to pass out, he would've already lurched across the desk and clasped his hands around her neck. . . . He found the mental image extremely satisfying, but he closed his eyes and breathed deeply enough to calm down and force away the desire.

"Let's be clear," the librarian said, sitting back and crossing her arms. "I am offering one thing and one thing only: to return the memories that have been taken from you. Those memories will provide the answers you seek, but after the memories are yours again, our business will be concluded."

Who *was* this woman?

She worked for the Secretum, that much was obvious.

But holding my memories . . . for what? Ransom? Who does she think she is?

"I imagine the ambiguity, the not knowing if they still draw breath," she said, "must be eating you alive. Kill me now, and you'll never know the truth."

"What do you want me to do?" he bit out, beginning to regain some of his strength.

"I wish you to accomplish two tasks," her calculating voice explained, "and in exchange, you'll get your memories back. Something requires fixing. And someone requires killing."

"I don't kill."

"Not my problem. The moral high ground always sounds good on paper, but this is the real world. Will you use your tremendous powers to take a life if it means saving those you care most about? I must admit, I'm eager to find out."

"You're not here by coincidence, are you?" Grant shot back, still light-headed but fighting it hard. "Your being here is about a lot more than coercing me into doing favors for you. And it may not even have anything to do with Morgan's past. It's this *place*. You're an operative of the Secretum, planted here for a reason. So what is it about this library that has kept you here for fourteen years?"

She ignored him. "My terms are thus. I want the barrier cutting London off from the rest of the world removed. Gone. And I want the prime minister dead, as he authorized its construction. His death will serve as a warning that nothing like this is to ever happen again. Both tasks are to be completed by sundown today, or no deal."

Grant examined her. "You're cut off from the Secretum inside the barrier, aren't you? That must really cramp your style."

If Grant's statement ruffled her, she didn't show it. "Sundown, Mr. Borrows. It's already midday. You should get a move on. One more thing . . . the rest of your traveling companions are to know nothing of this. If any of them find out I exist, or what I've assigned you to do, then the deal is off."

47

"Mr. Guardian, sir?"

It was the boy again. Stephan. He stood just outside the Library door.

"I know you said to go home, and I started to . . . But I felt guilty."

Grant walked beside the boy as they descended the stairs together. "Guilty about what?" he asked, distracted by other thoughts. He checked his watch. It was just after twelve noon. He had only seven or eight hours until sundown.

He kept trying to reach out to his friends. Why couldn't he sense Morgan anymore?

Maybe she really is dead.

"I took some pictures of you while you were asleep, and I was planning to post them on the message boards. But I just wanted you to know I deleted them, so if any pictures of you asleep turn up online, they didn't come from me, right? So me and my family are safe, right?"

Grant sighed, closing his eyes. "I'm sorry for threatening you earlier. I was . . . I didn't mean it."

Stephan smiled. "'S okay. You have to face things that ordinary people like me never even dream about."

Grant shook his head in confusion. "Slow down. You said something about message boards? What, are you one of those fan club people?"

Stephan smiled brightly. "Yessir, member in standing for over a month now. You're my favorite superhero."

"I'm not a superhero," Grant said wearily, then he stopped walking.

"Wait a minute. How did you find me in the first place?"

Stephan swallowed visibly. "Well, the club has a network of 'Guardian spotters,' see. Somebody posted that they thought they saw you climbing out of the river a few days ago. It being Saturday and all, this is the first chance I've been able to have a look around on my own, see if I could get a glimpse of you in action. Just about stumbled over you while I was walking through the square."

Grant took this in slowly, his thoughts still consumed elsewhere. An idea formed in his mind, and he retrieved a bloodied, crumpled business card from a jacket pocket.

"Anyway," Stephan was saying, "I wanted to give you something."

The boy handed him a spiral-bound notebook. Grant flipped through the pages and discovered dozens of pencil sketches of himself, in majestic, comic book-like spreads. There were action shots, superhero poses, images of Grant rescuing people in danger—he was looking at more than a boy's childhood fantasies. This was evidence of pure, childlike devotion.

He backpedaled. "I can't accept this," he said.

"No, you have to!" Stephan protested. "I don't need it anymore; I finally got to meet you in person. You're the greatest hero ever. And I got to *meet* you! I don't need anything else."

Grant was genuinely touched. He accepted the book while tussling the boy's blonde locks, smiling at him. It had never occurred to him just how much he needed a reminder of who and what he was, especially since Jerusalem and now this disorienting memory loss business.

"Thanks, kiddo," he said. "I've got to go . . . people to save, criminals to stop. You understand."

"Oh yeah, of course!" Stephan said. "Go!"

"See you around," Grant said, and then he was off to save the day. Or kill the Prime Minister. Whatever came first.

Grant searched the ground for nothing as he listened to Ethan talk, his ear pressed to his phone. He heard every word Ethan said, laying out the hard facts on the difficulties he was about to face, but Grant focused on his own thoughts.

Could he pull this off? What if he couldn't? What if killing the

Prime Minister was really the only way to ever find out what happened to Morgan and Alex?

No. He wouldn't accept that they could just vanish forever. Whatever had happened to them, wherever they were, he would find them. No matter what.

"This is a lot to ask," Ethan said on the other end of the phone line.

"Yes it is, Agent Cooke," Grant replied, playing with Ethan's business card between his fingers. He spun in place at the center of St. James's Square park, a plan taking shape. "But you offered to help, and this is one thing I can't do."

"I'm not sure I can either," Ethan muttered.

"I don't even know you," Grant reminded him. "You want *in*? You want my trust? Make this happen."

Ethan hesitated. "Even if I had the full resources of the FBI at my disposal, I don't know if I could make *this* happen."

"Then you're no use to me," Grant said with a coldness that surprised even himself. "This is the size of the playing field that I'm on. The stakes are always this big. If you can't do *this*, you won't ever be able to help us in any way that matters."

"Okay, all right," Ethan surrendered. "I'll pull every string I can. I'll be in touch."

Grant snapped his phone shut and scratched absently at the scar he'd suffered when the severed hand fell out of the ceiling a few days ago. It was strange how much the scar itched. He glanced down at it and saw that the scar had scabbed over, but the surrounding skin was deeply discolored. An angry red covered the entire back of his hand, as if he'd come in contact with an irritant, like poison ivy.

The scar itself wasn't really that big. It was a curved line, maybe two inches in length. And it itched like crazy.

He was scratching at it again when a terrible thought entered his mind.

"The end shall be marked by a scar revealing man's deepest hollow."

Could it be? The third Unholy Marker . . . was an actual *mark* on his skin? Was he branded now, as the Bringer?

From a hidden instinct, buried deep inside himself . . . he feared that this was no ordinary scar.

48

Grant closed his eyes and stood perfectly still, stretching out his senses. He needed to find the Upholders, and he needed to do it now.

He saw them in his mind. They were in some sort of attic. But where was this attic? What building was it in? The barrier surrounded a highly populated area that had to be at least a hundred square kilometers. There could be thousands of buildings with attics in that space.

Where. . . ? Grant concentrated so hard he began to sweat. *Where are you? How do I find you?*

This was probably a waste of time, the voice of doubt told him. He bore down harder, trying with all his might to get a sense of distance. He'd never used his connection to the Ringwearers in this way before, and he had no reason to believe it would work.

But it was all he had to go on.

Frustrated and tired, he plopped to a cross-legged sitting position on the grass and sat back against the cement base of the statue in the middle of the square. A quick glance at his watch—twelve forty-two in the afternoon—and he closed his eyes again. He began a breathing exercise that Daniel had taught him to calm his speeding pulse, and he was reminded of the last experiment he and Daniel had attempted in L.A. He never had a chance to go all the way with it. . . .

Okay, he thought. *If I'm going to do this, let's not rush it.*

One by one, he isolated all of the sounds surrounding him and cut them off in his mind. Birds chirping. Breeze blowing. Car engines.

Shoes clomping on nearby pavement. He shut them out, until all was silent.

He captured an image of the Upholders in his mind, but instead of merely peering at them as if through a hazy window pane, he tried to move within that space and go *inside* the image.

On his first attempt, he lost their image entirely and had to start over again, calming his heart, cutting off his immediate senses, and capturing a sharp picture of them in his mind.

The four of them were sitting around a card table in a makeshift kitchen, having what looked like a discussion of some sort. He couldn't hear what they were saying, but there was much gesturing and lips moving. He held the image of them there for a very long time, and it became sharper as time passed.

There really are *only four of them.*

So who is the fifth I sense?

How long did he sit there and watch them? His sense of time was distorted by this isolated place in his mind he'd retreated into. It felt like hours passed, though they were still sitting around their little table. Still talking.

Slowly, very slowly, he tried zooming in on the image of them. It was shaky and blurry at first, but soon he had it. He continued the movement until he found his viewpoint situated in the middle of the table. Rotating his view, he was centered among the four of them. They looked through him to speak to one another.

It was remarkable.

Okay, if I can go in, let's see if I can pull out . . .

Concentrating hard, he reversed the maneuver. His point of view began to pull out, away from them, but he pulled up instead of sideways. There was no formal ceiling here, only a slanted A-frame roof without insulation. He saw the angled ceiling approaching from his peripheral vision and pushed through it.

The four individuals seated in their kitchen vanished as shingles materialized before his eyes, then backed away from him. He pulled out farther and farther until he had a view of their whole building, and then the street they were on. The farther away he got from the four Ringwearers, the blurrier his vision grew. It remained in focus over the immediate area where they sat but became fuzzy in the periphery. He scanned the entire area, looking for something familiar, a landmark he could use as a reference . . .

There. A few blocks away and over from the small building with the attic was an enormous complex with numerous wings and even a helipad. *Hospital*, he decided.

And directly across the street from the hospital was a subway station labeled with the familiar circular red and blue "Underground" signs. Now he had two distinct reference points; it would be enough.

He released the image, the world around him and all its sounds returned, and he opened his eyes to the familiar St. James's Square park.

Gotcha.

Julie drummed her fingers on her armchair in the living room of their safe-house flat. If she'd possessed more energy, she would have used it to pace back and forth.

As she had off and on for the last forty-eight hours, she sat in her comfy chair watching the news, tapping her fingers. Grant, Morgan, and Alex had left for the London Library two days ago. Julie had been to the Library three times since then and found nothing. Her last attempt was early this morning; she was feeling the urge to try again.

But for now, she stewed. She fought the desire to tug at her hair, wanting to rip it out at the roots. *What if he's succumbed to the ring's influence? What if he's done something terrible? He could be out there all alone right now, thinking who knows what, doing who knows what. . . .*

Her fears grew with each moment that passed, but yesterday had probably seen the worst of it. That was the day the news had showed nonstop coverage of an unprecedented late season snowfall in northern Europe. The snow was so dense, and so much of it was falling so fast, that the affected areas were buried under meters of it in just hours. And that was just the beginning. The snow was still falling; parts of Norway, Finland, Sweden, and even the eastern coast of Iceland were close to entering a new ice age from the amount of winter weather they were experiencing.

The timing of this latest disaster—while Grant was missing—was not lost on Julie.

She glanced around the room. Nora and Fletcher sat nearby, watching the news alongside her. Hector hunched at the kitchen table, pretending to read a newspaper. In reality, he was watching Daniel and Lisa, who had spent every waking minute of their time in London doing their best to avoid one another.

Daniel had just hobbled into the kitchen without his cane, not realizing that Lisa was already there, fixing herself a sandwich.

He froze as she looked up and their eyes met.

Moments passed in silence. It was Lisa who found her voice first.

"Would you like one?" she said, indicating her freshly made tomato-on-whole-wheat.

"Yeah, okay," Daniel replied. She set about her task as he leaned over to the half-sized refrigerator beneath the cabinet by the sink and retrieved a metal pitcher containing fruit punch. She waited for him to finish and then withdrew the half of a tomato still inside the fridge.

Daniel didn't see her action as he was pouring his glass. With the juice still in his hand, he turned and slammed into her as she was still bent over. The red juice drenched her hair, soaked her clothes, and drizzled onto the floor. The pitcher clanged loudly as it floundered on the floor and finally settled.

"Oh!" Daniel cried. "I'm sorry—" his words drifted off as Lisa stood to her full height and he saw her face, her hair, her clothes . . . all soaked in red.

His complexion blanched. Horrified, he merely began shaking his head, as if to will none of this to be happening.

"All my fault . . ." His lips formed the words but no sound came out.

Lisa was perturbed by the bright red liquid soaking her hair and clothing, but she set that aside because she knew she was the only person in the room who realized what Daniel was seeing all over her.

And it wasn't juice.

"Daniel . . ." she said softly, trying to take his hand.

But he pulled away from her. The action was too fast, and he lost his balance and wound up on his rear end on the floor, the pool of juice seeping into his socks and pants. He was shaking all over and looked as though he might throw up.

"C'mon, it's okay," she said as everyone in the apartment looked on. "Let me help you up—"

"NO!" he howled. Appalled at everything around him, he clumsily returned to his feet and stumbled off toward the bathroom. Lisa, dripping red juice everywhere, chased after him.

He slammed the door in her face and locked it. She began pounding on it.

"Do you even CARE about my feelings?!" she shouted. After repeated attempts to get him to open the door, he still made no response.

"FINE!" she yelled at the door, livid, her face red—and not from the juice. "Hide from your problems and maybe they WILL go away!!"

Julie stood and made for the door. "That's it, I have to get out of here," she mumbled.

Lisa spun on her heel. "Where are you going? It's not safe to go out alone. I'll go with you," she offered.

"*No*," Julie replied emphatically. "You two are going to stay here and work out whatever's going on between you. I need a break from the drama."

Hector rose from his perch on the sofa and nodded an unspoken message to Julie, who nodded back to him. He would go with her.

They left, and Hector carefully and quietly pulled the door closed behind them.

49

Hector found that he had to walk faster than normal—which was already more rapidly than most people casually walked—to keep up with Julie. He always felt uncomfortable around Julie; he wanted so desperately to heal her from her illness, but no matter how hard he tried, nothing worked. It left him with feelings of repressed guilt every time he was alone with her, which thankfully didn't happen often.

Julie exhibited no desire to talk as they swerved through the anxious-looking Londoners trapped inside the barrier. Hector usually enjoyed hearing others talk since he never did it himself, but he was willing to settle for mutual silence now.

Nerves were frayed, and everything seemed to be falling apart.

If only Alex were here; she could soothe all of them by willing their emotions to calm.

They had barely made it two blocks when a wail and cry from a nearby pub stopped them cold. Men poured out into the streets, many looking shocked, some even crying.

When the crowd thinned, Hector and Julie squeezed inside, where a handful of patrons remained staring at a television mounted over the bar, their afternoon pints forgotten for the moment. The bartender, a beefy, balding lug in dark clothing, didn't even look their way.

"God save the Queen . . ." Julie heard him mutter to himself.

Julie caught sight of a scrolling banner at the bottom of the locally broadcast BBC channel, the only one still on the air inside the cordoned zone.

"PRIME MINISTER FOUND DEAD," read the enormous red headline.

Hector looked over her shoulder as Julie shook her head in disbelief.

The newscaster reported the few facts that they knew about this breaking story. The prime minister had been found at his desk, in his office, simply staring down at his desktop, eyes open. Reportedly, no one knew anything was wrong until he didn't answer a question from a female member of the opposing Parliamentary Party, who burst into his office. The woman called for help when he didn't respond to her, and he was found to have no vital signs.

"It was as if everything was normal one minute, and the next his heart had simply stopped beating," the anchor said, and Julie heard nothing more.

"No, Grant . . ." she whispered. "You couldn't have . . . I know you couldn't."

Grant didn't bother knocking on the door at the top of the stairs. He was in the apartment building that contained the attic he'd seen in his mind's eye.

The door opened before him and he walked through. He found the quartet of British Ringwearers still seated around the table in their kitchen, which was the very room the door opened into.

"I say!" The older man stood from the table in protest. "Don't you people know how to knock?"

"I don't have time for formalities," Grant said urgently. "I don't know how you're keeping this barrier in place around the city, but you're going to bring it down. Right now."

The woman in the hat faced him from her seat at the table, only today it was a yellow hat so bright it might have been colored by a highlighter. "Just like that?" she said, leaning back in her seat, dripping incredulity. "Simply because you say so? I'm afraid you have a mistaken idea of how things work here, darling. As well as how to present yourself in public," she added, taking in the dried blood stains all over him.

"For a group that's all about protecting your homeland, you should pay better attention to the local news," Grant replied.

At a glance from the hat woman, the spike-haired girl leaned back in her seat and turned on a small black radio on the nearby countertop.

A woman's voice was proclaiming the news about the Prime Minister with great urgency from a local news report—a station somewhere inside the barrier.

"It's true," Grant said, crossing his arms over his chest.

"*You* did this?" the old man asked, his fists clenched.

"I stopped his heart beating with a casual thought," Grant replied, his voice rising. "And I could do the same to each of you, simultaneously, right this instant, so don't bother trying anything. If you don't bring the barrier down, and I mean *right now* . . . I'll do it myself. I'll kill all four of you right here."

The woman in the hat and the older gentleman exchanged deadly serious looks. Finally, she nodded regretfully. The man took his seat once more and all four of them closed their eyes. They seemed to be meditating or concentrating, Grant couldn't quite tell.

Their silence stretched on for several minutes, and Grant began to feel uncomfortable. He kept his defenses up and close at hand should they try to attack him somehow.

Finally they all opened their eyes at the same moment.

"The barrier is done," said the woman in the hat. "But I assure you our business with you is not."

"If you're lying to me—"

"We're *not*," the old man cut him off. "We are honorable. And we will honor your actions in the manner most fitting. You have declared war on the sovereign nation of Great Britain with an illegal assassination. We will see you brought to justice, one way or another."

Grant turned to leave. He didn't have time for this. "Fine, whatever."

"It's done. The Prime Minister is dead. The barrier is gone," Grant barked at the librarian where she sat in her desk chair, unconcerned that he was making a scene in one of London's most revered establishments. "Now give me back my friends."

"Oh but you assign me far too much credit," the librarian replied smoothly. "I offered to return your memories, nothing more."

Grant seethed. "Then do so."

"Very well," she said, rising from her chair. "Follow me."

But she didn't move to exit the room via the door behind him. Instead, she opened her desk drawer and input a series of numbers into a calculator inside it. The narrow wall behind her swiveled on a pivot point in its center. She walked through one side and Grant followed.

On a whim, he glanced down at her right hand, just to be sure.

No ring there.

A metal grating floor behind the hidden door led them down spiral stairs. Their heels clicked on the steps, and they continued to wind their way down, much farther than Grant had expected. He estimated they were at least three or four stories below ground when they finally came to the staircase landing.

They were in a small room, about twenty feet by twenty. It looked like some sort of waiting room; bright wallpaper met a well-lit ceiling on top and stained wooden wainscoting on the bottom. A lush blue carpet gave Grant's feet a slight bounce as he moved. The stairs were in

one corner; cushy chairs and end tables lined the remainder of the
room except for an oak paneled door to his immediate right.

"What is this?" he asked aloud.

"Please, have a seat anywhere. I'll be right back with the antidote,"
she said, exiting through the side door and closing it behind her. He
heard the lock on the door click into place.

Grant felt ridiculous as he complied with her order to sit. Antidote?
He should be breaking down that door and following her, he thought.
But then he might never know what happened to Alex and Morgan . . .

A few minutes later, the door unlocked and she reentered the small
waiting room carrying a syringe.

"Roll up your sleeve," she said.

"So you did it with a chemical agent," he replied, folding back his
left sleeve.

"That's right."

It was so strange to look into this woman's cold face and know that
it was the face that had once been worn by his friend and mentor Morgan. Deep down inside, this was Morgan's true self as she knew herself
to be.

"Hold still," she said, pressing the needle roughly into his arm. "It
should only take a moment to take effect."

"What is it?" he asked. When she didn't answer, he asked another
question. "How were you able to selectively erase specific memories? I
would have thought that was impossible."

She smirked. "Your standards of science consider many things
impossible," she said as she slid the clear fluid into his veins.

The Secretum had different scientific standards? What was that
supposed to mean?

As soon as she'd drawn the needle out, Grant's vision began to blur.
A haze settled over his view of the room, and it was growing darker by
the moment.

"Do you think me *stupid*?" she said, her calm exterior vanishing,
replaced by a look of murderous revenge. "The Secretum of Six knows
everything there is to know about everything. And we know when we
are being lied to!"

Grant shook his head, trying to get his bearings, but he felt nau-
seous. Was it from whatever she'd put in his system?

He extended a hand in the librarian's direction and shoved her against the far wall with his mind . . .

Only nothing happened. The librarian still stood before him, syringe triumphantly in hand. She marched forward and smacked him.

"You only fulfilled half of the deal!" she shouted. "The prime minister's death was a hoax! Though enlisting the help of the local media to create your ruse was quite clever. I'd love to know how you pulled it off so quickly."

"I thought you knew everything about everything?" he slurred. His arm was still outstretched, his will still trying to push against her body, against the syringe, against anything. But nothing was happening.

"So you finally figured out that your powers aren't working?" she inquired with a mischievous smile. "They don't work anywhere inside this building. Not now, not this morning, and not two days ago. You already discovered this fact once, which is why I had to wipe your memory the first time."

How was it possible? Keeping his powers from working inside the Library? And more importantly, why? What was so important about this place?

Grant eyed the empty syringe, felt his blood pumping through his system harder than before, yet still his eyes glazed over and unconsciousness threatened to take him.

His muscles were failing, he could no longer keep his eyes open, sleep beckoned to him . . .

The librarian shook her head in disgust. "How did one so pathetic as you ever become the Bringer?"

"Sure wasn't *my*—" he began to respond, but then he was out.

51

Furious and outraged, Lisa packed her bag in the downstairs bedroom.

If Daniel wanted his problems to go away, that's just what she'd do. If she only served to remind him of his sins, she'd remove herself from his sight. If he was never willing to face up to what he did and accept her into his life . . .

She sighed, flopping onto the single bed beside her luggage. There were no more tears left in her. She couldn't keep hoping after Daniel forever, could she? Did he even know the extent of her feelings?

Did he *care*?

Indignant once more, she stood and continued her packing.

But the tug at her heart refused to go away. What if he was too far gone to know how much he needed someone else's help? What if he was thinking of hurting himself?!

She rolled her eyes, leaving the bedroom. The door to the bathroom had been closed since he'd locked himself inside.

"Daniel! I want you to come out of there! It's been long enough now. We need to talk about this."

She heard no response or even movement from inside the bathroom.

Searching the living room, she found a hairpin and picked the lock on the bathroom door. Fearing the worst, she swung the door open.

The bathroom was empty. No Daniel.

Opposite the door was a small window that was just big enough for a person to squeeze through. . . .

He's gone!

Before she could even think of her next move, something splintered nearby—a sound that could only have come from the front door being smashed in.

Julie and Hector were on their way back to the safe house when Hector stopped walking. He raised his arm and turned it in a circle, pointing in a complete three hundred and sixty degrees, encompassing the entire horizon, where the sun was already leaving the sky and stars were becoming visible. She wasn't sure what he was getting at, but then she noticed something.

That warm, fuzzy feeling of safety that came from being inside the barrier . . . was gone.

She considered leaving London and found it to be an appealing idea.

Was that what Hector was trying to tell her?

"You think it's gone?" Julie asked.

Hector nodded eagerly.

"Grant . . ." she said quietly. "He found a way."

Hector shrugged but seemed to agree with this assessment.

Julie's phone rang.

"Hello?"

"Ju—!——found us! We've——made!"

"Hello? What?"

It sounded like Lisa's voice, but the sound kept cutting in and out, so she couldn't be sure.

"Can—hear—? We——Grant!"

Click. The connection was cut off.

"Something's going on," Julie told Hector. "We've got to find Grant, *now.*"

Fletcher saw it with his own eyes but didn't believe it.

Armed men were approaching the safe house. He watched them on his laptop via one of the external cameras he'd planted out front. They were already at the front door.

His fingers danced over the keyboard as he activated a few final protocols he'd personally installed at the house, then he snapped the laptop shut, grabbed Nora by the hand from her perch on the couch, and dragged her to the stairs. Taking them two at a time, he arrived on the second floor just as he heard the front door crash in downstairs.

Fletcher glanced at his watch as he put a finger over his lips to signal silence to Nora and pushed her in the direction of the next flight of stairs. He looked quickly about for Daniel and Lisa, but they must've been in the downstairs bedroom. Too late to go back, he followed Nora to the third floor.

Shouting, crashing, and running could be heard from downstairs.

Fletcher checked his wristwatch.

Sixty seconds . . .

Lisa hid in the first-floor bedroom inside a small closet that was barely big enough to hold her.

She caught her breath in her throat and froze, listening to the footfalls just outside. It sounded as if the flat was being ransacked from top to bottom. There was no way they wouldn't find her here, she knew.

Lisa heard footsteps approaching and watched in horror as the closet's door handle turned . . .

Loud popping and crackling sounds came from somewhere outside the apartment. The door handle was turned loose and she let out a sigh of relief.

What was going on out there?

She shrieked as the closet door suddenly flew open.

"Hands over your head!" a policeman ordered, pointing a gun in her face.

On the roof, Fletcher shut and sealed the attic door behind him.

"What is going on?" Nora demanded.

"Just follow me," he whispered in reply.

He moved toward the far end of the adjoining apartments on this street. They shared rooftops, so it was a simple matter of walking the length of one apartment, stepping over a two-foot brick barrier, and continuing on to the next apartment rooftop.

As Nora kept moving, Fletcher carefully peered over the front edge of the apartment. Across the street, the cheap fireworks he'd planted there days ago had ignited just as he'd meant for them to, creating a juvenile but effective diversion.

At the far end of the adjoining apartments, they found a series of ladders and balconies that would lead them down to street level. From there, it was a matter of avoiding detection by the police, who had cars all along the street out front. But with darkness on their side, Fletcher was confident they could pull it off.

The only question remaining was where to go.

Lisa interlaced her fingers on top of her head, as instructed.

"Got one in here!" the patrolman yelled while the racket outside continued. The young man motioned for her to leave the closet, and she did so nervously. She'd never been arrested before. And she was in a foreign country . . .

What would they do to her?

The policeman marched her out of the bedroom, and she noticed that the living room was trashed but empty. She heard noises upstairs, and the popping and banging sounds still came from outside. She thought she heard voices out there.

There was a sharp clang behind her, and she turned around just as the policeman landed on the floor, out cold.

Daniel stood there with the metal juice pitcher in his hand—the same one he'd spilled on her earlier. There was a small dent in it where he'd banged it against the policeman's head.

"Come on!" he whispered and led her out the back entrance.

As they were running, Lisa said to him, voice low, "I thought you left!"

"I did," he replied, hobbling hard against his cane. "Needed to get some air."

"Then why did you come back?" she challenged him.

Daniel stopped short, and she followed suit. He studied her for a long moment, and for a brief second, a deep vulnerability passed over his face. In that moment, she witnessed the deep scars that had become his soul.

But the moment passed, and he looked away from her eyes once more.

"Fresh air's overrated," he replied.

52

Grant felt something sticking his arm. Again.

He was dizzy and queasy.

But he was awake, and he was still seated in the same chair in the waiting room at the bottom of the spiral staircase. Whatever was happening, the librarian hadn't erased his memory again.

He opened his eyes to see a boy in his late teens with an oval face and a permanently down-turned expression holding a finger to his lips. On his middle finger on that same hand rested one of the Rings of Dominion.

He's the fifth . . . the fifth Ringwearer I sensed in London . . .

The boy looked to the door while pocketing a syringe. "She'll be back any second," he whispered urgently. "Shake it off and get up, man!"

"Who are—"

"No time, no time!" the boy whispered, a crazed expression on his face. "Get up, will you! I gave you something to counteract what she used to knock you out, but if you're still here when she gets back . . . If *I'm* here with you when she comes in. . . !"

Grant allowed the young man to pull him to his feet from the waiting room chair he still sat in, and slowly his equilibrium began to return. The boy tried to pull him toward the spiral staircase, but Grant grabbed him by the arm and yanked up his shirtsleeve.

No tattoo.

"You're not one of them," he said.

"Of course not!" the boy said. "Come on, you have to go—"

"I'm not going anywhere," Grant replied, suddenly angry. "I want to know what this place is, and why my powers don't work here! And why you're wearing a ring!"

"Lower your voice!" the boy replied, resigning himself to Grant's stubbornness. "We've met already, but you don't remember—"

"You have no idea how sick I am of hearing that," Grant cut in.

"My name is Trevor," the boy explained, still whispering. "And yes, I'm a Ringwearer. Your powers don't work here because *I'm* here. Because of *this*," he indicated his ring, "my mind sends out disruptive brain waves that dampen the powers of other Ringwearers. The nausea and headaches you've been experiencing are a side effect. I can't control it; I can't turn it off. It just *happens* to anyone twenty or thirty feet away from me."

"But what is all this—?"

"This place is somewhere you shouldn't be. Ever. Please, you *have* to leave before she comes back and finds out what I've done."

"NO! You tell me what is going on here!" Grant whispered as loud as he dared. Enough was enough, and he had no more patience for these Secretum games. "Who are these people, really? What is this about?"

Trevor grabbed him by the shoulders and shook him. "Oh, what are you, barking mad? How can you not see it? No human was ever meant to wield the power you possess. It's a blasphemy! A blight, a perversion on the soul of Creation."

Grant wrested himself free of the boy's grasp, chills inching up his spine. "What are you saying?"

Trevor, this boy he didn't even know, who seemed to know everything about him, was the picture of frustration. "Don't you understand? No matter how much good you do, it will never be enough. Every action you take is a violation of the natural order of things. Continue to use this power, and everything will fall into ruin."

Grant looked at this boy Trevor anew. Maybe he wasn't quite as young as Grant first assumed.

Trevor glanced again at the wooden door, the same door the librarian had gone through earlier to retrieve the sedative she used on Grant.

"What's in there?" Grant asked.

"Something that shouldn't exist. Something I wish I didn't know about," Trevor replied anxiously. "Something dreadful."

Grant arched an eyebrow and approached the door. It was locked. He turned—

Trevor was gone, his footsteps echoing up the stairs.

Grant mentally kicked the wooden door in. It exploded into thousands of splinters.

He was pleased to see his powers were back; perhaps Trevor hadn't run away in fear but strategy?

On the other side of the bashed-in door was a very short hallway, shorter in length than the waiting room. At the hallway's end was a single wooden door matching the one he'd just forced open but with one difference.

A six-inch version of the symbol of the Secretum of Six had been carved into the door sloppily. Maybe with nothing more than a pocket knife.

He wasted no time and destroyed this door as well. The librarian was nowhere in his immediate field of vision.

What he saw instead was the last thing he expected.

53

Grant walked forward until he was in the center of a roughly rectangular room about ten times the size of the waiting room. There was no
décor here, nothing particularly special about its appearance. The walls
were bare cement, as were the ceiling and floor. Fluorescent light fixtures were attached to the ceiling. A handful of folding chairs could be
seen in what few open spaces there were along the walls.

The room was full of shelves. Row after row of them, filled not with
books, but three-ring binders. The bookcases down here were even
more cramped than the ones upstairs in the library, with less than two
feet of access space between them.

It was eerily silent, and it struck him then that he truly was underground. There was not even the hum of electric air conditioning. It was
more like an old bomb shelter, or a tomb.

Grant approached the nearest bookcase and grabbed the first
binder he could get his hands on. A man's name—was that Italian?—
he didn't recognize was printed on the spine and front cover of the
binder. Inside were hundreds of pages comprising nothing less than a
complete summary of this man's life.

He quickly rifled through the pages, all of which were stuffed inside
clear plastic page protectors with three-ring holes built into them. The
book began with a birth certificate. Subsequent pages included many
other official documents, such as a marriage certificate, driver's license,
and medical records.

Between those, in chronological order, were dozens of neatly typed pages summarizing any and all significant events or turning points in this man's life. His first date with his future wife was detailed on one page. Another recorded the circumstances surrounding a promotion at his job. Every report included a date.

Grant flipped to the back of the book. The last page was a death certificate.

Grant shook the cobwebs out of his head, certain that he'd read the page wrong. He looked at it again to be sure.

The death certificate was dated one week in the future.

"You're cleverer than I thought," said the librarian. She stood behind him, at least eight feet away, pointing a small pistol at him. "I'm afraid you've forced my final hand. I've triggered a mechanism that will reduce this room to ashes in a few moments. Don't worry, this room is entirely self-contained within its cement walls, fully protected and reinforced. The Library above won't even know anything's happened. But I strongly suggest you leave now."

Grant's heart skipped a beat when he smelled smoke already.

"Who are you?" he cried. "What *is* all this?"

"This is the *real* Library," she replied. "One of only three in the world. All identical. So few things in this world are certain; it's always a good idea to have backups, you know."

Grant's mind spun. "And all of these files . . ." His eyes traced the room and saw what must have been thousands of them lining the dusty shelves from floor to ceiling. "Each one represents a real person?"

"Yes," the librarian replied. "The files catalog their entire lives from beginning to end. And these are only currently living individuals. You should see the archives for the long dead."

"But . . . but this man's life hasn't ended yet!"

The smell of smoke was growing stronger by the second, and Grant saw the first visual sign of it near the ceiling above.

"The files are written in their entirety before the lives contained within them have even begun," she revealed.

"How comprehensive are these files?"

"Comprehensive enough."

"But that's—"

"Impossible? Yes, it is. As impossible as a man who can lift objects with his mind."

"Who are these people?" he demanded. "What does the Secretum want with them?"

"More important than what we want is what we believe. The people represented here are tools. Building blocks. Nothing compared to you. *You* are the reason for everything we do, and everything we've ever done."

"But *why?*" He coughed. The smoke smell was rising, as was the temperature in the room. There was a fire somewhere—perhaps inside the walls? He needed to find a way out of this place, but the librarian showed no sign of concern for herself, and he still had so many questions. . . .

There was one he was sure he already knew the answer to, but he didn't want to ask.

"Is there a file in this room about me?"

"Of course. The most important file of all. You are the Bringer."

No no no. . . !! They're doing it again . . . They can't manipulate me anymore! They can't*!*

"And the others?" he shouted over the rising flames. "The others like me?"

"Yes, I imagine they have records here as well, somewhere in all this."

"Show me!" he screamed, trembling in rage and anguish.

"You aren't meant to see that information," she replied. She was visibly feeling the effects of the heat and the flames, but she made no move to save herself. "Not yet. You must go now, while you can. Your file does not end here, Grant. Your destiny awaits elsewhere."

He snapped and lunged.

"*I don't have a destiny!!*" he thundered.

The gun went off, but Grant already had her on the ground, and the gun was pointed upward, over his left shoulder. A chip of cement fell from the ceiling.

He forced the gun out of her hand and placed it next to her temple.

"How can the Secretum know everything about my life before it happens?!" he shouted. "How can they know everything about all of these people? It's insane!"

"GRANT!!" screamed a voice somewhere in the distance, beyond the smoke. "Grant, is that you?!"

Alex.

Alex is alive!

The librarian used his distraction to grab the pistol with her own hand. Before Grant could stop her, she'd placed her trigger finger on top of his and pressed down.

Grant recoiled violently, landing backward on his hands.

She'd blown her own brains out with the gun still in his hand.

54

Sweating now from the growing heat, Grant caught sight of flames which seemed to have erupted from within the bookcases.

He jumped to his feet, closing his eyes both to block out the gruesome sight of the dead woman at his feet and to ward off the billowing smoke in this small, confined space.

"Alex!" he shouted.

"I'm in here!" came the reply from somewhere to his right. He followed the sound and found a small cupboard in a far corner of the room. It was just big enough for a small person to curl up in. A padlock held closed a latch that hung over the edge.

"Please get me out of this!" Alex pleaded.

Grant didn't hesitate. The padlock flew apart and the entire door to the cupboard exploded outward. Inside, Alex screamed and when Grant could finally glimpse inside, he saw her curled in an uncomfortable fetal position. Her dark locks were matted to her head, and she squinted hard against the room's light.

He helped her to wobbly feet.

"You all right? What'd they do to you?" Grant babbled, fear washing over him at her appearance.

"Been locked inside that thing since yesterday . . ."

"What about Morgan? Do you know where she is?" Grant asked frantically.

Alex shook her head. "She's not here, they took her. . . . I—I think she was dying. She was shot, and you gave her CPR, but I don't think she responded . . . It all happened so fast!"

That's where the blood came from, all over my clothes and hands . . .
It was Morgan's blood.

Grant's heart was pained at the thought of losing Morgan, but the
smoke was so thick in the room that they could barely see anymore.

"We have to *go!*" Alex shouted.

"Can you walk?"

"I don't know," she replied helplessly. She was so weak, she looked
as if she might pass out.

He scooped her up and ran.

They were at the top of the spiral staircase when he heard the
sound of footfalls below them on the stairs.

Where did they even come from? he wondered. He hadn't noticed
any other exits.

A handle at the top of the stairs swiveled open to reveal the rear
wall of the librarian's office, and Grant never stopped moving. Out of
the office, through the Library, he ignored the stares of the dozen or so
patrons between him and the exit. Still he heard the footfalls approaching from behind.

They dashed out of the Library's main exit and down the outer
steps. Less than fifteen feet behind, he heard the door slam open again
and more steps down.

He chanced a look behind as he ran through St. James's Square.
Three men in black jumpsuits bearing no insignia. They each had scab-
bards with swords attached to their hips. Though they were of different
heights and builds, and none were bald, they looked for all the world
the way Payton had the day they'd met.

The cover of darkness was their only ally, though bright street
lamps illuminated much of the small park. He noted with alarm that
his powers were out again. . . . At the far edge of the park he saw
Trevor, the kid who gave off the nullifying brainwaves, standing there
watching.

Something sailed through the air dangerously close to his right ear,
and with a twang a small throwing knife stuck into a tree twenty feet
ahead in his path. The action brought him up short. He turned.

The three men faced him down, encircling him. Holding their

swords in attack position, their stances looked remarkably similar to Payton's familiar fighting pose.

"Bringer," one of them began, "we have no quarrel with you. But the empath is a liability. Step aside and allow us to deal with her."

Grant dropped Alex to her feet but positioned himself in front of her. "You even think about touching her and I'll break your neck."

The one who'd thrown the knife tilted his head. "You have no powers. You think this is by accident? Your powers have been negated so we may perform our duty. This is how the Secretum works. The nature of the game is never made clear until the game is already won."

"Then you should consider playing something else," growled a voice out of the darkness.

Grant spun . . . that voice . . .

55

"Fellows," Payton approached, his sword extended and his stance ready for a fight. His weapon, with its elaborate engravings and extra-long handle, made theirs look like children's plastic toys. "I'm glad you're here. You have no idea how long I've been itching for a *real* fight."

The three men blocking Grant's path clearly recognized Payton; they were speechless, their eyes wide with recognition.

"You're late," Grant remarked.

"Came once the blasted barrier was down."

"You realize our powers don't work here, right?" Grant warned him.

"Why, do I look worried?" Payton shot back without looking in his direction.

"Thresher," one of the attackers acknowledged with a bowed head. "We do not wish to harm you, but our orders were exact. Secretum business must not falter at your hands again."

Payton smirked. "Oh, I think it must."

Payton placed himself between Grant and Alex, and the three swordsmen. He stood perfectly still, waiting for his opponents to make the first move.

As one, the three men lunged at Payton, but he dropped and rolled between them and came up behind. A vicious fist to the head, and the one on the far right was knocked out. The other two turned fast and their swords clanged together as Payton struck, but the blow was blocked by both men.

Grant had never seen anyone block Payton's attacks before.

Payton let his blade tilt forward until he was grasping it in a back-handed grip.

One of the attackers worked his way behind Payton and tried to stab, but Payton spun and slashed. When the move was over, the attacker placed a hand on top of his head and felt something missing. Payton extended his sword out to the side, where a large clump of black hair fell away from the tip of the blade.

Grant blinked and looked at the attacker who'd been shaved by Payton's sword. Where once had been a full head of dark black hair, now there was a bald patch; Payton's blade had shaved the hair right down to the skin.

The man's eyes widened at this realization, but Payton threw a disgusted expression at him that said without words, *Did you forget who you were dealing with?*

The second attacker lunged at Payton, but he whipped around with his other arm to deliver a wicked backhand that spun the man's head sharply. The man recovered quickly, sword at the ready.

Payton once again positioned himself between the two swordsmen and Grant and Alex, and as they swung their weapons, he leapt up high and pulled in his feet so that they swiped at nothing but air. Just as Payton landed he brought the broad side of his sword around and bashed it against the head of the attacker on the right.

The man staggered and bumped into his compatriot, and Payton used their off-balance moment to grab the man on the right by the arm and spin him clockwise until he was face-to-face with the man on the left.

Before the two men could recover, they looked down at the same time and saw Payton's steel sword protruding through both of their bellies. Payton extracted the sword just as quickly, and they slumped to the ground in unison.

Grant was amazed; Payton's speed enhancement certainly gave him a profound edge, but without it, he still had to be one of the most skilled fighters in the world. Payton cleaned the blood from his sword and sheathed it as Grant's eyes fell upon the men on the ground.

"You killed them!" he cried, just realizing it. He was still coughing up smoke from the underground library. "We don't *kill* people!"

"These men stopped being 'people' a long time ago," Payton replied.

He sheathed his sword. "Whose blood is all over you? Are you hurt? And why aren't our powers working?"

Grant's head turned to the spot where he'd seen Trevor, but the boy was gone.

"It's . . . something about this place," Grant faltered. He had no desire to explain the strange young man at this point in time, as he found himself fighting off the lingering effects of the nausea once more. His powers were already returning, he could feel it. Nor did he feel that this was the best moment to tell Payton about Morgan's disappearance.

But wait, the ground only held two bodies. . . . "What happened to the third man? The one you knocked out?"

There was no time to react as the third man raised up suddenly behind Grant and swung his sword at Alex's head. His sword never completed its arc; instead, there was the sharp bark of a pistol and a hole appeared in his head and dribbled blood. His body slumped lifelessly to the ground.

Ten feet behind him stood Ethan, his gun raised and steadied in both hands, his feet spread wide and knees bent.

"Who's this?" Payton inquired.

Grant was still hovering over Alex, making sure she was safe, but he cast a glance in Ethan's direction. "A friend."

Ethan held his gun at the ready and monitored the perimeter as he joined them in the center of the Square.

"Good timing," Payton remarked.

Ethan caught sight of the other two bodies on the ground. "Not as good as yours."

"We can't just take lives whenever we feel like it," Grant said, "or we're no better than—"

Payton turned to look upon him at last. "Those men had the same training I was given. *Secretum* training. Death is the *only* thing that will stop a Secretum operative from completing his mission. You should know this better than anyone."

Grant frowned, seeing the truth in Payton's words. Payton had almost killed him the day they met; only Payton's realization that he'd been lied to by the Secretum had halted Payton's attacks.

Ethan broke the silence. "This area is too open, too hard to defend, especially in the dark."

"Agreed," said Payton. "Alex is hurt; we need to move her someplace safe."

"Your safe house has been compromised," Ethan announced. "Can't be going back there."

Grant and Payton both eyed him curiously.

"I didn't do it," Ethan replied. "Heard about it from a connection inside MI–5."

Grant thought. "I might know a place we could—"

"Grant!" someone screamed from the edge of the park.

He turned in time to see Julie and Hector running toward them.

Half an hour later, the group neared its destination. Grant carried Alex in his arms and refused all offers of help. Hector did what he could for her back at St. James's Square, but her body needed nutrients he could not provide.

Someone's cell phone rang. The ringtone was the theme from *Mission: Impossible*.

"Mine," Ethan said, no sign of embarrassment at his choice of ringtone. "Been expecting this call."

He flipped open the phone. "Good evening, Director Stevens."

"I've just received a report here of some sort of confrontation between Guardian and three armed men in St. James's Park."

"Oh?" he casually replied.

"My report states that *you* were at the scene of this incident, Agent Cooke."

"Yes ma'am, your information is accurate."

"I hope this means that you've learned enough about Guardian to formulate a scenario for apprehending him."

"After careful consideration," he began, "I must recommend that the Agency reconsider its policy on this situation. If I may speak plainly . . ." He cut his eyes across at Grant. "Guardian is not what you think he is."

"You're off the Guardian case," she said, and there was no mistaking the smugness in her voice. "I want you on a flight home five minutes ago. Prepare for an immediate debriefing upon—"

"Actually, Director," Ethan boldly interrupted her and said, relishing his every word, "that last part's not going to happen. Check your email, and you'll find my formal letter of resignation from the FBI. Effective as of one hour ago."

Without waiting for her outraged reply, he hung up the phone and placed it inside his jacket pocket.

That was it then. No going back now.

He held no deep concerns that he might have made the wrong choice. This was how he made all of his biggest decisions: He went with his gut and never looked back.

He kept walking in step with this new group of extraordinary individuals—a group he felt honored to be a part of. No one bothered with questions about the conversation he'd just had. Their minds were on much larger concerns.

But no one questioned his place among them either. He was sure that time would come. They would need to know why he had sacrificed his career for them. Why he was so sure that it was the right thing to do. Why he was willing to give up everything to help them.

He wasn't sure what answer he could give. He simply knew that it was what he had to do. The same way he always knew. He trusted his instincts and had never made a wrong move yet.

But those questions would wait. For now, the group simply kept moving.

56

Payton chopped the handle off of the attic's outer door and marched into what looked like a rather small kitchen.

Grant was about to protest when the young girl with the spiky hair appeared. "Oh," she said, disappointed. "You again."

"It's the cretins," announced the other woman, rounding another corner to enter the room. Now she wore a bright green hat with fake sunflowers around its brim. "Weren't you warned not to return here?"

"We need your help," Grant began.

"Do you?" she replied, dripping in sarcasm. "With *pretending* to assassinate the Queen this time, perhaps?"

"Hey, I bluffed. You could have called it. You didn't."

"You play us for fools and then pretend it's our fault? Of all the nerve . . ." the woman was saying.

Payton was already bored. "You don't seem to have noticed the unconscious woman in his arms. We need a place to help her recuperate. And we're not asking."

The hat woman's eyes fell upon the unconscious Alex.

She frowned but said, "Very well, bring her this way before she makes a mess on the kitchen floor."

She led the way out into the main area of the loft. It was drab, largely unfurnished, with quite a bit of empty space. But there was a set of chairs and a couch in one corner; Grant put Alex down upon the musty old couch.

"Do you have anything to eat or drink? She's weak, dehydrated,"

Grant explained, taking a seat before one was offered.

The woman in the green hat nodded to the younger girl, who returned to the kitchen. The other two members of the British team appeared and converged on the sitting area.

"You *lied* to us, young man," the older gentleman with the mustache said, without any sort of preface or introduction. "In so doing, you coerced us into undoing a number of very carefully laid plans. In my day that sort of thing was punishable by public flogging."

Grant wasn't terribly interested in hearing more about exactly what "day" the old man was referring to.

"We need to let the others know about this place," Julie said softly, taking a seat next to Grant.

"Already done," he replied. "They're on their way. But you should try calling Daniel and Lisa; they're not with the others."

Julie walked away to a secluded corner to make her phone call.

The girl with the spiked hair returned from the kitchen bearing a glass of water and some kind of small biscuits. Hector set to work at getting Alex awake enough to get the water and crackers into her system.

"Thank you," Grant said to the girl. He turned to the other three who lived here. "I've given you plenty of reasons to hate me. I'm sorry for that. I am. But if you all know who I am, then you need to know that there are much bigger things at stake right now."

Julie returned to his side. "Daniel and Lisa are coming. They're okay."

The Upholders, it seemed, were not wholly unreasonable. They exchanged a number of glances and then found themselves seats in the circle around Grant, Alex, and the others. Ethan stood guard at a window, surveying the neighborhood. Payton maintained watch over the back door.

After just a few minutes, Nora, Fletcher, Lisa, and Daniel arrived and made themselves at home, taking seats wherever they could find them in the sparse room. Grant was relieved to see everyone was okay.

"Where is Morgan?" Payton suddenly asked, his hand reflexively clutching the hilt of his sheathed sword.

"I'm not . . ." Grant tried to think back. "I don't know."

Payton abandoned his post at the back door and stepped forward.

"What is going on?" he asked with a hint of menace in his voice.

Grant took a deep breath and let it out. Once again, he found himself longing for sleep when it was nowhere in sight. "We need to stop and catch our breath here. There's too much happening all around us; I need to try and connect the dots."

"What brought all of you to London in the first place?" asked the woman in the hat.

"We were searching for a secret society known as the Secretum of Six," Grant replied. "This group is responsible for giving us the rings that give us our powers. They have a headquarters of some kind called 'Omega Prime' that we're trying to find."

"I see. So you wish to thank them?" the woman asked.

"Not really, no, it's this whole destiny thing . . ." Grant replied, sensing the differences between the two groups coming to the surface. "Grant. My name is Grant. This is my sister Julie. Alex is the unconscious one. The rest are Hector, Nora, Fletcher, Ethan by the window, and Daniel and Lisa. Payton is the glowering one with the sword."

The woman in the hat stuck her chin up and looked down at them all, considering her response. Finally, she said, "You may call me Mrs. Edeson. The gentleman on my left is Cornelius. You've met our young Charlotte," she said, nodding at the spike-haired girl. "And the man in the back is . . . well . . . he's *special.*"

The man in the back corner of the room stood with his hands in his pockets, watching the scene before him play out with avid curiosity.

"Anyway, our search for this 'Omega Prime' place led us to the London Library. We found something underneath it—something I don't think you'd believe if I told you. And now one of my friends is missing."

"*Where is Morgan?*" Payton asked again.

"I don't know," Grant replied. "I can't remember." He recounted his story of the last three days, with Julie filling in some of the blanks regarding the false public perception that the Prime Minister had been murdered. Grant explained the help he got in pulling that deception off from Ethan.

Most of the reactions were reserved, at best, as Grant finished his story. Especially from the locals.

Grant ended with the hundreds of thousands of files representing people's entire lives that resided beneath the London Library, along with the librarian he met there who had once been Morgan before the Shift traded their lives.

"I still don't understand how they erased your memory," said Julie.

Grant's eyes scanned the others in the now-crowded loft as he thought back. He blinked and tried to shake the cobwebs out of his head; his memories of those two days were simply gone. He didn't even have snatches of mental images in his head.

Everyone was watching him with close scrutiny—Fletcher, Payton, Julie, Hector, Nora . . .

Nora.

Grant looked at the black woman, who was eying him with suspicion near the back of the room.

And suddenly, everything came into all-too-clear focus.

"You . . ." he whispered.

He watched as Nora floated off the ground, to the screams of nearly everyone in the room.

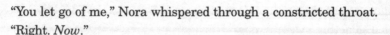

57

"You let go of me," Nora whispered through a constricted throat. "Right. *Now*."

"WHAT DID YOU DO TO ME?!" Grant thundered, rising to his feet and holding her in place against the wall with a concentrated thought.

"What are you doing?!" Julie screamed, her gaze bouncing between Grant and Nora, who was struggling to breathe.

Mrs. Edeson stood as well. "What is the meaning of this?"

"*She* did it!" Grant roared. "I can't remember two days of my life—two days when Morgan may have died—and *she's* the reason!"

Julie took Grant's hand, trying to calm him, trying anything. "Honey, you're not making any sense! Nora couldn't have done anything. She just puts people to *sleep*—"

"She erases people's memories!" Grant shouted, and the revelation fell over the room in a hushed silence. "The sleeping thing was a lie! We made it up! Her *real* power is selective, precise manipulation of memories! She can read your memory and erase any part of it she wants."

Everyone was speechless.

Nora still hung pressed against the wall, trying to peel invisible fingers away from her constricted throat.

"Grant . . ." Alex's weak voice spoke up for the first time since they'd arrived. "You're not a murderer. Don't start now."

Reluctantly, Grant slowly let go of Nora, who dropped to the ground and began coughing violently and sucking in air. Hector rushed to her side and placed his hand on her forehead.

Fletcher examined Grant. "Why did you lie to us about her powers?"

"Because . . . we felt that . . ." Grant stammered, "it seemed like—"

"We knew the truth was too dangerous," Alex put in, barely able to vocalize her words above a whisper.

"We?" asked Fletcher.

"Me and Alex . . . and Morgan," Grant replied. "Just think about it . . . the idea of someone who can alter memories with incredible precision . . . Our memories make us *us*. Nora could strip any one of us of our very identities without batting an eyelash. In a way, that makes her the most powerful one of us all. When she first came through the Railroad, the three of us decided it was in everyone's best interests if we didn't let out the truth of what she can do because she'd be blamed anytime something went wrong—"

"Just like you're doin' now," Nora rasped between breaths, a vicious look in her eyes. Hector's touch was helping her throat, but not her mood.

Mrs. Edeson pursed her lips. "It would seem that your predilection for lying is a chronic condition. I'm inclined to agree with my colleague that a public flogging might be in order."

Grant ignored her. "It had to have been her! Morgan and Alex went with me to the Library, and that's all I can remember. I woke up in St. James's Square two days later, with Morgan's blood all over me. Alex said Morgan was shot by operatives of the Secretum during those two days, but I don't remember any of it. There's only one person in the world who can completely erase memories, and she's right here in this room!" Grant thrust a finger in Nora's direction.

Nora was still catching her breath, but she shook her head. "It wasn't me. I swear it wasn't."

Daniel cleared his throat, much to everyone's surprise. "You may be assigning Nora too much credit. There are plenty of proven methods for brainwashing that are known to science. The specificity of this particular memory alteration is unusual, but I think it could be done by an expert—someone versed in the intricacies of brainwashing techniques." Daniel's eyes still searched the ground, as always. But everyone knew he was avoiding the eyes of just one person in the room.

All was silent for a few minutes as everyone became calm again. Grant and Mrs. Edeson returned to their seats. Nora walked to the kitchen, alone.

The first person to break the uneasy silence was Fletcher. "What's wrong with him?" Fletcher asked.

Grant turned to see who Fletcher was talking about, but saw Fletcher returning his gaze in an uncomfortable way.

Everyone looked at Grant, who had no idea what they were seeing. "What?"

Even Julie was visibly shaken, pulling away from him slightly. She tried to smile. "Your eyes . . . they're a little bloodshot, honey," she said reassuringly, but her face told a different story than her voice.

"More like blood-*soaked*," Lisa remarked. "That is not normal."

"What is everyone talking about?" Grant mumbled to Julie. "You got a mirror?"

She retrieved one from a compact in her purse. They were right; his normally blue irises had turned a deep, bloody shade of red.

"Did . . . did that librarian do something to you?" Julie asked, her face full of revulsion.

"I've seen it before," Alex whispered, an anguished look on her weakened face that kept her eyes from meeting Grant's.

Everyone turned in her direction. "His eyes turned red like that in Los Angeles when he was shot during the riot. And again in Jerusalem after we found the baby that died."

"Why didn't you say something to the rest of us?" Fletcher demanded.

Alex struggled to stay awake. "It was gradual . . . I kept trying to convince myself I was just seeing things. . . ."

"When was the first time you noticed it?" Julie asked, unnerved.

"It was the night Hannah died." Alex faced Grant with remorse. "Your eyes—they weren't blue *or* red, they were kind of purple. I didn't know what to make of it, but it only lasted a moment, and then it passed. But that was the same day . . ."

"What?" asked Grant.

She replied reluctantly. "That was the day of the fire storm. The fire that rained down from the sky in Los Angeles, and the terrible earthquake—it began when your eyes changed."

No one answered. An unspoken thought circled the room like the wind of a tornado. No one said it because no one had to.

Except for Fletcher. "He caused the firestorm. Could he be causing the worldwide disasters happening now?"

"Could he be *unintentionally* causing them?" Julie reworded his question, adding an important qualifier.

Everyone looked at Grant, awaiting an answer.

But he picked up on a strange vibe between Fletcher and Julie. "You two. . . ? You've been talking about this, behind my back. . . ." He was scratching the scar on his hand again. . . . "Even you?" he said to his sister.

He couldn't believe it. Julie was the one who constantly told him how good he was, how much she believed in him. She was the *last* person . . .

"*What happened to Morgan?*" Payton said once again.

Alex spoke up. "I, I don't . . . She was hurt, Grant tried to help her. . . . I'm not sure what happened after that."

Payton moved. He'd been standing statue-still, arms crossed, and listening to everything unfold. But now he walked away to the kitchen.

He returned dragging Nora by the arm, who was wriggling and trying to break free from his vise-like grip. "You said this one can read memories, so she can selectively erase them?" Payton asked.

Grant nodded.

Payton turned her loose. "Read his memory. Recover what's been suppressed."

Nora raised one eyebrow at this notion. She marched forward and punched Grant across the face as hard as she could. "Don't you *ever* touch me again," she warned him.

Tension mounted in the loft as everyone waited to see what Grant's response would be. He merely massaged his cheek.

Nora knelt in front of him. "Let's do this. You better bear down on something—this *ain't* gonna be pleasant."

58

Grant screamed.

The pain that surged through his brain was intense, like two hot pokers stabbed through both of his temples. Nora never touched him, never made physical contact of any kind.

Her mind reached inside of his and removed what was keeping hidden his memories of those two missing days. There was nothing gentle or delicate about her operation. She *ripped* free the memories that were cloaked behind the chemical agent used by the librarian and made them *more* than just easily accessible. If his memories had been words on a page, they would now have been visible in gigantic, bold, all-capital letters, outlined with a glowing neon highlighter.

"It's coming back to him," Nora announced. She unceremoniously stood and walked away.

Grant clutched his head with both hands, but the pain was slow in subsiding. "Alex, Morgan, and I spotted a woman at the London Library. Morgan knew her; she said that this woman, the head librarian, was *her*. Or who she used to be before the Shift. You get the idea . . .

"Morgan had never heard of any of the 'husks,' as my grandfather called them—the people we exchanged lives with—surviving long after the Shift. So we investigated this woman. We located her office on the ground floor and snuck inside. And Morgan was right: this woman in Morgan's old body still bore Morgan's birth name. We found plenty of papers on her desk to confirm this.

"That was about as far as we got before the librarian walked in and caught us in the act. I don't know what she did—hit some kind of fail-safe or something—but we were knocked out instantly. Probably some kind of fast-acting gas released inside the room; whatever it was, it was too fast for me to contain. The next thing I remember is waking up underground in the special room beneath the Library."

Grant stopped here to rub his head again and take a break from these fresh memories to explain to them what he'd found in that room. He told them all about the librarian's confession, the files and binders detailing various people's lives from birth to death—all before they were even born, no less—and the boy he encountered named Trevor, who had the peculiar ability to nullify the mental powers of others.

"Anyway," he resumed his earlier story, "Two days before, when I first woke up in that room, I had no idea what it was or where we were. I assumed the librarian had taken us somewhere off-site. We could have been *anywhere*. My powers weren't working, and the three of us were tied to chairs. The librarian was elsewhere in the room, and she was clearly agitated. Remember, the barrier around London was still up at the time, so she was cut off from the Secretum.

"Or so she believed. It wasn't long before a group of soldiers—some of the same men Payton and Ethan killed tonight—appeared from a far corner of the room."

"There was nothing at that end of the room?" Payton inquired. "No exit? No passageway of any kind?"

"Not that I know of," Grant replied. "But no one appears out of nowhere, do they? I guess there had to be something there. But the room was destroyed by fire, so it's all moot now anyway. So these soldier guys appeared, and the librarian was really unnerved by their appearance. I got the impression she *really* thought she was all alone as far as the Secretum was concerned and was trying to figure out what to do with the three of us by herself. She was seriously thrown by the soldiers' showing up. Morgan managed to wriggle herself free of her bindings, and she freed Alex and me while the librarian was distracted.

"As soon as we got to our feet, the librarian pulled out a gun and started firing. She was kind of crazed. Maybe she got bad news from the soldiers or something, I don't know."

He swallowed and tried not to look at Payton before he continued. "Morgan was hit. It was a stomach wound. The soldier guys got the librarian to stop firing so they could pursue us properly. I used CPR on Morgan—that's where all the blood came from on my hands and clothes. But the soldiers were running toward us and we were without our powers, defenseless. We had to go—"

"And Morgan?" Payton demanded.

Grant hesitated. "I don't think she was breathing. And she wasn't there the next time I visited that room two days later, so I have to assume they moved her—or moved the body."

"And you can't sense her?" asked Payton, his composure becoming increasingly severe.

"No, I'm sorry. It's like there's a hole where she's supposed to—"

Payton turned and made for the exit.

Hector stepped in front of him and held out a hand.

"Out of my way," Payton said in a warning so soft no one else heard it.

"Where are you going?" Grant called out.

Payton turned. "You people need to get something straight about me. I may lend a hand when our interests run parallel. And I can play the hero as well as the next man. But there's really only one thing I'm good for. And it's time I got back to it."

"What are you going to do?" Grant called after him as he turned and strode away.

Payton never answered. He moved into superspeed and was out the kitchen door before anyone realized he was gone.

Grant was surprised by his reaction. Payton hated Morgan with a genuine passion. Of all the ways he could have responded to the possibility of Morgan's death, this was the last thing Grant expected.

"Should we go after him?" Julie asked.

Grant shook his head.

"You didn't finish the story," Alex said weakly. "You should tell them about how we met Ethan."

Grant was surprised to see her awake again. Ethan was listening from his station at the window, but he turned at hearing his own name.

"Right," Grant replied. "Well, we ran. There were stairs to climb,

and we found ourselves back inside the librarian's office. We opened
the window there and escaped through it. That was when we met
Ethan. He had suffered recent blood loss and was pretty weak himself,
but he helped us find a place to hide in an abandoned building about
two blocks away from the Square.

"He explained who he was and that he wanted to help. We didn't
believe him at first, of course. Alex was particularly suspicious after we
realized he had led the strike team on the warehouse just before we
left L.A. But he told—"

"I told her," Ethan spoke up, "that I thought you all were a threat.
But it was a mistake. And I'd come here to correct that mistake."

"Somewhere along the way," Grant continued, "Alex and I fell
asleep. I'm ashamed of it now, that we didn't try harder to go back and
determine what happened to Morgan. But the drugs weren't completely out of our systems, and we were both feeling physically ill from
our exposure to Trevor. We found out the next morning that even
though he wasn't feeling well himself, Ethan had popped some uppers
so he could stay awake and keep guard while we slept safely through
the night."

This news settled throughout the group. Even the four Upholders
seemed a bit more at ease looking upon Ethan now.

"In the morning we decided to go back inside the Library, but I
refused to let Ethan come with us. That was *my* mistake. I doubt any
of this would have ended as it did if I'd allowed him to come with us. I
didn't contact any of you because I didn't want to worry everyone until
we knew Morgan's fate for certain.

"We made it back inside, but as soon as we got to the librarian's
office the soldiers reappeared, and they pursued us throughout the
Library. It's a maze in there, and eventually we made our way outside
to the square. But they were waiting. The librarian and the swordsmen
trapped us in the small park there. Neither Alex nor I could access our
powers. The librarian pulled out a hypodermic needle and tranquilized
Alex on the spot. Then she jabbed me in the neck really hard with
another needle and all the strength went out of me.

"That's it. I passed out and then woke up the next day with my
memories erased. I guess she saw an opportunity, knew I'd be desper-

ate to know what happened to Morgan and Alex, and tried to use that desperation against me."

"Clever plan," Fletcher remarked.

"Yeah," Julie added, "but we still don't know what happened to Morgan."

Grant stood. "They took her. Dead or alive, they've got her. To find Morgan, I have to find the Secretum."

Julie stood as well. "So where do we start looking?"

Grant's pulse raced, angry and disappointing thoughts rushing back to the surface. "I've got this. You all sit tight."

"Grant!" Julie called out as he crossed the loft toward the kitchen and the exit. "We have to consider all the possibilities; you *know* that. We have a responsibility—"

"Stop it," Grant spun on his heel and faced her. "I know you mean well, but I don't have any way of *proving* that I'm not somehow causing the world to fall apart with all these crises. And I don't have time right now to figure out how I can."

A sad look crossed Julie's face. "Your eyes are back to normal."

"What?"

"Your eyes," she said. "They're blue again."

"Good." he turned and the back door opened itself before him. "Maybe blue-eyed Grant won't rain fire down on London."

"That's not fair!" Julie shouted. She'd stopped moving and stood by the small kitchen table. "You think I *want* to fear the worst about you?"

He was already out the door but looked back inside one last time. "Life isn't about what we *want*. It's about what we're willing to *do*!"

Tears appeared around Julie's eyes. Grant wasn't sorry to see them. She was willing to believe *this* about her own brother? What did that say about *her*?

"By the way . . ." he said. "That was a direct quote from Mom."

The door shut itself and Grant was gone.

59

Payton flung open the main entrance to the London Library and stalked inside. A smiling young woman asked if he'd like to purchase a membership. He didn't respond.

A distraught young man, taking note of Payton's sword, which was sheathed as usual at his side, tried his best to maintain a helpful tone as he said, "Sir? May I help you find something?"

Payton didn't respond. He moved forward into the Library methodically, unstoppable.

"Er, well, be sure to let one of us know if we can be of help. . . ." The man's voice trailed off, uncertain what he should say in this situation.

Payton followed Grant's description to the letter and walked to the door of the head librarian's office.

Only there *was* no door. A blank wall greeted him instead.

A trick, he thought. *They've covered it up.*

Payton whipped out his sword and began slashing at the wall. He came up against bricks, mortar, wood, and other standard wall materials, but nothing more.

"Sir, no! Sir!" called the young man, who had come to see what all of the commotion was. "You mustn't do that, sir!"

Payton continued his work, hacking away at various areas of the empty wall.

"Sir, I will summon the authorities!" the man said, seeming to grow a backbone before Payton's very eyes. He stationed himself between Payton and the wall.

Payton shoved him flat against the wall. But the young man's impact against the wall was much louder than expected; it sounded shallow.

"Sir, this is *the* historic London Library, and it must not be damaged in any way!" the young man said, as if explaining to Payton where he was would deter his actions. "We've already had a difficult few days, and I can summon the authorities quite easily—"

Payton extended a fist, and the man thought he was about to be hit in the face, but instead Payton knocked on the wall just above the librarian's shoulder.

"Stand still," Payton growled.

The young man's eyes widened as Payton made three swift slices— two vertical and one horizontal. He'd cut a shape into the wall the size of a door, outlining the space where the young man stood frozen with fear.

"What are you—?" the man cried before Payton had finished his task, but he was interrupted as he suddenly fell backward through the drywall Payton had just dissected.

Payton stepped over him and into the head librarian's office.

"Thanks for your help," he snarled. "This is exactly what I was looking for."

Grant glanced inside the spiral notebook one last time to confirm the address and rang the doorbell.

The book of sketches given to him by that young boy he'd met in St. James's Square had the boy's address written inside the front cover.

Grant heard footsteps inside that sounded like someone running down stairs.

"Mum, I've got it!" called a voice inside.

The door opened, and the boy stood there in his pajamas. Grant had forgotten how early it was; the first signs of dawn were just spilling over the horizon.

But the boy wasn't upset by the early morning visitor. His jaw hung loose from his mouth at the sight of Grant, and he said nothing.

Grant offered a modest smile in return. "Hi, again. It's Stephan, isn't it?"

Stephan stared at him bug-eyed and nodded without blinking.

"Do you remember that Guardian message board you told me about? I was wondering if you wouldn't mind showing it to me?"

Alex's strength returned slowly, and she sat up now on the couch next to Julie with her arm around her. Lisa was on Julie's other side.

Daniel sat nearby, staring at the floor as usual. Nora stood in a corner all alone.

The Upholders were in the kitchen by themselves. Ethan remained at the window, ever watching.

Julie, seated between the two women, tried to blink back her tears, but was unsuccessful. She was shaking now, her illness asserting itself more than usual. She couldn't get her arms to stop moving, even when they were resting in her lap.

Alex knew Julie probably needed a hug or some words of comfort, but at the moment she didn't feel much like soothing anyone. Let alone the woman who seemed to be blaming Grant for everything. Alex tried to convince the others that this theory that *he* was the one responsible was nonsense . . . but they wouldn't listen to her.

Her thoughts went to Grant, out there alone. It wasn't his fault. Couldn't be his fault.

I should be with him.

And what about Morgan . . . Was she really dead?

How could the team go on without her?

Distractedly, Alex watched as Hector made himself busy using his powers on the people here he hadn't yet met. He walked up to Ethan and smiled. Then he suddenly placed his hand on Ethan's forehead. Ethan started to protest, but then he stopped and closed his eyes. He was giving in to a pleasant sensation; Alex could still remember the first time Hector had touched her.

When Hector pulled away, Ethan opened his eyes and looked down at his wrists. The scars from his ordeal on the subway train were gone. "Incredible!" he said, smiling. "You didn't even leave a scar."

"He never does," Fletcher remarked from nearby, where he was fiddling on his computer as usual.

Ethan almost laughed. "Can he do anything for an old football injury to the neck?"

"I would imagine he already did," Fletcher explained without emotion.

Ethan pivoted his head down, turned it back and forth, and looked up at the large man in astonishment.

"A single touch is all it takes," Fletcher continued, though he never looked up from his computer screen. "Hector can heal any injury that's not too far gone. Illnesses are much more challenging for him, but he continues to try."

"Man, where were you three days ago?" Ethan laughed.

"You want to can the celebration?" Nora scowled from her corner. "Show some respect, man. We just lost one of our own."

Ethan blushed. "I—I'm sorry." He was at a loss. "I, um . . . I'm not much use to you all here. Maybe I should see if my MI–5 contacts could help turn up something on Morgan. . . ."

He glanced nervously around the room and then exited the loft. Alex knew she should stop him from leaving, but she found herself watching and saying nothing as he went.

"So," Fletcher looked up from his computer, "are we really going to just 'sit tight' like good little sidekicks?"

"What else can we do?" Lisa replied.

"We have no leads to investigate, do we?" Daniel offered.

A thought popped into Alex's head. Something she'd forgotten about.

"The Museum," she blurted out. Everyone faced her. "The British Museum. Morgan mentioned it the other day. There's supposedly some secret room there named 'the Secretum'."

"Works for me," Lisa said, standing. "Anything's better than just sitting here."

Payton surprised everyone by storming through the outer door. He brushed past the Upholders in the kitchen and entered the main area of the loft.

"You must come with me, all of you," he announced, his features grim. "Where's Grant?"

Alex stood from her seat, and Julie moved to help or brace her, but Alex motioned that she was fine.

"You found something at the Library?" Alex asked.

"What's he on about?" Mrs. Edeson asked, appearing from the kitchen.

"I found something that could lead us to Morgan and the Secretum," Payton stated. "It concerns us all," he added, glancing at Mrs. Edeson.

"I think we should look into this Museum thing first . . ." Fletcher said.

"I haven't time for this. We're going now," Payton replied.

"Shut up, both of you!" Alex shouted, fire returning to her for the first time in days. "Doc, you and Lisa go check out the Museum. The rest of us will go with Payton."

Daniel looked up, but at Alex, not Lisa. "I . . . I don't think that's a good—"

Alex cut him off with a wave of her hand. "I don't want to hear it. Whatever the deal is between you two, I know I speak for everyone when I say I've had enough of it. The Museum is the least dangerous assignment we've got. It should give you two loads of time to work out your personal issues."

Daniel looked deflated and downcast, but Lisa appeared rather smug.

She turned to Mrs. Edeson and Cornelius. "Will you come with us?"

"What is this about, dear?" Mrs. Edeson asked.

"You want to know where that ring on your finger came from?" Payton stepped in. "Or who put it there? Then come with us."

60

"Here we go," Stephan said, taking a seat behind one of the computers in the Internet café.

They were lucky to find an open terminal. Patrons jammed the place, and everyone turned to look as Grant entered and took a seat opposite Stephan at one of the tiny tables. His appearance was ghastly, but he still had the world's most recognized—and now most *wanted*—face. He kept a close eye on everyone around, should any of them try anything. But they all seemed too dazed and awed by his presence to act.

They shouldn't stay long . . . One of these people was bound to dial 911, or whatever number Londoners dialed for emergencies. . . .

Stephan's fingers tapped the keyboard as he logged into a remote account. In only seconds, he'd pulled up the "Guardian Fans" website and began scanning through the most recent postings.

Grant knelt beside him. "Where are the 'Guardian Sightings' you mentioned?"

"One sec . . ." Stephan replied, clicking with his mouse. He pulled up a secondary page that looked like a standard Internet message board with brief paragraphs written by users detailing how and where they had seen Guardian. Stephan scrolled through the list, and two things caught Grant's attention.

First, more than half of the reports were unfactual nonsense. Nothing more than sad attempts at grabbing fifteen seconds of fame.

Second, the majority of the valid reports were signed by someone
named Levi.

"Who's this Levi person?" Grant asked.

Stephan shook his head. "Dunno, man, but he comes up with more
reliable sightings of you than anyone. Don't know how he does it."

"So you don't know him?"

"I know his name; he's on here all the time. Never talked to him.
But he's the one who wrote the report I saw the other day that led me
to you. Everybody wants to know who he is. Some friends of mine even
think he could be a member of your team," Stephan added.

"He's not," Grant replied confidently. "Can you tell if Levi is online
right now?"

"Yeah, he's on."

"I want to talk to him."

Lisa and Daniel entered the British Museum, an enormous building
in classic Greco-Roman style, in silence. Daniel hadn't said a single
word since they departed from the loft. Lisa had tried to start a conversation a few times, but she quickly gave up.

She gazed about at the enormous expanse before them. The sheer
vastness was mind-boggling.

"Where do we start looking?" she asked.

Daniel merely shrugged.

Lisa rolled her eyes and turned to her right. "It's probably off in
some remote corner . . ."

Behind her, Daniel turned and set off to the left.

Lisa's shoulders slumped as she noticed his action and turned to
follow him. "Or . . . we could look over that way. . . ."

"Tell me you were undercover, Ethan," Chief Inspector Walden said,
rounding on him. "Tell me it was all part of one of your wild schemes to
infiltrate Guardian's ranks and discover his secrets."

Ethan met Walden's eyes evenly. His hands were cuffed behind him.
He was seated in a folding chair in the large police workroom, amid
desks, filing cabinets, and over a dozen of Scotland Yard's finest. Several MI–5 agents were also present.

Things had not exactly gone according to plan. Apparently, Director

Stevens had issued an international warrant for his arrest. Ethan had unknowingly walked right into her clutches.

"No comment," Ethan replied.

Walden knelt on one knee before Ethan and grabbed him by the shoulders. "You listen to me, lad! This man you're protecting is a wanted terrorist capable of, literally, almost anything. Your people are coming all the way over here to retrieve you, and I don't think they're going to be as friendly with you as I am. It'd be best to make your confession to me now and get it over with."

Ethan looked into his friend's eyes. He was grateful for the older man's concern, but he'd gotten himself into this mess and would have to figure his own way out. He couldn't reach Grant or any of his people for help, and he sure wasn't about to drag another good law enforcement officer like Walden down with him.

"I have nothing to say," Ethan mumbled and looked away.

His self-pity was for show only; in reality, his eyes were searching the room, his mind formulating various means of escape. He'd gotten out of tighter spots than this. . . .

Walden walked away sadly, and several of his officers followed him. Two were left to guard Ethan, remaining by him on either side.

Ethan waited until Walden was clear of the room, allowed at least three minutes to pass, and then he acted.

"I need to go to the rest room," he said.

The two guards looked at each other. "You'll have to hold it," one of them said.

He stood, and one of them made a move to force him back down into his seat, but Ethan kicked backward against the chair, which hit the other officer, knocking him off guard. Ethan head-butted the man before him in the stomach and took off running for the nearest exit, his hands still cuffed behind his back.

He made it to within ten feet of the nearest door, which would lead to an outer hallway, a front desk, a foyer, and then the exit. This wouldn't be easy, but then, that was the way he liked it.

"Hold it!" someone yelled from behind. He heard more than one set of footsteps.

He didn't stop. He made it to the hallway and ducked inside a water fountain alcove. When the running officers approached, he tripped them. He stepped over them and kept running.

He was halfway through the hallway when someone slammed into him from his side. Tackled and wrestled to the ground, Ethan looked up into the eyes of his friend Walden.

"What are you *doing*, lad?" Walden shouted. "Did you really think you could escape? You're just making things worse—"

His words stopped when the electricity went out all over the building. Emergency flood lights came on, augmenting the natural sunlight shining through the windows. Ethan looked up; Walden still had him pinned to the ground, but his attention was elsewhere.

Ethan heard a *zip* sound, and Walden's eyes grew wide. He passed out, his heavy weight holding Ethan to the ground.

More silent shots were fired, but Ethan's trained ears knew he wasn't hearing the sound of bullets firing—even ones from a silencer. This was some sort of tranq dart or Taser fire, and it seemed that everyone in the building was getting one. It happened so quickly and efficiently, Ethan couldn't believe it when he couldn't hear anyone speaking or any shoes hitting the tile floor. Everyone was out cold in mere seconds.

Walden's unconscious form was peeled off of him, and someone helped Ethan to his feet.

"Ethan Cooke?" said a voice to his right behind a black ski mask. The man was clad all in black, head-to-toe, and there was another man on his left dressed exactly the same.

"Yeah," he replied, no idea what was going on. "What is this?"

"You are needed," the man in the mask said. It was a voice he had never heard before.

The two men grabbed him by his restrained arms and dragged him toward the exit.

"Wait!" Ethan cried. "Who are you people?!"

"We're the good guys, friend," said one of the men. "And you've just been drafted into war."

Ethan shook himself free. "There is no way I'm going back to the FBI."

One of the men chuckled, amused. "We don't answer to any government. We work for . . . a higher power."

"What higher power?" Ethan demanded.

"*The* higher power."

61

"You going to tell us what we're about to find?" Alex asked Payton as the group walked together through the main doors of the London Library.

"No," Payton replied.

"I kind of despise you," Alex said with a sigh.

They marched without incident to the librarian's office and down the spiral staircase. Mrs. Edeson proved Grant's theory about her control over willpower correct by ensuring that none of the patrons inside the Library looked in their direction. Nora erased the memories of the one or two that caught a glimpse of them anyway.

"I don't understand," Mrs. Edeson said as the group stepped through the blown-in doorway and into the charred remains of the Secretum's file room. "What's a filthy, poorly lit room such as *this* doing underneath the finest library in all the world?"

"We're not here for the room," Payton bit out.

He led the way to a distant corner, where he knelt and pointed at a small pockmark on the wall. It was less than an inch in diameter, but as Alex leaned in close to see it, she recognized it.

It was the six-pointed symbol of the Secretum.

She stood straight again. "So it's their symbol? So what?"

"What symbol?" asked Cornelius, twirling his mustache in what might've been a nervous gesture.

Fletcher summed it up. "The Secretum of Six. That ancient underground conspiracy Grant told you about that's screwed with our lives.

They call him 'the Bringer.' They have some kind of big plans for Grant that have been written in stone for seven thousand years. Literally."

"Why are we down here, Payton?" Alex asked, wanting to get back to the point.

Payton touched the tiny six-pointed star with his forefinger, and it depressed inward, revealing the seams of a round button that was set into the wall. He stepped back as three square feet of corner space swiveled open, pivoting on the corner itself.

It revealed a dank cubbyhole inside, no larger than the corner that had swiveled open. At its bottom was a hole that had been dug out of the ground. The top rungs of a cast-iron ladder stuck out over the top edge of the hole.

"Where does it lead?" Alex asked.

Daniel and Lisa's search of the British Museum turned up nothing. By early afternoon, they had covered most of the building's surprisingly modern interior.

But they were both far too distracted to take in the rarities the Museum held, simply proceeding in silence from one area to the next.

Lisa watched Daniel almost as often as she searched the exhibits. More than anything else, this proved how different a person he was. The old Daniel would have been alive with excitement. He would've wanted plenty of time to marvel at the ancient relics, the comprehensive collections, the perfectly preserved artifacts from dozens of ancient civilizations. The British Museum held one of the finest collections of cultural antiquities in the world.

Now, his gaze seemed to skim over the surface of everything he saw, like water running off of an oily surface. Nothing registered, nothing mattered.

Under different circumstances, their visit together to such a prominent British tourist attraction could have qualified as a date. She'd once longed for such a possibility, but she still couldn't reconcile her feelings for this man with what she'd seen him do. Daniel had used a handgun to drill a hole in the center of Detective Matthew Drexel's forehead.

She couldn't help thinking that if he would simply talk to her, they could sort things out somehow. But he refused, retreating further and further inward.

They concluded their tour of the facility in the central Great Court. A magnificent glass and steel roof covered what once had been an outdoor space, and in the center of this courtyard was a building completely separated from the rest of the Museum, yet enclosed by it on all sides.

It was a round building labeled "Reading Room." As soon as Daniel saw it, he rolled his eyes.

"I'm an idiot," he said.

"What?" Lisa asked.

"This place—the Reading Room—contains a library of reference materials on all of the Museum's collections and many volumes about the cultures represented inside the Museum. We should've started here. I'm so stupid. . . ."

Her eyes were drawn upward to the dome that reached high above them as they entered the round room. Detailed with beautiful gold, white, and blue décor, the ceiling was a work of art in and of itself. Shelves lined the curved walls all the way around, and every shelf was filled to the brim with books.

The room's center was filled with straight desks, shelves, and other resources extending from the middle of the chamber out to the edges. The desks were topped with individual fluorescent lamps that illuminated the room in a soft, reverential way. The combined effect gave an unspoken command to visitors: *Please be quiet.*

Visitors were here and there about the room, researching or merely appreciating what could be considered another of the Museum's collections.

"This won't take long," Daniel said, wandering off.

Whatever, she thought. Lisa allowed herself to wander as well and soon came upon a computer screen containing a digitized version of the Reading Room's card catalog.

On a whim, she sat and typed in the word *secretum.*

An entry came up, but it wasn't about any sort of secret repository. It was the name of a book, a very old book. Something about it captured her attention immediately, and she got a tingle across her skin— a remnant of the same sensation she felt when she and Daniel used to make a breakthrough back at their lab.

She printed out the reference and read over it again before rising from her seat to locate Daniel. She spotted him facing the bookcases against the wall about forty feet away, flipping through the pages of one volume after another. She fought the urge to run with excitement as she approached him.

"Did you know there's a book called *Secretum* by somebody named Petrarch?" she said, still reading over the page in her hands.

"Mm," he nodded absently, not looking up. "It's a classical Latin philosophy piece written by a disciple of Augustine. Dates back to the fourteenth century, if I'm not mistaken."

Lisa cursed him in her mind. Why did he always have to know everything she didn't? Frowning, she said, "Yeah, but do you know what it's *about*?"

"I don't recall the specifics," he replied, still not turning away from his book.

"According to this, it's a self-examination of man's free will."

A moment passed, and Lisa almost thought Daniel hadn't heard her. Then he slowly turned his head and looked into her eyes—*truly* looked into her eyes for the first time in months.

Her heart fluttered as she felt an old emotion surface—the thrill of shared discovery.

"Let me see that," he said softly. She handed him the printed page. "Man's free will . . ." he repeated, whispering the phrase. She studied him, knowing the look in his eyes so well. It was intense concentration, and she could practically see the wheels turning inside his head, processing.

She felt it as well, her mind going over and over the words on the paper. He looked at her again, his expression severe. There was something to this.

They both knew it. "We're on to something," she whispered.

"I think so, yes," Daniel replied, his mind still spinning.

Lisa looked past his shoulder. There was something else bothering her, a vague sense that only now was forming into a genuine thought as she said it aloud. "Don't look, but there are two men on the other side of the room who've been watching us since we walked in here."

He faced the book in his hand, pretending to read. "Are you sure?"

"Positive," she replied, her adrenaline surging. "They're trying to hide it but not doing a very good job."

"Feds or locals?" Daniel whispered.

"Can't tell." She stared at her piece of paper, trying hard not to look at the men again.

"I want you to work your way around the outer edge of the room until you're near the exit. Don't look at them again," he instructed her.

"What about you?"

"Just go, *now.*"

Frustrated, she turned away and followed his instructions, slowly browsing through the collected books along the outer wall until she was within ten feet of the exit.

The room's silence was broken by the sound of feet running across the carpeted floor. Alarmed, Lisa turned to see Daniel coming toward her at a dead sprint.

"GO!" he shouted.

She fell into step right in front of him as they mashed against the door and ran out into the Great Court.

62

Having started at what must've been over one hundred feet beneath the surface, Alex and her companions were surprised at just how many rungs this ladder had—and how far down it went.

It didn't seem to end.

All of them—Alex, Payton, Julie, Mrs. Edeson, Cornelius, Nora, Fletcher, Hector, Charlotte, and the young guy whose name Alex still didn't know—held small flashlights, but still none of them could see the bottom. Not even Payton, who led the way at the bottom of their procession downward.

"Helloooo!" Alex called out. Her voice echoed down through the cylindrical hole and then back up at them.

"That can't be a good idea," Fletcher whispered. "You really want to let the evil conspiracy people *know* we're climbing down their tiny little hole?"

"You think that's what we're going to find down there? Substation Omega Prime?" Julie asked. "Maybe we should call Grant. . . ."

Fletcher replied, "At least we've got our powers. That Trevor kid must have vacated the premises."

"Give me that," Payton said. He snatched Alex's flashlight and dropped it.

Alex opened her mouth to protest but then waited in silence for the flashlight to find purchase on something beneath them.

Long after the light had faded from their sight they heard a tiny *clink* from far below.

"I hate climbing," Alex muttered as they continued to slowly descend.

"This isn't climbing," Fletcher replied. "Climbing is going *up*."

"I hate *you*," she said miserably.

"You all are giving me a frightful headache," Mrs. Edeson said. "Could we not observe silence until we reach the bottom?"

Alex replied, "How's about you tell us about your powers, instead?"

Fletcher chimed in as well. "Yeah, I'm dying to know how you pulled off the barrier."

"It's called ingenuity, darling," Mrs. Edeson replied. "I control will-power, as I demonstrated in the Library above. I can make anyone do anything I so choose. Cornelius has the peculiar ability to establish a perimeter of thought around himself—he causes everyone around him to think about what he *wants* them to think about. And Charlotte is a broadcaster—she can control the transfer of all forms of electronic information. Wired or wireless, as the case may be."

"She's how you were able to regulate the flow of information going in and out of the city," Julie offered, catching on.

"*And* why satellites covering the area inside of the barrier returned images of static," Mrs. Edeson added. "She's quite clever."

"But how were you able to create and maintain such a complex desire—not wanting to leave the city—in so many minds all at once?" Fletcher asked, wanting specifics.

Cornelius answered. "Well, consider my ability and that of Mrs. Edeson. If you multiplied them by one another, you could create a bar-rier of thought or will that forces others to do as you wish."

"I get it," Fletcher replied. "That's what the other guy does—Mr. Special. He joins your minds together, allowing you to use your powers as if they were one and the same. Remarkable. In this case, you removed the desire from outsiders to enter the city, and the desire from those on the inside to leave."

"More or less correct," Mrs. Edeson replied.

It was ten more minutes before they reached the bottom, which opened into another cubbyhole of a room, much like the one above. It was far too small to fit them all, but there was a door opposite the bot-tom of the ladder. Payton reached the bottom and hopped off the lad-der, examining the door before he opened it.

It was tremendously ornate, carved out of solid oak, with another version of the Secretum's symbol etched into it—this one as wide as the door itself. The remainder of the door was carved with intricate scroll-work, patterns inside of patterns that dazzled the eyes. In the center of the Secretum's symbol was a number, carved so that it stood out from the symbol.

"What is it?" Alex asked as she neared the bottom of the ladder and the door came into view. "What's it say?"

"It's just a number," Payton replied.

Alex stepped forward and read for herself. The number "17" was inscribed in the center of the symbol.

Maybe it's the 17th Substation? she pondered. *But no, there weren't numbered doors like this at the last two substations. . . .*

Payton pushed open the door.

Stephan's eyes lit up. "Hey, I got him! We're on with Levi."

His fingers raced across the keyboard.

"Um, can you come around here a sec?" Stephan said. Grant stood from his chair and circled the table to stand behind his young friend.

He saw Stephan's visage in a tiny window on the screen and himself stepping into view behind him. It was a live video image Stephan was sending over the Net. He typed words as Grant watched:

    see? believe me now?

"He didn't believe I was really with you?" Grant asked.

Stephan shook his head, grinning. Grant returned to his seat.

"Tell him I would like to know where he gets his leads from on my whereabouts."

Stephan typed the message. Grant waited impatiently for the response to come through.

"Says he has an inside source," Stephan relayed.

"Inside what? My people? Some government agency?"

Stephan clicked the keyboard again.

"No, from underground," was the reply.

Underground? What's that supposed to mean . . .

Unless. . . ?

Daniel and Lisa's escape had progressed outside to a remote parking area when their efforts were cut short by gunshots fired just over their heads.

Lisa wanted to keep running, but Daniel shook his head no. He put his hands up and turned around.

The two men approached, weapons trained on them both.

"Turn around, down on your knees!" one of them barked.

"What's the charge?" Daniel asked as handcuffs were roughly placed on his wrists.

No response.

"I demand to know what we're being charged with! Who are you? Scotland Yard? MI–5?"

The men forced him and Lisa down onto their knees, facing away from them. "Neither, actually," one of them hissed. Daniel caught a glimpse of one of the men's hands as he was roughly shoved down.

The symbol of the Secretum was tattooed on the man's wrist.

Guns appeared, silencers already in place, and the muzzles touched the backs of Daniel's and Lisa's heads.

"Wait, why are you doing this?!" Daniel cried.

"Sorry, Doctor Cossick," the man behind him said. "But you've been classified a 'loose end,' and our orders are to remove you from the picture."

Two gunshots rang out, but Daniel discovered much to his shock that he was still alive. And something wet was all over the back of his head.

He turned cautiously to see a man wearing an overcoat and a woman in a pantsuit, both with guns raised, carefully approaching the attackers, both of whom were already falling to the ground, dead.

"Sorry for our tardiness," the woman said. "But you're not an easy pair to locate."

Satisfied that the two attacking men were dead, they holstered their weapons and pulled out badges. MI–5, both of them. They helped Daniel and Lisa to their feet but didn't remove their handcuffs.

"I don't understand," Lisa stammered nervously. "What's going on?"

"You're under arrest for aiding the wanted criminal known as 'Guardian.'"

Lisa and Daniel glanced at the dead men on the ground. "Then who were *these two?*" he asked.

"We were expecting you could tell us," the woman replied.

Nothing else was said. The British agents led Daniel and Lisa to an unmarked sedan and drove them away.

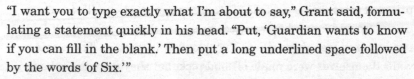

63

"I want you to type exactly what I'm about to say," Grant said, formulating a statement quickly in his head. "Put, 'Guardian wants to know if you can fill in the blank.' Then put a long underlined space followed by the words 'of Six.'"

Stephan seemed curious but sort of shrugged and typed in Grant's words.

"What's a 'Seekretoom'?" Stephan asked, trying unsuccessfully to sound out Levi's reply.

"He knows about the Secretum?!" Grant asked, massaging his forehead, thoughts spinning rapidly. "Ask him if he knows where to find 'Omega Prime.'"

He waited impatiently as Stephan typed the question. "He says 'Omega Prime' is located at the heart of the Secretum. They're waiting for you to come and enter their world."

Grant's breaths were coming faster and faster now. This was it . . . The end of his search was so close now. . . . "Where do I find the entrance to their world?" he whispered.

"Don't have to, mate," Stephan replied, reading the screen. "Says you just have to find the nearest Entry Node."

"The nearest what?"

"What do you see?" Fletcher asked as he neared the bottom of the ladder. He brought up the rear of the group, so everyone else was already at the bottom and moving through the ornate wooden door by

the time he saw the small foyer. Dim light protruded through the doorway, but he couldn't tell what was inside. "What's in there?" he called
out, rushing to catch up.

No one responded.

Carefully, he stepped off the bottom rung. He brushed his hands off
against each other, displeased at the rust and soot that had accumu-
lated on them from the climb down. He turned.

Stepping through the door, his breath caught in his throat and his
jaw fell.

A small tunnel, just wide enough to accommodate the door, opened
into a cavernous space like nothing he'd ever seen.

The shape of the space was like two horizontal cylinders that
passed through one another. It was an underground chamber, comprised of intersecting tunnels of staggering proportions. The walls
curved up and around in a perfect circle, reaching a pinnacle at least
two hundred feet above where they stood at its bottom. The curving
walls themselves were made of solid rock, but they were braced every
twenty or thirty feet with gleaming silver struts that went all the way
around.

Fletcher noticed that the walls were made of far more than just
rock. Pieces of metal and electronic circuit boards were scattered
throughout, as if sewn directly into the structure of the walls. But
there were no wires, no cords leading from one panel to another. Whatever this was, whatever made it work, it was all buried inside or built
into the rock.

The chamber hummed quietly as the ten of them merely turned in
their own circles, taking in the enormity of it all. Alex and Julie stood
out at the very bottom of the chamber, near a T-beam that jutted
upward; the others remained closer to the door.

Fletcher stepped a little farther in and realized that the humming
was coming from the T-beams. Were they electromagnetic?

Alex opened her mouth to break the silence when a high-pitched
whistling sound was heard from one of the tunnels. It was so ear-
splitting, no one realized that there was something in the tunnel moving. Something huge, headed straight for them. A tremendous gust of
wind rushed at them, so hard the flesh on their faces pressed inward
and distorted against it.

"Down!" shouted Payton, and then he vanished in a blur, reappearing on top of Alex, who was now lying on her stomach, Payton pinning her down. An enormous gold-tinged object darted through the tunnel at lightning speed. Its belly soared through the space where Alex's head had been only a second ago, and then it was long gone, down the other end of the tunnel.

It went by far too fast for any of them to get a good look, but it was clearly huge—and it seemed to have *floated* in the exact center of the tunnel.

Fletcher thought it might've had a cylindrical shape, matching the tunnel, but rounded on the ends.

Like some sort of high-powered subway train or monorail, able to move faster than anything he'd ever seen—maybe even faster than Payton.

He watched the others recover from this astonishing sight, and Alex and Payton peeled themselves up off the ground. He waited as recognition lit their eyes—why couldn't they ever understand as fast as he could?—and they turned to look at each other in shock.

They all knew exactly what they were looking at, what they had just seen, and what they were standing inside of.

But not a single one of them could form any words adequate for their discovery.

It was unbelievable.

"Is this?" Alex began.

"Wait a minute . . ." said Fletcher, looking around. "Where's Julie?"

Alex spun in place. "She was just here, right beside me! Right before that thing—!"

Alex looked up at each of them in horror.

Payton shouted, "JULIE!" His voice echoed through all four tunnels, but no other sound was heard.

"We should call Grant," Alex said.

Payton turned to Alex and the others. "I dove for you *both*," he said. "I don't understand. She was standing right here beside you."

"They grabbed her," Fletcher stated. It was the only logical conclusion. If that "train" thing had hit her, there'd be smashed bits of her all over the tunnel. But there weren't.

"Are you insane?" Alex asked. "Did you see how fast that thing was moving?"

"Then maybe somebody else grabbed her from the ground while we were distracted, I don't know. It was loud enough that we didn't hear her shout," Fletcher replied. "All that matters is, she's gone. And now the team is down by two."

"Yes, but up by four," Mrs. Edeson noted, a knowing glimmer in her eye.

"Whatever they did with Morgan, this is how they traveled," Nora noted. "Maybe she and Julie will be held together someplace?"

"But where does this *go*?" Alex asked, exasperated.

Fletcher's attention was elsewhere. "I bet I know a way we can find out."

The others rejoined him in the small tunnel that led to the wooden door. A small panel outside the door held a lever, several LED lights that were currently turned off, and words written in various languages.

"I think it's a call button," he said.

He pulled the lever.

64

"We'd better get you home," Grant told Stephan as they exited the café together. He absently scratched at the scar on his hand and noted that the red marks had died down considerably. But they'd been replaced by an odd blue discoloration that surrounded the scar. He'd never seen anything quite like it.

A wave of nausea suddenly came over him, and he found himself holding Stephan's shoulder for support to keep from losing his balance.

"What's wrong? Guardian?" Stephan asked, his eyes looking around their surroundings as if he were about to call for help, right there in the heart of downtown London.

"It's my fault."

Grant turned right. Trevor stood there.

"Sorry," he said.

"Who's he?" Stephan asked.

"Trevor," Grant replied. "He's . . ." Grant grappled with how to explain it simply, "he's another like me."

"Cool," Stephan replied eagerly. "What's *your* superpower?" he asked Trevor.

Trevor didn't answer him. His attention was fixed on Grant.

"What are you doing here?" Grant asked, while his stomach cramped under the terrible pains that accompanied being so close to Trevor.

"I was sent."

"By your masters in the Secretum?"

Trevor appeared mildly stung by the words but tried not to show it. "I can't stay long; they're expecting me back rather quickly."

"So they're coercing you somehow, that it?"

Trevor didn't reply to that question. He merely looked on Grant with a sad expression.

"They've got you tagged, don't they?" Grant said softly. He didn't wait for Trevor to reply; there was no need. Somewhere in his clothes or implanted somewhere in his body there was a tracking device. Possibly even a wire, listening in to everything they were saying right now.

"I was instructed to tell you that they have just picked up your sister," he explained. He fished a piece of paper out of his pants pocket and handed it to Grant.

"Who? The Secretum?" Grant cried. "They have Julie?!"

Grant snatched the paper and unfolded it. It contained a map depicting a view of the Middle Eastern nation of Turkey. In the central southern portion of the map was the asterisk-like symbol of the Secretum, marking some unidentified mountain range. It was exactly what Morgan had expected them to find at the London Library.

Grant stared at the page, a knot building in his stomach. Then he looked up at Trevor, anger coloring his face. Trevor recoiled slightly, and Grant guessed from the boy's reaction that his eyes had turned red again.

Let's hope no more cities are getting swallowed up into the earth right now—

Good grief, now they've got me believing it!

Grant's phone rang.

"It's him," Trevor said, locking eyes with Grant.

Grant flipped open the phone. "Is my sister alive? For your sake, the answer had better be yes."

"She lives," Devlin replied through the phone in a heavy Russian accent.

Wasn't he South African? That's how it sounded when he called me in L.A. . . .

"I wish it weren't necessary to take her from you," Devlin continued, "but it is the only way we could ensure you would come. There are parts of what we do that are most repugnant. But sometimes questionable ethics must be employed for the greater good to be accomplished.

I'm not telling you anything you don't already know."

"What about Morgan?" Grant asked, dreading the answer because in his heart, he already knew it. He'd known it since he woke up in St. James's Square and could no longer feel her presence.

"I am truly sorry, Grant," Devlin replied. "We did everything we could, but she was too far gone by the time she reached our surgeons."

Grant was surprised that despite the empty feeling he felt inside, no tears formed in his eyes. Why couldn't he cry for Morgan? She was gone! What was wrong with him? Was he too preoccupied with his sister? Or was it something else?

"I know this will mean nothing to you, coming from me," Devlin continued, "but you have my deepest condolences. I knew enough about Morgan to know that her loss must be deeply felt by all Externals who knew her. Casualties are an ugly reality, in any army," Devlin said, echoing something Grant's grandfather had told him about the Loci.

"Package deal. They're your army. Created to suit your specific needs as the Bringer."

"Yeah," Grant struggled to get any words to come out.

What's an External?

"She was a remarkable woman, and not just because of her gift of memory," Devlin offered. "But I'm afraid the three of you caught our librarian quite off guard, and she panicked. After all, we honestly believed Morgan would never, *ever* return there—"

"What does the Bringer bring?" The question burst from Grant's lips before he knew he was saying it. He regretted disrespecting Morgan's death, but now that he'd said it, he was desperate to hear the answer.

"I have never lied to you, Grant, and I never will. But this is *the* crucial question of your existence, and I simply cannot answer until I see you in person."

Grant scratched at his scar. "Just tell me if I'm the cause of all these disasters threatening to rip the world apart. Please."

"The global disasters are not your doing," Devlin replied. "They're mine."

What??

"You?!" Grant cried, oblivious to the amount of attention he was drawing on the streets of London. Trevor stood rock still and watched his phone exchange. "How could you *possibly*—?"

"I told you before that it was my duty to finish the work your grandfather started, and that's precisely what I've been doing. He prepared you for your arrival into the world. *I* have prepared the world for your arrival—the arrival of the Bringer."

No . . . it's not true, it can't be . . .

NO!

"You . . ." Grant stammered. "You couldn't have . . . This was all about me? . . . But you drowned New York, you killed all of those innocent people in China! You destroyed Jerusalem!! Millions of people are DEAD!!" he raged.

"They don't matter," Devlin declared with a simple, casual air that gave Grant chills. "Our plans were in place seven thousand years before you were born. That's a very long time, Grant. Long enough to develop and apply technologies for things like the manufacture and release of a devastating pathogen . . . or tectonic manipulation to cause earthquakes, landslides, volcanic eruptions . . . or taking control of your man-made satellites and causing them to crash to the earth. The fire we spread in your hometown of Los Angeles was the easiest to accomplish, but it brought perhaps the highest rate of success."

Some part of Grant knew Devlin was telling the truth, but he still couldn't quite swallow the reality of what this man was saying. "I don't believe you. It's impossible . . . No one has that kind of technology or resources."

"*We* do, and a great deal more," Devlin replied. "But none of that matters anymore. All of our plans have been completed. It's time now, Grant. We expect to see you within the next twenty-four hours. We'll be waiting for you. As will your sister."

"I'll be there," Grant replied, snapping his phone shut.

How could this be happening?

More importantly, how had he not seen it? For two whole months he believed the Secretum's influence had been absent from his life. Yet there was no break in their activity. Their plans had continued to unfold right before his eyes. And he never made the connection.

"There's one last thing you should know," Trevor said uneasily, nodding at the paper Grant held. "That map in your hands? It came from your file."

"My file? You mean like the files in that room under the Library?" Trevor nodded. "They kept me down there for a long time. Long enough for me to read many of the files down there. Including yours."

There was something else, something he was holding back. . . .

"And?" Grant coached him.

"The stuff in those files is placed in chronological order, from a person's birth on the first page, until . . ." Trevor didn't finish his thought, swallowing nervously. "That map was the last page in your file."

This map of some remote mountain location in Turkey was the final page in his file in the Secretum's records of his life?

"Wouldn't that mean this is the place where—where I'm supposed to die?"

"I don't know," Trevor replied, his body language becoming increasingly antsy.

Grant felt like he'd been punched in the gut. "Yes you do," was all he said.

"I gotta get back," Trevor said. "They aren't the sort to forgive and forget if I'm late."

Grant studied Trevor as he walked away.

He pored over the map for a long time, weighing his options. The mark on the map wasn't far from what looked like a rather large city called Antalya.

"What are you going to do?" Stephan asked in a small voice.

Grant turned. He had forgotten that his young friend was still there.

"What do *you* think I should do?" he asked, wistfully taking in the boy's wide-eyed optimism.

Stephan looked at his feet. "I was just thinking . . . Shouldn't this be the part where the hero saves the world?"

Grant placed a hand on the boy's shoulder. "I hope it is."

"MY FRIENDS. THIS IS the day that generations of our people gave up everything for."

"It comes to this, at last."

"Everything this Secretum has ever done is about to converge in one pivotal event."

"Yes. But we've never discussed in detail what follows. I can't stop wondering . . . What will tomorrow bring? With this task accomplished, what will we do after?"

"There may *be* no tomorrow. We go wherever he takes us."

65

Antalya, Turkey
12 hours later

Grant felt like a walking corpse as he disembarked from his red-eye flight. *Red-eye.* That term had new meaning now. . . .

Since learning of Morgan's death, he had refused to allow his mind to reach out to the Loci. He knew it was irrational, but he feared the despair in his heart might somehow seep into theirs. And the comfort of community that sensing the Loci usually gave him now only grieved him.

He had to finish this alone.

Morgan was dead. All of her vast knowledge and wisdom, a terrible loss. But not as great as the one Grant felt in his heart. Morgan was his teacher, his guide. His friend. She was the first to believe in him, yet she was ever the pragmatist, always prepared to do whatever was required to see something through to the end.

Their search for the Secretum had almost reached its end, but she would not be there to see it.

And Julie . . . If she was still alive, as Devlin claimed, then that blasted illness was still taking her from him a piece at a time.

Without her, he wasn't sure there would be anything worth living for.

Grant bypassed the airport's baggage claim area, as he'd boarded the plane with only the clothes on his back.

Well, he thought, *that's not entirely true.*

Before leaving London, he checked out a book about Turkey from the London Library. He considered it a terrific irony that he'd finally put to use the membership Morgan purchased for him.

She would like that. She'd laugh.

Never mind that this book he'd borrowed was undoubtedly one she could have quoted to him verbatim. He spent the entire flight giving himself a crash course on the nation of Turkey. He'd never had reason to find out anything about it before, and six months ago never would he have imagined he would be walking through the Antalya International Airport.

He'd learned that Antalya, this beautiful resort city situated on the Mediterranean Sea, was just one of hundreds of ancient cities throughout the Taurus Mountains—the mountain range that had been unnamed on the map Trevor had given him. The Taurus Mountains contained numerous peaks rising over ten thousand feet into the sky, including the famous Mount Ararat. And beneath those mountains, he'd discovered with interest, rested the largest caves in all of Asia.

The next fact to catch his eye cemented it. He knew exactly why it was here that the Secretum brought him when he read that this region had been home to over *nine thousand years* of human civilization.

He left the book on the plane.

Morgan was right. The Secretum of Six had placed its base of operations beneath a place of tremendous influence and power. Situated in the very heart of human civilization for thousands of years.

As he strode warily toward the airport's exit, he spotted a number of individuals holding placards and signs for arriving guests. Most of the names were written in Turkish or Arabic, but one sign caught his attention.

In English was written the word "Borrows."

We will expect to see you within the next twenty-four hours, Devlin had said.

The man holding the sign was at least twice Grant's weight, a massive thug of a creature who could probably crush Grant's entire neck with a single hand. A hand, Grant noted, that was branded with the symbol of the Secretum just below his wrist.

He approached the big man and said, "I'm Grant Borrows."

"I know," the man coldly replied. He turned on one heel and marched away, no further instructions given.

Grant fell into step behind the big man, following him out of the airport and to the darkened parking area, where they arrived at an unmarked white van.

The giant unlocked the rear double doors. He merely stood there, his implacable expression leveled on Grant.

Grant understood and climbed inside the van, but the big man didn't close the doors. Grant knelt on his knees; there were no seats in the back of the van, so he wasn't quite sure how he was meant to endure this ride. He hoped it wouldn't be a long trip.

The big man retrieved a small black box from the front passenger seat and brought it around to the back. He climbed in behind Grant and shut the doors behind him.

Grant backed away from the big man as far as he could, uncomfortable about this turn of events. But the other man's attention was focused on the box.

He opened it and retrieved a hypodermic needle containing a clear liquid. A liquid that looked an awful lot like the one the librarian had injected him with at their second meeting, when he'd been rendered unconscious . . .

"No," Grant said, defensively outstretching his hands. "No way. Not again."

The big man was unperturbed. "You will take the needle or you will get out of the van."

Grant remained motionless, his hands still raised, as he considered this.

The big guy tossed him the needle and got out of the van. "Close the doors and inject yourself. Even in the muscle is fine."

Grant knew he could refuse, he could effortlessly send the needle flying into the bulging neck of this gigantic man and commandeer the van. But it would get him no closer to his goal. Even if he could find this mountain range depicted on the map Trevor gave him, how would he ever find Substation Omega Prime on his own? Access from the surface would be too well hidden.

Grant glanced at the rear doors of the van and they closed themselves. He didn't bother rolling up his sleeve; he stuck himself with the needle in his upper arm and mashed the fluid into his system.

The last thing he saw was the big man climbing into the front seat of the van. His vision blurred and he fell against the van's floor.

Unconscious.

Lisa paced.

Her cell adjoined the one they'd put Daniel in. It was otherwise quiet in the small police station's jail. She believed they were the only prisoners here this night.

There was nothing to do here; even the paper she'd printed off at the Museum about the book named *Secretum* had been confiscated, though they'd allowed Daniel to keep his cane. Iron bars separated the two of them, so she had a full view of his movements.

Or lack thereof.

Daniel was reclined on his back on a small cot in the far corner, and his eyes were closed. It was dark out and Daniel was asleep.

How can he sleep at a time like this?!

So she paced, not knowing what else to do.

She wanted to wake him but told herself it was a bad idea. She couldn't do that to him. He'd been through so much . . .

No! Stop making excuses for him!

"Daniel!" she shouted.

Daniel awoke with a start. "What?!" he cried, a fearful expression on his face.

"Why are you sleeping?" Lisa asked in frustration.

"Because I'm tired."

"I can't believe you can just go to sleep like that. Now, of all times."

"What should I be doing?" he replied, still lying flat on his back.

"*I don't know!!*" she yelled, pent-up feelings boiling over. "We don't know how long they're going to hold us here like this, and after that who knows if we'll ever even see each other again! Don't you think we have some things we should say to each other?!"

Daniel sat up and watched her walk back and forth.

"I'm sorry," he said softly.

"What?"

"I'm sorry. I'm sorry we're here. I'm sorry I've withdrawn from you and everyone else and made everything worse. Mostly, I'm sorry for the person I turned out to be."

"For who you are?" she repeated, sitting down on the ground by the bars that separated them. "Do you have any idea how much I care about who you are?"

Daniel looked down. "You don't understand," he said. "I'm not sorry for killing Drexel. I wish I was. I wish it *so much*. But I'm not. No matter how much self-loathing I feel for being the one that pulled the trigger . . . I know without question that I'd do it again. Right here, right now, if I had to. He was pure evil, and he got what was coming to him."

Lisa felt tears stinging her eyes, but made no effort to will them away. She sat silently, waiting for him to continue. He'd taken a long time to get this off his chest, and she wasn't about to interrupt him before he was done.

"I'm a murderer," he said miserably, as if hearing the words for the first time. "I murdered a man. I used these hands to end someone else's life. I *killed* him. And I . . . I'm *glad* I did it! I'm not sorry. I'm not sorry! *I'm not!*" his voice rose at the end, just as he got up from his seat.

He turned his face toward the ceiling, stretched out his arms, and shouted at the top of his lungs, "I'M NOT SORRY AND I NEVER WILL BE!!" Then he let out an enraged, wordless howl that made Lisa's skin crawl.

When he was done, he collapsed to the ground, spent. He shook his head slowly and kept his eyes on the ground.

"*Why* am I not sorry?" he whispered.

The tears spilled out of Lisa's eyes at last, and she saw that Daniel was crying quietly to himself as well.

She let out a shuddering breath and finally opened her mouth to speak again.

"Do you remember how we met?" she asked.

Daniel didn't respond. He continued weeping.

"It was so hot that summer. I answered your want ad for a research assistant, and the ad was so small, I thought I would be the only one there. But it turned out I was your fifth interview of the day. I figured I didn't have a chance, especially after I dropped those microscope slides you wanted me to examine." She almost laughed at the memory.

"But instead of complaining or dismissing me, you knelt down and helped me clean up the mess. And you said something about wishing you had a dollar for every time you'd done that yourself. I never found out why you hired me over all the others, but in my mind, I liked to think that you saw a kindred spirit in me and decided that maybe it was meant to be."

"It wasn't anything like that . . ." Daniel admitted. "You were the only applicant who pronounced my last name correctly."

Lisa smiled, wiping tears out of her face. "Whatever your reason, I still think it was meant to be. Not long after I started, your personal funding began to run out and we had to look for private investors to fund the research—do you remember that?"

"Of course," Daniel said, still looking at the ground. "I still don't know how you managed to find someone so willing to part with their money as fast as you did."

"I didn't find someone," Lisa replied.

Daniel finally looked up and met her eyes.

"*I* was the investor."

Daniel was speechless.

"Before he passed away, my father was the COO of a Fortune 500 company. I was an only child and my mom died when I was young, so everything was left to me. I was in college and had no idea what to do with myself *or* the money, and I just wasn't interested in his business— the automotive industry—so I decided on a whim to switch majors to science."

"*You* funded our research? Out of your own pocket?" Daniel cried, incredulous. "You believed in the work *that much*?"

"No," Lisa replied. "I believed in you."

Daniel opened his mouth but nothing came out. He crawled, on his hands and knees, until he was close enough to touch her through the bars. He took her hand in his and looked deep into her eyes, still not understanding or believing her words.

"Why?" he sincerely asked.

She squeezed his hand. "You know why."

Daniel looked down, tears threatening to seize him once more. He turned his face all about, searching for answers, searching for words, but he was greeted only by the empty jail cell's walls.

"I have nothing to offer you . . ." he whispered, grappling with the words. "I'm not good enough . . . I don't *deserve* you."

"I forgive you, Daniel," Lisa replied, "for everything. I forgive you."

67

Grant awoke to find the van rolling to a stop. They'd come to rest on what felt like a steep incline.

The back door swung open, and the big guy stood there gesturing for Grant to get out of the vehicle.

When Grant stumbled out, still groggy from the drugs, he saw they'd stopped on a rough dirt road a quarter of the way up a mountainside in the heart of the Taurus Mountains. A majestic nighttime view greeted him both above and below. The stars shown very bright, and very far off in the distance he could see a halo of lights that must have been Antalya.

Without a word, the large man turned and began to walk farther up the mountain. Grant followed. There was no path, no signposts telling them where to go. It was a desert mountain of peaks and hills and dirt and boulders. A few sparse trees dotted the landscape, but there was little else.

Half an hour later, they were still climbing a steep incline when the big man veered in a new direction. Grant didn't dare let the man get out of his sight; the only light came from the moon and stars. He scrambled to keep up.

The big man led him another fifty meters around the mountain's side until they reached an outcropping of large rocks surrounding what had to be a twenty-ton boulder. Without a word, Grant's escort reached between the base of the boulder and some of the large rocks, and once his hand was inside the crack, Grant heard a soft *click*.

This was followed by a *hiss* as the boulder began sinking into the ground. As it went, Grant spotted a mark at its base that until now had been obscured by the other rocks surrounding it. It was the symbol of the Secretum scratched into the boulder, no more than an inch in size.

The boulder lowered until it was out of sight, and the hole it left behind led to a spiral set of stairs descending into the darkness.

The big man took the lead, stepping over the rocks.

"Thanks," Grant said, breaking the silence they'd observed since he had regained consciousness. "But I think I can take it from here."

The man turned and squinted his eyes at Grant.

Grant flung a hand at him, and the man was hurled high up into the air and off into the distance toward the mountain's peak. Grant didn't bother watching him soar away. Instead, he entered the hole in the ground and began to descend.

It was dark along the spiraling stairs, but a flicker of light at the bottom caught his attention, and he focused on reaching that light. Once at the bottom of the stairs, he found a single torch jutting out from the rock wall which Grant grabbed as he moved on.

Inside the mountain, it looked much as Grant had expected it to. Carved-out spaces, ranging from very large to very small, one leading to another and another. A steep downhill corridor, just wide enough for a body to fit through, led him on an hour-long trek deep into the earth.

In the shifting light of his torch, he noted that not far ahead, the corridor appeared to give way to a much larger chamber, which was lit brightly. In the distance, he could see more torches lining the round chamber's stone walls.

He felt a familiar tingle at the back of his mind before he heard the voice.

"Took you long enough to get here," Alex said, waiting just beside the entrance to the large chamber as he walked through.

She wasn't alone. Payton was here too, along with Fletcher, Hector, Nora, and their British counterparts—Mrs. Edeson, Cornelius, Charlotte, and that strange, child-like man whose name he'd never learned.

"What are you—?" Grant managed.

Alex spoke up first. "We found something. It brought us here. But Grant, your sister, she—"

"I know," he responded. "They have her."

Alex sighed, and Grant looked closer at the others. They showed evidence of being worn, but not yet defeated. He wondered how much they knew about Morgan but elected not to mention it yet.

The large round chamber they were in was plain and bare. It was nothing more than a hollowed-out cave, with a flattened ground surface to walk on. Aside from the entryway he'd just come through, there were two more archways leading away from the chamber in opposite directions on his left and his right.

"Come here," Alex said, leading him toward the exit on his left. "Let me show you something."

The others followed as she led him in silence on a meandering path through another tunnel. Shorter than the one he'd traversed, it brought them to their destination in less than five minutes. The tunnel opened into an enormous, cylindrical, horizontal tube cut out of the mountain's rock.

"This is how we got here," she explained. She quickly detailed their discovery beneath the London Library—what they could only assume was some sort of "underground transit system." As hard as it was to believe, the nine of them had used this transit system to get there in less than an hour's time.

Grant was amazed but not surprised. "I'm just starting to understand for myself the true breadth and depth of the Secretum's resources. This is incredible," he remarked, studying the colossal tunnel.

As Alex led the group back to the round chamber, Grant offered his own story of how he'd located this place with the help of the young boy, Stephan, his online contact, Levi, and the mysterious Trevor.

"The new Keeper called me," he said, and Payton looked at him with sudden interest. "He's the one who told me Julie was here. They're waiting for me, and from what he said, it sounds like everything the Secretum has been planning—all their schemes and manipulations and plotting for the Bringer—it's all supposed to culminate when I meet them here."

"This new Keeper," Payton inquired. "Did he give you his name?"

"Devlin," Grant replied, keenly watching Payton's reaction.

Payton offered only the subtlest of shifts in his eyes, but said nothing.

They reached the chamber and as a group walked toward the third and final corridor opposite their current position. It was the only remaining place to go, so it had to lead to Omega Prime.

"Devlin told me . . ." Grant began. "He said that the Secretum was behind all of the disasters happening around the world. It was them, all along."

Fletcher did a double take, but Alex merely nodded and took him by the hand. He was electrified by the gesture, his heart suddenly pumping faster.

"I knew it wasn't you, Grant," she said softly as they continued to walk hand in hand. "It couldn't have been. It's not who you are."

He turned loose of her hand, fear clouding his thoughts. "What if it is, and I just don't know it yet?"

68

The group of ten Ringwearers looked out upon an expanse that was beyond anything they ever dreamed possible. A few recoiled in fear, but Grant, Payton, and Alex steeled themselves at the sight.

The final corridor from the entry chamber led them, single file, steeply downward, farther inside the mountain. Indeed, they were no longer inside the mountain; now they were certain they were far *under* it. They knew when they reached a large rock outcropping-like balcony that looked out over . . .

Over something they had no words to describe. Something that quite possibly, no words had ever been invented to describe.

A subterranean cavern stretched out beneath them that was roughly hexagonal in shape and about five miles in diameter. From its ceiling, hundreds of feet above their heads and probably more than a thousand feet above the ground floor below, descended the most enormous stalactite any of them could comprehend. At the top, it was easily half a mile across; at the bottom, where it now touched the ground, it was about two hundred feet wide.

That any of this was visible at all was its own miracle. It wasn't dark inside the cavern. Bright lights were scattered randomly throughout, illuminating it with a warm glow, like stars shining in the night sky. And as their amazement slackened, more details became evident.

Buildings populated the ground floor, mostly single-story and a blend of Mediterranean and Persian design. Many of them were circular in shape with lotus-style "onion dome" roofs. They ran the full spectrum of sizes. Some seemed quite large, as if they were community buildings, but the majority were small enough to be modest homes.

It was an underground city, Grant realized.

What looked like train tracks of some kind—only with one iron track instead of the standard two—extended the full diameter of the city. There were three such tracks, and they intersected in the center of town, beneath the great stalactite, and when looked at from this vantage point above, the tracks formed a very familiar six-pointed shape.

The city boasted an odd conglomeration of the archaic and the ultra modern. Six mammoth power cables came up through the ground floor, branched out from the great stalactite in the center of town, and touched the outer walls of the city. Smaller cables forked away from the big ones and down to all parts of the city.

A water reservoir or lake of some kind took up a full sixth of the city between two sets of train tracks.

Its scale and proportions made Grant feel infinitesimal. And the very idea that something like this could exist beneath the earth, and yet no one knew about it . . . Grant's mind said it was preposterous, but his eyes told another story.

Until now, he had believed the Secretum to be some kind of secretive organization. But *this* . . .

His gaze followed the slope of the outer walls until he realized that closer to the bottom, the walls had been carved out. About eight levels of hollowed-out structures lined the outer walls; it was as if all the space on the ground floor had been used up, so the Secretum had taken to expanding into the walls themselves.

The group stood dead silent. For minute after awestruck minute, no one spoke a word.

Grant was the first to assert himself. "We have to do something," he said.

One by one, the others tore themselves away from the sight before them and woke up to what Grant had said.

"There are stairs over here," Fletcher pointed to an archway to their far left. Beyond it a set of steps descended into a tunnel that looked as though it ran parallel, behind the curve of the outer wall.

"Look out there at the center," Alex said, and everyone turned.

"That looks like a series of elevators to me, surrounding the point where the tracks intersect."

Grant saw that she was right. Where the great stalactite met the ground, tunnels had been carved out for the tracks to pass through, and outside of the tunnels, at even increments, were several sets of parting doors. Even now, people were passing through the many sets of parting doors, getting on or off of the vertical cars.

"But do they go up or down?" Nora asked.

"Down," said Grant and Alex at the same time, without hesitation.

Alex pointed at the gigantic power cables. "See how the cables poke up out of the ground? They're coming from somewhere beneath all this."

"Then that's where I have to go," Grant declared.

"The Secretum went to enormous trouble to bring you here," Payton reminded everyone. "They *know* you're on your way. They may even know we're standing right here."

Fletcher stepped closer to the edge of the balcony, addressing Grant. "There have to be more than ten thousand people down there. Short of caving in the entire cavern, that's more than even *you* could get past."

Grant's mind turned quickly. He faced Alex. "How would you feel about creating a diversion?"

Her eyes danced. "Downright giddy."

"Then I'll make my way through the town and hitch an elevator ride while you make with the distracting," he explained to everyone. "Alex is in charge; make sure you do whatever she says, and make *sure* you do it big and loud."

The group was shaken and unsure, but nonetheless they were already moving toward the stairs.

"Wait," Payton interjected. "You've said nothing of Morgan's fate. You must have asked Devlin about her."

Grant waited until the others were already descending the stairs. Only he, Alex, and Payton remained on the balcony overlooking the underground city. He closed his eyes and turned down his head. "She's gone. I'm sorry—"

Payton swore, and in a flash, his sword was sailing through the air. It jammed into the solid rock wall beside the stairway entrance and vibrated back and forth there like a spring.

"I'm coming with you," Payton announced, his face harder than the stone surrounding them.

"The others need you here," Grant replied.

"I am not coming to assist you," Payton retorted. "I have business of my own with the Secretum tonight."

Leaving no room for argument, he retrieved his sword from the rock wall and proceeded down the stairs.

Grant rolled his eyes and sighed. He was about to say something when Alex took his hand in hers again.

"I've never been afraid of walking into danger beside you," Alex said, her voice lower and more restrained than Grant had ever heard it. "But *this* . . ." she glanced back over the balcony again.

"I know," Grant replied. "I'm scared too."

She looked deep into his eyes, as if staring at his soul. There was a sad longing in her own face that he couldn't turn away from.

Suddenly a rush of adrenaline coursed through his veins, a wave of fresh bravery washing over him and preparing him for what was to come.

"Now you're not," Alex said with a brave smile.

"Thanks," he whispered, realizing that she'd just used her powers on him.

"You should get going," Alex said, letting go of his hand. "Julie's waiting for you. And you're going to bring her back to us. I know you will."

He smiled at her, the strength she'd just given him in more ways than one refreshing his determination.

"Be careful," he said simply and then vanished down the stairway.

69

Everything went according to plan. As Alex and the rest of the team stirred the underground city into a frenzy, Grant and Payton covertly made their way to the elevators in the center of town.

They were inside an elevator with the doors closed before anyone could stop them. It was just the two of them.

"What exactly are you planning on doing when we get there?" Grant asked, watching as Payton stood perfectly still in a quiet fury. Grant could practically feel heat emanating from him.

"What do you *think* I plan on doing?" Payton spat.

The elevator car descended.

"I would appreciate it," Grant remarked, "if you could hold off dispatching any of these people until they show me where my sister is."

"I've told you before," Payton's gravelly voice intoned, "that the individuals you are about to meet are not *people*. The Secretum of Six is comprised of individuals unlike anyone you have ever encountered, save for your grandfather. The members of the Secretum are cunning in ways you cannot conceive of and dangerous in ways you don't want to know. Don't bother trying to reason with them. Don't *argue* with them. And whatever you do, don't *lie* to them. They will ensnare you with any vulnerability you allow yourself to present."

Grant swallowed this. "So the only solution is to kill them?"

"Unquestionably," Payton seethed without remorse.

The doors to the elevator opened at what they guessed was the bottom-most floor. Another circular chamber greeted them, much like the one near the entrance high above. It was donut-shaped, with elevator access in the center and a dozen tunnels leading outward from every direction.

A tunnel to their left was marked with the symbol of the Secretum carved into the rock wall overhead. They entered that tunnel without comment. It was wide enough for them to walk side by side.

"Part of me still wants to believe that violence is not the best use of our gifts," Grant pondered. "As intelligent, self-aware, *moral* beings, shouldn't we be able to find better ways to resolve our problems?"

"You are describing some abstract, romanticized notion of existence," Payton replied with cold authority. "Reality is not found in such thoughts. Morgan once told me, years ago, of a quote by Edmund Burke. 'It is necessary only for the good to do nothing for evil to triumph.' If the Dominion Stone is to be believed, then battle lines were drawn in this universe long before man entered into it. And the war rages on, all around us. We have only to decide which side we will be on."

Grant stopped walking. He couldn't deny the wisdom in these words.

"And which side are you on?" he asked.

"Today," Payton replied, "it would seem that I am on your side."

The tunnel opened into another gigantic circular chamber, twice as large as the last one. The "ceiling" was at least twenty meters above their heads. Stalactites reached down from it like craggy old fingers.

Unlike the other cave corridors they'd passed through, this room was lit by electric lights on stands, circling the perimeter of the room.

They must be powered by the same cables and conduits that feed into the city above us. But where does the electricity even come from, in a place like this? We must be almost a mile below sea level by now. . . .

A set of large, nickel-plated double doors were closed at the far end of the room. They were like stalwart gates outside some medieval castle.

But they stopped walking as the doors creaked and groaned and swung slowly open.

A full battalion of Secretum soldiers spilled into the room and blocked their path. They wore black jumpsuits and carried swords. Like the attackers Payton had killed in St. James's Square, these soldiers had the same training Payton had. They weren't Ringwearers, and they didn't have his speed. But there had to be more than fifty of them.

This fact was enough to give Grant slight pause, but Payton never slowed his pace, walking straight for them. "Go around. I'll handle this."

"Are you sure?" Grant replied. "I could just take them all out with a blast of energy."

Payton whipped out his sword and faced Grant with more anger and malice than Grant had seen on anyone he'd ever known.

"Right," Grant mumbled. "You'll handle this."

The soldiers were twenty feet away as Payton spun, and Grant saw something he'd never seen Payton do before.

Slowly, deliberately, Payton's left hand came around to join his right. He clutched the overlong hilt of his silver sword with *both* hands.

He marched straight into the middle of their line, where they stood with swords in hand and bloodlust in their eyes. Payton vanished in a burst of speed, and the soldier in the middle of the line had no time to react as Payton reappeared in the air right in front of him, roaring with murderous ferocity and slashing down diagonally with all of his might.

One down.

He twirled to the right and took out another with the momentum of turning, then he dove for the ground and disappeared in a blur again. Three converging soldiers stopped short, before their heads fell off and plopped on the ground, shortly followed by their bodies. Payton stood in the center of them with a broad stance, both arms and sword out thrust straight ahead. The blade was still horizontal from the beheadings, but his own head was downturned.

His eyes popped up, his head unmoving, as he spotted a new group of attackers moving in.

Payton twisted to his left but flipped his sword backwards, thrusting it in reverse at an oncoming soldier on his right. The sword slid into the man's gut, and Payton let go of it there, leaving the man skewered and in shock. Another man facing him slashed his sword sideways, but it froze unexpectedly in mid-arc. Payton was clasping the broad sides of it with both hands, and with a sudden jerk, the soldier he faced was disarmed.

Still holding the other man's sword awkwardly with both hands, he flicked it over his shoulder, where it tumbled twice in the air before it shot like a lance into a soldier near the far edge of the crowd. Payton reached behind himself without looking and retrieved his own sword with both hands. With a new burst of speed and another unholy roar of vengeance escaping from his lips, his feet stepped up onto the disarmed man before him like he was climbing a ladder. The sword still behind his back, he swung it down and then up in a perfect arc. The sword connected with the soldier vertically, and Grant looked away to avoid seeing the man cleaved in half, from tip to toe.

When he looked again, Payton was already on the ground, his sword twisting ninety degrees, and slicing around wide like a tennis racket.

A dozen men were already down, and it had happened in a steady stream of furious moves that lasted no more than ten seconds.

70

Grant snuck past the fight by hugging the outer wall.

He'd just reached the still-open double doors when a searing pain tore through his shoulder.

He turned; a soldier stood clutching a bloodied sword.

Instinctively, Grant willed a stalactite hanging from the ceiling to come loose in self-defense. He dove through the doorway for cover as the giant rocky tendril bored into the earth at the spot where the soldier stood.

Pleased with his success, Grant returned to his feet and applied pressure to the cut on his shoulder.

That was when he felt the ground begin to rumble.

Another stalactite fell twenty feet away inside the chamber. And another farther away, crashing into some of the soldiers Payton was squaring off with.

The entire cave was coming down. . . .

Grant ran back through the doorway, concentrating on trying to make the shaking stop, *willing* the cave to steady itself.

"Payton!" he yelled over the quaking.

His view was obscured by falling dirt and rocks, but he heard Payton's voice reply, "Go! Finish it!"

Grant looked up just in time to see a massive fifteen-ton boulder break loose from the ceiling. It was above the area where Payton continued to hack and slash his enemies.

"Look out!" Grant called out. He put out a hand to stop the boulder, but another stalactite broke free right above him, and he was forced to dive through the doorway to escape it.

On his hands and knees, he looked back. The doorway was covered over by the rockslide.

Grant stretched out with his mind; he couldn't get a strong sense of Payton. All he could see was darkness where Payton should be.

He was trying to convince himself that Payton could have gotten clear with his speed when he heard a deep, booming voice coming from the path ahead of him.

"Hello, Grant."

Grant recognized the voice, though today it spoke in a simple American accent. Grant wondered if this could be Devlin's real one.

Grant worked his way to his feet, but as he was getting up, he saw familiar lettering carved into the rock on the ground right beneath him that said:

SUBSTATION OMEGA PRIME

Grant placed one hand on his aching shoulder, wishing Hector were handy. Another narrow corridor of rock extended before him, but a man stood there, blocking it.

The man wore a trim, custom-tailored pin-striped suit. He had white hair and showed obvious signs of age, yet his face was remarkably smooth. His hands clasped in front of him with manicured fingernails, his demeanor was the personification of calm.

"We've been expecting you," the man said. "My apologies for the guards. A necessary evil, deployed to prevent Payton from accompanying you any farther. You alone may venture where we are about to go. Even very few of our people have ever been to your destination."

"I don't know what you think I'm here to do," Grant replied. "But all I want is my sister. Hand her over, and I won't explode your heart inside your chest."

"Yes, of course," Devlin answered. "Julie is quite safe. If you'll allow me, I'll take you to her."

Grant watched the man with unbridled suspicion and made no movement to follow.

"Grant," Devlin prodded, "I have been nothing but truthful with you since our very first conversation, and I've no intention of changing that policy now. So I would like to make you a deal."

"Why would I make a deal with you? If you don't give me my sister, you have to know I'll tear this entire place down until I find her myself."

"Because," Devlin replied, "we both know your sister is not the only reason you're here. You want to know what it's all been about. Since that first day you stepped off the bus in Los Angeles and saw yourself walking to work. Since you met Morgan and your friends, since you met your grandfather and learned of your parents' involvement with the Secretum. Since the world began to crash and burn all around you."

Grant said nothing.

Devlin took a step closer. "You. Must. Know. The truth."

Grant hated this man already, with his polite charm and all too helpful mannerisms.

"What are you proposing?" Grant asked.

"I need to show you something," Devlin replied. "Along the way, we'll stop and retrieve your sister, and you can see for yourself that I've been true to my word. She's perfectly fine, she's well fed, and she's been treated like an honored guest. But once she's at your side again, you must see what I wish to show you."

"In exchange for?"

"As we are walking to our destination, you may ask me any questions you like and I will answer them truthfully. Ask me anything— about the Secretum, the Rings of Dominion, your family tree, anything you are curious about—and I will tell you all you want to know."

Grant considered tossing Devlin down the corridor like a rag doll and got an internal charge at the mental image. But he stifled the impulse, his sister taking precedence in his mind.

"Agreed," Grant answered and walked toward Devlin.

The elder man turned and began to walk, and Grant followed. Down the corridor, Devlin found a crack in the cave wall that Grant would never have noticed and pushed on it. It was a door that slid inward with a *click* and then moved to one side. Devlin entered, motioning for Grant to follow.

They walked on in silence through another narrow corridor carved out of the rock, and Grant's mind raced against this insanity. Why was he following this man so willingly into what he knew would be a trap?

Was he so sure of himself and his abilities that he believed nothing could take him down?

The press believed he was "fearless."

If they only knew . . .

A bullet nearly ended him just two weeks ago, and the more recent brainwashing made him feel more helpless than he'd felt in a very long time. Just weeks ago, rescuing L.A., he'd felt invincible. Now he felt . . . like a marionette on a string.

And this place. It felt familiar somehow. He was positive he'd never been here before, but there was something . . . *comforting* about being inside these walls. Was that the right word for it? Maybe not.

Grant's eyes shifted to Devlin's right hand . . .

His finger.

Devlin was wearing a ring made of silver, with a blue gemstone inset.

Grant knew that ring. He'd seen it before.

"He who wields the weapon of purest silver will stand between the Bringer and the day of torment."

That's the ring my grandfather wore when he was the Keeper of the Secretum.

How did Devlin get it. . . ?

71

"You haven't asked me any questions yet," Devlin observed, drawing Grant's attention away from the silver ring. "Our walk will take some time, but it won't last forever."

"Fine," Grant replied. "Let's start with, who *are* you people? I mean, really?"

"We are the embodiment of a question," Devlin replied.

"What question?"

"The only question that truly matters: *Is there more to this existence than what we can see or hear or taste or smell or touch?* In essence, the question is simply, *Why?* Why are we here? Why is the average human temperature ninety-eight point six degrees? Why is the universe larger than the human mind's ability to conceive? And why does it all happen the way that it does? *Is . . . there . . . more?*"

Grant was reminded of a conversation he'd had with Daniel months ago on a similar topic. *"Every scientist in the world,"* Daniel said, *"studies the natural order of the universe. But the one thing they can never explain through reason or logic is why that order exists."*

Finally, as the silence dragged on and Devlin waited patiently, Grant was forced to offer the only answer he could. "I don't know."

"No one on this plane of existence does. An answer has never been given in any definitive, infallible way. But here, in this place, *you* will answer the fundamental question of existence . . . once and for all. We are the question. You are the answer.

"*This* is why you are here, Grant Borrows. This is why you were born, and why you have been drawn to this place from your very first breath. You are here to answer the unanswerable question."

"I don't understand . . . I thought you were some kind of secret society, like the Illuminati or the Masons or something."

Devlin let out a chuckle. "The Masons . . . The Knights Templar . . . The Illuminati . . . These are constructs of the imaginations of Externals based around vague historical accounts—products of your unending fascination with the unknown."

They turned a corner and entered another corridor.

"Externals," Grant said. "You used that word before. What's it mean?"

"Externals are what we call your kind, and I don't mean the Ringwearers. We live and work below the surface of this world, therefore everyone above the surface is external to us."

Grant found that the questions were compounding in his mind, coming faster and faster now, and it was difficult not to forget any of them. "So were you born here? Underground?"

"Born and raised. Did you know that the Taurus Mountains contain approximately *forty thousand* caves? Only eight hundred of which have ever been explored by Externals?"

"Why do you keep talking about those of us who live on the surface like we're a different species than you are?" Grant asked. "You *are* human, are you not?"

Devlin laughed again. "Yes, of course. But the Secretum is not merely an organization or a 'secret society.' We are our own civilization. We have been here, in this place, for millennia, and our society developed and evolved independently from any External influence. We have our own rules, laws, and hierarchies of power. We are wholly self-sufficient and we are not in any way members of your society."

"But my grandfather said you've been manipulating events on the surface for years."

"True enough," Devlin conceded. "And when necessary, our methods have been quite overt: catalyzing civil uprisings, initiating revolts, igniting wars, altering election results.

"But on the whole, our tactics are far more subtle than any of your conspiracy theorists want to believe. A whisper in one man's ear. Making sure a young woman of promise attended *this* school instead of *that* one. Providing the spark of an idea that would lead to an invention that would change the way the world does business.

"*This* is our task. The Secretum has been at work for thousands of years, tailoring this world's fabric by pulling at a mere handful of its millions of threads. Coercing the very path that history takes. It can't be done with sloppy, casual moves; it requires an understated, elegant attention to detail that no External could possibly grasp."

The corridor grew wider, and Grant saw that they were nearing a much larger opening up ahead.

"Is that why you built your file 'repositories'—like that room under London with files on people from all over the world?"

"Yes, our work is quite meticulous."

"The librarian in London said there were two more repositories."

"One of them is here. Along with the complete archives—seven thousand years' records of the Secretum's influence on External lives."

Grant stopped walking. "But . . ." He scrambled to phrase his next question. "To what end? Why do you do all this?"

Devlin glanced at him. "As long as there has been time, there has been the Secretum of Six. We were there at the beginning, and we will be there at the end. We have orchestrated key events in the history of this world for as long as history has been recorded, for one reason and one reason only. To prepare for the coming of the Bringer, at the appointed time."

"And when is this appointed time?"

"I assumed you knew," Devlin replied, looking at him. "It's today, of course."

They began walking again. The corridor opened into a chasm at least a hundred feet in diameter. They stood at the top of a precipice above a fathomless drop. To their right was a set of very modern metallic stairs, and Grant could see across the well-lit chasm that the stairs spiraled along the wall, down farther into the darkness below that went much deeper than he could see. Doors were inset in the wall every fifty feet or so along the spiral staircase.

"This is where we keep . . . *guests*," Devlin said.

They proceeded down the stairs, and Grant was glad to find a handrail to keep them from stumbling over the inner edge. They descended the stairs faster than Grant had expected. Soon the ceiling was very high above, a blurred vision of bright light beaming down through the expanse.

After passing about twenty doors—Grant had lost count—Devlin stopped and opened one. A guard stood inside a short hallway at attention. Devlin ordered, "Open it," and the guard promptly went to the door at the far end and inserted an iron key.

The door swung open and Julie sat at a table inside a well-lit room with basic furnishings. The tiny room contained simple furniture, including two chairs for the table and a bed, as well as a small sink and a toilet. A single light bulb dangled from a chain affixed to the ceiling.

Grant tore down the hallway—forgetting Devlin, forgetting everything—and scooped his sister up into his arms.

72

Julie embraced him fiercely and began to cry.

"I'm okay," she whispered. "Really, I am. I'm sorry. I'm so sorry . . . I'm sorry I doubted you, back in London. I should have known you'd never—"

"It's okay, it doesn't matter," he comforted her.

Julie shook in Grant's arms as he held her, and for a quick moment he thought she shivered out of terror . . . but then a more worrying realization dawned on him. She'd been without her medication since her abduction, many hours before.

Grant turned to look back down the hallway and met Devlin's eyes. "Can you give us a minute?"

Devlin peered at him with a dutiful expression, checking his expensive-looking watch. "Five minutes. Then we must press on. The door to the cell will be left unlocked."

The guard closed the door.

"Morgan, she's—"

"I know," Julie said tearfully. "I saw her body. They showed it to me."

"Then it's really true," Grant said, resigned.

Julie put a finger to his lips. They sat next to each other, using the chairs from the table.

"Honey, listen to me," Julie said with an urgency in her voice. "There's something you and I have never talked about, and we may not get another chance."

Grant already knew what it was. His mind went back to deep beneath the Wagner Building, where he'd flashed into a time outside of time, where his mother and his comatose sister had spoken to him and given him the strength he needed to go on.

"The safe house thing," Grant said it for her. "That dreamscape, where we talked the day I met our grandfather in Los Angeles."

"Yeah."

"What needs to be said?"

"You've never talked about what happened there, not once. You never even told Morgan." Julie paused. "You *do* believe it was real, don't you?"

He smiled. "You were there even though you were in a coma, and you remember everything that happened as well as I do. Of course it was real."

"But Grant . . . Haven't you ever wondered about the implications? I mean, *Mom* was there. And she's dead. Doesn't that *mean* something?"

"I guess," Grant agreed but had no idea what else to say.

"There's something else," Julie whispered. "Don't bother asking how I know this . . . I think maybe it's some kind of leftover intuition from that whole experience."

"What?"

"Mom can't come to you like that again," Julie said softly. "That's why she hasn't been back since the day of the fire storm. The two times she appeared to you were . . ." she struggled for the words. "They were more than either of you had any right to, in a cosmic sense. I don't know how it works, but I know beyond a doubt that she can't do it again. You're on your own now."

"No, I'm not," Grant replied, holding her hand tighter. "I just wish I knew what this was all about. All of this. I don't know if I'm strong enough to withstand whatever they're going to throw at me."

"You will," Julie replied without any trace of condescension. "You're fearless, and everybody knows it."

"Everybody's wrong. I'm afraid all the time. I'm afraid of losing the people I care about most."

Julie looked upon him with eyes of wisdom and love. "I think you have the wrong idea about this fearless thing. Being fearless doesn't mean having an absence of fear. It means you press on in spite of the fear."

"But I'm not sure I know how to do that."

"You do it every day, you just don't realize it. Every time you put one foot in front of the other, it's an act of trust. A belief that the ground will still be there when that foot comes down.

"The day I first met her," Julie went on, "Morgan told me that everything happening to you was happening for a reason. I realized over time that she was saying that if I could trust in that, that everything would unfold as it is meant to. All we have to do is trust that nothing happening in the here and now is an accident, or is without purpose. Believe that, and you will be truly fearless."

He smiled anew, swallowed her words, and stood to his feet. Carefully, he helped her to do the same. "I think our five minutes are up. We should go."

"I'm proud of you, you know," she said. "You know what they say about a life that's wasted. You're living proof that it's never too late."

These words caught Grant off guard. "What did you say about a life that's wasted?"

"You know, that saying . . . 'A life that is wasted is not truly lived,'" she recited.

"Where did you hear that?" Grant asked.

She thought. "Come to think of it, it was at your funeral. I mean, Collin's. The priest presiding over the ceremony said it."

"Huh," Grant commented, thoughts drifting back to that day. It felt like a lifetime ago. In some ways, he supposed it was.

"I wish Alex were here," he remarked.

Julie froze, and Grant pulled up short in front of her, right at the unlocked door.

Wait, he thought to himself. *What did I just say?*

He'd said it without thinking.

But it was true. He *did* wish Alex were here, at his side. . . .

Where did that come from? I mean, she's Alex.

Of course, I don't have feelings for her.

Unless—

"Took you long enough to figure it out," Julie said, wearing a crooked smile as if she knew exactly what he was thinking.

"So you knew this whole time? Does anyone else know?"

"I don't know. I think Morgan did. Remember back in L.A., the day before we left town, when she gave me that book, *The Remains of the Day*? You were standing right there when she gave it to me, and I suspect it might have been more for your benefit than mine. *The Remains of the Day* is a story about a man who wastes his life and lets his one true love slip through his fingers."

Grant looked at the ceiling, stunned at all this new information. How had he missed it? "Does Alex really feel the same way about me?"

"I think so," Julie replied, nodding. She walked forward and opened the door. "Let's finish this so you can go find out."

73

"Come," Devlin said smoothly as Grant and Julie rejoined him on the downward stairway. "There's something close-by I want you to get a look at."

They walked on in silence, Grant holding Julie's quivering hand. She looked so tired. . . .

At the bottom an enormous set of double doors awaited them. Crafted with tremendous attention to detail, these doors were four times the size of the metallic ones back at the substation's entrance, where Grant had met Devlin. These were made of wood and were framed by an equally ornate doorway. Extremely intricate carvings offered another variation on the six-sided Secretum symbol.

Two soldiers like the ones Payton had fought above stood at attention before the two doors, and as Devlin approached them, they clasped enormous, round iron handles and pulled until the massive gateway was fully open.

A blast of sweltering hot air hit them as they approached the giant doorway, but Devlin kept walking until he'd gone through. Grant and Julie saw no choice but to follow.

"There are other ways to reach our destination, of course," Devlin said, acknowledging the immense heat. "But missing this would be like traveling to China and not seeing the Great Wall."

On the other side of the doorway was a chamber of boundless proportions—even larger than the cave that held the underground city far above. It had no distinct shape; Grant guessed that this room had not been carved out of the rock like the ones above. It was used as the Secretum had found it.

And with good reason. A slender bridge stretched out before them farther than they could see. The bridge fluctuated at various points, making its width anywhere between six and twelve feet wide, depending on where you stood.

Red light flickered on the craggy ceiling of stalactites. Grant stepped forward and peered over one side of the bridge. Three hundred feet below, a sea of molten lava stirred, casting an eerie crimson glow over the entire space and pouring heat out upon them.

"Careful on the bridge," Devlin instructed. "We've never managed to perfect it, so it's full of small stalagmites and rocks you can easily trip over. A few centuries ago, someone nicknamed it the 'Scar Bridge,' because it was so easy to get hurt on."

Grant and Julie slowly and cautiously stepped out onto the bridge, holding tightly to one another and staying as close to the center as possible. The temperature easily soared above one hundred degrees the farther in they went.

"Geothermals such as the one beneath us," Devlin explained, following them onto the bridge, "are our primary means of powering our technology, though we have also embraced power sources that the External world has not yet mastered, such as the electromagnetics that govern our Conveyor system."

"Is that the transport tunnels I saw above?" Grant inquired. "Where else can it go?"

Devlin smiled, clearly proud. "It reaches from one end of the world to the other. It allows us to conduct our affairs most efficiently. We can get to the farthest Conveyor stop from here in less than four hours. Jules Verne dreamt of traversing around the world in eighty days. We can make the entire trip in eight *hours*."

Julie's ankle twisted slightly, and Grant held onto her even tighter, steadying her as they walked. He hoped their journey would be over soon; it was wearing her out.

"That's how you were able to follow us from Los Angeles to Jerusalem so easily," Grant realized. "But how is it possible? How can you have such enormous tunnels running under all of the world's civilized regions without anyone *knowing* about it? How could a project of that size have been built in secret?"

"To answer your first question, yes, I used the Conveyor to visit Los Angeles during the riot. That was the same day, if I'm not mistaken, that you met someone from your past."

Someone from my past? What was that supposed to mean?

Did he mean that strange old man at the nursing home?

They continued walking across the bridge as Devlin breezed past Grant's confusion. "As for our technology and construction . . . Come now, it's not so hard to believe, is it? Your own people have developed monorail systems that work on technology ancestral to our electromagnetic Conveyor. And it was not very long ago that the British and the French dug an enormous tunnel under the English Channel for a subterranean train system of their own, was it not? We're using the same technology they're headed for; we're just further along the curve.

"As I said before, the Secretum is not a part of your world, and therefore it is not subject to the same history. We have developed independently of External civilization, and in many ways, at a much faster rate. Our scientists estimate that our technology is at least fifty to one hundred years ahead of the surface world. It used to be a wider margin than that, but your scientists have made huge strides in recent decades. Of course, with our resources, we have access to every new discovery your people make, so we can take advantage of any advances we might have missed."

Grant estimated they were around the halfway point on the bridge now.

"So what are these substations for?" Grant asked.

"They are observation points and places where our plans are carried out by acolytes like your parents."

Grant's mind was still tugging at something he'd noticed earlier. "You're wearing the same silver ring that my grandfather wore when he was the Keeper, aren't you? There's only one of them, right?"

"That's right," Devlin said.

"But my grandfather and his ring were buried under tons of earth when I destroyed that substation. How on *earth* could you—?"

"When you take in the sight of this place you're standing in right now," Devlin cut him off, "is it really so hard to accept that the

Secretum has technology advanced enough to accomplish all of these things you consider impossible? The disasters, the repositories, the Conveyor, the drastic shift in global power. Your entire worldwide economy has collapsed, thanks to us. Even down to the simplest of things, like the memory-altering drug our operative in London used on you. Every detail has been seen to, every piece of the puzzle is perfectly in place. And now, at last, we have come to the end of the journey."

Past the bridge, the path split, with multiple hallways opening up before them.

Devlin selected the one in the center and they continued on to another downward slope, this one at a much greater angle than the one Grant and Payton had used earlier. It wasn't long before Grant found that this slope was circling around on itself, spiraling similar to the stairs above. He held Julie's hand in his, carefully keeping her steady as they traversed the slope.

"Considering where the rings come from, and who originally wore them . . . Why do the rings give us enhanced mental powers? Why don't they come off? And why do they *glow*?"

"I understand your need for there to be an explanation for everything, Grant," Devlin said patiently. "I really do. Better than you think. But sooner or later we must all accept that there are some things that even *our* science down here cannot neatly justify, quantify, or explain.

"The rings and where they come from is not a mathematical riddle for science to answer; it is much, much bigger than anything our finite minds could ever place into a nice, tidy explanation. Put simply, there are some things we will *just never know* the answers to."

"I can't accept that."

"I know," Devlin replied. "Consider this. The rings come from a reality that exists beyond our own. They originate somewhere behind the curtain of this life, in a place and time that is far outside our knowledge as mortal beings. Can you swallow this as a possibility?"

"Okay."

Devlin nodded. "Good. Think about it this way. If you were to give a microscope to an infant, what would the result be?"

"I don't know," Grant said slowly. "The kid would probably damage it somehow."

"More likely he would try to ingest it," Devlin explained. "All infants know very few reflexes, and the drive to eat rules them all. But this is not the point. The microscope is simply a tool, and regardless of what the infant might decide to do with it—whether he tries to bite it, hurts himself with it, or makes it into some kind of tactile toy—he *will* find a use for it. But the fact remains that the microscope was not made nor intended for *his* use."

Grant was starting to catch on. He thought back to what Trevor had tried to tell him the first time they met, about his ring never having been meant for use by a mortal human. "So you're saying the rings are a tool of some kind that weren't intended for us."

"Precisely," Devlin replied. "They were never made for use by human beings, so when a man or woman comes into contact with one of them—when we *wear* one of the Rings of Dominion, as you do now— it is an improper . . . or perhaps an *impure* . . . mixture of this object from a reality beyond our comprehension and human flesh here on the mortal plane. The results are dangerous, unpredictable, and we may never fully understand them.

"What we do know is that the Rings of Dominion are linked to a source of power beyond anything the intellect of man is equipped to grasp. When brought into contact with humans, the rings interact with the mortal body in ways that can't be anticipated or explained. By some, that union is considered a desecration, a distortion of the natural order because the effect that they have on their wearers is to allow them to distort the natural order at will."

"If you knew how powerful they were, then why did the Secretum give the rings to us?" Grant said, straining with serious effort *not* to raise his voice. "Why not wear the rings yourselves?"

"Because it was commanded of us," Devlin replied. "As you probably know, the Secretum has awaited your arrival for seven millennia. And we have done so . . . under orders given to us seven thousand years ago."

"Why? What am I here to do?"

"The Bringer brings the future into being."

74

They continued walking downward. Grant feared for Julie's health, even though she was doing her best to put on her bravest face.

Devlin never slowed his pace, nor showed any signs of weariness.

"This planet and all of its inhabitants were forged millennia ago as the greatest calculated risk in all the universe," Devlin went on. "Call it an experiment. Some have referred to it as a grand cosmic wager. Call it whatever you like, but the secret of our existence boils down to this: *Would a race of sentient creatures, granted unequivocal free will, willingly choose the path of light?*

"One need look no further than the Internet or your daily newspapers to see that this question has been answered. Man is *incapable* of choosing the correct path on his own. Put simply, this grand experiment called humanity was a horrendous failure. The worst mistake ever made.

"The Secretum of Six was formed seven thousand years ago to set things right. To undo the incalculable damage that mankind's free will has wrought. Around that same time, it was prophesied that a man would someday be born who would complete the Secretum's great work. And this man would be called the Bringer."

"Wait—hold on . . ." Grant stopped. "Who *made* this prophecy?"

Devlin eyed him with a bemused smile. "You would *never* believe me."

The slanted corridor gave way to a small alcove-type landing. Double wooden doors waited to their immediate right, but these doors were normal sized and unadorned with any sort of marking or carvings. They appeared ancient in the extreme.

"This," Devlin said with reverence, "is the Hollow. We have arrived at our destination."

Grant's eyebrows scrunched up as something tickled the back of his brain. Something about this sounded very familiar. . . .

The Unholy Markers! it came to him.

"The end shall be marked by a scar, revealing man's deepest hollow."

Scar Bridge . . . and now the Hollow . . .

Oh, no.

The third Marker wasn't the discolored scar on his hand. It was happening right here, right now.

The doors parted and before them lay darkness. It was a dimly lit space about one mile in diameter. Like so many chambers in this underground complex, this area was circular as well. Firelight was the only source of illumination, coming from torches affixed to the walls at evenly spaced intervals.

They stepped slowly inside.

The entire room, if it could be called that, had been sculpted from a different kind of rock than he'd seen anywhere else under the mountain. This rock gleamed black as onyx.

There were no walls here, in the traditional sense. A domed ceiling of solid black rock stretched over two hundred feet into the air at its apex, arching down until it met the floor at the outer edges of the vast room. The floor was a shallow dome as well—a perfectly symmetrical mile-wide hill that rose very gently to no more than ten feet high at its center point.

Carved into the floor were grooves of various sizes that cut about two inches into the ground. Grant couldn't quite figure out what the point of the grooves was, but they converged in the center of the Hollow.

A cold wind blew around them, though Grant could see nothing that the blast of air might be coming from. It seemed a stark contrast to the intense heat from the geothermal lava flow above.

Grant took in all of this peripheral data in a blink. The room's true focus stood at its center, and he could barely tear his eyes from it. Like a mirage of oil and heat on a highway, something solid and dark swam there before the three of them, but there wasn't enough light in the room to make it out properly.

"What is it?" Grant whispered, finding himself timid at the thought of speaking loudly in this intimidating space.

Julie squeezed his hand harder than before.

"Holy ground," Devlin replied. "We are at the bottom-most level of Substation Omega Prime, which was built above and around *this room*. You are looking at the very reason the Secretum exists."

Grant made no attempt to move inside beyond the handful of steps they'd taken to clear the doorway.

Devlin walked a few paces farther and then turned to face them.

"Do you have any idea where we are, geographically speaking?" he asked.

"*I* don't," said Julie.

"I know we're under the Taurus mountain range in Turkey," Grant offered.

"Before there *was* a Turkey, before the mountain range had a name, this Hollow existed. Thousands of feet above us is the Euphrates River, the place where it forms and empties into Syria. The site in question is no longer accessible, but at the dawn of time, it was *right here*, a few miles directly above where we now stand."

"What site in question?" Grant asked, though he had a feeling he knew where this was going.

"Eden. The birthplace of mankind," Devlin replied as though it were obvious. "The Garden."

Grant couldn't stop himself from gasping. "'A place of great power . . .'" he quoted to Julie.

This was bigger than either of them could have imagined; it was huge and dangerous and they were meddling in things and places and powers that man was never meant to touch. . . .

Julie squeezed his hand again, and this time there was no mistaking the message the gesture carried: *We have to get out of here. Right now!*

"Where better," continued Devlin, "to subvert the Great Experiment than the site where it first began? This place was prepared for us thousands of years ago so that we could carry out the prophecy of Dominion and arrange for the Bringer to perform his function."

"And *what is* the Bringer's function?" Grant cried desperately.

"Come," Devlin replied. He turned and began walking toward the center of the room, toward the blurry object that resided there.

Grant took a step forward, but Julie held him firmly back.

"No!" she cried. "Something *terrible* is going to happen here! You can't let them do it! You *know* you can't! Don't, Grant! Never give up!"

Grant barely heard her, all of his senses trained on this remarkable, terrifying room. Something deep and powerful had begun to stir in his core. It pulled at him like a magnet.

He had to get to the center of the room.

"Never give in," he offered the response she waited for at last. "I won't, Julie. I'm in control of myself. But we've come this far, and something about this place is what all of this has been about! I *have* to know! I have to!"

He let go of her hand and followed Devlin.

75

Slowly, the object in the room's center began to take shape as they drew closer. It grew darker the closer Grant came. It was still hard to make out, but he thought he saw a dark black circle marked on the ground about twenty feet across.

He sensed that Julie was behind him, so he turned and grabbed her hand once more.

"We're going to make it," he whispered. "It's going to be okay."

She hesitated a moment but eventually followed, clinging to Grant's hand as if her life depended on it.

It began faintly at first, but with each step he took toward the center of the room, it grew. A rumbling. A minor vibration beneath his feet that developed into a miniature earthquake.

Julie squeezed his hand, but he turned to her and shook his head. "I'm not doing it."

Grant moved farther toward the center, and the rumbling grew. "What's happening?" he called out.

Devlin stopped at the edge of the black circle and faced him. "Destiny is happening!" he shouted back.

"Grant, we have to turn back. Don't do this!" Julie cried.

But he couldn't turn away. He was meant to be here. He knew it; he felt it. Down to his bones, the same way he felt connected to the ancient, primal power that was part of his ring. He was sure that everything in his life had been leading to this moment, to this place.

There was no going back. Not now.

He came to within ten feet of the circle, and as the quaking beneath his feet grew stronger, Grant realized that what he was moving toward wasn't a mark on the ground at all—it was a hole. Lining the rim of the hole was a ring of small rocks and rubble, rising no more than a few inches off the ground.

Here, at the top of the mile-wide mound, in the center of this round hole in the earth, Grant gained a new perspective on the grooves carved into the floor, and he recognized the shape immediately. Six lines that stretched from the center out to the far edge of the floor, equally separated from one another. Six more lines were situated between them and extended half the distance between the center and the room's edge. Six more followed this same pattern, and six more after that, and so on.

It was the symbol of the Secretum, and somehow he knew that this Hollow was the place where the symbol had originated. This was the first place it had ever been seen by human eyes.

Alex watched with satisfaction from inside one of the small homes as the order of this underground city was rendered into chaos thanks to her team's actions. And she had to admit, their new British friends had been instrumental in pulling it off.

She just hoped it was enough to give Grant the opening he needed to grab Julie and get out.

He'd been gone quite a long time. Maybe she should venture to one of those elevators herself, give him some backup . . .

Who cares if "the path of the Bringer must be walked alone"? Since when have we ever played by the rules, anyway?

She was just exiting the tiny house when someone grabbed her from behind and pulled her to an alcove between buildings.

She wrenched herself loose and saw the man who had grabbed her. He was wearing a black jumpsuit and a matching ski mask that hid his face.

Alex was just about to make him terrified of the dark when the man pulled off his mask.

"Wait!" he said. "It's me!"

"Ethan?!" she nearly shouted. "What are *you* doing here? You scared the crap out of me! How did you even find this place?"

"I was sent," Ethan replied, shaking his head as she was about to ask more questions. "I'll explain later—there's no time! Where's Grant?"

"He's gone to find his sister and confront the Secretum."

Ethan looked like he'd just lost an Olympic marathon. "Alex . . ." he said, struggling to explain. "I was wrong about him. Grant's not what you think he is. He's a threat. A terrible threat, bigger than anything you could possibly imagine. We have to find him and stop him before it's too late—"

Alex was about to interrupt him when the ground began to tremble. A bright light was growing in time with the trembling, and she realized it was coming from her hand. And it wasn't just her. She saw more beams of light emanating throughout the city from her teammates.

The Rings of Dominion were glowing.

Brighter and brighter . . .

Lisa was stirred awake by a rumbling beneath her. *What was that? An earthquake?*

Her consciousness caught up with her reflexes and she remembered she was on her cot, all alone in a jail cell in London, England.

The entire building trembled, and above that sound, higher in pitch, she heard a squeaking.

Groggy, she sat up on her cot and rubbed at her dried-out eyes. The bed, as it was laughingly called, was not exactly conducive to rest. She would never complain about the beds at the warehouse ever again. If they ever got *back* to the—

Squeak, squeak.

She stood, straining to see in the darkness. Nothing out in the hallway. She turned to her right to see into Daniel's cell, where his body was hanging limp from a rope attached to the ceiling.

Lisa gasped. Her body lost all its strength and she fell to her knees.

His bed sheets had been rolled tightly and tied into a noose, which was squeezing against his neck. His face was red, and his limp body swayed back and forth in the empty air, squeaking against the light fixture the makeshift rope was affixed to.

Lisa screamed.

Daniel's lifeless, pale body swung from the ceiling light above, tied off at his neck.

"*SOMEBODY HELP!!*" she shouted as loud as she could over the growing noise of the earthquake.

Even after all she'd said, all she'd done for him . . . after his big step forward in admitting his feelings of guilt . . .

Daniel had coiled his own bed sheets and fashioned a noose and stretched it out by jumping from—

Wait a minute, Lisa's breath caught in her throat. She wiped away the tears so she could see more clearly. *There's nothing here that he could have jumped off of, nothing he could have stood on to get high enough to do this himself!*

Her whole body jumped when Daniel's eyes snapped open. He started gagging and flailing about like mad. The noose choked too tight; he couldn't get any leverage on it. . . .

And then his eyes locked onto hers.

That one look was all it took. She knew in her heart that he hadn't done this to himself. It had been done *to* him.

"Help me!" Daniel croaked desperately, his face turning now to purple.

She looked about her cell, searching for something, anything she could use . . . But there was nothing.

Lisa glanced back up at Daniel, and his eyes were closed again, his body hanging limp as before.

He wasn't breathing.

76

In London, the young man known as Trevor paced, terribly confused.

He wanted desperately to feel relieved that his masters in the Secretum of Six seemed to have abandoned their hold over him after he'd delivered Devlin's message to Grant Borrows. But long experience taught him not to get his hopes up; they had to still be out there with new plans for him.

It made no sense. They should have contacted him hours ago. Yet he wanted so badly to believe that maybe, after all this time, they had finally just let him go.

He was sitting on an old gray wooden bench in St. James's Square, pondering these things under the light of office windows around the square, when his ring began to glow and the ground trembled. A piercing white light grew until it illuminated the entire square, drawing unwanted attention from the handful of pedestrians still out and about at this late hour.

Not knowing what else to do, he ran, fear propelling his steps into the night.

In Jerusalem, Wilhelm rested in a bunk provided to him by his Jewish friend Amiel Yishai after a long day of helping restore power in various parts of the city.

The smiles he brought to faces throughout his days remained with him through the night, coloring his dreams with reminders of all the good he had done here, all the hope he had created. He saw, too, the sorrow of these people and shared in their misery over so many lost lives, lost homes, and lost pieces of a treasured history.

He was in the midst of one of these dreams when he was awoken by what he initially thought to be one of the rescue operation's flood-lights shining straight into his tent. Had to be an accident, or maybe an emergency?

Wilhelm awoke fully in seconds as the ground of Jerusalem shud-dered for the first time since the terrible collapse that had caused its destruction. He jolted awake, realizing that the floodlight he thought he'd seen was not outside of his tent.

And it wasn't even a floodlight.

In Los Angeles, the burly muscle man Henrike attended a Lakers game at the Staples Center. He was seated in the lower balcony in the midst of a frenzied crowd. He'd spent more of the game on his feet than in his high-priced seat.

It was so loud and bright in the room that it was five minutes or more before he realized his ring was glowing. It grew so bright that soon everyone in his entire section was reacting to the phenomenon. They began with curiosity but quickly grew fearful, scrambling over each other and out of the way as the ring's glow grew more and more blinding. And then the building started to shake.

Henrike couldn't stop the light or shield it from anyone's view with his other hand. It wasn't long before the glow overshadowed everything in the entire arena, even stopping the game and forcing the players to gaze up into the balcony at the light brighter than the sun.

In San Diego, a gifted painter and Ringwearer named Lilly sat along the shore absorbing the beauty of the harbor. Her thoughts drifted far from the assassin known as the Thresher, a man she'd helped out a few times in the past with information in exchange for his money. Most recently, she'd seen him a few months ago, when she tipped him off about the Bringer's location in Los Angeles.

Such concerns were miles away this night. Tonight she thought of her younger sister, who Lilly had been forced to leave behind when she'd been Shifted into a new life. As Lilly's eyes traced the darkened shoreline, she wondered who her sister had grown up to be and if she would ever see her again.

Her reflection in the water below changed. Subtle at first, it glistened in the rippling ocean surface as if a white full moon bloomed from the horizon behind her.

She didn't notice the tremor of the ground until her ring was ablaze, bathing everything in a half-mile radius in pure white light.

Just outside Los Angeles, in a reserve safe house Morgan and Lisa had established for the team months ago in case anything went wrong at the warehouse, a group of sixteen Ringwearers sat glued to the news coverage as they awaited word from Grant and his team. The hiding place was little more than a small run-down single-floor house whose roof creaked threateningly at the slightest gust of wind.

The group consisted mostly of Ringwearers whose powers wouldn't prove much help in danger. Nigel, the "human calculator" Grant first met at the asylum the day Morgan showed him the Dominion Stone, waited there. As did Thomas, the young boy who had been held at gunpoint by Drexel when the detective first tried to get his hands on the Dominion Stone.

The television was quickly forgotten when all sixteen rings in the room lit up, casting dazzling beams of light out of the house's windows and into the surrounding neighborhood.

A powerful earthquake built in strength as the otherworldly glow pushed through every barrier in its path.

"Watch your step!" Devlin warned as Grant and Julie stepped closer to the center of the Hollow.

Grant looked past the bright white glow of his ring, the Seal of Dominion, at the unsteady ground and saw that his next footstep would fall in a depression—a bit of sunken ground as if a layer of the black rock had been removed and then a smaller hole dug into the dirt beneath that.

The missing section of the ground formed a familiar shape.

"The Dominion Stone?" Grant shouted over the roar of the earthquake. "It came from *here*?"

Devlin nodded. "The rings were entombed beneath it. All two

hundred and ninety-nine of them. Along with the Seal, your ring, which was buried at the very bottom."

A blast of cool air poured out from the massive hole in the ground before them. It was a constant flow, an unending river of wind that never let up.

"I don't understand," Grant shouted over the crippling din of the quaking earth. He stepped to the edge of the massive, central hole and peered down inside. "What is this?"

He could see nothing within the hole. It was pure blackness.

"Poor Grant," Devlin said in a sad voice, so softly Grant almost didn't hear it. He nodded with his chin toward the ring on Grant's finger. "Did you really think you could play with fire and not get burned?"

"We have to get out of here!" Julie screamed at his side in a panic. Cold wind poured up from the hole. Combined with the earthquake, it forced Julie to hold tightly to Grant's hand to keep from being pushed over backward. "Grant, *don't do this!*"

Grant's heart was pounding so hard he could feel it reverberating through every vein in his body.

He looked beyond Devlin and saw that a crowd had gathered around the three of them. They stood in a perfect circle surrounding the center of the room. Each of them bore the Secretum's symbol on his or her wrist. And they were chanting . . . something.

This is *the Secretum*, Grant realized. *They're here to witness something.*

He listened closer, trying to make out what they were saying.

"Pario Atrum Universitas . . ." they were saying.

"GRANT!!" Julie screamed for no reason other than mortal terror.

But he was unmoved. Something about the chanting, the room they stood in . . . It felt familiar, yet utterly new to him.

"Pario Atrum Universitas . . . Pario Atrum Universitas . . ." They chanted it over and over.

Grant had no idea what it meant, but he thought it might have been in Latin.

Devlin joined in with a mighty roar, *"PARIO ATRUM UNIVERSITAS!!"*

Grant's heart leapt into his throat. He turned to Devlin just as the silver-haired man reached into his inner jacket pocket. . . .

Devlin revealed a glistening black 9mm pistol. He took aim . . . It was happening too fast. Grant's reactions were dulled by the sensory overload around him . . . the earthquake . . . the chanting, which was rising in intensity . . . the glow of his ring, which was brighter than it had ever been, *blindingly* bright . . . his own heart beating the beat of destiny . . .

"Pario Atrum Universitas! . . . Pario Atrum Universitas! . . . Pario Atrum Universitas! . . ."

Devlin pulled the trigger, his eyes placid, pleased.

The blast caught Julie square between the eyes. She fell without a sound. And Grant, cheeks spotted with his sister's blood, stared in anguished horror.

"BEHOLD, HE HAS COME!" Devlin thundered. "OBLIVION, THE BRINGER OF ENDINGS!!"

Devlin's voice rose ever louder with each word, and the choir of rage and sickness swirled around them as Grant stared at his sister's lifeless body on the ground. Furious, his eyes turned completely red, blazing as if on fire.

Devlin stepped forward and put a hand on Grant's shoulder. Grant was just about to rip the man's body to shreds when Devlin gave him a gentle shove.

Grant tipped on the edge of the great black chasm, unbalanced, his arms flailing. But he couldn't hold on; it was too late, and a single thought seared at the neurons of his brain as he fell . . .

She's dead!

The earth swallowed him whole.

The earth shook down to its foundations. Many were those who feared it might shake itself apart.

Until the quaking suddenly stopped.

At that moment, every living being on the planet could feel it.

Wherever they lived, wherever they breathed, they simply *knew* . . .

Something had just changed.

Very possibly *everything*.

One by one, across the globe's four corners, they paused whatever they were doing.

They stopped to look at something impossible.

Every clock of every kind throughout all the earth . . .

. . . had stopped ticking.

AND DON'T MISS!

MERCILESS

THE FINAL CHAPTER IN THE DOMINION TRILOGY

by ROBIN PARRISH

ACKNOWLEDGMENTS

Thanks to . . .

- My family: Mom, Larry, Evelyn, Ross, Melissa, Scott, Kara, Kaylee, and Skyler, for always, *always* believing in me.

- The wonderful staff of Bethany House Publishers, and especially my editor David Long, for making me feel like a valued member of the family.

- Everyone at Creative Ministries and *Infuze Magazine* for your unwavering dedication and support.

- My friend and right-hand man, Matt Conner, without whose efforts I would never be able to find time to write. Your passion and dedication are inspiring.

- Mrs. Marsha Presson and Mr. Tim Goodrich, teachers from my high school years whom I've recently had the pleasure of reconnecting with. Apart from my parents, *no one* supported, nurtured, or believed in my talents without fail during my formative years as much as the two of you.

- Ashley Morgan, the photographer who took my publicity shots for *Fearless*. You actually made me look like a *real* author. Don't know how you managed it, but I'm grateful.

- My Father above, without whom nothing is possible. This is quite a ride we're on; I'm glad you're at the wheel.

- Most importantly, my beautiful, amazing, supportive, patient, encouraging, helpful, understanding, loving wife, Karen. You are my sunshine, my joy, and my treasure. I love you forever.